# Finding Home

## A Rehoboth Beach Novel

Deborah Smith Cook

Atheseus Press

Published by Atheseus Press, Springfield, Virginia



This book is available in print at most online retailers.

ISBN: 978-1-963838-01-5 (ebook)

ISBN: 978-1-963838-00-8 (paperback)

ISBN: 978-1-963838-02-2 (large print paperback)

Library of Congress Control Number: 2024904621

Cover Design by 100Covers

Author photo by Candace Boissy Photography, LLC

*For Joel —*
*my love, my loon, my everything*

# Chapter One

Katherine drew in a deep breath and savored the brisk salt breeze. The pain in her neck eased — she always carried her stress in her neck — as she strolled down the wooden boardwalk. It was quiet. The beach shops and hotels were still shuttered since it was barely dawn. The sky, pink and orange, blushed as the sun peeked over the horizon. A few dedicated fishermen and the occasional seagull swooping down for their breakfast dotted the shoreline.

*This is what I need.* Away from all the bickering and tension her almost "ex," Stan, put her through in the last few months after he announced he wanted a divorce. Blaming Katherine for his affair because she "just wasn't interesting or exciting anymore." After thirty-seven years!

Katherine shook her head. *No, I'm not going to think about that right now. I came to Rehoboth Beach to escape from it all. Let the ocean work its magic.* The beach never failed to sooth and relax her. The sand between her toes. The shush of the waves coming in at low tide. When the water was warm enough, bobbing up and down in the waves. The seagulls' cries and the sandpipers' titters in their syncopated harmony.

There were so many great beaches in Delaware, but Rehoboth was her favorite. Coming here evoked childhood memories of blissful and uncomplicated times. Her family started taking their only annual vacations to Delaware when she was three or four years old — as long as she could remember.

They rented the same old dilapidated, unairconditioned cottage with a great view of the beach from the front porch. How many hours did she sit on the front steps simply watching the waves? Or playing on the edge of the water, building architecturally unsound castles that collapsed with the first rambunctious wave? Or swinging lazily in the weathered rope hammock reading and rereading her favorite books? *Life was so much simpler then.*

Too bad the cottage was gone now, replaced with a monster six-bedroom "cottage." The cost of Rehoboth being "discovered." Many of the quaint little beachfront cottages had been torn down and replaced with expensive beachfront homes.

Reaching the grandstand at the midpoint of the mile-long boardwalk, Katherine looked away from the softly waving sea grass and the aquamarine ocean and searched for Dolle's Candyland sign. *Where is it?*

A vague memory of a news clip from the Rehoboth Chamber of Commerce struggled to surface. She drew close to the counter window to read the sign. "We're moving. We've been in this location since 1927. Our new shop is about sixty feet to the west down Rehoboth Avenue. Come see us there."

*Right.* She remembered the article now. Their rent had doubled so they were forced to move from their prime location on the boardwalk. *More changes.*

Thinking about their key lime taffy, her favorite, made her tongue tingle with anticipation. Katherine scurried down the block only to be disappointed that they didn't open until 11:00.

Dejected, she retraced her steps to the boardwalk. At least the beach was still there. She needed to put her feet in the sand and walk along the water. Stopping at the clunky white wooden benches that lined the wooden promenade, she slipped out of her shoes and rolled up her pantlegs. The smooth wooden boardwalk gave way to the prickly black rubber mats that were new since her last visit. The red picket snow fence kept her off the sand berm. The berm, covered with dune grass, was higher than she remembered. The storms of recent years required a higher barrier to protect the homes and businesses from the rising tides and waves.

She dropped her shoes at the end of the mats and plodded through the long expanse of soft sand, still marked by the beach cleaner rake lines and occasional seagull footprints. The rasp of the cool sand smoothed her feet. She squeaked when a few late-hiding ghost crabs scuttled sideways out of her way.

The soft sand gave way to hard-packed sand and shells washed up by last night's tides. One toe at a time, Katherine waded in the icy spring surf. She hopped from foot to foot until her feet were frozen enough to be numb. And as she focused on her cold feet, Stan and the mess she left at home faded.

Katherine sniffed the air. A hint of salt. This early in the season the scent of the ocean was crisp and faintly metallic, reminiscent of the Cancale oysters she loved so much. Panning for treasures, she meandered along the shore, capturing a calico scallop shell and translucent jingle shells. Pouncing on the real find, a particularly lovely cobalt blue piece of sea glass, she carefully squirreled it away in her pocket.

She shivered, pulled her collar up around her ears, and buried her hands in her pockets. *What am I going to do? At least I've got some time to think about it. I didn't know when I applied for my sabbatical that I would need it so badly now.* Katherine wrapped her arms around her middle for comfort.

Her stomach growled, reminding her that she hadn't eaten since lunch yesterday. Arriving too late and too tired last night when she checked into the Boardwalk Plaza Hotel, she'd skipped dinner and dined on a stale granola bar she dug out of the bottom of her purse.

*Enough thinking. Time for breakfast.*

Sammy's Kitchen was calling her name. Taco Omelet or Sammy's French Toast. Either would fill her tummy. Mostly, Katherine needed the warmth and comfort of the family restaurant to shake the blues. And she desperately needed coffee. Sammy's wasn't fancy — red vinyl booths, linoleum floors. But Sammy's was the locals' favorite. And it had become Katherine and the kids' favorite, too.

Katherine trudged back to retrieve her shoes. Stopping to brush the sand out from between her toes, she stuffed her feet into her sneakers, the grittiness telling her she hadn't done a very good job of getting all the sand off.

Now the boardwalk was more crowded. Joggers. Power walkers. Young parents with strollers whose babies didn't know that vacation meant sleeping in. Quiet murmuring conversations. Katherine caught a word or phrase. "Scones or eggs?" "Did you remember the sunscreen?" Katherine remembered the days when those were the questions to be answered, not what she was going to do with the rest of her life.

# Chapter Two

Jeff watched as the pretty woman walked along the beach, stooping to pocket a shell every now and then. Shoulders slumped, she looked like she was carrying the weight of the world. Once in a while she stopped, turned to the water and lifted her arms in a kind of sun salutation. He laughed softly when a wave caught her by surprise and her rolled-up pantlegs got wet.

He slowed his pace so he wouldn't startle her as he came up behind her. Cooling down from his run along the shore, he had time to relax and amble along. He wasn't needed at the restaurant for another couple of hours. And this was his favorite time of the day when the beach wasn't too crowded.

His restaurants were all doing well, although the staffing problem was a real concern. During the winter, he followed local practices and only opened Tuesday through Saturday, so he could make do with a skeleton crew and still give his staff enough hours to make a living. But in April, all the local restaurants started opening on Sundays and staying open longer hours. He needed more staff to cover all the shifts.

This spring had been particularly tough for Jeff, especially in his newest restaurant in Rehoboth. One cook, Jerry, took leave to care for his father who had fallen off a ladder. Joyce, a full-time waitress normally, was filling in some shifts for Jerry. But Joyce was finally pregnant after a long struggle. Her doctor was already making noises that she needed to cut back on her hours or he would put her on bed rest.

His main cook, Tim, wasn't due back for another fourteen days from Key West where he spent his winters. His other waitress, Allison, was working double shifts. Jeff was filling in as waiter or bartender or cook — whatever was needed. Thank heavens, some of the college kids would be starting in a couple of weeks when their semesters were over. He had to hang in there until then.

Engrossed in his labor problem, he almost ran into the woman as she abruptly turned around to head back to the path. He sidestepped to avoid the collision. She was so lost in thought, she didn't even notice.

Her cheeks were slightly flushed pink. Wide brown or maybe green eyes, rimmed with long lashes. Soft brown curls framed her face. Jeff was surprised at the flash of attraction. Divorced for ten years, he had occasional relationships during that time, but he had been off dating for a while. He didn't have the energy for it while he was launching his latest restaurant up and running. And whatever free time he had he spent with his teenage daughter who lived with his ex-wife in Wilmington. He didn't have time for a social life.

Jeff turned to watch her make her way back to the boardwalk. She walked heavy, like it was an effort, like she was sad. *What is it about an unhappy woman that makes me want to cheer her up?* Frowning, he waited until she disappeared behind the berm. *I don't have time for this. Too many things to worry about with the new restaurant.*

# Chapter Three

Pleasantly sated with French toast, Katherine wandered into Browseabout Books, her favorite store in Rehoboth. One side was cases and cases of books. The other side was a treasure trove of delightful gifts and cards. She couldn't count the many thoughtful hostess gifts she had brought home from here.

Of course, she treated herself as well. Her favorite shirt with the quote, "Women who read are dangerous," purchased here several years ago, had attracted many approving comments. Now the collar and cuffs were frayed and the color dulled to a gray seafoam green, but she still wore it, and no doubt would until it dissolved into threads. Especially now since it was one of Stan's least favorite shirts.

Bypassing the board games and toys, she aimed straight for the bookshelf of staff favorites. An elfin, golden-tanned, silver-haired woman greeted her with a smile and a "Welcome! Let me know if I can help you." Katherine returned the smile and reflected on how friendly everyone was.

*Ahh, there's the latest Elin Hilderbrand.* Katherine read the jacket blurb and put it in her basket. She supported independent bookstores wherever she went. In fact, she had a quest list of independent bookstores across the country, and even around the world, that she wanted to visit. Wherever she travelled, she made a point to find an independent bookstore there. She might only buy one or two books, but if everyone did that, it would go a long way toward helping these bookstores survive and thrive.

Continuing to browse the staff picks, she was drawn to a new author she hadn't read before. She liked to expand her portfolio of authors. Seeing the world through someone else's eyes helped her escape from the craziness of everyday life and gave her new insights into other people's lives. Adding this new book to her basket, she approached the counter where the woman looked up expectantly.

"It looks like you've found a couple of page-turners. I read the Hilderbrand book and it's quite good. I won't spoil it by telling you what happens," she laughed. "I'm Beth, by the way. Are you here for the weekend or a day visit?"

"I'm Katherine. I'm here for the week at least. Graduation was yesterday — I teach at a university in Washington, D.C. And now I'm officially on sabbatical until January. I don't have a clue what I want to do for the next eight months. I thought this would be a good place for me to think. I'm hoping my next step will come to me." Katherine paused. "Listen to me going on and on. Sorry about that."

"No worries. This is a great place to unwind and see where the current will take you. Have you walked the boardwalk yet?"

"I did this morning. That's the first thing I do. The second is to come here." Katherine laughed. "I've vacationed here quite a few times, first with my parents when I was growing up and later with my own children over the years. I'm amazed at the number of changes, but fortunately, my favorites, like Dolle's and Browseabout, are still here. I tried to hit up Dolle's at their new location, but they're not open yet. My visit will not be complete until I've visited them."

"I've probably seen you in here since I've been managing the store for almost ten years. What do you teach?"

"Literature with a specialty in early American literature, and creative writing."

"Great stuff. A long time ago, I was an English major, too. My first job after college I worked for a publishing house, editing mostly. Now I feed my love of reading by working in a bookstore."

"Kind of a dream job if you love to read." Katherine laughed. "If I worked here, I wouldn't earn anything. I'd spend everything on books."

Beth nodded. "Where are you staying? How long did you say you were staying?"

"I'm at the Boardwalk this time. We stay either there or The Avenue Inn for shorter visits. We've rented several cottages over the years when we can stay longer."

"Did your children come with you this time? Your husband or partner?"

"No, I'm by myself this time." She paused. "Actually, this is the first time I've been here alone. My kids are all grown and I'm in the middle of a nasty divorce. I needed a break."

"Well, I'm sorry you're going through that. Divorce is hard."

Katherine tapped her credit card to pay for her books. Beth handed her a purple insolated canvas Browseabout bag.

"We don't usually give these out unless you join our loyalty program but think of it as a welcome back to Rehoboth."

"Thanks. That's lovely. I should join the loyalty program anyway since I'm here often enough."

"Happy to sign you up. It's free and only takes a minute."

Katherine nodded her agreement. "What do you need?"

"Phone number or email address." Beth added, "You earn dollars on every purchase and when you reach a goal level, you can use it on your next purchase."

Katherine wrote down her email and then asked, "Do you have any recommendations about new places for lunch or dinner? I know there's always Blue Moon and Back Porch, but I'd like to try something new."

Beth grabbed one of the free Rehoboth maps. "Those are always good choices. There are a couple of newish places. My friend, Jeff, runs a great bar and grill here on Wilmington." She circled a building in the first block off the boardwalk. "Not fancy, but the food is great." She tagged another place on the map. "And Salt Air is the new up-and-coming restaurant. It's won several awards."

"Thanks. Do you think they're good for a woman dining alone? I guess I need to get used to that."

"Absolutely." Beth hesitated. "Hey, if you're still around on Sunday evening at 6:00, a few of us women meet at one of the local restaurants downtown to talk books and drink wine if you want to join us."

"I'll still be here. Are you sure I wouldn't be intruding?"

"Of course not. It's very casual. I never know who exactly is going to show up, but you'd be welcome. This week we're meeting in the back room of Blue Moon."

"Well, then count me in. I'll see you then."

# Chapter Four

Katherine left Browseabout feeling good. Beth seemed very nice, and it was great meeting another book lover. Besides Shawna, her neighbor and best friend, Katherine didn't have many close female friends. There were women at the university, but schedules were complicated since the faculty lived all over the place in D.C., Virginia, Maryland, and even West Virginia. It was hard to catch coffee or happy hour with those commutes and conflicting teaching schedules. Since people were finally back in the office after teaching remotely because of COVID, she was at least reconnecting with her colleagues at departmental meetings.

Of course, COVID hadn't stopped Stan from having an affair with his former doctoral student. What a cliché! Taking up with a woman twenty-five years younger than him. She was almost the same age as Vanessa. *How could he do that to his own daughter? How could he do that to me?*

*I should have seen it coming.* Looking back, she saw the signs. The late nights working in his office, allegedly working on a research paper. The frequent dashes to the office to pick up a book he "forgot." The phone calls he rushed to take behind the closed doors of his home office. Departmental meetings that ran "late" so he had to miss dinner with the family.

Even worse were the passive-aggressive comments. "Are you really going to wear that dress? It doesn't do anything for you." "Do you think you should be eating that cake?" "I can't make the award ceremony. I have an important meeting with our doctoral students." "I don't have time to discuss your research. I have my own paper to complete." He chipped and chipped away at Katherine's self-esteem.

He said she wasn't interesting anymore. Funny. He thought she was plenty interesting when they were doctoral students at Yale.

He told her he wanted a partner who was more driven, more focused on her career. Chrissy was a rising academic star in marketing with offers from several A-list universities. He went on and on about how he and Chrissy shared the same aspirations in life and in their careers.

He argued that he needed an intellectual equal who understood the big economic and corporate questions like he did, not some ivory tower romantic English professor like Katherine. It didn't matter that Katherine was very well respected professionally having published four books and earned a PEN/Robert W. Bingham Prize for her short story collection.

Or that she was selected from the whole faculty for the University Teaching Award, the most prestigious honor at the university. Stan, of course, poo-pooed it saying that of course an English professor would win this. It was easy to teach English, not like economics. He scoffed that no one would award economic professors a fluffy teaching award, nor would they want it. Further diminishing the teaching award's significance, he said smugly, "And who cares about teaching anyway? Research is the singular criterion of success for academics."

He battered and battered her with words so often, she stopped talking to him about her work, not even telling him about the scholarly success of her publications. When had he become so critical of her career? When had he started minimizing her accomplishments?

He told her that he wasn't attracted to her anymore. He blamed her weight. She had put on a few pounds, but she was still size fourteen. It wasn't that bad. He said she didn't seem to care much about her appearance since she let her hair go gray during the pandemic. *Lots of women chose not to dye their hair, for heaven's sake.* He maintained he hadn't been happy with her for years.

Katherine still reeled from the blows. How could she have missed his increasing dissatisfaction? She thought they were happy enough. True, they were a little more like roommates than lovers, but they went out to dinner, to the Kennedy Center for the symphony and Arena Stage for plays. They had fun walking on the weekends. They cooked together every now and then.

And they loved spending time with the kids whenever they came to visit. Or so she thought. He had been away at "conferences" a few times when Vanessa and Anthony and his family came for dinner. And he had begged off their season tickets to the symphony more than once and encouraged her to take Shawna, her best friend, instead.

*How was I so blind? How did I miss all these clues?*

She realized she was race-walking as she turned Stan's hurtful comments over and over in her head, reliving the pain with every repetition. Taking a breath, she slowed her pace. Escaping to Rehoboth, even for a few days, felt like the right next step. She was free from Stan's belittling comments.

She noticed the curly-haired toddler dragging her sand pail and shovel toward the beach while mom corralled two grade-school siblings, and dad followed with a beach wagon laden with chairs, umbrella, cooler, all the necessities for a day at the beach. Their excited chatter was a balm to Katherine's troubled thoughts.

Katherine smiled recalling her own trips here with her children and sighed because it would have been her pulling the wagon and wrangling the two kids. It wasn't Stan's "thing" to vacation at the ocean. *Is that when this started? All those years ago when Stan preferred to travel to Europe or stay in Washington while we went to the beach? Is that when we drifted apart?*

She cringed when she thought about Vanessa, their daughter. She was furious with her dad. "Typical mid-life crisis, an affair with a younger woman," she ranted. "Good grief. Chrissy is *my* age. What is he thinking? It's just plain disgusting."

Vanessa was pushing Katherine to move on with her life and show him what he was throwing away. "Don't sit around doing nothing, waiting for Dad to come back." That was easier said than done. How do you "go on" when the whole future you had planned isn't your future anymore?

*I'm not sitting around waiting. Why would I want him back after what he's done?*

*But everything I've believed to be true is not anymore. I'm not going to be married. I'm not going to grow old with Stan. We're not going to enjoy our lives together.* Katherine frowned. *Don't I deserve some time to grieve?*

Watching the harried father wrangle the beach wagon over the sand, Katherine's son, Anthony, and his wife, Sonja, and their new baby, Lucas, came to mind. Anthony was aggressively "encouraging" her to move to Atlanta where they lived. They wanted to help her. *Help her do what?* She was only sixty-one years old, in pretty good physical shape, and in complete control of her mental capacity. *Good grief! Do they think I'm going to fall apart?*

*I know their hearts are in the right place, but it's insulting to think that I'm not capable of taking care of myself, even if I don't know exactly what I want to do right now. I understand that their lives are in Atlanta, their jobs, friends, and my grandson, but I'm certainly not ready to move in with them. And I have a job, two jobs, actually, if you count the work I'm doing with the incubator.*

So many decisions to make. Should she stay in their home in McLean, Virginia? Stan was exceedingly glad, almost a little too glad, like he thought he was pulling one over on her, because she wasn't contesting the divorce. He magnanimously agreed to give her the house since "that's where the kids grew up."

But what was Katherine going to do with the big house? What was she going to do with five bedrooms? She was the only person living there now. Vanessa and her guy had a place in Georgetown, and they finally got their first overseas assignments with the State Department where they both worked. They would be moving to Africa in the spring. Anthony and his family had already moved to Atlanta. It was a lot more house than she needed. But where would she go if she moved?

Yet the house still brimmed with good memories — the gigantic Christmas trees in front of the Palladian window, Vanessa and Anthony clattering down the stairs for pancakes on Saturday mornings, the sounds of the swim meets at the pool across the street on Monday evenings and Saturday mornings, the tot lots where the kids demanded to be pushed higher and higher in the swings. Sadly, Katherine saw how few memories involved Stan. Where had he been all those years?

Katherine sighed. *I don't have to deal with that right this moment. What I have to do now is figure out what I'm doing tomorrow. And where I'm going for lunch. I'll try the new place Beth recommended.*

# Chapter Five

Katherine peered in the window of Brews and Bites. It was just 11:30. Many tables were already filled. She liked the look of the place, a few booths, but mostly tables with dark green, purple, and silver patio chairs. A long ebony lacquer bar, polished to a high sheen, ran down one side of the restaurant framed by well-lit shelving showcasing the impressive array of liquor. The black walls and ceilings were a nice relief from the blinding sunshine. *I might as well give it a try. Beth said it was good.*

*Seat Yourself.* Obeying the sign, Katherine found a table tucked between the front window and the bar. The waitress acknowledged her with a quick nod as she dashed into the kitchen. Katherine watched as she quickly returned with a tray and headed to a table filled with scowling, toe-tapping customers. Katherine heard her apologizing for the delay. And heard the customers grumbling that they didn't have all day. The table next to them leaned over and asked the waitress when their food was going to be ready.

"I think your order is up right now. Let me go check." She looked around frantically at the four other tables impatiently waiting for their lunches. Turning abruptly, she hurried into the kitchen.

*Poor woman. This is a huge room, and she seems to be working it by herself. I wonder where the other waitstaff are.* Katherine spied a menu on the bar and stood up to grab it. The bartender rushed in from the back room carrying a keg. He muttered, "Of all the times for this to go dry, why now?" He fussed over it, moved the hose thing to the new keg, and ran a little beer in a glass evidently to make sure it was working.

Impressed with how quickly he had swapped out the barrel, Katherine thought he would look up and ask for her order. But he turned back to the line of tickets in front of him and started making drinks and pouring drafts. Katherine sat back down. *He could have at least asked if I wanted a drink.*

The waitress bustled out of the kitchen, grabbing the drink tray from the bartender. "Thanks, Jeff." She nodded toward Katherine. "Do you think you could take her order?" He kept pulling beers for her next tray and shook his head yes.

Katherine glanced at her watch. *I've been here for twenty minutes. That poor waitress is never going to take care of all these tables. Perhaps if I sat in front of him, the bartender would take my order.*

Katherine moved to the bar, making a bit of a production of pulling out the chair and letting it scrape across the floor. She dropped the menu on the bar with a thud and cleared her throat several times. "Excuse me. I'd like to have a draft and a burger."

"Hold your horses. I'll get to you in a minute. Can't you see I'm busy?" he snarled.

*Well! This place isn't going to be in business very long with that kind of behavior. I've been here this long I'll give him another five minutes. If he doesn't wait on me by then, I'm leaving. I'll be sure to leave a bad review on Yelp and let Beth know that her friend's place needs some improvement.*

"What do you want?" the bartender tossed over his shoulder as he pulled two more drafts.

Katherine looked over her shoulder to see if he was addressing her or another party. Since no one else was there, she presumed he was talking to her. "I would like to order lunch. A draft and the peppercorn steakhouse burger with sweet potato fries. Medium. Hold the mayo. I've had time to memorize the menu," she said with a hint of sarcasm.

*Why is he staring at me like he knows me? I've never seen him before.* Katherine pulled her phone from her purse to read her emails. Watching him through her eyelashes, she saw him frown, puzzled, and then shake his head as he submitted her order and poured her drink. She turned back to her emails and grimaced at the barrage of emails from Stan about the divorce. *Why can't he leave me alone for a few days!*

Katherine looked up and caught him watching her. He had nice eyes, tired but nice. Muscle shirt over a well-toned body. Sleeve tattoos. Gray-streaked ponytail. Black leather pants. *Probably rides a Harley.* She knew she was stereotyping him, but she didn't run into many professors who looked like him.

He smirked when he saw Katherine checking out his pants. And then smiled smugly when he saw her blush. He disappeared into the kitchen and returned with her food. The burger was as delicious as Beth had promised. *Too bad it came with such bad service.* Katherine finished her beer and pulled out her wallet.

"May I have my check, please?" She raised her voice to be heard over the blender. "Excuse me, my check?"

"I'll get to you when I can," he snapped. "Geez, lady, wait your turn. Can't you see I'm working as fast as I can."

*The burgers are good but not good enough to put up with this rudeness. I can't think of the last time I've met such an unpleasant person.*

# Chapter Six

After spending the last couple of days lazing under the beach umbrella in the sand, devouring her Browseabout books, Katherine was ready for conversation and company. When she wasn't reading, she was in her head thinking about Stan and what went wrong with her marriage.

*It's Sunday. Beth invited me to join her and her friends. I don't know if I should go or not. But she did invite me...*

Katherine didn't want to sit in her hotel room tonight. *I'm going to go and if it's awkward, I'll just have one glass of wine and leave.*

She surveyed the meager collection of clothes she brought with her. *Good thing I bought that cream linen sheath the other afternoon when it was raining. Everything else I brought is better suited to the classroom than the beach.*

She threw on the dress and a clunky wood bead necklace and matching earrings. She surveyed herself critically in the mirror. *Not bad.* The touch of sun looked good on her. And the circles under her eyes were not so noticeable. She looked less stressed than when she got here last week. Grabbing her purse, she set out for Blue Moon.

The bright blue and yellow house, lined with rainbow flags, gave way to a surprisingly neutral and calm interior at the Blue Moon. Katherine stood inside the door waiting for the host with his crisp white shirt and tailored black pants to finish taking a reservation. Through the double French doors, she could barely make out the slightly raucous bar side of the restaurant, but the dining room was quiet and peaceful.

"May I help you?" the host asked.

"I'm meeting a group of women. Beth, from Browseabout, said it was in the back room?"

"Of course." He led her through the softly lit dining room. The tables were filled with couples and groups laughing quietly and enjoying what must be delicious dinners judging by the wonderful smells wafting up as she passed. Just past the service station, there was a little alcove with one round table in it.

"Here is your party," he said with a flourish. "Sammy will be over in a minute to take your order. Enjoy."

Beth stood up and moved to Katherine's side. "You made it! Let me introduce you to everyone."

Conversation dwindled as Beth got the attention of the other women at the table. "First, let me introduce Katherine — I don't know your last name?" She turned to Katherine.

"It's Lewis, Katherine Lewis."

"This is Katherine Lewis. Another book lover—I met her the other day at Browseabout. You know me, I like to surround myself with people that read. That's why I hang out with you all," she laughed.

"I invited her to join us tonight. Other than she loves books, I don't know a lot about her except she's visited many times and she's here now to relax and rejuvenate."

Choruses of "welcome" went around the table from the other three women.

Beth continued. "This lovely lady here is Isabella. She owns the biggest brewpub in Delaware, one of the few female-owned and operated in Delaware."

"Actually, one of the few in the country," Isabella interrupted. "Happy to meet you."

Katherine smiled at the striking Hispanic woman with her red lipstick, bright yellow top, and halo of black curls.

"Next to her is Cassandra. She and her partner own Bikes for Life, a bicycle shop for everyone but with particular emphasis on female bike riders." Cassandra nodded and raised her glass.

"Finally, Michelle here is one of our top real estate agents in the area. She can help you find whatever property you might be looking for." Katherine admired the thin, exquisitely dressed woman with every auburn hair in place.

Katherine smiled at the lively faces. "It's great to meet you all. Thank you very much for including me."

Sammy appeared at her elbow. "Would you like something to drink?"

"I'll have a glass of cabernet." She slid into the chair between Beth and Isabella.

Isabella asked, "What brings you to Rehoboth?"

Katherine looked around at the open and welcoming faces of the women and plunged in. "As Beth said, I'm here to relax and rejuvenate. My semester ended last week." She paused. "And I'm in the middle of a messy divorce. I had to take a break."

Michelle murmured sympathetically, "Been there. My

divorce was final a few years ago. You picked a good place to relax."

Isabella jumped in. "Relaxing is good, but it's also good to have fun! Let's order appetizers and maybe another round. Isn't living well the best revenge? Not that I actually know since I've never been married. Bringing the brewery to life has taken all my time. Let's get this party going!"

Katherine chuckled. "You're right. Enough of this moping around. Tell me about you all. Cassandra, what do you do for fun?"

Cassandra was quiet. Katherine knew from her teaching experience that she had to draw the quiet ones out and give them a chance to participate. They were often overshadowed by extroverts who needed to talk out loud to process what they were learning. And yet it seemed like the quiet ones would bring great insights into the discussion. Katherine liked all her students, but she was particularly drawn to introverts.

Cassandra, tall, slim, with short blond no-nonsense hair, straightened up and drawled, "Well, I think you can relax *and* have fun. At least that's what happens with me and Penny when we ride our bikes. Do you ride?" she asked Katherine.

"I used to." *I used to do a lot of things,* Katherine muttered under her breath.

Cassandra studied Katherine. "If you want to give it another shot, stop by the store. I've got bikes I'm cleaning up to give away. I can let you borrow one and see how it feels. I don't have to deliver them to the Newark Bike Project until next week."

"Newark Bike Project?" Michelle asked.

"Their mission is to give donated bikes to adults for transportation or to kids who can't afford them. I collect bikes here, tune them up, and drive them to Newark. It saves them the work of fixing them up so they can concentrate on providing bikes to people who need them."

"That's a great idea. I've got a couple of bikes in my garage that I don't use anymore. I'll drop them off, and I'll let the people in my office know about what you're doing, Cassandra. I'm sure they can help out, too," Michelle said.

Katherine smiled at Cassandra. "Thanks for the offer. I'm only going to be here for a week, but I might take you up on it. They say you never forget how to ride a bike."

"Are you teaching this summer?" Beth asked.

"Not this summer. I'm on sabbatical until January. Technically, university faculty members earn a one-year sabbatical every seven years to concentrate on their research, but I haven't taken one in forever. I decided it was time. Instead of the whole year, I'm taking a half-year."

"I've never heard of a sabbatical. What is it?" Isabella asked.

"It's a standard university practice. And it's beginning to be offered by corporations as well. There are at least seventy-five companies that offer paid sabbaticals. AARP. Adobe. McDonald's. Bank of America. General Mills. The sabbatical length and eligibility vary, but it's a great addition to their benefit package."

Katherine continued. "It's time off either with full pay for a short period of time, or partial pay for a longer period."

"Sounds like a great idea. Why do they offer it?" Isabella continued to quiz Katherine.

"It counters burnout. Reduces stress. It lets the faculty member or employee explore a new research interest or learning experience." Katherine paused. "There's quite a bit of research that shows that it also benefits the company because employees are more engaged and productive when they come back from their sabbatical."

"What are you going to do during yours? Are you staying in D.C.? Working at another university? Traveling?" Beth asked.

"To be determined — research for sure, and hopefully some creative writing, or...I don't know. Figure out which end is up? I'm feeling a little unmoored. I do know that I don't want to spend my sabbatical in Atlanta with my son and his family, and I'd really rather not spend it at home either."

"Why don't you spend it here?" Michelle asked.

"Here?"

"Sure," Michelle continued. "Why not? As I said before, it's a great place to relax. And Isabella is right."

Isabella grinned. "Fun is important, too. You can have both here."

*Why not, indeed.* Katherine weighed the idea. "It would be impossible to find a place to live this late in the season."

Michelle raised an eyebrow. "Were you not listening to Beth?" she teased. "Didn't she tell you that I'm one of the best? Actually, she undersold me — I am *the* best real estate agent in the area."

Katherine felt her resistance begin to fade and her excitement increase. "You truly think you can come up with a place for me to stay through the first of January? It wouldn't have to be fancy or even that big."

"I've got a couple of places in mind that I think would be perfect," Michelle said smugly.

"I can't believe I'm considering this. It's the most impulsive thing I've thought about in a long, long time. Here, text me your number. I'll call you tomorrow."

"I'm hungry," Isabella said. "Anyone want to split the Crispy Octopus or the Short Rib Nachos with me?"

"Ugh. You can keep the octopus, but I'd go for the nachos." Michelle scanned the menu. "How about the Cajun Egg Rolls?"

Katherine watched as the women negotiated. They were so comfortable with each other. She relaxed and sipped her wine.

"Anything look appealing to you, Katherine?" Beth handed her the menu.

"The Mozzarella Burrata looks good to me."

Taking charge, Beth called Sammy. "We're starving and unless you want us getting silly from drinking on empty stomachs, would you bring us the octopus, egg rolls, burrata, and two orders of the nachos?"

"And I could use another." Isabella held up her glass.

"Me, too." One by one the women held up their empty glasses.

"Coming right up." Sammy disappeared into the kitchen to place their order.

"So Katherine, what do you like to read?" Michelle asked.

Katherine chuckled. "You're asking an English professor what she likes to read? How much time do you have?"

Isabella jumped in. "Romances? Thrillers? Mysteries?"

"Yes. Yes. And yes," Katherine responded. "What authors do you like?"

For the next hour, they debated who was better — Baldacci or Child. Mallory or Hilderbrand. Katherine laughed at Isabella's passionate defense that Coben was really the best while Cassandra was Lee Child all the way. Michelle was a dedicated Picoult fan. Beth refused to pick her favorite child — she loved them all.

Katherine basked in the warmth and acceptance of these interesting women. It was the most pleasant evening she had enjoyed in a long time. She wondered if there would be more nights like this if she stayed in Rehoboth.

# Chapter Seven

After thanking Beth profusely for inviting her to the wine get-together, Katherine strolled down Baltimore Ave toward the Boardwalk Plaza. Lost in thought, she didn't notice the couples walking arm in arm, heading for the boardwalk for a romantic moonlight stroll, or the group of young teens, hormones on full alert, laughing, "accidentally" bumping their current crush, rushing to make it back before their curfews. Her mind whirred with Michelle's suggestion that she spend her sabbatical here.

*Of course, I can't do it. It's just crazy. I have responsibilities at home. Who would keep an eye on the house?*

She stared blindly at the art gallery window, not seeing the beautiful seascapes, thinking instead about the obstacles to this hare-brained idea. But her usual optimistic and pragmatic self came up with solutions as well.

Shawna, her neighbor, lawyer, and best friend, could keep an eye on the house. For that matter, Vanessa had a key. She could pick up packages if Shawna had to go out of town. *Check.*

Katherine had the locks changed on Shawna's advice. Stan

no longer had access to the house. She wouldn't have to worry about him entering without her permission. *Check.*

Lawn care and pool maintenance on automatic schedules. *Check.*

Her negative side popped up again. *I have things I need to do for the divorce. Shawna asked for more financial information and she wants to review the prenup I had her draw up when my parents sold their business. And she said we'll have to meet with Stan's lawyers to iron out the details of the settlement.*

She squared her shoulders. *Four or five hours of meetings over the next few months — it's about a four-hour drive back to D.C. I can go back for a day or an overnight when I have to.*

It would be great to be away from Stan — very important to her mental health. *Check.*

*Wouldn't the department think I was being frivolous, taking my sabbatical at the beach? They'll probably think I'm not taking it very seriously and won't accomplish anything.*

She paused on the corner where Jake's Seafood Restaurant used to be and wondered idly why they had moved from their downtown location all the way out on Route 1. She'd heard they shut down that restaurant, too, because of COVID. Bad luck or bad decisions? She didn't want to make a bad decision and she didn't trust herself much right now. She continued her internal debate.

*But why couldn't I be productive here? Fewer distractions from Stan and all his drama. People go on writers' retreats all the time at the beach and they write. Being here might break my writer's block. And I can access all my research and resources remotely. I can work on my research from here as easily as from home.*

Katherine stopped to inhale the dianthus' clove-like, spicy scent, and the heavy honeysuckle-like perfume of the purple Hosta flowers. Instantly, she was transported to her mother's garden and the lazy summer nights Katherine spent lying on a blanket in her backyard, counting stars and catching fireflies. And bathing in the sensual pleasure of darkness, scents, and warmth.

*Anthony wants me to come to Atlanta "to take care of me."* She scowled as she crossed the street. *I don't need to be taken care of. And I have to stand on my own two feet. I let Stan rule our house for too long. It's time for me to take charge of me.*

She argued with herself. *Isn't the real reason you're resisting is that you haven't done anything this spontaneous... frivolous...in a long time?*

Wrapped up in her head, she caught her toe on a raised brick and almost tumbled, caught herself just in time. *Ha — See? I can take care of myself.*

She mused. *My life has become so predictable. I've worked hard and done well in my academic career. And I've been a good mother. And a good wife, despite what Stan says.*

Wincing, she thought, *I used to be a risk-taker. Going to Yale instead of staying close to home. Pursuing my doctorate instead of joining the family business. Taking the teaching job in a non-tenure track position, hoping that it would convert. Which it did.* She silently saluted herself.

She sighed. *But stability became more important. Tenure. Insurance. Raising a family. The right priorities at the time.*

Katherine stopped abruptly when she reached the boardwalk. *Now I don't have those constraints. I can do anything I want. Even spend my sabbatical in Rehoboth.*

*How come you're not jumping on this?* She shook her head and drew in a deep breath. *It's scary. What if it's a disaster? What if I'm miserable and lonely here? What if I don't get anything written? What if...? What if?*

She scolded herself. *You're awfully good at catastrophizing. What if it was great? What if you made more new friends?*

*You've already met a group of great women. What if being here gave you the space to write and research? What if...? What if...?*

She gazed at the moonrise over the ocean, the light shimmering over the low tide, the full moon making it almost light enough to read. As far as she could see in the moonlight, the gray-black ocean dotted with tiny whitecaps gleamed. *It's so vast. So full of possibilities. That's what I want. I want to explore and learn and live boldly.*

*But what about finding a place here?* she worried.

*Michelle said she had a few places in mind.*

She mused. *I guess it wouldn't hurt to check them out.*

She smiled and felt lighter and happier than she had in a long time. *I'm going to do it.*

# Chapter Eight

Katherine slumped on the floral blue and salmon loveseat in Michelle's office. "How did you pull all this together? I only called you yesterday morning. You do this every day? I'm exhausted."

Michelle laughed. "It's all in the training. I don't have to go to the gym to work out when I'm showing houses. What did you think?"

Katherine grimaced. "I haven't looked at houses in almost forty years. I had no idea how complicated this would be. You know those shows on HGTV where you are shown three houses and then you have to choose one? And they have to make a decision in a half hour show? That's where I am right now. We're going to cut to commercial and I'll have to tell you my choice in sixty seconds. And you showed me four places. That makes it even harder to make a decision."

Michelle laughed out loud. "You realize they tape those shows over several days, sometimes even weeks. Then they edit it. It has to fit in a twenty-five-minute time slot by the time you add all the commercials."

She pointed at Katherine. "And you put yourself under this time pressure, by the way. Are you afraid you'll change your mind about spending your sabbatical here?"

"Busted," Katherine lamented.

Michelle handed her an iced tea and a protein bar. "Here, drink this and eat the bar. You can change your mind. I'm not going be upset if this is not the right time to do this."

"No." Katherine stopped. "I am committed to do this and I want to move on with my life. I'm going to make the house decision right now."

Michelle pulled up the pictures of the first house. "What did you think of this one?"

Katherine scrolled through the photos. "This one was the least expensive and the furthest from the beach. It would take me forty minutes to walk to downtown and the boardwalk, and the neighborhoods are not that interesting."

She checked her notes from their tour. "It's a basic apartment — nice pool and tennis courts — but it doesn't excite me. I'm crossing this one off the list."

"Good. That's one down. How about the loft?" Michelle turned the monitor to Katherine again so she could review the property.

"That one was cool — do we say that anymore, 'cool'? I'm probably showing my age. Anyway, it was very chic with the polished concrete floors and the exposed metal beams with the shop lighting. I liked the patio out back, although it felt a little closed-in with the tall privacy fence to block the road noise." Katherine rapidly flipped through the listing.

Michelle interrupted, "What did you think of the location?"

Katherine studied the map. "It's about a twenty-minute walk to the beach. That's doable for me. And it's close to Dogfish Brewing — one of my favorite places — that's a plus."

She grimaced. "But the road is always busy with people rushing to park close to the boardwalk. It's the main drag into downtown and I've seen the traffic on summer weekends. It's pretty bad. I don't think I want to live that close to such a busy road. I'm going to eliminate this one, too."

"Look at you, making all these decisions." Michelle applauded. "I know you were concerned about making these choices on your own. For my money, I think you're doing a great job — using both your head and your heart to decide what's right for you."

"Thanks, Michelle. Two more to go and these are the hardest. I didn't expect to find anything I liked in Dewey, and I can't thank you enough for showing me these great opportunities." Katherine straightened her shoulders and said, "Okay, let's look at the one on Jersey Street first."

"Dewey has a reputation of being the college kids' spring break playground, but families love it there, too. The house on Jersey Street is very nice."

Katherine reviewed the house room by room. "I love the screened-in porch in the back. I can imagine sitting out in the evenings with a glass of wine. And the inside of the house is calming with that soft gray wide beadboard walls and gray and white furniture. It's like living in a cloud."

Michelle nodded. "It is very soothing."

"But I'm not crazy about the natural knotty pine paneling in the bedrooms — definitely not my style." Katherine paused. "The kitchen is great, and I love the windows and the vaulted ceilings in the living room. Someone put impressive work into the design."

"It sounds like this is a strong contender." Michelle checked the listing. "A couple of other people have looked at this place today. If you think this is the one, we'd better move on it quickly."

Katherine hesitated. "Let's talk about the Carolina Street house."

Michelle clicked on another tab and brought it up. "This one is a beauty."

Katherine leaned in and slowly reviewed every photo. "It is. I can't believe it's available to rent. It's lovely. What's wrong with it?"

Michelle smiled. "Nothing. The owner gave me the listing the other day. He's launching a new business and since he's spending most of his time there, he decided to stay in the apartment above the business."

Katherine gazed longingly at the brilliant blue house with the blinding white trim surrounded with lush plants and shrubs. It was an oasis. When she was touring it, everything fell away. She felt cocooned, wrapped in soothing tranquility. The porch with its thick cushioned wicker chairs invited her to breathe and sit back and relax.

Trying to be rational, Katherine said, "It meets most of my needs. Close to downtown —a thirty-minute walk to the boardwalk. The Trolley stops somewhere close by if I don't want to walk. With three bedrooms, I would have plenty of room when the kids come to visit, if I could talk them into it. And I could use one of the bedrooms as an office."

Michelle smiled indulgently. "And..."

"Oh, you know this is the one I want! My heart said this is where I belong as soon as I walked in and saw the porch, the pool, the waterfall, and the bathtub," she gushed. "Did you see that shower? It's like a spa." Katherine took a deep breath. "Where's the dotted line? I want to sign the contract."

Thirty minutes later, Michelle shook Katherine's hand and handed her the keys. "Now we celebrate with a glass of champagne. My treat, of course!"

# Chapter Nine

Katherine thought back over the whirlwind week. Meeting Beth at Browseabout last Friday. Sunday night with wine and book women at Blue Moon. Deciding on Monday to stay in Rehoboth for her sabbatical. House hunting on Wednesday. And now today, heading back to Virginia to pack up some stuff. It hadn't exactly been the quiet, relaxing time she was expecting at the beach. But for the first time in a while, Katherine was looking forward.

The drive flew by. Before she knew it, she was back in McLean, Virginia, the suburb of Washington, D.C., where she and Stan had lived and raised their children for over thirty years.

*The lawn looks good,* she noticed as she turned into her driveway. But the house looks...sad or abandoned, maybe lonely. Since Stan had moved out and the kids were already out, it was just Katherine rambling around alone.

Stan hadn't wanted the house in the divorce settlement even though it was more his style than Katherine's. When he and Chrissy got back from his year at Oxford University, they moved to a condo at the Watergate — two bedrooms, all glass and chrome — very different from the Frank Lloyd Wright-style house in McLean.

Katherine entered the kitchen from the garage and felt the silence. The house was huge — five bedrooms, formal living room and dining room, fully furnished recreation room with an in-home movie theater. Yes, it felt lonely. When the kids were growing up, it brimmed with life and activities, but now it felt too empty.

Startled from her revelry by the insistent ringing, she grabbed the phone. "What are you doing home? I didn't think you were coming back for a couple of days." Her best friend and neighbor, Shawna, immediately launched into a conversation. "I saw the front lights go on."

"You caught me as I was walking in the door. If you have a minute, come on over and I'll catch you up," Katherine invited.

"Be there in a flash. Can't wait to see you."

Katherine emptied the car of the moving boxes she had collected. As she finished the last load, "Yoo-hoo? Where are you?"

Shawna stopped short when she entered the kitchen. "What's with all the boxes?"

"Well, that's what I need to catch you up on. I decided to spend my sabbatical in Rehoboth. I've already rented a place. I'm here to pack up a few of my things and I'll head back on Memorial Day."

Astonished, Shawna said, "What! Not so fast. How did this all happen?"

Katherine smiled. "I know. It's been a blur. I made the decision Monday after drinking a little wine Sunday night, but not too much wine. I was thinking clearly. I called a realtor I met Sunday night — I'll tell you more about that later. She pulled together four places for me to look at on Wednesday and

I rented a place that day. Wait till you see it. The shower is fantastic."

"But what about your work? And what about the divorce?" Shawna asked.

"You're my lawyer. You can handle the divorce. I'll be here whenever you need me."

"That's true. You can count on me for that."

After a quick fist bump, Katherine continued. "As for my work, I can do it remotely. I can access the library and my research materials online. And I think the change will be good for my writing, especially my creative writing."

She searched the refrigerator for something to offer Shawna, settling for a bottle of vin gris and some brie. "And I need the space from Stan. He nags me and nags me about the settlement. He wants this thing from the house, that painting, that piece of furniture — it's endless. I need breathing space, away from Stan."

Shawna put her arm around her. "I understand that, and if staying in Rehoboth can do that, I'll support you however you need me."

"Thanks. Would you keep an eye on the house?" Shawna nodded. "Oh, and what are you doing Monday morning? I could use help loading my car." Katherine grinned. "All that gym time you've been putting in can be put to good use hefting boxes."

"No problem. By the way, I've been getting calls from Stan. He's been asking weird questions like 'how committed is Katherine to staying in the house' and 'do I think Katherine would be more interested in a cash payout from the house?' I'm not sure what's going on."

Katherine frowned. "I don't know either. I sure don't want to reopen the settlement discussion."

Shawna handed her the wine opener. "Let's not worry

about that now. Come on, open the bottle of wine. Tell me about this place you've rented."

"It's fantastic. You can see for yourself when you come visit. You will come visit me, won't you?"

"Of course. I'm already feeling the sand between my toes."

# Chapter Ten

"Mom," exasperated, Anthony continued, "What are you thinking? Why would you spend your sabbatical in Rehoboth? You don't know anyone there."

Katherine explained patiently, "That's not exactly true, I've already met a number of delightful individuals. You remember Browseabout — the bookstore? Beth, the store manager, invited me to join her and a group of women for wine the other night. Interesting group — Isabella, one of the few female brewery owners in the country, Cassandra..." Katherine could hear Sonja in the background cooing at the baby and encouraging Anthony to stay calm.

Anthony interrupted, "That's nice, Mom, but they're not family. You need your family around right now. You're vulnerable and I don't want anyone to take advantage of you."

Katherine chuckled and rolled her eyes. "Thank you for caring, Anthony, but I'm sixty-one years old. Not ninety-seven. And I'm perfectly capable of tending to my own affairs. I need to be more self-reliant right now. I've been so caught up in taking care of your dad, and then later you and

Vanessa, which I don't regret for a minute, I've forgotten who I am."

Anthony whined, "But I thought you wanted to spend the time with us here in Atlanta. And we could use your help with Lucas."

"Much as I adore Lucas and love being with you, I don't think it's what I need right now. I'm hoping you'll come visit me and maybe stay for a week or so?" Katherine continued brightly. "You used to love to spend time on the boardwalk in Rehoboth."

Anthony huffed. "Traveling with Lucas is pretty complicated — you remember all the paraphernalia that goes with a six-month-old. And I don't think I can take the time off this summer. This case I'm working on is a bear. I'm putting in hours of overtime. Sonja has started asking for my ID when I come in the house. Seriously."

Even though Anthony couldn't see her over the phone, she shook her head. Katherine was glad that Anthony had a job that he loved, but she feared he was making the same mistake as his father — putting his career ahead of his family.

"Mom, I think this is a mistake. And it's not like you. You're not impulsive. And you just decided last week that you were going to do this? Uproot your whole life? Move to a strange place?"

Anthony, ever the logical lawyer, continued to list all the reasons why Katherine should not do this. "You probably won't even be able to find a place to stay and it'll be expensive. And don't you have divorce things to do at home? And we could use you here in Atlanta. And while you're here, we could make sure you're safe and not lonely."

"Anthony, honey — I have a place to stay already."

"What? How did that happen?" Anthony exploded.

"One of the women I met last week is a realtor and she

found me a great little house between Rehoboth and Dewey, a couple of blocks from the ocean. It's a bungalow with three small bedrooms. Plenty of room for you to stay when you come. There's a darling little pool in the backyard — more like an oversized bathtub — and a fountain. And a flagstone patio lined with flowers and shrubs and it's about a mile from the boardwalk," Katherine gushed.

"A mile from the boardwalk. Is it a safe neighborhood?"

"Anthony." She was exasperated now. "Give me a little credit. Michelle, the realtor, showed me all the crime statistics and it's fine. And I won't be walking around in the dark all night long, going to bars, hanging out on the street corners." Katherine tried a little humor. "You should be happy I didn't decide to spend my sabbatical in Paris."

Horrified, he exclaimed, "You wouldn't do that, would you? Then I'd worry about you all the time."

Katherine smiled. Her son was a little too protective. He always had been the sensitive one, the one who made sure she was included in his life, the first one to call when he thought she might be lonely.

She assured him, "No, I'm not doing that. *This year*. And I'm going to be fine. I need this, Anthony. I need the mental space. And I do hope you'll come visit — if not this summer, then maybe in the fall. Or for Thanksgiving. Actually, I'd love to see you anytime. I'll be there through New Year's."

Resigned, he said, "It sounds like your mind is made up." She imagined him tugging on his ear, like he used to do as a kid when he was frustrated or unhappy. "You know I love you, Mom. And I want you to be happy and taken care of. I'm sorry Dad is being such a jerk. We'll try to figure out when we can make a trip."

"Thanks, honey. I love you, too. And I'm so glad you're my son."

# Chapter Eleven

Vanessa, eyes flashing, crossed to the kitchen cabinet and plucked a coffee cup from the shelf. "Mom, I think you should definitely do it. It would serve Dad right if you had a great adventure this summer."

Katherine peered at her daughter, an incredibly strong and independent young woman. She knew Vanessa was furious with her dad. She constantly ranted that he was having a typical mid-life crisis — such a cliché, an affair with a younger woman.

"I am doing it. I've already rented a little cottage. And I'm not doing it to spite your father. I'm doing it because I want to." Katherine topped off her coffee and slipped back on the counter bar stool. This kitchen was her favorite room in the house — one of the few that she liked. The rest was all Stan — all decorator perfect, with very few personal touches.

But the kitchen was hers — from the white oak table to the sunshine yellow walls lined with her copper pans to the cobalt blue and white tiles. She'd modeled it after Monet's kitchen and dining room in Giverny. This room had always been the hub of the family with Vanessa and Anthony doing their homework on that white oak table. It made sense that this is where Vanessa settled when she stopped by this morning.

Vanessa considered her mother. "I'm glad you're doing something and not sitting around waiting for Dad to come back. You deserve better than this."

Katherine was glad that Vanessa approved, not that she needed it, but she appreciated it. Deciding where she was going to spend her sabbatical, not where Anthony, Vanessa, or Stan *wanted* her to, was a positive move. Of course, Stan thought she should stay in D.C. to make it easier on him while they ironed out the divorce settlement.

No more. She was going to live her life her way. She didn't regret putting her children first nor taking time out from her career when they were little. Going to Rehoboth — she was going to rediscover who she was and what she wanted to be since she would soon no longer be a wife and her kids didn't need her the way they used to.

Vanessa cleared her throat, drawing Katherine's attention. Vanessa, dark-haired bundle of energy, was her adventurer. She always had been since she was a little girl. She was forever going off exploring, sometimes much to Katherine's dismay since she didn't always know where Vanessa was. And now she was about to embark on a huge adventure — one very far from home, all the way to Africa. But she wasn't afraid. *I want to be as brave as she is.*

"What did Anthony say when you told him you decided to stay in Rehoboth for your sabbatical?" Vanessa asked.

"He wasn't happy about it. He wants me to come to Atlanta and stay with them. He said he thought he 'needed to take care of me'."

Vanessa grimaced. "He takes the older brother protector role too seriously. He, of course, is crazy mad at me for taking the assignment in Ethiopia. He said, 'don't you read the travel alerts? Reconsider travel to Ethiopia due to conflict, civil unrest, crime, communications disruptions, and the potential for terrorism and kidnapping.'"

She paced to the coffee pot. "Well, duh — I work for the State Department — of course I've seen the alerts. But this is my job and I'm still going. I've been waiting for an overseas assignment for a year and a half."

"I'm happy for you. But as your mother, I'll still worry about you and Curt. I'm extremely relieved he was assigned to the same place, too. That's quite a coup — both of you assigned together."

Vanessa squeezed her mom's hand. "I know you're concerned, and I appreciate your support." She reached for her car keys. "It helped that I'm an Economic Officer and he's a Political Officer. And we both listed Ethiopia as our top choice. Because the situation is complex, we didn't have as much competition for the slots."

She hugged her mom. "Being married would have made it easier. We talked about it, but we're not quite ready to do that, especially given what happened with you and Dad. I know Curt is not anything like Dad, thank God, but it has made us super cautious."

"Oh, honey, don't let what happened between your dad and me color your thoughts about marriage. You two are very different people than we are...were. You guys are real partners. I wasn't as strong as you are, and I put my career on hold while I supported his. Now I have a chance to do something different."

"Do it, Mom. Go do what you need to do."

"I am, Vanessa. I am."

# Chapter Twelve

Katherine crossed off the last item on her list. Papers stopped. Mail forwarded. Security system set.

The rental was furnished, albeit in a shabby chic kind of style that probably wasn't on purpose. Except for the shower. The owner put all his money into that shower. She loved that shower.

She counted the boxes and suitcases — not that many. She had packed mostly her summer clothes and a couple of sweatshirts for cool nights. And a few things from the kitchen that she loved. And her books. And her plants.

*Is that too many books?* she fretted. *Nah.* She needed all those books for her research even though she could read academic articles online. These books were seminal works, critical to her research.

Shawna, her fiery red hair tied back with a red and white polka dot bandana, rang the bell and barged in. "Are you ready for the cavalry? Well, at least one recruit reporting for manual labor. This doesn't look like very many boxes."

"A few more boxes in the bedroom and a couple of suitcases. I hope it's all going to fit in the car."

Shawna counted the boxes. "It's going to be a tight fit."

"I'm just taking clothes for this season. I'll be back to collect my fall and winter things later."

"Do you have to take any dishes or pots and pans?"

"The kitchen in the rental has all the basics — no need for me to duplicate any of that. And what's not there, I'll do without. I'm taking my coffee maker since you know I love it."

Shawna nodded. She knew that Katherine couldn't start her day without her fancy Nespresso machine.

"And pictures of Vanessa and Curt, and Anthony and his family. My laptop and printer, and of course, my books."

Shawna groaned. "Boxes of books are the worst."

Sheepish, Katherine winced. "I know. I'll carry those."

Shawna flexed her muscles. "Fine. Let's do this. But whenever I move, you're helping me and I'm going to have a lot more boxes than this."

"Are you moving?" Katherine was worried.

"No, but if I was, you'd be helping me." Shawna grinned.

The two women made quick work of loading the car. "I've got lemonade left," Katherine said when they finished. "Would you like a glass before I hit the road?"

"Sure. Hey, how did Vanessa and Anthony take your news?"

"Vanessa was very supportive and Anthony, well, he still thinks I should spend my next seven months with him in Atlanta under his concerned attention. He fears that I'll fall apart."

Shawna laughed. "Even as a little boy, he was always so concerned about you. He just can't help himself."

Katherine handed her a glass. She scowled. "Anthony told his father about my plan. Stan called me to tell me how irresponsible I was being, that I wasn't taking this divorce seriously, and that we still had things to talk about and how was I going to do that all the way in Delaware."

"Like Delaware is on the other side of the world. It's a four-hour drive." Shawna smirked. "What a drama queen."

"Do you think I should block his number? I can't take his badgering much more. I don't know what's going on with him." Katherine rambled on, her stress mounting as she recalled Stan's last phone call.

"As your lawyer, and your friend, let me look into it and circle back to you. I'll talk to his lawyer and have him tell Stan that he needs to communicate through his attorney to me."

"Thanks, Shawna. You're the best."

"You better hit the road. You'll want to be settled in your new place before it's dark." Shawna gave her a hug. "Text me when you get there."

Katherine took a last look around. The house looked like a model home — not a real home with people living and laughing in it. Her little house in Rehoboth had more character and felt more alive. She glanced at the clock. *Arghh, how is it so late?* She locked the door, climbed in her car, and without a backward glance, headed for her new home.

# Chapter Thirteen

*Late. Why does it always feel like I'm late?* Katherine wheeled out of the driveway. It had taken twice as much time to load her Volvo Cross Country as she expected even with Shawna's help. And, of course, they had to have one final chat over lemonade. She would miss her so much.

She made the turn onto the access road. Flap. Flap. Flap. Flap. *What the hell is that?*

Katherine pulled over. The weather stripping on the twelve-year-old Volvo on the passenger side was loose. *Darn Stan! He was supposed to have this fixed the last time he took the car in. And how come he got the new SUV and left me with this old clunker?*

*Where is that last box of stuff I threw in? Ha — duct tape.* She fished her Swiss Army knife out of her purse and taped the weather strip down. *Another half hour gone. At this rate, I'll be lucky to arrive before dark.*

Traffic was thick on 495. Maniac drivers still passed her on the right and the left in the bumper-to-bumper traffic. They had to be going seventy or eighty miles per hour even though the speed limit was fifty-five. Katherine flinched every time one blew past her. She finally reached Route 50 and headed to Annapolis. With traffic a bit lighter, Katherine breathed a sigh of relief.

The sun was low in the sky behind her, backlighting the trees that lined the highway. She was making steady progress until she spotted the construction sign — "Right Lane Closed Ahead." And then she noticed the "Left Lane Ending, Merge Right" sign. Four lanes collapsing into two. The light traffic turned into brake lights as far as she could see. Katherine fidgeted and fumed. *More delays.*

She groaned. *Stan, of course, would have checked the traffic and known about this. He would have left earlier, too. I should have left earlier. Oh, stop "shoulding" on yourself as Shawna would tell you. You're doing the best you can.*

Finally clearing the construction, Katherine zoomed along at the sixty-five miles per hour speed limit until she reached Annapolis. The sign overhead read, "10 miles, 60 minutes to Bay Bridge." She slammed on her brakes and came to a screeching halt.

She pounded the steering wheel. *Why is there so much traffic going east over the Bay Bridge? Everyone should be heading back to the city from their Memorial Day vacation at the beaches.*

She turned off the air conditioning and rolled down her window, hoping to catch a breeze. But the air was still and perfumed with exhaust. The guy in the "rolling speaker" next to her was going to lose his hearing playing his music that loud. In a spurt of movement, he pulled ahead only to be replaced with a van full of a mom and dad and four kids, clearly tired of sitting — two were crying, and mom had a hand on a third who looked like he was ready to hit back, while the fourth made faces at the criers.

Katherine remembered her trips to the beach with Anthony and Vanessa. With only two of them, they each got their own row in the van. Thinking back, she realized Stan was rarely with them. She took the kids on her own and Stan promised to come later. But he never did.

She sneezed and quickly closed the windows and hoped the good old Volvo wouldn't overheat. Another thirty minutes and she would be at the bridge.

*Oh geez, I have to move into the left lane.* Katherine was terrified of driving in the railing lane on the bridge. Then she could see how high up she was over the water. She shuddered.

*Why won't anyone let me over? I'm being nice. I've got my signal on.* Frustrated, she tapped her horn to attract the attention of the driver next to her. He just ignored her.

Double yellow lines and a flashing yellow sign telling her to "Stay in Your Lane." *Story of my life.* Stan always told her that he would manage everything else — she needed to mind the kids and the house. *Stay in my lane and don't venture into his. That didn't work out very well, did it?* Now she had to do everything she'd always done *and* learn how to do everything that Stan did — like the taxes.

Resigned, Katherine turned off her blinker. *I can do this. I can't close my eyes until we reach the other side — almost four and a half miles — like I do...did...on the rare times that Stan drove. But I can do this.*

White knuckled, she clutched the steering wheel. *At least, we're moving. This will be over soon.* Traffic crept along at ten miles per hour and climbed the slope to where the bridge leveled off almost 200 feet above the water. She shivered. *Just focus on the car in front of you. You can do this.*

*No! No! No! Don't stop here!* Sweat broke out on her forehead. She was stuck — traffic came to a dead halt right in the middle of the bridge. Like being trapped in the top car on a stopped Ferris wheel.

Both hands gripping the wheel, Katherine looked around wildly. Next to her on the guardrail was a seagull, calmly regarding her with interest. The slight breeze ruffled his feathers, but his claws firmly attached to the railing. Not bothered a bit by the traffic nor the breeze nor the fact that he was clinging to a two-inch railing 200 feet in the air. He bobbed his head at Katherine as if to say, "Chill. Doesn't the sun feel great? Doesn't the breeze feel nice? And take a look at all those boaters on the water having fun."

Relaxing, Katherine laughed at the bird's antics. The boats were beautiful as they flew back and forth with their multicolored spinnakers. Safely inside the car, Katherine appreciated the view.

Kent Island, the first English settlement in Maryland, was straight ahead with its many marinas and condos. Over her shoulder to the right, she caught the tip of Annapolis. Turning back the other way, if she craned her neck just so, she could see Sandy Point Beach where they did the Polar Bear Plunge every February. Well, at least a surprisingly large group of crazy people did if the newspaper pictures could be trusted. Not her. Even if it were for a good cause, it was too darn cold.

A gentle beep startled her. Glancing up, she realized traffic was moving again. *Huh. Thanks to that bird I forgot to be scared.* Speed picked up and soon she was over the bridge. Yachts for sale lined up like mail-order brides waiting for their forever homes. Marinas jutted into the Chesapeake, their berths full of motorboats and sailboats. Marsh grasses bled into bays.

After a quick stop at The Lovely Little Coffee House in the Queenstown Outlet Mall, Katherine sailed along Route 50 past the old St. Peter the Apostle Catholic Church, founded in 1765. Just a mile past St Peter's, she passed the turn to the Aspen Institute Wye River Conference Centers. President Bill Clinton led negotiations there in 1998 that resulted in a step toward peace between Palestine and Israel. Old history and new history — one of the reasons she loved this area.

Sailing along Route 404, she crossed the Underground Railroad. Harriot Tubman was born not too far from here. She reflected on Tubman's strength and wondered how such a small person in stature could be extraordinarily brave. It made her realize that her own problems were nothing compared to what Tubman had faced.

Katherine flipped her lights on as she took the bypass around Denton, Maryland. This was the last four-lane road of the trip until she got to Route 1 that led to the Delaware beaches. The rest of the trip was on a curvy two-lane road with very few places to pass.

She rolled her shoulders and rubbed her eyes. The last few days were catching up with her. She replayed the bitter conversation with Stan before she left. He didn't give her credit for thinking through this decision and thought she was being selfish — only thinking of her own needs and not caring what he needed. Which was to be divorced quickly and with a settlement that met his needs, of course.

Lost in her thoughts, Katherine didn't notice she crossed the Delaware state line. Flashing blue and red lights drew closer and she pulled over to let the policeman pass. Instead of passing, he pulled up behind her.

"Ma'am, are you aware of how fast you were driving?"

"I don't know — maybe fifty-five or sixty? I'm on my way to Rehoboth from Virginia and I got caught in traffic on the bridge and it's getting dark," she stammered. "What is the speed limit? I think it's the same as Maryland."

"No, ma'am. Our speed limit here in Delaware is fifty miles

per hour on these rural two-lane roads. Maryland's is fifty-five miles per hour. I clocked you going sixty-one miles per hour."

"I'm sorry, officer. I was thinking and not paying attention to my speed, and I didn't see the sign. I promise I'll be more careful."

"I'm sure you will. License and registration, please." Katherine's face fell. He was going to give her a ticket. *Damn, could this day get any worse?*

Religiously driving the speed limit as she passed through the last little town before hitting Route 1, she noticed dark stoplights and streetlights, and big branches littering the yards. The houses were all dark, too. *There must have been a big storm here. The power's out.* She fretted. *I hope everything's okay at my new place.*

She sighed with relief when she hit the main road to the beach. Surely, she could make up some time now. Dismayed, she saw flashing red stoplights. Traffic was backed up at every single light as drivers tried to decide who had the right-of-way. Cars inched along past darkened restaurants and strip malls.

She waited to make a left on King Charles Ave. and breathed a sigh of relief. She was almost to her new home. Four blocks later, she turned right on Carolina. *It's awfully dark. Where is the driveway? They need a light there.* She stopped short as she started the turn into the rental.

An enormous tree covered the driveway. It looked like it missed the house but caught the edge of the carport. She would barely be able to squeeze by to reach the front door. She'd have to walk on the grass and leave the car parked on the street.

*Oh. Come. On. First the traffic and then the ticket and now this? Is the universe trying to tell me something? Maybe this whole thing is a bad decision.*

Katherine couldn't decide whether to laugh or cry. Exhausted, she sat there, stunned.

# Chapter Fourteen

Katherine climbed out of her car and rubbed her back. What was supposed to be a four-hour trip had taken six hours. She was tired and hungry and now she had to deal with this tree.

"Michelle, this is Katherine. I just got back into town and I'm guessing you had severe weather over the weekend."

"We sure did. High winds and torrential rains. Lots of downed trees and lines all over the place. Do you have power?"

"I don't know. I haven't been inside yet. I think so — I see lights across the street. The thing is...a tree or a big branch fell down on the driveway. It missed the house, but the carport is pretty wrecked."

"Oh no," Michelle interrupted. "Was anything of yours damaged?"

"No, I haven't even gotten out of the car yet. I got a late start today and ran into a little trouble on the way."

"Can you get into the house?"

"I think I can slide by on the grass. Let me check." She

found the flashlight app on her phone and made her way to the front door. *Which key is it? The red or blue one? There was one was for the back door and the other was for the front door.*

"It's the red key," Michelle said. "Blue is for Back — b and b. Get it?"

Katherine sighed. *Why couldn't one key open both doors?* The first thing she would do is rekey the locks if this were her place, right after she put a light at the end of the driveway.

The door creaked open, and she reached inside for the porch light. Light flooded the sidewalk and the edge of the driveway.

"Good news. The power is on." She walked through the house checking for more damage, turning on lights as she went. "It doesn't look like anything else was hit — only the carport from what I can see now."

"Do you feel okay staying there tonight? I could try to find you a room somewhere but with all the tourists and the people without power, most everything will be full."

She shook her head. "No, I'm beat. I'll be fine here. I'm going to bring some bedding, one suitcase, and my laptop and leave everything else for tomorrow. A quick shower and I'll hit the sack."

"If you're sure..."

"I'm sure. What are we going to do about the carport?"

"I'll talk to the owner tomorrow and see what he wants to do. He'll probably want to come see the damage and then ask for a couple of bids."

"That's fine. If he comes tomorrow, tell him not too early. And Michelle, you don't think this is a sign I wasn't supposed to stay here for my sabbatical, do you?"

"No, no, I'm sorry you're having a rocky start, but I listened to all your arguments about why this was a good idea when we were looking at all the apartments and houses. It seemed like pretty good reasoning to me. You've had a hard day. Get some rest and I'll talk to you soon."

# Chapter Fifteen

Katherine rolled over and grabbed her Fitbit. *8:00! Who the heck is pounding on my door?* She grabbed her robe and stumbled to the door. "Who's there?"

"Katherine, it's me, Michelle."

"And me, Beth."

"And me, Isabella." Voices caroled. Katherine unlocked the door and gaped in surprise. "What are you all doing here?"

"We brought you coffee and the best scones in Rehoboth from Rise Up. They're deliciously moist and yummy. Have you been there yet? And we're here to help you unload your car."

Katherine struggled to keep up with Michelle. She raked her hand through her already bed-headed hair. "Could we start with the coffee and then tell me again what you're doing here?"

"Michelle called us last night after she heard about the tree." Isabella bounced into the kitchen. "Damn, that's a big tree. It's amazing it didn't hit the house."

Katherine looked out at the carport and realized how close it had been to a real disaster. It had barely missed the house.

"Michelle invited us to come over this morning and give you a hand," Beth continued. "We've all got to open places at ten o'clock so here we are. Sorry we got you out of bed, but it's now or never."

Michelle laughed at Katherine's face. "Close your mouth, Katherine. Have a scone."

"But why?"

"Because they're delicious scones."

"No, why are you here? Why would you do this?"

Beth took in the circles under Katherine's eyes and her pale skin. "Because you needed the help."

Katherine ducked her head and wiped her eyes on her sleeve. She took in the women surrounding her. "Thank you," she whispered.

Isabella jumped up. "Where are your keys? Enough of this lollygagging. I've got places to go."

"Right. Give me a minute to change. The keys are on the table by the door." Katherine pulled herself together. *Maybe this is going to be all right after all.*

Michelle was a drill sergeant. By the time Katherine got back, Michelle had Isabella assigned to unloading the car and delivering the boxes to the living room. A perpetual motion machine, she whizzed back and forth so fast, Katherine got dizzy watching her. Before she could even help, the car was empty.

Beth worked the inside. She methodically moved the boxes to whichever room they belonged based on Katherine's careful labelling. Gently slitting the tops of the boxes with her safety handle boxcutter she used all day at the bookstore, she left the boxes ready to unpack.

Cassandra rushed up as Isabella closed the hatch.

"Perfect timing, girl," Isabella teased.

"Sorry! Sorry! I don't know what happened to my alarm."

"Here. Grab the monstera plant and earn your scone," Isabella directed as she pulled the last suitcase over the gravel.

"Cassandra, how are you? Put that plant over by the sliding door. There's one coffee left and I think there might be one scone left if Beth didn't snag it." Michelle winked at Beth.

"Hey, I only ate one." Beth insisted. "Nice of you to show up, Cassandra." She grinned and inched toward the last scone.

Cassandra grabbed the scone as Beth tried to slide it onto her plate. "I know. I know. I'm sorry. My alarm didn't go off."

Katherine smiled at the easy relationships between these friends, each very different from the other. Isabella — all fire and energy. Michelle — polished and chic. Beth — warm and intellectual. Cassandra — shy and quiet. How lucky she was to be included in this group. How lucky to be with friends.

"Thank you, guys, for everything. Now you all better head to work, or your bosses will have my head. Oh wait, you are the bosses." She laughed. "When I've sorted out these boxes, I'll invite you over for dinner."

"Deal," said Michelle. "And I left a message with the owner about the tree. He hasn't gotten back to me yet, but he works tremendously long hours. I'm sure he'll call me back later today."

"Are you up for lunch today?" Beth asked.

"Would tomorrow or the next day work? I'd like to be settled and put my stuff away."

"Sure, no problem. I'll give you a call."

# Chapter Sixteen

*First things first,* Katherine thought as she entered City Hall. *I have to register my car before it gets ticketed.* Since the tree was blocking the driveway, she had to park on the street. Darn inconvenient. Why couldn't the owner find someone to clear the tree at least?

Michelle gave her a temporary parking permit when she signed the contract, but she had to have a permanent permit for the whole season through September. That required proof of registration, vehicle registration number (including the state in which the vehicle is registered), make/model, and year of vehicle. It seemed like rigmarole, but parking was at such a premium with all the summer visitors, it had to be done. And she needed an extra guest permit when the kids came to visit.

Katherine walked the halls of the new City Hall looking for the parking office. *This is an exceptionally well-designed building — it looks quite new — lots of windows, blond wood, marble floors reflecting the sun from the floor-to-ceiling windows. Fancy staircase and great art. They need better signage so I can figure out where I'm going.*

Just as she turned back to ask the guard where the Parking Office was located, she bumped into a handsome gray-haired man in perfectly creased Todd Snyder khakis, Brooks Brothers turquoise polo shirt, Manolo Blahnik boat shoes. No socks, of course. She recognized the brands since her husband wore the same pretentious names.

"Oh, excuse me. I'm sorry. I was looking for the Parking Office and didn't watch where I was going."

He smiled and caught her elbow to steady her. "Well, I guess it's my lucky day because that's where I'm headed. I'll show you where it is."

Katherine took a step back and hesitated. "You don't need to do that. Point me in the right direction."

"I wouldn't dream of letting such a lovely lady wander these halls alone. Who knows who you could run into?"

She reluctantly let him take her arm and lead her around the stairway and out the back door. "The Parking Office is in a separate building behind City Hall —across the driveway. I'm Richard Ferry. And you are?"

She replied, "I'm Katherine" without sharing her last name. She wasn't sure she liked his familiarity.

She could feel his head-to-toe perusal assessing her diamond earrings and Burberry bag. His gaze flashed to her bare left ring finger and then lingered on her right hand where she wore the flashy diamond ring that Stan had given her for their twenty-fifth anniversary. It felt like he was calculating her net worth.

"Katherine, are you here for the season?" He lightly touched her arm and gazed into her eyes.

*A little too smarmy. Is this guy being friendly or is this creepy?*

"Yes, I'm here for the season this time. Usually, it's only for a week or two."

"Oh?"

She didn't take the bait and explain why she was staying in town.

Richard dropped it when they entered the Parking Office. They each took a number to wait their turns. Katherine turned to thank Richard for his help. He beckoned her to the only two empty chairs by the window and settled down close beside her. she shifted away to keep their legs from touching.

"How long have you been in town? Have you found any new restaurants you like?" he asked, leaning in as if he couldn't wait for her answer.

"There are a couple of new places I like — Goldie's over on Olive Ave is a great place for brunch. Fantastic eggs Benedict and crab Benedict and peach Bellini's by the pitcher. And a little hole-in-the-wall on Delaware Ave, The Hideaway. They're kind of a best-kept secret with great Greek food — souvlaki, moussaka, baclava." She laughed. "You can tell food is one of my passions."

Richard quickly glanced at her hips before replying, "Oh, mine, too. Eating together is one of the most intimate things a couple can do together."

Katherine frowned and looked away. "Are you a seasonal resident, too?"

"No, I'm permanent. I have a place on the ocean in North Rehoboth where I spend my summers and holidays when I'm not traveling for work. I've misplaced my permit, unfortunately, so I need to replace it."

Katherine's number was called and shortly after, Richard's was. Her tasks didn't take long to complete. She turned to thank Richard again and found him standing behind her.

"Would you like to grab a cup of coffee? There's a great coffee shop in the Mews down the street."

Katherine hesitated. There was something that didn't quite

sit right with her about him. "I'll have to pass. I need to run a few other errands."

"Okay, lovely to make your acquaintance, Katherine with no last name. At least give me your phone number. Maybe we can try again later?"

She was feeling hustled. She had never liked pushy salespeople and this guy was coming on too strong. She hadn't had this kind of pressure since she first met Stan and he insisted on walking her back to the dorm until she agreed to go out with him. And look how that turned out.

"Thanks for the offer. Perhaps we'll run into each other again." Katherine turned to leave. *That's not going to happen.*

# Chapter Seventeen

Beth waved to the bartender who nodded without smiling and went back to pouring drinks. *At least it isn't just me that he ignores,* Katherine thought.

Bellying up to the bar, they watched as he slapped four glasses on the bar. Scooped the right amount of ice. Grabbed two bottles of liquor and poured down the line like a machine. Slipped the garnish on each glass. Hit the bell. Maybe fifteen seconds for four drinks. Almost like watching a ballet — every move had purpose and efficiency. Katherine grudgingly admired his skill. *If only his people skills were as good.*

"Hey, Beth, how's it going?" He smiled at Beth. Katherine gaped in surprise at the difference his smile made. His chiseled face, brooding mouth, cool brown eyes softened as he regarded Beth.

"Hi, Jeff. Not too bad. How are you?"

*This is Jeff? He's not just the rude bartender. He owns this place according to Beth. What's he doing bartending?*

"This is my friend, Katherine. She moved to town the other day and I thought I'd show her where the best food is."

He turned to her and grimaced.

"Oh, we've sort of met," she said.

"Yeah, you were in here last week and couldn't wait to be served," he sneered.

"Well, I was waiting quite a long time," Katherine responded sarcastically. "It looks like it might be the same today from the looks of your poor waitress. Is she covering the whole restaurant again?"

Beth watched the exchange like a tennis match with each player hitting killer shots just inside the line.

"I didn't know you had already been here, Katherine."

"I came last week after you recommended it."

"What's going on, Jeff? You usually have two or three people covering lunch." Beth asked.

He cast a quick glance over his shoulder to see if he had any new orders to fill. Scrubbing his scruffy face with both hands, "One of my cooks had to go home last week to take care for his dad who broke his leg. My main guy, Tim, just came back from the Keys where he winters. I can usually scrape by with a skeleton crew until school is out and the season really kicks in. When Jerry had the emergency, I had to scramble."

Katherine watched as he pulled two drafts and mixed three gin and tonics while still talking to Beth. No wasted motions as he deftly filled the drink orders. *He moves like an athlete — controlled, elegant. And he had a really nice chest.*

"Is Tim coming in today?"

"No, he got in quite late last night. Got caught in the bad weather we had the last couple of days. It took him an extra day to make the trip. I told him to sleep in today and get his butt in here tomorrow. Joyce, my other waitress, is still filling in as cook which leaves me and Allison to cover the front."

"Isn't Joyce like twelve months pregnant?" Beth laughed.

"Only seven and a half but she's having all kinds of Braxton-Hicks. I hope she hangs in there until my college kids are done with the semester or I can hire a few more seasonal folks to join the team. But you know how hard that's been."

"It has been a real problem for us, too. We all depend on the tourist revenue and if we can't find people to work during the season, we may have to cut our hours at Browseabout."

He nodded. "Us, too. I don't want to do it, but I might be limited to staffing dinners exclusively. I'll have to open at 5:00 instead of 11:00."

"No," Katherine interrupted, looking at Beth. "That would be terrible. You can't reduce the Browseabout hours — where would people buy their morning newspapers?"

Beth shrugged. "I agree, but we may have to open later or close earlier or something. I can't work any more hours than I am. We've got a couple of high school kids coming in a few evenings and weekends, but they can't be in charge. I need someone more mature."

Katherine's ears perked up.

"Looks like Allison needs me. Do you want a drink? Something to eat?" He tapped the order pad on the bar impatiently.

"I'll have the Rueben — I'm always looking for the best one. Although it will be hard to beat the ones I had in Madison when I was teaching there." Katherine paused. "And do you carry Isabella's beer?"

"Of course. What'll you have, Beth?"

"I'll take the blackened rockfish BLT and iced tea. Have to go back to work so no alcohol for me."

Katherine and Beth chatted about their favorite authors and argued whether it was better to see the movie first or read the book first while they finished their lunches. Since Beth had an in with the owner, their checks came out before they asked for them. He knew Beth had to dash back to Browseabout.

They blinked as they walked out into the noon sun. Beth asked. "I'm sorry you had such a bad experience the first time. Jeff's not usually like that."

"I can see Jeff was not at his best the other day. He's still not the warmest, nicest guy I've ever met. And don't tell him his Rueben was one of the best I've had — his ego doesn't need anything more."

Beth chuckled. "He doesn't lack self-confidence, that's for sure. He's working like a dog to keep his people employed. If he has to reduce hours or close more days, the people he has working for him now would be hurt. And he tries to take good care of his staff. Even provides benefits."

"It sounds like it will be better soon if his new hires all come through. Staffing is one of the biggest problems entrepreneurs have." Katherine said.

Beth frowned. "We all are facing a crisis if we can't hire more summer help. We're not getting the applicants like we used to even when we're offering a good salary and more benefits for our part-time people. Restaurants are hurting for sure, but all retail is feeling the pinch."

"About that...how mature are you looking for? Is sixty-one mature enough?"

"What are you saying?" Beth asked hopefully.

"I've always loved Browseabout. And I can't think of any place I'd rather spend time. Do you think I could work part-time, a couple of evenings and maybe even the weekends? It's not like I've got a wild social life."

"Oh my...are you serious?" Beth bounced with excitement. "If you're serious, when can you start?"

Katherine said, "Don't you want to think about it? Interview me? Check my references?"

"Sure! But I can already predict you'll ace the interview. Why don't you come by in the morning, and we'll discuss the details? Oh, this is a dream come true for me. You have no idea how much I've been worrying about finding someone I could trust with the store."

# Chapter Eighteen

"Katherine? This is Michelle. How's it going?"

Katherine looked around the comfortable house, satisfied with loading the bookshelves, putting up Vanessa and Anthony's pictures, and situating her plants for the best sun or shade required.

It wasn't a fancy place and the owner certainly had not put much effort into decorating, except for the primary bathroom which would give many high-priced spas a run for their money. No expense had been spared — teak floors, a rainfall shower with fourteen jets, stone bowl sink, skylights. Ten-foot windows made it feel like you were showering outdoors. A nine-foot redwood enclosure outside the windows filled with lush plants and flowers provided privacy. There was nothing she needed to do — it was perfect. For the rest of the house, colorful pillows and throw rugs had substantially improved it.

"It's going well. I've got all my boxes unpacked and did a little sprucing up — all temporary stuff. My landlord shouldn't be bothered."

"I'm sure he won't mind. That's why I called. I spoke to

him, and he wondered if he could stop by this afternoon and take a look at the damage. I spoke to him yesterday and he's called several tree removal companies and a couple of contractor friends to see when they'll be available to do the work."

"It's about time. It's been three days. Of course, he can come over this afternoon. What time is he coming?" Katherine asked.

"That's just it. He wants you to call him and let him know a good time for you. Is that okay?"

"Sure. What's his number?" She scribbled the number on her pages-long to-do list.

"Thompson!" the voice barked. Katherine could hear clanking and music in the background. It almost sounded like a bar.

"Michelle Schneider gave me this number to speak to my landlord. I'm over on Caroline Street."

"Yeah, that's me. What do you want?" He sounded frazzled and grumpy.

She stared at the phone in exasperation. "Michelle told me you wanted to come over and take a look at the tree that's fallen on your property? This afternoon?" she explained. *Sheesh —  were all the men in Rehoboth grumpy and brusque?*

"7:30 work for you?" he said abruptly.

"Yes, that's fine." She started to continue, but he interrupted, "I'll see you later," and hung up.

She fussed he could have been a little nicer. After all, it was his house. And she had been patient. She was the one being inconvenienced. She had to park her car in the street and walk all over the grass. She was going to give him a piece of her mind this evening when he showed up.

Katherine had barely finished loading the dishwasher when the doorbell rang insistently. *Good grief! Don't break the bell.* She dried her hands and went to open the door.

"What are you doing here?" she asked Jeff, not very politely. He looked disheveled. His ponytail was coming loose from its rubber band. His jeans looked like he had been barbecuing and spilled grease on his pants. His chambray shirt with the sleeves rolled up to the elbows was wrinkled and stained.

"I could ask you the same thing." Jeff scowled. "I own this place."

"You're Thompson? You own this place! You're my landlord?" Katherine was incredulous. *Of all the bad luck...*

"Ah, shi...I mean, damn. Michelle told me she had rented the place out to an English professor from D.C., but I didn't make the connection. I thought you taught high school or something when you said you were a teacher."

"Well, I don't. I teach at a university in Washington, D.C. Michelle never told me my landlord's name. I've been working directly with her."

"Let's just get this over with. Can I come in and see if there's any other damage? I took a look at the outside already. I know what needs to be done there."

"Of course," she said not very graciously. "I've already checked but you can check again."

# Chapter Nineteen

Jeff strode through the house, noting the homey touches Katherine had added. He liked the red and black pillows in the living room, and the vases of colorful zinnias she had everywhere. She must have cleaned out the farmer's market.

His pride and joy — the shower — smelled different. It didn't smell like his shampoo anymore. It smelled like lavender and eucalyptus — must be her scent.

She had filled his bookcases with books and pictures of a small family and a couple. There was a fancy coffee maker on his counter. And fruit in his favorite bowl that was his grandmother's.

She had turned one of the bedrooms into an office. She made a desk out of a couple of short filing cabinets and a door — functional, if not pretty.

It looked like she was settling in quite comfortably.

He didn't see any other damage, but he would have the contractor check it out more carefully when she came to fix the carport.

She stood just inside the open front door. *Jeez, did she think he was going to attack her or something?* She looked like she was poised for a quick getaway.

He supposed he hadn't given her much reason to be comfortable with him, but he was darn tired and stressed. The situation at his latest restaurant wasn't getting better. Joyce's doctor had told her today she had to quit working and go on bedrest for the last few weeks of her pregnancy.

Tim was back and working but Jeff was still one cook short. He might have to move someone from one of his other restaurants temporarily until he could hire someone else or until Jerry got back. He didn't have many spares at his other places either. He didn't know what he was going to do.

"Did you find anything else?"

"What?" Jeff looked up in surprise. He'd forgotten she was there. "No, nothing else."

He stepped toward the front door and she looked up anxiously.

"I'm going to take off now. Terry, the tree guy, is going to be here tomorrow. I had to beg and plead with him to make it soon. There's extensive damage all over the county — he could be working twenty-four hours a day. As it is, he's putting in fifteen, sixteen hours every day trying to clear everything out."

"Thank you. I'd appreciate being able to park in the driveway."

He swiped his hand across his eyes. He knew he should apologize for being so rude the other day, but he was so darn tired he could hardly think straight.

"I have a contractor friend who's going to try to fit the carport in the beginning of next week. Whatever Terry doesn't clean up tomorrow, I'll have someone come over the next day so you can park in the driveway. I don't think you should park in the carport yet — it looks like it's still structurally sound, but I don't want to take any chances." He glanced at her old Volvo and thought it probably wouldn't matter with as many dents and scrapes as it already had.

"Thanks. Just being off the street will be nice."

He stuck out his hand to shake. His eyes widened as warmth flowed through him and gave his manly parts a rush. *What was that?* She looked as taken aback as he was.

Dropping her hand like it was a hot frying pan, he gave a brief salute as he strode to his motorcycle.

# Chapter Twenty

*What the hell just happened?* Jeff snapped his helmet in place. He didn't have to wear a helmet after he turned twenty. He loved his bike and the freedom it gave him, but safety was always first and that meant wearing a helmet every single time he rode.

Thank God, he did. He had too many friends with scarred heads, or worse, because they didn't want to wear a helmet.

*What the hell? I don't even like that woman.* But he couldn't deny she had lit up his impulses. There was something about her prickliness that attracted him. Or maybe it was the contrast between the sadness in her eyes and her bitching at him for the poor service.

*Geez, what did she want?* It's not like he wanted people to wait in his restaurant. Did she not understand everyone was short-staffed?

She was so curvy and soft. He caught himself imagining what her plump pink lips would taste like.

*Whoa! Where is that coming from?* It had been a while since he'd kissed anyone, but he didn't usually jump to thinking about kissing whenever he met a new woman.

He was careful about who he got involved with now. He waited until he was forty-one to marry. Too busy getting established in the business, first with updating and expanding his grandparents' diner, and then acquiring or building more restaurants. He'd thought his ex-wife was okay with his hours when they got married. It turned out she wasn't, especially after their daughter was born. He didn't really blame her, but she knew going in people like to eat out on the weekends and at night.

Shannon, his ex-wife, didn't want to live like two ships passing in the night. She wanted her husband to work "regular" hours. She wanted to do more than sleep in the same bed for three hours a night — he got home at 2:00 AM by the time he closed and did the books, and she had to be up by 5:00 AM to get to her hospital shift by 6:00. They parted, mostly amicably.

His daughter, Chelsea, was the one who had suffered the most. Six years old when they divorced, she didn't understand why Daddy wasn't home in the mornings to make her pancakes and take her to school. They had especially loved summers when they could spend the whole morning together. They had built many forts and sandcastles before he had to go to work.

When Shannon got married and moved to Wilmington, Delaware, Chelsea stayed with her mother during the school year and Jeff took her on some holidays and summers. They still got to spend their days together until he had to go to work. He made sure she had friends and play dates in Rehoboth. She loved his neighbor who fed her dinner with her own family and then put her to bed. When Chelsea got older, Jeff's neighbor's teenage daughter spent the evenings with her.

Now that Chelsea was sixteen, she didn't need a sitter. And her summers were so busy she didn't come to Rehoboth for the whole summer anymore. In fact, this summer she was earning college credit by taking two classes at the local community college.

Reflecting on the jolt Katherine gave him, *that's why I don't date much. Chelsea is my first priority. I missed so much time with her when she was younger. I don't want to miss any more. She'll be graduating soon and going off to college.*

*But those lips. Rich and full. And I could get lost in those big green eyes.*

# Chapter Twenty-One

Katherine stared morosely into her coffee cup, not noticing the sun peeking up over the trees. Tossing and turning all night, she finally decided to get up and sit in the chaise lounge on the patio, hoping the fountain would soothe her. Wiping a tear from her cheek, she mourned all she had lost.

She missed Stan — or rather the husband Stan used to be. She missed being part of a couple. She missed having someone to talk to in the evenings. She missed sleeping next to someone. And yes, she missed the sex, even though it had become less and less frequent. *When was the last time he kissed me on the lips?* She couldn't remember.

Friends weren't sure whether to invite one, or both, or neither of them to their parties. Last week when she was talking with Shawna, Shawna let it slip Stan had brought Chrissy to the neighborhood barbeque. *What was that about? He's not even living in the house anymore and he won't be since he "gave" the house to me.*

She checked the time and decided it wasn't too early to call Shawna before she headed to the office.

"Hey."

"What's wrong?" Shawna asked. "You sound down."

"You can tell that from one word?"

"Yeah. For one thing, it's the crack of dawn and you're usually not up this early. And second, it was the saddest 'hey' I've heard in a long time."

"I miss my old life. And I'm sad and mad at the same time. How could Stan throw our whole marriage away? I feel like such a failure. I'm embarrassed I didn't see what was happening right in front of me. How could this have happened?"

"Well, kid, you're not a failure. You're an accomplished person, a wonderful mother, a great friend whose marriage fell apart because your husband had, and is having, an affair with a woman almost thirty years younger than you."

"But maybe if I'd been more...more interesting, sexier, thinner, different — he wouldn't have had the affair."

"Come on, Katherine, you can't own his behavior. You loved him. You trusted him. And he broke your trust. And even when you guys went to counseling, do you think he was all-in to try to repair the damage he had done to your relationship? I don't think so. Considering he went right back to her."

"I know. I know. I never thought I would be divorced. I thought my marriage would last forever." Katherine sighed deeply. "And I'm lonely. Some days I'm fine. Other days I can't stand being alone here."

"You know you have to give yourself the time and the grace to grieve. And the time to focus on yourself and figure out what you want to do. What are you doing for self-care?"

"I'm trying a few tools my divorce coach has given me.

Journaling. Long walks. Getting out to meet new people. All that helps sometimes."

"That's good. Are you doing any writing?"

"Other than the journaling, no. I have a writer's brick wall — not writer's block."

Shawna chuckled. "I'm sorry to hear that, but at least you still have your sense of humor."

"Yeah, that's me. A barrel of laughs."

"Look, I need a vacation. Do you have an extra room if I come down and spend the weekend?"

"Would you? That would be great. I don't know what I'd do without you. Your support means the world to me."

"You're my best friend. You know I'll be there whenever you need me."

# Chapter Twenty-Two

Katherine answered the door, finding a silver-haired woman with twinkling blue eyes, poised to knock again.

"Oh, sorry, I wasn't sure you could hear the knock, especially if you were in the back yard. I'm Susie Lincoln. Jeff sent me to look at the carport."

Katherine regarded the diminutive woman in front of her with a bit of skepticism.

"Don't let my size fool you. I've been doing this for a long time." Susie smiled.

Katherine was not thinking about her size, but wondering if she was seventy or eighty years old.

"And I'm seventy-five, in case you're wondering." She winked mischievously.

Katherine blushed. "Come in. Jeff said he was sending a contractor. You aren't what I expected."

"I get that a lot." She shrugged. "I need to look at the west end of the house to see if there was any structural damage. The roof looks good — I've already been up and checked that out — except for the carport."

Katherine looked out to see if there was anyone else with her. Another woman — also gray-haired — waved from the truck. The two of them must have wrestled the ladder up to the roof. And why shouldn't they? Wasn't she irritated when Anthony made the same assumption she was "too old" to be by herself? *Shame on me for having the same ageism bias.*

Katherine stood back as Susie thoroughly examined the main bedroom and bathroom as well as the other bedroom on the west end. "No hairline cracks, no nail pops, everything looks square, but I'll keep an eye on everything while we do the work. Hey, what do you think about the shower?"

"It's fantastic. Why?"

"I built it. Last winter. I've done all the construction for Jeff's restaurants, and when we had a lull last winter, he asked me to do his shower."

Katherine stared at the woman with admiration. "It is one of the most beautiful bathrooms I've ever seen."

"I put a lot of time into it. He gave me my first break when I started my company almost thirty years ago. He was opening another restaurant, and he took a huge chance on me. New business. No track record yet. Woman, 'older' woman no less. I never would have made it without his support. We hit it off and my company grew with his. He's helped so many start-ups over the years — trusting his instincts and often going with someone who needed a boost."

*That's what Terry said yesterday after he cleared the tree and picked up all the debris.* He told her Jeff had hired him to clear his property and carefully take out as few trees as possible for one of his new locations. Terry was getting started after several years of bad luck, but Jeff hired him even though he didn't have any references yet. He said Jeff was all about second chances, or first chances if you were starting up.

Katherine struggled with the contradictions. She was

impressed with this information about Jeff. So far, she hadn't seen this good side. The other night he hadn't been particularly civil, like it was her fault the tree fell down. The jury was still out on him, but more evidence was piling up he might have some redeeming qualities.

"It should take me a day or so to put up new supports on the carport and replace the shingles. I might even have a few of the original shingles from when I redid his roof a couple of years ago. He's been upgrading this place a little at a time — most of his money and time go into his restaurants."

"When do you think you'll be able to schedule it?"

"I put Jeff's work at the top of my list — I owe him. I'll be here tomorrow morning at 7:00." With a quick tip of her hat, Susie scurried back to her truck.

Katherine struggled to mesh this new information about Jeff with her own interactions with him. *Doesn't make much difference. I probably won't see him once the carport is fixed.*

# Chapter Twenty-Three

Disturbed, Katherine looked up from her blank computer screen. The phone rang again. Irritated, she snatched it up.

"Hello," she growled.

"Katherine?" a deep voice rumbled. "Katherine, this is Jeff. Did I catch you at a bad time?"

"No, it's okay. What can I do for you?" she mumbled.

"I wanted to see if the carport was done, and if you were satisfied."

"It's fine. Susie did a great job. You can't see where the damage was."

"I wonder if you would mind if I stopped by to take a look?" he asked.

"Now?" She looked down at her ratty T-shirt and torn jeans.

"In a half hour or so?"

Calculating she could grab a quick shower, she agreed. "That's fine. I'll see you then."

She hung up and dashed to the shower, not that she was

trying to impress him, but she'd spent the day weeding and pruning the jungle outside the cottage. The plants were wildly overgrown, covering the stone path to the backyard. She thought the physical work would help her break through her writer's block, but the screen was still blank. *What is it going to take to make my creative juices flow again?*

Right on time, the doorbell rang. She opened the door to find him in clean jeans, clean-shaven, and a Guns & Roses T-shirt.

"Would you like to come in?" she asked, noticing her pulse jumped at the sight of his heavily muscled arms.

"Sure. I checked out the carport, and it does look good. Susie does such great work — I was lucky to find her thirty years ago."

"She told me you helped her out when she was getting started."

He looked away. "Look, I want to apologize for being grumpy."

"I would have said rude," she interrupted.

"Okay, rude and grumpy."

She looked up in surprise.

"I shouldn't have taken it out on you, but it's been a shitstorm of stuff happening at the restaurant."

She nodded. "I heard you telling Beth about the trouble you were having with your staff. Is it resolved?" She paused. "I've got lemonade or beer if you want something."

"Lemonade would be great." He slid onto one of the bar stools in the kitchen. "It's getting better but I'm not out of the woods yet. Tim is back full-time now, and my other cook, Jerry, thinks he'll be back next week. His dad is almost recovered enough he can drive himself to his appointments."

"That's good. Is your waitress, Joyce, still covering for him?" She pushed his glass of lemonade toward him.

"No, her doctor told her just after you and Beth came in she shouldn't be on her feet as much. She had to quit and do bedrest until she delivers — about a month." He rotated his shoulders. He looked tense. And she couldn't help but appreciate the way his shirt tightened over his pecs. "I took over her shifts and I got another guy to cover the bar for me. It's like musical chairs."

"Good grief — have you cooked before?"

"Sure. I've done about every job in the restaurant at one time or another."

"What about your poor waitress? You were running her legs off when I was in there."

He smiled. "That's the good news. I've got two college kids starting Tuesday and a couple of high school kids the week after. One of the college guys has worked in one or another of my restaurants since he was sixteen. He knows the ropes. He'll train the others. And I moved one of my bartenders from the Dewey shop up here so I can stay in the kitchen."

He continued, "I am sorry about my behavior. I know we got off on the wrong foot. Can I make it up to you? Have you had dinner? Have you been to Grotto's yet? You know they make the best pizza on the Delaware coast. Can I take you out for pizza as an apology?" He paused, looking hopeful.

She had already decided she wasn't going to have any more to do with him than she had to. Yes, he was attractive, but he had been rude and surly every other time she'd seen him. This nice, new behavior could be an act — maybe because Beth had said something to him.

He pleaded, "Really, I'm sorry I acted like a jerk. Beth read me the riot act, too, about the way I behaved. You know, she's like my older sister, even though she's only fifty-nine, a couple of years younger than me. She acts like an older sister if I had one. I don't want to be crosswise of her. Please. Let me try to make it up to you."

"And there it is...Beth put you up to this."

"No, this is my idea." He tossed out another incentive. "They also have Red Stripe beer there — great Jamaican beer and great pizza — and we can sit outside and watch the waves. Wouldn't that be nice?"

She looked into his warm brown eyes and gave in. He seemed to be authentically sorry.

"Fine. I haven't been to Grotto's since I've been here. And I do love their pizza. Let me grab my wallet and a sweater."

"Do you mind riding on my bike?"

"Do you have a bicycle built for two? I'm not riding on your handlebars."

He laughed. "No, I mean my motorcycle. I've got an extra helmet."

"Uh. No. No motorcycle. We can take my car or walk — it's about a half-hour walk."

He looked disappointed. "I'm too hungry to walk. Let's take your car."

Parking was such a challenge downtown. After driving the side streets, they finally found a place a few blocks away from Grotto's. Their brightly lit patio was still packed with pizza lovers. Waiting a few minutes, they managed to snag a table right on the railing next to the boardwalk. With Katherine's consent, Jeff ordered a four-beer bucket of Jamaican Red Stripe.

"What kind of pizza do you like?" he asked. "I'm a meat lovers fan myself, but I could live with sausage and pepperoni."

"Well, you're in luck because when I get to choose, it's meat lovers for me."

"I thought this would be a tougher negotiation. Most women get all fussy about too many calories or too much fat."

"Not when it comes to pizza. Why bother to eat it if it's plain cheese, or worse yet, a veggie pizza?"

He saluted her with his beer. "My thoughts exactly,"

"Does your restaurant serve pizza?"

"No, there's no reason to compete when there's already good pizza here." He sipped his beer and watched the teens at the next table flirt with each other. "Ah, young love, or young lust, anyway. Do you have children?"

Katherine looked at the young people next to them and said wistfully, "Yes, but mine are all grown up now. My son is happily married and lives in Atlanta with his wife and my first grandchild. I don't get to see them often enough." She sipped her beer and watched the sun sink into the water, bathing the sky in oranges and reds. "My daughter and her partner live in D.C. They both work for the State Department and are about to take their first overseas assignment in Africa."

# Chapter Twenty-Four

Katherine stopped talking as the waiter slid their pizza on the stand. Jeff watched as pleasure rolled over Katherine's face. Eyes closed, she took deep breath after deep breath, sucking in the rich tomato and oregano scent.

"Ahh! That's what I remember. Do you know that your sense of smell is most closely linked to memories? Smelling this pizza takes me right back to our beach trips with the kids. Every time we spent any time here, we always had Grotto's pizza the first night we arrived. What were we talking about?" she asked, finally opening her eyes.

"Doesn't matter." He grabbed the plates under the pizza stand and picked up the pizza cutter. Katherine watched hungrily as he made three fast swipes across the pie and then slid a piece on each plate. Pausing long enough to sprinkle red pepper flakes and Parmesan cheese, she bit the nose off her piece.

He stared as she moaned. *That should be illegal. I didn't think eating pizza was that sexy, but that sure was.*

She looked up and blushed. "Oh, my goodness. Excuse my manners, but I love their pizza."

"No need to apologize. I love to see a woman enjoy food." He regarded her speculatively. He hadn't been that turned on in a long, long time. How could a schoolteacher eating pizza have this effect on him?

He asked Katherine about her research and her teaching. He listened intently to her discussion about the issues she was addressing in her next book. He laughed at her stories about her students' excuses for why they hadn't finished an assignment. The best one was the student who said he had to take his goldfish to the vet because she wasn't acting herself.

"That did not happen."

"I swear it did," she said. "And the kid told me that with a straight face."

"What did you do?"

"I told him he had to bring me a note from the vet or else he'd fail the assignment."

"And did he?"

"Nope." She grinned. "And he got a zero on the assignment, although I was tempted to give him a few points for creativity. It *was* a creative writing class."

"What else do you like to do when you're not teaching or writing?"

"You know, I've been so caught up in my work, I've neglected other things I enjoy — like walking, traveling, reading." She paused. "Do you know Cassandra? She owns a bike store in town." He nodded. "She's trying to get me back on a bike — I mean, a bicycle. I haven't ridden in a while, but I think I'm going to give it a shot."

"I put away my bicycle when I got the Harley. Maybe I should pull it back out — there's something more relaxing in a quiet bike ride along the shore."

They debated the merits of motorcycles versus bicycles. She was firmly in the bicycle camp while he saw value in both.

"One item on my bucket list is to ride all ten of the best motorcycle roads in the United States. I've already done the East Coast rides — the Mad River Loop in Vermont, the Pig Trail Scenic Byway in Arkansas, Deals Gap in Tennessee and North Carolina, and the Natchez Trace Parkway from Tennessee through Alabama and Mississippi."

"Do you ride by yourself? Is it dangerous?"

"I usually ride with a group of guys I went to high school and college with. We stay in decent hotels along the way — we're too old to rough it."

"You aren't that old, are you?" She poked his arm. "You're what? My age? Sixty?"

"Almost fifty-nine. I thought women didn't like to talk about their age," he joked.

"I'm sixty-one. I don't think I'm too old. I would sleep in a tent. There are lots of things I would do yet."

His eyes lit up. "Does that mean you'll go for a ride on my motorcycle?"

"Let's not get ahead of ourselves," she countered. "I meant, I don't think I'm 'too old.'"

"Got it. Can't blame me for trying."

"Where are the other five rides? You said there were ten?"

"Mostly out west in Washington, Utah, Montana, California, and Colorado. There's one that's supposed to be spectacular — great scenery, nice winding room, well-paved so it's safe — in Texas. My buddies and I are planning a trip next summer to hit the West Coast rides."

He told her how much he liked to travel by driving. She argued she liked to fly to a destination and then drive. He agreed when he took his trip to California and Washington, he would fly to California and rent a motorcycle there. It wasn't the same as riding his own bike, but it beat riding from Delaware to California. They both agreed they were not fans of travel tours, preferring to scout out their own destinations and sights.

He was surprised at how easy it was to talk to her. Looking around, he realized the restaurant was closing and their waitress had cleared all the tables but theirs.

"We should head back. We're keeping the waitstaff from going home," he said reluctantly.

"This was a lot more fun than I expected," she said. "That didn't come out right."

"I know what you mean." He chuckled. "I wasn't expecting much. That didn't come out much better. Maybe we should try this again and see if we can do better."

# Chapter Twenty-Five

"You sure this is what you want to do on your sabbatical?" Beth asked Katherine as she completed the last of the paperwork to make her an official part-time employee at Browseabout.

"Yes, I think it's just what I need right now. This whole divorce process is stressful and enervating. I need something like this to get out of my head."

Beth nodded. "I know, I spend too much time there, too. People accuse me of being an over-thinker," she said laughing.

"I've been told that as well," Katherine said ruefully. She got up from the desk. "You already know I love books. This will be like a kid working in a candy store."

"I love that attitude." Beth opened the tiny office door and headed to the front counter.

"Are you okay with me only working Tuesday and Thursday evenings, and Saturday or Sunday?" Katherine took her position in front of the cash register, reviewing how to ring up a sale. "I have to work on my research. And I'd like to see if I can get back into my creative writing if my muse ever comes back. Right now, I've got a blank screen and a blinking cursor. I'm hoping working here will be the mental break I need to clear my writer's block." She greeted a customer with a smile.

Beth asked, "Do you know about the Rehoboth Beach Writers Guild (RBWG)? You might want to check them out. They have lots of programs — classes, something they call 'freewrites' where participants get together and respond to writing prompts, writing and coffee, book clubs — something for everyone. It's a great group of people. We co-sponsor events with them frequently. That will be one of your responsibilities."

"What's that?" Katherine directed one harried father to the children's section in the back of the store. Beth smiled her approval at how quickly Katherine was fitting in.

"We hold six to ten book signings or conversations a month — mostly local authors, but we also have a few 'big names' like Elin Hilderbrand." Beth straightened the piles of stickers on the counter. "And we often have RBWG events here like 'how to self-publish.' I've got the schedule done for the next three months but it's a blank slate after that."

"That sounds like fun. I know a woman in Washington who books author events — I'm sure I can contact her for ideas. I'll connect with RBWG to see who is publishing soon. What else?" Katherine jotted a note on the note cards she always carried in her pocket.

"Working the front desk like you're doing now. Supervising our high school and college kids. How does that sound?"

"Very doable. Thanks, Beth, for hiring this 'mature' woman. I've been a little adrift since this divorce started. I'm going to enjoy this very much."

"That's great. For me, you're a godsend. I can take a day off now."

# Chapter Twenty-Six

Michelle took the last stool at the high top near the bar. "What's everybody drinking?"

"I was about to order a Podere Montepulciano d'Abruzzo," Katherine said. "We're in an Italian restaurant after all."

"Me, too," piped up Cassandra.

"Sounds good to me. Should we order a bottle?" Michelle said.

"I'll join you. Let's go for the bottle," Beth agreed.

"Ashleigh, how are you?" Michelle asked as a very toned fortyish blonde woman wearing a skintight red knit dress walked up.

"Got room for me? I know you all have been getting together on Sunday nights, but I've never been able to catch you."

Michelle glanced at Cassandra and rolled her eyes. "Sure. Pull up another stool. Ashleigh, do you know everyone? Have you met Katherine?" she asked. "Ashleigh, Katherine. Katherine, Ashleigh. Katherine's spending a few months here."

"Hi." Ashleigh, after a quick survey, dismissed Katherine

quickly and turned back to Michelle. "I thought you were going to stop in for one of my Body Pump classes?"

"Ashleigh runs the fitness center on the other side of the Boardwalk Plaza Hotel," Michelle explained to Katherine. "I will — but I've been busy getting all the summer renters settled. Everybody wanted to come this week. I hope to have more time next week."

She turned back to Katherine and changed the subject. "Katherine, are you getting settled? How's the job working out at Browseabout?" she asked.

"I love it. Beth is giving me free rein on the author talks. And I've graduated to doing the closings myself. I'm hopeful that Beth will have a whole day off soon."

"I'll drink to that!" Beth laughed. "Did I see you at Grotto's last Sunday with Jeff?"

Ashleigh snapped to attention. "Jeff Thompson? You were with Jeff? As in? Out on a date?"

Katherine was surprised at Ashleigh's tone. "No, not a date. He was treating me to pizza for being such a jerk. Every time I've seen him, he's been most unpleasant. He apologized and took me to Grotto's to make up for his bad behavior."

Ashleigh smirked. "That's a surprise. He's one of the nicest guys I've ever met. He's never been rude to me." She shrugged. "Of course, I can never manage to get him to ask me out. Not that I haven't tried. He's not interested in dating, not even me." Ashleigh flipped her highly bleached blond hair over her shoulder.

Isabella, ignoring Ashleigh, said, "That doesn't sound like the Jeff I know either. He was very helpful when I was setting up the brewpub. He has incredible expertise from all the restaurants he's opened and operated successfully. He spent hours with me making sure I had all the right licenses and filled out all the paperwork. He helped me hire my staff. I hadn't done any of that before." She fiddled with her empty wineglass. "He wouldn't take any money for his time either. He gets a free beer whenever he comes in. Which, unfortunately, isn't very often."

"All his restaurants?" Katherine asked.

"Yeah, didn't he tell you that he owns five restaurants from Lewes to Ocean City?" Ashleigh said smugly. "They're all extremely successful — named the best restaurants on the Delaware coast."

"No, he didn't say a thing about that. Beth told me he owned the restaurant here in Rehoboth and he told me about his grandparents' diner, but I didn't know he had others." Katherine was shocked. "He doesn't look the part of a successful businessman."

"Don't let appearances fool you," Beth said. "He might not look like it, but he's one of the best restaurateurs around. People study how he operates, and he always mentors several interns from the University of Delaware Hospitality Department."

"So, he probably didn't ask you to go out again? Since he apologized and all," Ashleigh sniped, smoothing her already perfect hair in place.

"Actually, we had such a good time he suggested we do it again."

Ashleigh scowled. "Well, he's going to my Fourth of July party, so I'll see him then. I've got this new outfit that's going to knock his socks off."

Beth grinned at Katherine. "Jeff usually works on the Fourth of July. Most restaurants are packed that day."

Ashleigh stared at Beth and then Katherine. She climbed off her stool and snarled over her shoulder as she headed for the door, "I have a hot date tonight so I guess I can't hang out with you ladies. Sorry you all don't have dates." She flounced out of the restaurant.

Katherine raised an eyebrow. "What was that about?"

"She and Jeff dated for a New York minute last year. She still thinks Jeff is into her. I can tell you that he's not," Beth said. "She doesn't seem to hear the message."

"I haven't seen her at the other Sunday meetings. Does she usually come?" Katherine asked.

"She's not actually part of our group. I don't think reading a book is high on her preferred activities list," Isabella smirked. "It's another reason we move our meetings around. Makes it harder for her to find us."

"Isabella!"

"I know. That's not nice. And my mama told me, if I can't say anything nice..." Isabella shrugged. "But she's so full of her perfect hair and perfect body, I can't stand her."

"Okay. Who's read the latest Elin Hilderbrand?" Beth asked. "And does anybody want something to eat? I'm starving."

"Food for the body first and then the mind. I want the calamari," Isabella stated.

"How about the prosciutto and peach burrata?" Cassandra put in. "And the garlic bread?"

"I'm good with all of that but I need a little more protein. You know you need more protein as you age? At least 60-70 grams per day for a 150-pound person," Beth said. "Could we have the chicken parmesan, too?"

"It's hard to eat that much protein in a day," Michelle lamented. "An egg is only six grams of protein. You'd have to eat three and a half eggs to get a third of your protein for breakfast."

Beth called their waiter over. "Can we order the calamari, the prosciutto, and the garlic bread? And the chicken parmesan with all the other appetizers, please?"

"And we need another bottle of the Montepulciano."

"Now. How about that Elin Hilderbrand?" Katherine said. "You know she's going to be at Browseabout next month?"

"I wonder how many Hilderbabes will show up," Beth asked.

"Hilderbabes?" Isabella laughed. "What's that?"

"They are Hilderbrand superfans. Last year, about 130 of her readers flew to Nantucket Island for a weekend of reading, yoga, and dancing with her. They greeted her like a rock star."

"Why haven't I heard about this?" Cassandra asked.

"You like Hilderbrand's books, right? But would you spend $700 for the event fee? That doesn't include lodging — about $500 a night. Or transportation," Beth added. "The women who go say it's worth every penny."

"I could read all her books for that," Cassandra responded.

"Why do you suppose she's so popular?" Beth asked.

"Her characters are relatable. They face real-life issues and find solutions," Michelle said. "But she also allows me to escape real life. Everyone is happy in the end. There are some days I really need happy endings."

They pounced on the appetizers and chicken parmesan, snarfing down even the garnishes. They debated the merits of Hilderbrand's work, dismissing the critics saying it was fluff. Not arguing that it was serious literature. But it filled a need for the readers.

Katherine and Beth were the last ones to leave.

"Beth, I don't know if I've thanked you enough for inviting me to that first wine meeting," Katherine said. "I love being with you all — debating books, drinking wine —hanging out."

Beth hugged her. "You don't need to thank me. You add so much to our group. I'm glad you joined us. And I'm really glad you decided to work at Browseabout. I am so going to enjoy my time off."

# Chapter Twenty-Seven

Isabella two-finger whistled loudly when Katherine and Beth walked into Eden Sunday night. Cassandra winced when the bartender shook her head in disapproval. Isabella shrugged.

Eden was one of their favorite go-to's for good wine. They had an award-winning selection — one of the best in Rehoboth.

The dark green walls framed with votive candelabras brought a warm glow to everyone at the table. *Everyone looks nicer by candlelight,* Katherine thought. In the dining room, the fairy light-draped bare branch heightened the exotic and romantic environment. Soft music played, not loud enough to disrupt conversation. It provided the right background vibe.

Isabella greeted them with a warm smile. "Katherine, do you know Penny? She decided to join us tonight. Penny is Cassandra's life and business partner."

Katherine smiled at Penny and Cassandra. "Pleased to meet you. I have to visit your shop and see what kind of bike I can borrow or rent."

They settled in and perused the wine-by-the-glass list.

Isabella already had a Hindsight 20/20 and Cassandra was drinking Chateau Gruaud-Larose Sarget.

Katherine teased Isabella, "I'm surprised you're drinking wine. You make your own excellent beer at your brewpub."

"It's good to broaden my palate," she laughed. "You never know, maybe I'll have my Brewmeister make a wine-flavored beer. My chocolate beer and the peanut butter beer are big sellers."

Cassandra interrupted, "Ugh! Those don't sound good to me at all. If I want chocolate or peanut butter, I'll eat them, not drink them."

"Katherine?" A man's voice startled Katherine.

"Richard, how are you?"

"Not bad, not bad. It looks like you all are having a good time." He looked expectantly at Katherine and glanced at the others. They were looking at Katherine with curiosity.

"Richard, this is Beth. She manages the great bookstore on Rehoboth Ave. Cassandra owns the bike shop also on Rehoboth Ave almost to the train tracks. And that's Penny, her partner. And Isabella owns the Gallina Azul Brewpub. Michelle is the best real estate agent in the county. Ladies, this is Richard Ferry. I met him at City Hall when I was registering my car for the parking permit."

"Delighted to meet you all. I won't keep you from your fun." He looked over his shoulder at the young man waiting for him by the door. "I need to give Mark a ride home."

He leaned close to Katherine. "Katherine, what do you think about that cup of coffee?"

Flustered, Katherine replied, "I'm sorry. I've been busy getting settled. Why don't you give me a call tomorrow and we'll set something up?"

He smiled at the others and stroked Katherine's arm lightly. "Until tomorrow then."

"Woohee! Is it hot in here or is it the way he was looking at you, Katherine?" Isabella fanned her face. "That's one fine-looking man. How long did you say you've known him?"

"I don't know him. I met him the other day."

"Well, he seems to want to know you a whole lot better," Cassandra chimed in.

Katherine shook her head emphatically. "I'm not ready to go out with anyone yet. I'm not even divorced."

Isabella replied, "He's asking you out for coffee. You don't have to go to bed with him."

"Who's going to bed with someone?" Michelle asked as she swung into the last empty chair. "What did I miss?"

"Katherine has this hot guy after her and she won't go out for coffee with him." Isabella turned to Katherine. "If you don't want him, can I have him?"

Katherine laughed. "Be my guest. He's not mine to give you." Isabella raised an eyebrow. "Okay, okay, I'll go out for coffee with him. What could it hurt?"

"Are you talking about that silver-haired guy I saw leave?" Michelle asked. "He looks familiar, but I can't place him."

Katherine nodded. "He says he has a place up in North Rehoboth."

Michelle looked thoughtful, like she wondered where she had seen him before.

# Chapter Twenty-Eight

Striding purposefully down the boardwalk, dodging other walkers and baby strollers, Katherine turned when she heard her name called.

"Katherine!"

Jeff loped gracefully toward her. Katherine couldn't help noticing how good he looked even wearing a ratty, torn-sleeve sweatshirt from University of Delaware and sweatpants falling down on his hips. Long, lean legs. Broad shoulders tapering to a narrow waist.

Katherine caught a glimpse of his very solid abs, just enough to be tantalizing. She looked down and wished she were wearing something other than her stretched out yoga pants and slightly tight T-shirt. At least the chambray shirt covered her tummy rolls. *Who cares anyway? I'm not trying to impress him.*

He fell into perfect step with her as Katherine continued her morning walk. "Why haven't you been back to my restaurant?"

Katherine retorted, "Why didn't you tell me you were a restaurant mogul? How many restaurants do you own?"

"I thought it was more fun for you to think that my business was not that big," he teased. "Why? Does it make a difference that I own five restaurants?"

"No, but I don't think you were very honest with me. I've had enough of people lying to me."

"I wasn't lying to you as much as not telling you everything." At Katherine's raised eyebrows, he said, "Okay, it wasn't all that honest, but I didn't mean any harm."

"Dishonesty of any kind causes harm." She looked out at the ocean and sighed.

Jeff hesitated. "Sounds like there's a story behind that statement."

"My almost ex-husband cheated on me with one of his former doctoral students. He lied all the time about where he was going, who he was going with. I was blindsided when he told me he wanted a divorce."

She looked down at her shoes. "Shame on me for being so gullible, but I didn't see it coming. If he had told me he was unhappy, we might have been able to work it out. I don't trust my own judgment anymore and I don't like it when it feels like people are hiding things from me."

"That's fair. What do you want to know about me? I gather you found out I own the Black Pony. Did you also find out I have restaurants in Lewes, Dewey Beach, Bethany Beach, and Fenwick Island?"

"Yes, Beth told me the other night." Katherine eyed him sternly. "How did you get into the restaurant business?"

"How much time have you got? Want to sit on the beach? I'll give you my whole life story."

She looked at her watch. "I've got time."

# Chapter Twenty-Nine

They followed the wooden staircase to the beach, shooed away the seagulls looking for a snack, and sank down in the sand on the water's edge.

"Well, my granddad owned a little mom-and-pop diner in Dewey Beach. He and my grandma did everything. He was the cook — not a chef, by any means, a good old-fashioned meat and potatoes cook. My grandma was the waitress, the hostess, the bookkeeper — everything else. They only had ten tables. They could manage that fine." Jeff gazed out at the sand, remembering the little diner.

"As soon as I was old enough, I started bussing tables and doing prep work in the kitchen. Chopping up lettuce. Peeling potatoes. All the grunt work. Granddad wanted me to learn the business from the bottom up."

"He sounds like a smart guy."

"He was," Jeff replied. "Finally, when I was in high school, I started doing the food and supplies ordering for them and working with the vendors. I wanted to learn the business side of the diner."

Katherine chased away a sandpiper. "Go on."

"And by relieving Granddad on the grill, I learned his recipes. He was finally able to take time off when I could work the grill full-time. By that time, Grandma was only doing the books. Her arthritis made it too hard for her to be on her feet all the time. We were doing well enough by then that we hired a couple of waitresses."

"Sounds like you got a good education from them."

Jeff leaned back on his elbows and smiled slightly, remembering his grandfather's patience in teaching him the business. "After high school, I went to the University of Delaware." He pointed to his raggedy sweatshirt. "I should probably buy a new one of these."

Katherine lifted the edge of his torn sleeve and nodded. "My favorite Yale sweatshirt looks a lot like this."

"Are you sure you want to hear all this?" He rolled over on his tummy.

"I'll let you know when I've heard enough."

"Okay, but you asked for it." He told her he got his undergraduate degree in hospitality management, and he worked all through college in restaurants and hotels in Newark. "It was the best on-the-job training."

"How did you manage to work so much and go to school at the same time?" Katherine asked. "I worked in the library part-time at the research desk. When I didn't have any requests, I could work on my homework."

"My grades were not the best — and I didn't have any social life." Jeff sat up. "The summer after I graduated, my granddad and grandma told me they were ready to retire and do their wish list of traveling. They sold me their restaurant for a dollar."

"A dollar?" Katherine asked, astonished.

"Yes, they were going to give it to me, but I insisted they sell it to me. I still send them a percentage of my profits every month. They're living well in Florida."

Katherine nodded her appreciation of his behavior.

"I took their little diner and gradually expanded it. Now I have seating for seventy-five and an indoor/outdoor bar. It's very popular in Dewey with the college kids." He flicked away a sand cricket that was encroaching on their spot.

"Sounds like it would be fun. How did you end up in Rehoboth?"

"Actually, Rehoboth is my newest restaurant. I moved to Bethany Beach next. Took a tired fish market on the bay and made it a gourmet fish place."

Katherine said, "I've eaten there. It's great. I love the big fat crab cakes."

Jeff glowed with pride.

"Where did you go next?"

"Lewes. Then Fenwick Island. Finally, the Black Pony came up for sale in Rehoboth a few months ago. I changed the name to Brews and Bites and reopened recently."

"I'm impressed that you can manage all these places."

"I've been fortunate to hire great managers." He stood up and brushed the sand off his pants. "Okay, is that enough about me? I need to start heading back." He held out a hand to help her up.

# Chapter Thirty

They climbed back over the berm and retrieved their shoes from the bench. Jeff stepped close to Katherine. "It's your turn to tell me about you next." He lowered his head to kiss her. She held her breath. *I haven't been kissed by any man other than Stan for over thirty years.*

"Yoohoo! Jeff!"

They sprang apart as a beautiful blonde jogged up beside them in her hot pink running tights and sports bra. "I'm glad I caught you. Are you going to make my Fourth of July party?" she simpered, barely glancing at Katherine. "I was hoping you could get away from the restaurant."

Jeff looked down at his shoes. "Ashleigh, I'm not sure. Let me get back to you when I find out if I have enough staff to work that day. Have you met Katherine?"

"Yes, we met the other night. Are you still here? I thought you were headed back to D.C.?"

"I think Michelle mentioned that I'm going to be here a while. In fact, I've rented Jeff's cottage. I'll be here through the first of the year since I'm on sabbatical."

Ashleigh glared at Katherine. "Well, aren't you lucky that you can take all that time off? Too bad the rest of us have to keep working for a living."

She touched Jeff's arm. "You know I'd love to see you," she whispered seductively. "I better get going. Can't keep a body like this without serious exercising." She glanced scornfully at Katherine's hips and flabby arms. "Katherine, I'd be happy to whip you into shape if you wanted to. Stop by my gym and we'll work those extra pounds off." She smiled falsely and took off jogging, making sure that she brushed her perky breasts against Jeff's arm.

"Sorry about that. Ashleigh and I dated briefly, and I do mean briefly, over a year ago. It's been over for me almost before it started. Sorry she was rude."

"No worries. She doesn't seem to think it's over. And she is in awfully good shape."

"Physically, maybe, but she's not for me." He stopped. "Would you go out to dinner with me? Like on a real date out to dinner?"

"I don't know." She toed the hole on the boardwalk while she thought about it.

"I promise to be on my best behavior. Didn't you have fun at Grotto's? Let's go have a good time."

*Well, what harm could it be?* It's not like she was falling for him, even though he was growing on her.

"Fine. A date. Just to have fun. I'm not interested in a relationship, you know, but I do have to eat so, why not?"

# Chapter Thirty-One

Shawna snuggled down in the chaise lounge on Katherine's patio. "I could get used to this. Between the fountain and the ocean breeze, I really feel like I'm on vacation."

"I've missed talking with you. Thanks for driving up to Rehoboth." Katherine pulled the beach blanket over her lap. The breeze was still a little cool for early June. "Talking to you on the phone isn't the same."

"That's why I'm here, so we can have a real chat and you can tell me what's going on."

Taking a sip of her wine, Katherine murmured, "It's the loss of control. And you know how much I like to be in control." She refilled Shawna's glass. "I feel like I'm in a kayak with no oars — drifting wherever the current takes me. I just hope I don't end up out in the middle of the ocean."

Shawna plucked a stem of grapes from the platter Katherine set out. "I know I can't really understand what you're feeling, but I know your whole world is topsy-turvy."

Katherine grabbed a chunk of cheese. "I don't know who I

am anymore. I'm not a wife — I'm going to be an ex-wife. And people look at ex-wives differently than they do married women or even widows. They think, 'what's wrong with her?' or that I'll be after all their husbands." She snorted. "As if. That's the last thing I'm interested in now — getting involved with someone."

Munching on her grapes, Shawna asked, "What about that guy that asked you out for coffee? Richard?"

"He's okay, but a little too smooth. He reminds me too much of Stan," Katherine exclaimed vehemently. "And it's coffee. Not a date."

"What about that other guy? The one that took you to Grotto's?"

"He's my landlord. And he's very rude. And I think he feels sorry for me."

Shawna observed Katherine. "Why are you blushing? Is there more to this story?"

"No, no, no," Katherine protested. "Well, I thought he was going to kiss me the other day on the boardwalk and I was going to let him."

"This is interesting," Shawna teased. "How long has it been since you've gotten any?"

"Shawna!" Katherine swatted her.

"What? You're not dead."

"Yes, but I'm not divorced."

"On paper only. You haven't lived with Stan for almost a year. I'd be getting horny by now."

"Shawwnaa!"

The voluptuous redhead shrugged. "I'm just saying..."

Katherine blushed. "Can we get back to my crisis, please? As I was saying, I have to check a new box when I'm asked if I'm married or single. I have to file my taxes as a single person.

A different capital gains tax exemption if I ever decide to sell the house."

Shawna raised her hand. "I know a good accountant who can take care of that for you."

Katherine sighed. "That's not the point. Most of my friends are 'couples.' And most of the world is about pairs — double occupancy, double beds, plus ones, restaurant tables are two-tops not one-top."

Shawna interrupted. "All that is true, and..." She walked to the heated mini-pool and dangled her feet in the water. "Look at the single people you've met since you've been here. And the Silver Pickleball Club you've joined. They offer ways for you to find other singles who want to play pickleball. You don't have to have a partner."

"I know. I know. And I've been looking into this solo travel group that doesn't charge you more for a single occupancy room." Katherine muttered, "But that's not how I thought I'd be traveling. I thought I'd be traveling with my husband, doing the things I thought we were going to do when the kids were out of the house and our careers were settled. Now I have to rethink my future. It's not what I thought it was going to be." She joined Shawna on the side of the pool.

"That must be the hardest part — reimagining your future." Shawna patted Katherine's knee. "I know this is hard. It's turned your world upside-down. Have you decided what you want to do about your name? Are you going back to your maiden name?"

Katherine started when the patio lights came on. It was getting dark. "Arghh, that's another problem. I've done all my publishing and academic work with my married name. That name is my professional identity. I don't want to lose that. Even my doctoral diploma is in my married name," she moaned. "And of course, the kids all have my married name. I think it would be too confusing to go back to my maiden name, much as I'd like to shed Stan's name."

Shawna reached for a beach towel to dry her feet. "I can see where that would be a problem professionally, but your colleagues see you as you, not as Stan's wife, don't you think? At your professional conferences, they may not even know if you're married or not. As for your kids, Anthony will obviously keep his name and Vanessa will have to figure out what she wants to do with her name if, or when, she gets married." She handed the towel to Katherine and started tapping her toe.

Katherine lingered in the warm water for a few more minutes. "What do you think our neighbors will do? Do you think they'll pick sides? I know Stan's colleagues will side with him, and mine in the English department will favor me probably. But what about the friends we've made through PTA and marching band?"

"I don't know." Shawna shook her head. "There are going to be friends that choose Stan, but maybe they weren't good friends anyway. At some point, you may have to let them go and move on to other friends. Like me. You know I'm going to support you however I can. And Steve will, too. He may not be the handiest husband, but if you need someone to catch a mouse, you can borrow him. My husband is a fierce mouser!"

She laughed and then sobered. "I don't mean to make light of this. This is a very real thing you're dealing with. Your social network is getting totally rewired."

Katherine grimaced. "Well, as long as I've got the mice covered, I'm all set." She straightened up. "Enough moping. Let's go find dinner and then take a walk. I bet you haven't touched the ocean in a while."

"Now you're talking. Are we going to see that hottie that was going to kiss you?"

Katherine swatted her friend. "You are incorrigible. I'm

glad you came for the weekend. Do you think you can stand being away from your husband that long?"

"I brought my trusty battery friend if I can't."

Katherine blushed again and wondered if she would ever have a relationship like Shawna and her husband, Steve. They loved each other passionately.

# Chapter Thirty-Two

Katherine approached Bikes for Life with trepidation. *They say you never forget how to ride a bike but who are "they"? And what do they know?* What if she couldn't ride a bike anymore? That would be embarrassing, not to mention dangerous. *I'll probably break my neck or something.*

Cassandra opened the door and with her quiet, calm voice said, "Come on in, Katherine. These bikes won't hurt you." She smiled and turned aside to let Katherine in.

"That's what you say, Cassandra. Do you know how long it's been? Twenty? Twenty-five years at least? The bikes I remember are those old fat tire things. You know, the ones where you put streamers on the handlebars. They might have had three-speeds in my day, but I'm not sure."

Cassandra laughed. "Stop! You're not that old — I'd guess we're about the same age — and I know they had three-speeds when I was first starting out. Don't dismiss doing something you enjoy because of your 'age' — it's just a number."

Katherine gazed around the store, noting the louvered doors on the dressing rooms — a much more private option for women than the skinny curtains in most bike stores. Women's bike shirts and shorts were displayed at the front of the store while the men's clothes were in the back. Women's shoes and helmets were also displayed first, followed by the men's selections — opposite of most bike stores that promoted men's products to the front of the store. It was subtle, but a clear nod to highlighting women's needs first. Both men and women were served but the shop design meant to help women feel comfortable.

The bikes were arranged from the smallest frames to the largest, again putting the emphasis on female riders. Casandra said, "Bikes have come a long way since you probably bought or were gifted your first bike."

"How did you get into this business, Cassandra?"

"My partner, Penny, and I have been riding bikes for thirty years. When we first started racing, we had to scour the bike stores and expos for size XXS men's shorts and then the padding was in all the wrong places. And forget about finding a bicycle that fit me well."

Katherine examined Cassandra's petite frame.

Cassandra conceded, "Penny didn't have the same problem since she's 5'11" but traditional girls' bikes were not built well enough for racing and men's bikes weren't designed for female bodies."

"What did you do?" Katherine asked.

"We went to every expo we could afford and talked to every woman we could find. The problem was universal for all women. There weren't many manufacturers who realized women's needs were different. Then we ran into Georgena Terry at an expo in Massachusetts. In 1985 she designed the first bike specifically engineered for women. Her slogan was to tell women to 'have a fit,' a nod to all the women who were trying to shoehorn their bodies onto men's bicycles. Get it?"

Cassandra air-quoted, "Have a fit." She chuckled. "I loved it — 'have a fit' because the men's bikes don't fit and 'have a fit' because hers did." Puzzled, Katherine raised her eyebrows. Cassandra finished dryly. "Maybe you had to be there."

Cassandra rested her hand on a bike. "Terry's design innovations in her bicycles, saddles — seats — and clothing have won numerous awards and been recognized by the Museum of Modern Art. She received the Pioneering Women Award in 2010 from Outdoor Industries. Her saddle design is now the industry standard for women's bikes."

"That's very impressive," Katherine agreed. "How did you end up here?"

"We're from Milton — a little north and west of here. We liked the LGBTQ acceptance in Rehoboth.. There's already a great bike culture here. Even though there were already a couple of terrific bicycle shops, there were none that catered specifically to women. So we decided to open our shop here."

"Wow! That was really bold. Was it hard to get started?" Katherine walked over to flip through the bike shirts.

Cassandra pulled out a blue and green impressionist looking shirt and held it up for Katherine's approval. "We had a good nest egg built up and our families 'invested' in us. I'm not going to lie — the first few years were tough. But we got help when we first started out from Terry and other women in the bicycle world. We couldn't have done it without their mentorship and support."

Katherine nodded her head at the shirt and picked up a pair of black and white bike shoes. "These are cute." She added, "You were very fortunate. So many entrepreneurs don't have that kind of support."

"I know. We also studied several successful women's bike shops. There weren't very many women-focused bike shops, but we did find a few. One of the best we found was BFF in

Chicago. Their goal was to create 'the kindest and most approachable shop in Chicago.' That's what we wanted to create here."

Katherine wandered over to the coffee machine. "What a great story! And from the looks of it, you're doing pretty well. I especially like that you can buy a cup of coffee and a protein muffin here. What a good idea that is!"

"Serious bike riders love to ride early in the morning sometimes even before the other coffee shops are open. We don't make a ton of money on the coffee and sweets service, but it's a service our customers appreciate."

Katherine snagged one of the muffins and poured herself a cup of coffee, putting three dollars in the cash cup. "These muffins are really good. It's hard to believe they're actually good for you."

Cassandra laughed. "One more thing about Terry. She didn't know if she would be considered a feminist, but she wanted women to think for themselves." Cassandra steered Katherine to the used bikes. "That's our philosophy here, too. We'll give you the information you need to make a good decision."

Katherine pondered that statement. "I think I'd like to try one of her bikes. I like the way she thinks."

Cassandra said, "I thought you were going to pick up one of my used bikes." She stopped. "If you want one of Terry's bikes, you have to have it custom-designed since that's the only way she does bikes now." Disappointed, Katherine looked back at the row of shiny bicycles. Cassandra walked over to the new bike area and pulled out three contenders. "But we do carry several brands inspired by Terry that are designed to fit women better."

"I want to stop doing things halfway. If I'm going to take charge of my life, I need to be all in. No used bike for me. I need to make a commitment to do this, and a new bike will help me."

"Okay. Let's take a few measurements and see if we can find the right bike for you."

Katherine stood patiently while Cassandra did her job and then valiantly strapped on a helmet to take the first option for a test drive. She tried two other bikes and on the third, feeling a little like Goldilocks, said, "This one is just right!"

Cassandra laughed. "I thought that would be the one for you, but I wanted you to try the others so you could feel the difference. What did you like about it?"

"I felt more in control. The brake handles are smaller. It's easier to brake and the smaller front wheel makes the angle of the frame more comfortable. I love this saddle — it fits my behind perfectly," Katherine raved. "I'll take it."

"Are you sure? We can still set you up with a used bike. You can decide if you really want to ride a bicycle," Cassandra said anxiously. "I don't want to push you into anything."

"Nope. This is the one for me." Katherine took off the loaner helmet and put the kickstand down on her new bike.

"Okay then. You're going to need a helmet. What about shorts and a top?" Cassandra led her back to the front of the store.

"I liked that top you showed me before — it looked like a Monet Water Lilies painting."

"Good eye. It's called Summer in Monet." Cassandra sorted through the bike shorts to find the coordinating bottom.

A half hour later, Katherine was decked out with a new bib, shorts, shoes, and helmet. And of course, her new bicycle.

"Now that you've got your new bike and everything you need to ride, when are you going to start?" Cassandra steered the conversation back to biking. "I find it helps to have a plan."

"I don't want to push it so fast that I get discouraged. What do you suggest?"

Cassandra plucked a sheet from the rack. "This is an 8-week training plan for a twenty-mile ride. It's very moderate — you ride every other day, and you do a long ride on Saturday. Your first Saturday of the plan is four or five miles and then you add two miles for the next seven Saturdays until you reach twenty. I suggest you build up a mile a week until you reach four miles and then start the plan. What do you think?"

Katherine took the plan and studied it briefly. "This looks good. I'll start this week."

"A good target might be the twenty-mile Wild Goose Ride in early October. It's a race founded by Terry in 2008 and raises funds for the Blackwater National Wildlife Refuge. Hundreds of women from all over come to participate."

"I like that idea. Do you ride it?"

"We have in the past. If you commit to do it, we'll do it with you."

"It's a deal." They sealed the commitment with a fist bump.

# Chapter Thirty-Three

Katherine stormed around the kitchen, slamming cupboard doors, throwing silverware into the sink. "Unbelievable! I can't believe Stan would stoop so low. 'Let's do this amicably,' he said. 'We don't need to pay the lawyers' fees,' he argued. 'We could do this on our own.' What a crock!" She tossed the dishrag into the sink, knocking over a metal glass with a clang. "Boy, was I wrong!"

"Ouch. What are you doing? You're hurting my ears," Shawna complained.

"Sorry. I can't believe that he's trying to take half the money my parents left me from the sale of their business. He can't do that, can he?" Katherine panicked.

Shawna reassured her, "No, he can't touch that money. We put it in a trust for you, Vanessa, and Anthony like your parents wanted. He's being a bully. Or maybe he's using this as a tactic — he'll back off from this if you give him something else. What do you suppose he's after?"

Katherine huffed in frustration. "I don't know. We already

went through the whole settlement thing. He 'gave' me the house because he didn't want it. He got the Porsche and vacation home in the Antibes, which is fine since he paid for them with his consulting earnings from the World Bank and IMF. His sole requests from the house were a couple of paintings and a few things he bought that I never liked anyway, or ugly stuff his mother gave us as gifts. There's no other joint property. I don't have any idea what he thinks he deserves."

"Don't worry. I'm not going to let you be taken advantage of," Shawna said in a soothing tone. "You've been more than equitable in the settlement."

Katherine nodded, thinking gratefully that Shawna was not only her best friend but a terror in divorce cases. Men trembled when they heard their wives had engaged Shawna as their divorce attorney. She settled down on one of the bar stools and reached for her coffee. "Did I catch you before you had time for breakfast?" She could hear running water and the refrigerator door opening and closing.

"I'm making it now. No worries." Shawna continued, "You brought a lot into this marriage, too. You've been a full-time faculty member for the past twenty-five years, pulling in a reasonable salary, not as much as Stan, but your two salaries together gave you a nice standard of living in this area. And you worked part-time for the first ten years of your marriage, supporting him, and then taking care of the kids."

Katherine gazed thoughtfully out the window, barely seeing the brilliant blue morning sky flecked with wispy white clouds. She growled, "I'm not interested in more than my fair share — I don't want half of his retirement or half of his anything. But I don't want him taking half of my retirement or my parents' trust either. This just sucks! You think you know someone and then he starts doing this crap!"

She leapt off the stool and starting pacing again. She ranted, breathing heavily. "You know I thought the anger and resentment would go away, but he keeps doing this stupid stuff and tears the scab off again. He makes me so damn mad."

"Katherine, I hate to see you this upset." Shawna's voice sounded alarmed. "Are you getting any help? What does your divorce coach tell you?"

"Anger is a normal reaction. Well, duh," Katherine said scornfully as she sat down on the sofa.

"What does she tell you to do about it?" Shawna coaxed. Katherine heard the microwave bell go off and could 'see' Shawna moving around her kitchen. She had been there so many times she knew it almost as well as her own.

Katherine reached for the notebook where she was keeping the coach's recommendations. "She says to make a list of all the things that I'm angry about with Stan and the divorce. And then think about what, if anything, I can do about the things on the list."

"And then what?" Shawna prompted.

Katherine flipped a few pages to find the one she wanted. "If it's something I can't control, like Stan asking for a divorce, then I'm supposed to put that in one column. If it's something I can control, like having to pay my own bills, then I put it in the other column and figure out a system that makes paying the bills easier — like paying them online through my bank."

"How's that working for you?" Katherine could hear that Shawna was on the move — dishes in the sink, milk back in the refrigerator.

She sighed. "On the days I'm feeling good, it works. Some things are getting better. On a day like today when I'm just mad, not so good. She also says it's going to take time. It's been nine months since he asked for the divorce. I thought *it* — I mean, 'I' — would be better by now. It doesn't help that he keeps making these unreasonable demands."

Katherine heard the beep of Shawna's car being unlocked. "I know you need to go to the office."

"I always have time for you," Shawna replied. "And you don't have to heal on anyone's schedule but your own. As long as you keep doing what works for you, you'll heal at your own pace. Look at all the things you've done — moved, working at the bookstore, writing, made new friends, riding your bicycle, and walking..."

Knowing Shawna couldn't see her, Katherine nodded her head anyway. "You're a great friend, Shawna, as well as a killer lawyer. I needed to hear all that. I have to stop focusing on what I lost. Now, what are you going to do about Stan's latest request?"

"I'll talk to his lawyer and let him know that Stan doesn't have a leg to stand on with respect to the trust. And I'll see if he can shed light on what Stan is up to."

Katherine walked down the gravel path to the beach. The soft breeze whispered through the sea grass. Hidden critters scurried deeper away from the path. She clicked off the flashlight and waited until her eyes adjusted to pale moonlight. The half-moon lit the sand enough that Katherine could pick her way across the loose sand that taxed her leg muscles. The tide was out, and the waves lapped softly against the shore. She plopped down at the edge of the hard packed sand.

The waves lulled her. She shook her head to dispel the troubling Stan thoughts from her mind and drew in four cleansing breaths. *Too much power. I'm giving Stan too much power.* Katherine reflected on Shawna's conversation this morning. *What could Stan want?*

She lay back in the sand and looked up at the sky full of stars. She could make out Orion's Belt and the Big and Little Dipper. And there was Cassiopeia. That was the extent of her star knowledge. She could see the constellations when they outlined them at the planetarium, but out here, her knowledge was limited. Still, the vastness of the sky and the millions of twinkling lights put things in perspective. In the big scheme of things, Stan was one tiny insignificant little star in the whole universe.

She rested quietly, watching the stars and listening to the waves brushing against the shore until she was calm.

She tapped her watch. Midnight. *He's probably home by now. And he told me to call anytime...*

Katherine pulled her phone out of her pocket and scrolled down her list of contacts.

"Hello?" Jeff's deep voice hesitantly answered the phone.

"Jeff, this is Katherine."

"Is everything okay?" he asked, sounding worried.

Katherine stuttered, "I'm sorry. Everything's okay. You said to call anytime."

"I did. I did. When the phone rings this late at night, as the father of a teenager, I get a little anxious." Katherine nodded empathetically. She could hear him opening the refrigerator. "I just got home and I'm thirsty. Need a bottle of water. What's up?"

Katherine buried her toes in the cool wet sand. "Can I ask you a couple of questions? About...how you got through the divorce, how you treated your ex-wife. I'm trying to understand this from a guy's perspective."

"Did something happen?" Jeff asked. She heard him open the screen door to his patio and then settle in a creaky chair.

He had told her he didn't have much furniture in his apartment.

She puffed out a long sigh. "My lawyer called, and my soon-to-be-ex has changed his mind about what he wants in the divorce. But I don't know what he wants. How did you handle splitting up your property?"

"We didn't have an abundance of property," Jeff said dryly. " I suspect it was not as big a deal as it sounds like it is for you." The water bottle clattered to the floor.

In a more serious tone, he went on to say. "Even though we had joint custody, Chelsea was going to be spending more time with her mother than me so she wouldn't have to change schools and be disrupted. So, Shannon got the house and everything in it, and a portion of the value of the restaurants since I couldn't have built them without her support. I paid alimony until she got remarried, and I still pay child support. It's only fair."

"You sound awfully rational." Katherine brushed the sand off her toes and then buried them again, digging little tunnels and watching them begin to fill with water.

"And your soon-to-be-ex — what's his name?" She heard him slap something and then open the screen door. "Darn mosquitos. I have to go back inside."

Katherine hesitated. *Did she want to get into all this with him? Let him know all her business? Why not? He's a guy — not that he seems anything like Stan — but maybe he can give me some perspective.* "Stan."

"Stan isn't being fair?" He opened and closed the refrigerator again. Katherine heard him pop the top on a beer.

Katherine picked up a shell and started drawing circles in the sand. "I thought he was, but this latest call has thrown me. Our situation is different than yours since our kids are grown. I have a bad feeling he doesn't define 'fair' the same way I do. I don't want more than I should get, but I don't want to feel used either."

Jeff was quiet. "How are you doing on the divorce diet?"

Startled, Katherine asked, "What?"

"Some people gain weight when they're going through a divorce. Others lose it. I saw you the other day and it looks like you've lost weight. How much have you lost?"

"Just about 9 pounds," she said. "But some of that is probably from all the walking I'm doing." Her pile of shells was getting bigger as she mindlessly gathered them close.

"How about sleep?"

Katherine murmured, "Not so much."

"Listen, Katherine. You have to take care of yourself. Find ways to relax and get some sleep. Where are you right now?"

"Sitting in the sand just out of the water by your house." She looked around. "I don't see anyone else on the beach."

"That's a safe neighborhood. I'm not trying to tell you what to do — just don't stay out too late," Jeff said, concerned.

"I couldn't sleep. I'm so angry. Angry with him for breaking our vows. Angry with him for tearing up my life and our kids' lives. Angry about everything." Katherine didn't want to cry, but she could feel the tears gathering.

"You should be. This isn't fair. It isn't right."

"I'm sorry to throw all this at you. You're probably exhausted." She brushed away the tears and stood up.

"No worries. If you need a shoulder to lean on, I've got two that you're welcome to."

"Thanks, Jeff. I'm going to head back now." *He makes me feel better.* She flipped on her flashlight and started back to the beach house.

"Do me a favor and text me when you're safe inside the house?"

Katherine walked quickly through the sand, catching the

ghost crabs scuttling for cover. *That's been me, hiding to avoid conflict. No more. I'm going to strengthen my backbone. Stan can't take advantage of me.*

When she was safely indoors and all locked up, she texted Jeff and thanked him for listening. *He is truly a kind and decent person,* she mused as she fell asleep, a smile lingering on her lips.

# Chapter Thirty-Four

K atherine rushed down the Mews, the little pedestrian alley that connected Rehoboth Ave and Baltimore Ave, glancing at the colorful windows of Bella Luna as she rushed by. *Hmm, I'll have to stop there and check out those beautiful Murano style wine glasses. Jeff's cottage could use a little more sprucing up.*

She smiled when she thought about Jeff. Their walk on the boardwalk. The surprising sweetness of their conversation last night. His endless collection of 60s rock band T-shirts. *He's certainly a contrast to Stan. And Richard.*

Her heart raced thinking about the warmth of his breath as he almost kissed her. Not that she wanted him to kiss her, but it had given her a bit of a tingle. If Ashleigh hadn't shown up when she did, no telling what would have happened. Did she want anything to happen? It might be nice, and it'd been such a long time since she'd been kissed or felt any kind of affection — Stan had been cold and rejecting for over a year.

Drawing closer to the Coffee Mill, she saw Richard lounging at one of the four café tables, the only one shaded from the sun. With his sunglasses, she couldn't tell whether he had spotted her or not.

It was blisteringly hot already. Fishing for a Kleenex, Katherine thought, *why do I have to sweat excessively? I hope I've got a minute to wipe my brow.*

No such luck. He stood up and pulled out the other chair for her.

"Hi. I'm glad you made it!" he exclaimed. "I was wondering whether I had the times mixed up."

"No, I'm sorry. It took me a bit longer to walk over here than I planned." She flushed. "Whew! It got hot. Yesterday was in the seventies and today it's already eighty and it's not even noon."

She patted her face with a tissue. "I know women are supposed to glow in the heat. I blame my mother — she felt the heat as much as I do."

"Let me get you some water. And how about an affogato — expresso and gelato?"

Katherine tucked away the Kleenex. "That sounds good. Do you suppose they have chocolate gelato?"

"If they don't, I'll run to the store and buy some for you." He disappeared into the shop, gently closing the door.

*He is very gentlemanly,* Katherine thought.

He, of course, looked as cool as a cucumber. Every hair in place. No sheen on his face. His Tony Bahama shirt dry as can be. Katherine sighed as she patted her hair in place and pulled her sticky shirt off her back.

Richard came back with her coffee drink and a huge tumbler of ice water. Katherine took a big water gulp and then pressed the cold glass on her wrists. "I love this coffee shop. When I came here with my parents when I was in high school, we would always stop here on the way out of town to grab a coffee for the road and a pastry to tide us over until we got back to Bethesda."

"Did you come here often?" Richard leaned forward as if to capture every word.

"We started coming here when my brother and I were three and four years old. We mostly came at spring break. I think now it was probably because the rents were lower then." Katherine tasted the affogato. "Mmmm...so good. And so cooling. Thank you."

Richard shifted his chair so he was closer to her.

Katherine slid her chair away from him and moved closer to the fan. "There was a fifty/fifty chance that we'd have nice weather or freezing rain at spring break. It's probably why I love the beach in any weather. How about you? How long have you been coming here?"

He covered his mouth with his hand and stroked his chin and closed his eyes. "My family has had an oceanfront place for as long as I can remember. My mother and I, and my sister, would come for the summer while my father stayed in Wilmington and worked during the week. He came down on weekends and spent his two-week vacation with us."

*Odd — I just read that people cover their mouths or close their eyes when they're lying...that was weird.* "Do they still come down?" Katherine asked.

"No, they passed several years ago. They left the house to me and my sister. I bought her out since she's living in California now." He sipped his coffee, holding his pinkie out, and then patted his mouth delicately. He looked at the nicely dressed woman at the next table.

Katherine raised an eyebrow. She drew his attention back to her. "Where do you live, and what do you do, when you're not summering here?"

"I'm an investment banker in Wilmington." Richard caught

her glancing at his left hand. "And I'm not married, in case you're wondering."

Katherine blushed. "No family?" She finished her coffee and set her cup down in the saucer with a clank. He looked up with a disapproving glance. Katherine shrugged her shoulders.

With a blasé tone, he said, "My divorce was final a few years ago. My kids are grown up. My son and his wife live in Colorado, and my daughter and her live-in are in Austin. They come here for a week during the summer if they can."

He scooted his chair closer and gazed into her eyes. "What about you?"

*Good grief. What's with this guy? He acts like it's love at first sight. Only he's the only one in love here,* Katherine thought, picking up her water.

Choosing her words carefully, she said, "Our families are somewhat similar — my son, daughter-in-law, and my first grandson live in Atlanta, and my daughter and her boyfriend work for the State Department. They're looking forward to their first overseas assignment next spring." She paused. "My divorce should be final in the fall unless my ex decides he wants to renegotiate the settlement again. House in McLean. Investments. Retirement accounts. Unraveling our lives is a mess. He had the affair. And I'm left dealing with the fallout," she said bitterly.

"That's terrible. I'm sorry you're facing this," he said sympathetically. "If you want me to go over the settlement or assist with any investments, I'm more than willing to lend a hand."

Katherine schooled her face not to show her reaction, but inside alarm bells were going off. *Too fast. Not really sincere. I don't trust this guy.* "That's nice of you to offer, but I'm confident my lawyer will make sure it's equitable. In addition to being my lawyer, she's my best friend and neighbor."

"What's her name?" Richard asked.

"Why?" Katherine said cautiously. She reached for her purse and got ready to leave.

"Oh, I know lawyers in the area — I was wondering if I knew her," Richard said in a casual tone.

"It's Shawna McKinley."

"No, don't know her." Richard covered Katherine's hand and changed the subject. "What's your favorite restaurant in Washington?"

They chatted about their favorite places to dine — Richard loved all the high-end restaurants, especially Imperfecto and Fiola with their Michelin stars. He favored traditional steakhouses like Maestro's Steakhouse and The Capital Grill, waxing poetic about their tender filet mignons. He was quite animated about all the rich and important people he had seen dining at these places including former presidents and current senators and representatives. Katherine laughed at his story about bumping into the former chair of the House Ways and Means Committee in the men's restroom. She thought he was actually quite entertaining.

He finally wound down and asked her again about her favorites. She admitted she had dined at a few of the places he mentioned, but when given a choice, she liked Le Diplomate. It was like being in Paris at a cozy bistro with its red vinyl banquettes and white marble-topped tables. Noisy and boisterous, the restaurant rocked with energy when they dined there with her neighbors. And Dauphine's was the place to go for a taste of New Orleans. "Ah, the Oysters Dauphine!" She brought her fingers to her mouth, smacked, and said, "Magnifique!"

Richard stared at her. "Would you like to have dinner with me next week?"

She shook her head. "I'm afraid you might have the wrong

impression. I'm still raw from this divorce process. I'm not at all ready to date."

He looked disappointed. "We could be friends. Everyone needs a friend, especially with all the trauma you're going through now. How about if we just enjoy each other's company and see if anything develops?"

Everyone had been telling her that she should go out. Test the waters. Have some fun. Despite her misgivings about Richard, she thought, *It's only dinner. And maybe I'm wrong about him.* "Okay, we can have dinner, but strictly as friends."

"Great. How does next Friday work for you? I'll see if they have a table available." Richard pulled out his phone, thumbed in a number, and quickly sent a text.

"How about the week after? I'm still getting settled and I've started working at Browseabout." When he looked puzzled, she added, "The bookstore?"

Shaking his head. "I don't think I've been in there." He checked his calendar. "No, I can't do it that weekend. I'll be out of town."

Katherine looked up her Browseabout schedule. "I can do the next Saturday, but not Friday."

He sent another text. His phone chimed. "We're all set for two weeks from Saturday, 7:30."

*How could anyone come to Rehoboth without going to the bookstore?* Katherine wondered.

She stopped. "Where are we going? Casual? Dressy?"

Richard clasped her hands in his. "It'll be a surprise. It's beach chic and you'll need a light wrap. It gets cool on the water."

Katherine pulled her hands away and resisted wiping them off on her skirt. "Well, now I'm intrigued."

# Chapter Thirty-Five

*My god, could she not have been more disgusting? Sweating like a horse!* Richard pulled a starkly clean and white linen handkerchief from his pocket and wiped his hands thoroughly. *And she looked ridiculous with her tomato-red cheeks. I was almost afraid she was going to have a heart attack.*

He retrieved his Porsche 911 from the valet at the hotel. He wasn't a guest but when he slipped the attendant a couple of twenties, the kid was happy enough to park the car for him. He carefully examined the car for any scratches. If there was even one, the kid would have to pay for the repair.

*And the way she couldn't resist the affogato. I knew she couldn't.* With her hips — at least forty to forty-two inches — she should have. He had seen the indecision on her face and could almost read her mind. *She must be self-conscious about the extra weight she's carrying.* But from their earlier conversation in the parking office, he also knew that she liked to eat and wouldn't be able to resist the gelato.

*Boring. Who cares if she came here when she was a kid?*

Richard gunned the car around the corner on two wheels, narrowly missing a guy on a bicycle. "Get off the road, you moron."

Richard mentally tallied up her assets. She had been to some of the most expensive restaurants so either she or her husband had some dough. *House in McLean* — McLean is an expensive neighborhood. She's probably got money built up in that house. *Investments* — she didn't say how much, but the size of that rock on her right hand says they're probably extensive. *Retirement accounts* — she should get some of that in the settlement. *Jewelry* — if that big marquise cut diamond ring and those earrings are any indication, there's money there. *She could be just what I need right now. If I can get hold of her assets, I can get the early investors paid off and off my back.*

She was pretty cagey. She had backed off quickly when he offered to take a look at her portfolio. He would have to tread slowly if he didn't want to scare her away. *Yes, I need to be smart about this and win her trust.*

He wrinkled his nose. The thought of wooing her made his stomach turn. The idea of kissing her sweaty face made him gag.

The lawyer could be a problem, too. He lied when he told Katherine he didn't know about Shawna McKinley — she had a reputation of being a barracuda in the courtroom. And if she were a friend and neighbor, she'd be even more protective. He hoped she wouldn't do a background check on him — there were things in his past he would rather stay there.

He congratulated himself for getting her to go to dinner. They say the way to a man's heart is through his stomach. Well, evidently that was the way to her heart, too. The way she talked about food. *All. The. Time.* She'd be better off talking about getting a personal trainer. But at least she agreed. In the meantime, he'd be so attentive, nice, and reserved if it killed him. *She's my golden goose.*

Richard pulled into his driveway. *She wouldn't be bad looking if she lost a little weight. Too bad she's let herself go. The women I usually date are stick thin. But I can put up with a lot if I can get my hands on her money.*

# Chapter Thirty-Six

J eff watched the two smartly dressed men settle into the booth at the end of the bar. Allison flew by and dropped menus on their table and promised to return with water. The older, gray-haired man frowned. "We're on a tight schedule. Make it snappy."

Jeff signaled Allison that he would take the table since she was covering the rest of the dining room.

"Can I help you?"

The older man sneered at Jeff's long hair, tattoos, Steppenwolf T-shirt. The younger man shot a nervous glance at the older guy as if to ask permission to order. The older guy barked, "We'll have two of your Signature Burgers — hold the cheese and the tomato, and serve it on a regular bun with ketchup, not that onion-poppy seed crap or shallot aioli, whatever the hell that is. Instead of the fancy salad, we'll take French fries and onion rings. And two rye Manhattans, up."

*Ordered that way, not our signature burger anymore — just a plain old burger.* Jeff glanced at the younger guy who timidly handed his menu to Jeff.

"Yes, sir. I'll put that order in for you right away."

"We don't have all day." He turned to the younger man, dismissing Jeff curtly. "Mark, I told you that I have it under control. All you have to do is keep sending out the updates that I gave you to the other investors and keep them happy."

"But..."

"No buts about it. Your job is to keep feeding them the information I give you. I've got a line on another investor who could get us out of this mess. She's a dumb broad — she's getting a divorce from some rich guy. She told me he had an affair so she's the injured party. I'm betting she'll get a pretty good settlement. And she said she's keeping the house... What do you want?"

Jeff was waiting quietly beside the table. "You didn't tell me how you want your burgers cooked."

"Oh, for god's sake, medium well," he snarled at Jeff.

Troubled, Jeff headed for the kitchen.

"What's up?" Tim asked.

"This customer I'm waiting on is a jerk. I can handle that, but it sounds like he's running a scam on someone."

"Who?"

"I don't know. Some woman who's getting a divorce. And the way he was talking about her makes my skin crawl." Jeff pinned the order on the ticket rail and counted four orders ahead of his. "He's going to pitch a fit if he has to wait too long."

"Don't worry. The next two are almost ready." Tim checked the next ticket. "This one won't take long. His will be ready quickly." He asked, "Do you know who he is?"

"Nope. Never seen him before. Hopefully, he'll pay with a credit card so I can get his name. I want to keep an eye on him."

Jeff mixed the drinks and quietly approached their table. He heard the older guy say, "She's also got some money from her parents. I told her I'd be happy to help her with her investments, promised a big return like the others. If I can get control of her money, I can placate the other investors with a token return..." He looked up. "Well, what are you waiting for? Gimme the drinks. And where's the food?"

"It's coming up right now." Jeff hurried back to the kitchen and picked up their lunches. Passing Allison, he asked, "Have you ever seen the guys at the table I'm taking care of?"

"Never seen them before. But I think I saw the older one hanging around the bar at Eden a few weeks ago. He was talking to your friend, Beth, and some other women she was with."

That worried Jeff. *Was Beth the one the jerk was talking about? That can't be because she's not getting divorced.*

"Thanks, Allison. I'll check in with Beth and see if she knows this guy. There's something about him that isn't right."

The older guy was making a point. "I took her to coffee last week. She was sweating like a pig when she showed up. It was all I could do to not throw up. But I convinced her to let me take her to dinner..."

Jeff tried not to interrupt him, but he stopped short when Jeff appeared with their food.

"It's about time." He grabbed the ketchup bottle and covered his fries and his burger. Taking a big bite, he sneered around a mouthful of burger, "Get us the check."

# Chapter Thirty-Seven

Closed toed shoes. Check.

No loose scarves or belts. Check.

Katherine marked off Jeff's clothing requirements. He had been very specific about what she could and could not wear. It was a little irritating. If he told her where they were going, she could have figured out what to wear herself. But nooo, he has to make it a big secret. *What is it with guys and their surprises? First Richard won't tell me where we're going and now Jeff won't either.* She still wasn't even sure why she was going out with him, but he had pleaded so nicely when they ran into each other. *What the heck — it's only one night.*

*I'm here,* Jeff texted. *Come on out.*

"Oh no," Katherine muttered out loud. *You have to come to the door, buster,* she texted back.

He replied with a sad face emoji.

"Good grief. How old is this guy? You'd think he was in high school, or even middle school," Katherine grumbled.

She texted. *A grown-up would come to the door...* The doorbell rang insistently.

"Okay, I'm here. At your door. Let's go. We don't want to be late." Jeff pulled her in for a casual hug. She melted for a moment against his warm body and shivered when he pulled away. *Good grief. Get ahold of yourself.* She stammered, "Where are we going?"

"Hurry up. We're going to miss it."

He dragged her to the corner of Carolina Street. "Come on. We can just make it." They jogged toward Silver Lake and stopped on the corner of Chesapeake Street and Route 1, the main drag into Rehoboth Beach. It was one block, but Katherine was winded and sweating. "What are we doing?"

"Turn around."

Katherine jumped back a step as the red and gold Jolly Trolley rumbled to a stop. "Hi, folks. Headed to town? Hop on," the driver shouted from the front. The open-air trolley, lined with a double row of purple seats, was mostly full of laughing and chatting people.

Jeff punched their tickets and found two seats in the back across the aisle from each other. Katherine sat next to a scowling young boy while Jeff took the seat next to an equally scowling young boy. As they were dressed exactly alike and looked exactly alike and were sticking their tongues out in exactly the same way, it looked like Jeff and Katherine were in the demilitarized zone of twin warfare.

"This is my first time on the Trolley," Katherine said. She stuck out her tongue at the twin behind Jeff. Shocked, he shrank back behind Jeff.

"Really?" Jeff grinned. "You've never ridden the Trolley? Don't you know it's Rehoboth Beach's Original Mass Transit?"

"Well, I usually walk along the water to go downtown. Or ride my bike. Or drive. The schedule doesn't work with my job at Browseabout."

"How's that going anyhow?" Jeff blocked his twin's view of his brother.

"It's perfect. Beth has turned over a substantial number of responsibilities to me. I'm closing the store a couple of nights a week. She actually gets to go home early for a change. And I open the store on Sundays, her one day to sleep in. She seems a lot more relaxed now."

"I'm glad you're enjoying it and I'm glad Beth is getting a break. I've been a little worried about her."

Katherine regarded Jeff thoughtfully. "How did you two become such good friends?"

Jeff hesitated. "Right after my divorce, I was kind of a hot mess. I knew Beth casually from the Chamber of Commerce meetings but hadn't spent much time with her. She figured out that I was beating myself up for working so much and losing my wife and my child. I was furious at myself and depressed. She took me under her wing and made me do things."

"Made you do things?" She emphasized her skepticism with air quotes. "That sounds weird."

Jeff laughed. "She made me rent a bicycle built for two and ride her around. She took me bowling. She introduced me to Isabella who was getting started and told me to help her get her business off the ground. Helping Isabella got me out of my pity party. Beth never let me stew and mope. I don't think I'd be where I am now without her support."

"Did you two ever date?" Katherine asked.

"No, we never did. Beth has her own story. Maybe she'll tell you sometime."

"I'm really enjoying getting to know her and appreciate her support so much. She's already helped me immensely. I'd like to return the favor if I can."

Jeff looked up and jerked the stop cord. "Okay, this is it — our stop." Jeff finger waved at the twins. "Now behave yourselves." Their parents gave him a grateful smile. He helped Katherine down from the Trolley. "It's down this way." Racewalking her down the boardwalk, he held her hand to make sure she stayed with him. "Here it is!" he shouted gleefully.

"Funland?" Katherine said quizzically. "We're going to Funland?"

"Yup. This is where all the fun happens. I worked here a couple of summers in addition to working at my grandparents' café. I know all the best rides and best games. I bet I can win the biggest stuffed animal for you."

"What do you mean 'rides?'" Katherine said cautiously.

"You're not a wuss, are you?" Jeff teased. Noting her anxious look, he said, "We'll start with the kiddie rides first and then see how you do."

Jeff rushed over to the ticket booth and bought two books of fifty tickets. He handed Katherine one book. "Here, this one is yours. The tickets are good for life. If you don't use all of them tonight, you can come back anytime and use them."

Excited as a little kid, Jeff said, "Let's go. The line at the Carousel isn't very long." Jeff pulled two tickets from his booklet and waited for Katherine to give hers to the attendant. "I always ride the red horse with the blue saddle."

Katherine stared at him in astonishment. "You have a favorite merry-go-round horse?"

"Of course, don't you?"

Katherine shook her head and took the shiny black horse next to him.

From the Carousel to the Helicopters to the Mad Tea Party, they bounced from ride to ride. Katherine finally said, "How about the Tilt-A-Whirl?"

"You want to go on that?" Jeff asked. "You ready for a little more adventure?"

"Of course. Just because I haven't done this in a while doesn't mean I can't handle the big rides."

Jeff got an evil gleam in his eye. "Okay. Let's do the Tilt-A-Whirl and then we'll go for the really good ones."

Katherine didn't like the look in Jeff's eyes. "You're not going to hurt me, are you?"

Jeff said seriously, "I would never do that, Katherine. You can trust me."

The Tilt-A-Whirl seemed tame after the Superflip, which stood them upside down as they dropped to the ground. Katherine wasn't sure who screamed the loudest — her or Jeff. After the Sea Dragon, Katherine said, "Enough. My stomach is still doing barrel rolls. How about something a little more sedate?"

"I've got just the thing," he said as he led her to the Haunted Mansion. They got belted into their car and Jeff, oh so casually, put his arm around Katherine's shoulders. She studied him for a long moment and then snuggled in. "You will protect me, won't you?"

"Count on it." He gently kissed her forehead.

By the time they reached the end of the ride with all the screams and creatures jumping out without warning, Katherine had her head buried in Jeff's neck while Jeff had both arms around her. When they burst out the door onto the brightly lit platform, Katherine disengaged and said with embarrassment, "I wasn't that scared. I thought you needed comforting."

"Uh huh." Jeff smirked. "Had enough? Ready for some ice cream?"

"Wait — I thought you promised me a stuffed animal?"

Jeff led her over to the Goblet Toss. "Hi, Joe, you're still working here?"

"You know I can't get enough of this place. You're not going to win all my merchandise, man?"

Jeff flexed his muscles and nodded at Katherine. "Man's gotta do what he's gotta do to impress my girl."

He collected the six balls he needed to win the biggest prize. He stretched and postured, and said to Katherine, "Watch this."

First one, then two, followed by three balls plopped directly into the goblets. The fourth ball hit the rim and looked like it was not going in, but at the last moment, it dropped in.

He leaned over to Katherine. "How about a kiss for luck?"

Surprised, she gave him a prim peck on the cheek.

"That does not cut it," he complained and pulled her in. "This is how you do it." He laid his lips on Katherine's gently at first and then increasing the pressure, forcing her to open her lips and let his tongue dance in and out. "Hey, get a room!" someone shouted.

Jeff broke the kiss and turned back to the game. Ball five right in the goblet. Katherine held her breath as ball six circled the cup. In it went as the crowd cheered. "We have a winner!" Joe said. "Pick any prize on the top row."

Katherine studied Jeff for a moment and then turned to the prizes. "That one. The cow. I love cows." Cow under her arm, she said, "Now I'm ready for ice cream."

The boardwalk was still teeming with people. Couples strolled arm in arm. Parents walked slowly several feet behind their pre-teens who wouldn't be caught dead hanging out with the 'rents but for the fact they were too young to be out on their own yet. Katherine slipped her arm through Jeff's.

"I can't remember the last time I had so much fun. Thank you for taking me there. And for winning my cow. I think I'll name her...Jessie. Close enough to 'Jeffie'." She giggled.

"You're naming your cow after me?" he laughed. "I'm honored."

Katherine craned her neck to look around Jeff.

"What are you looking at?" Jeff turned to look.

"Oh, nothing. I see someone who said he was going to be out of town this weekend." She frowned.

Jeff caught a glimpse of the guy who had been bragging about scamming some woman. "Do you know that guy?" he pointed to Richard.

"Yes, I met him when I was getting my parking permit. We had coffee the other day. Why?"

Jeff scowled. "I don't think he's a nice guy. I don't think you should see him anymore."

Katherine bristled. "What do you mean 'I shouldn't see him anymore'? You don't get to tell me that."

"I heard him in my restaurant talking to another guy about how he was going to take advantage of some woman. He was going to try to get her to invest her money with him and then he was going to use it to pay off some other people. It sounded like a Ponzi scheme to me," Jeff warned. "And he was pretty rude."

"You should talk about being rude," Katherine fussed. "He was a perfect gentleman when we had coffee."

"Perfect gentleman, my ass. He's a snake. Because he looks good doesn't mean he is good."

Katherine fumed at Jeff's high-handed manner. *Who does he think he is? Telling me what to do.* "It's getting late. Can you call an Uber? I'd like to go home now."

Jeff tried to apologize on the way back to her place. Katherine wasn't having any of it. He said he was just saying she should be careful. She sat in stony silence looking out the window. When they reached her house, she got out without a word.

"Katherine, wait! Please." She inserted the key in the door. "I am really sorry. I don't want to see you get hurt or taken advantage of."

"Stan already did that. So far Richard hasn't done anything

to make me too suspicious of him, although I am now concerned that he told me he was out of town this weekend, and there he was in town, with a woman. I'll ask him about it when I have dinner with him and see if he has an explanation. Stan has made me very cautious — he destroyed my trust in him, and men in general, with his shenanigans. Right now, trust is not a given. It has to be earned."

Jeff looked as though he had something else to say, but he visibly restrained himself. "Good night, Katherine. I enjoyed Funland. And I'm sorry to end on this sour note," Jeff continued. "Why am I always apologizing to you?"

Katherine sighed. "I'm sorry, too. I might have overreacted. I let Stan control too much of my life before and I'm determined to not let that happen again."

Jeff pulled her in for a quick hug. "Sleep tight, Katherine." He gazed at her thoughtfully. "I meant it back at Funland. I'll never hurt you. Please don't compare me to Stan."

Jeff was different than Stan. Katherine could sense that he would never cheat on her or lie to her. But that still didn't mean he could tell her what to do.

# Chapter Thirty-Eight

Beth and Katherine powerwalked down the boardwalk, dodging early morning meandering strollers and dog walkers. With a professional-looking thirty-five-millimeter camera clutched in her hands, a trim silver-haired woman dashed out of the condo on their left and ran smack dab into Katherine.

"Oh, my heavens, I'm terribly sorry," the woman exclaimed. "I was chasing the dolphins and wasn't watching where I was going. I missed them yesterday and I wanted to be sure to catch them this time."

"No problem. No harm done." Katherine laughed. "I do the same thing when I see them go by. They probably wonder about that crazy woman running along the water's edge. Although I don't have a camera like that – I just use my cell phone."

The woman held up the Nikon. "I'm still learning how to use it. It's a new hobby."

"I've lived here forever, and I never get tired of looking at them. Look, there they are!" Beth pointed north of where they were standing. "Quick! You can still take some pictures."

The woman spun around and zoomed the telephoto lens as much as she could. She waited a moment and caught the pair as they surfaced. "They are beautiful. I love the way the sun reflects on their fins in the morning."

She dangled the camera around her neck and held out her hand. "I'm Brittany Spencer, by the way. And I'm sorry to have stopped your walk. You looked like you were having a very serious conversation."

Katherine grinned at Beth. "Oh, we were. We were trying to decide where to have coffee." She sat down on the bench to retie her shoe. "I'm Katherine Lewis, and this is Beth Standish. We were just finishing our walk and we always reward ourselves with coffee when we're done."

"Have you tried The Coffee Mill? It's a few blocks from here. They have some of the best coffee I've had."

Beth glanced at Katherine who nodded. "Actually, that was one of the places we were considering. Want to join us?"

"I would love to. And buying you a cup of coffee would be the least I could do for plowing into you and breaking your rhythm."

"Totally unnecessary. And to be honest, I was glad for the break." Katherine stood up. "Beth is a speed walker — I have to hustle to keep up with her."

Brittany headed for the condo lobby. "Let me put my camera away and grab some money. I'll be there in a minute."

Katherine and Beth went on to the end of the boardwalk and touched the mile marker for good luck. Walking back around the duck pond, they checked to see if the ducklings were still there. They stopped to watch them waddle after the mama duck and laughed at their antics.

The sun was higher now. The heat and humidity were

rising. Reaching the coffee shop, they nabbed the last table for three in the shade just as Brittany strolled up.

"What can I get you? My treat, remember," Brittany said.

"Just black coffee for me." Beth tilted the umbrella to make sure all the chairs were shaded.

"I'll help you carry them." Katherine stood up.

"I've got it. What would you like?" Brittany asked.

"Medium roast, black, one sugar." Katherine emptied her water bottle in one swallow.

Moments later, Brittany doled out their choices, black coffees for Beth and Katherine and a crème brûlée flavored coffee for herself. She shrugged. "I know. I know. It's a sissy coffee but I love it, so I indulge every once in a while."

"How long have you lived in the Star Colony?" Beth blew on her coffee, inhaling the rich aroma of the Jamaican Blue Island brew.

"Two years, although I didn't spend much time here the first year," Brittany explained. "My husband passed away suddenly. After I retired, I decided to sell our house and move here."

Beth and Katherine murmured their sympathy. "I'm so sorry. What happened, if it's not too hard to talk about it?" Beth asked.

Brittany winced. "No, it's okay. He died in a motorcycle accident right after he retired. He had always wanted to ride a motorcycle and never had the chance. He took lessons and everything — always wore his helmet and protective clothing — but he hit some loose gravel on a badly banked curve and wiped out. He was gone even before they got to the hospital."

She teared up. "I want to be mad at him because we had so many plans about what we were going to do in retirement, but of course, I can't. He loved riding his motorcycle and I wouldn't have denied him that pleasure."

"Oh, that's awful. Are you retired also?" Beth asked.

"I kept working another year and then decided to retire a little early. Life is too short — I learned that the hard way when my husband died. We put off doing things we wanted to do and places we wanted to visit. And then look what happened..." Brittany dug in her pocket for a Kleenex. "You'd think after three years that it would be easier..."

Katherine handed her a package of tissues. "Three years isn't that long. It must be so hard to lose someone you love."

Brittany wiped her eyes and went on. "I sold our house in Wilmington and bought the condo here. We came here as a family several times so Rehoboth was familiar, but not so familiar that I saw Bob on every corner. I've been mostly reading and knitting and chasing dolphins. Kind of wasting time — but it's evidently what I need."

"We have a lot in common," Katherine interjected. "My husband didn't die, however. He's divorcing me after thirty-seven years of marriage. My family used to come here all the time when I was a kid, too, just like you. Rehoboth is comfortable for me also."

"Thirty-seven years? What happened?"

"He had an affair and now he's marrying her," Katherine said dully.

"Well, that sucks."

Katherine squared her shoulders. "Yup. I came for a long weekend in May and decided to stay until January when my sabbatical is up." She continued, "I've been drifting along this summer. Beth was kind enough to give me a job — she's the manager of Browseabout Bookstore. Working there has given me enough structure — and it's great fun — that I'm getting things under control."

"Maybe that's what I need," Brittany said, lost in thought. "Something to make me want to get out of bed in the morning."

Beth asked, "What kind of work did you do in Wilmington?"

"I was in advertising — account management. It was a very high-pressure job — clients are always right, but sometimes, it's tough to satisfy them. When I decided to leave, I was pretty tired of the corporate rat race."

Beth sat up straight. "If you'd like to dip a toe back in the business, I could use some advice about our advertising strategy. Do you do any consulting?"

Brittany stirred her coffee. "You know, I've been thinking about that. I haven't done any yet, but the thought has crossed my mind with the right clients and right businesses. Would this be for the bookstore?"

Beth ducked her head, and said shyly, "No. I haven't told many people about this yet. My secret passion job would be working with authors to help them finish their books. Do you know how many people I talk to in a day that say they've got a book in their heads? A lot. I want to help them get their books out on paper. At some point, I'd like to do this full-time but right now I only take a few clients. I could use some help figuring out how to reach my market besides word of mouth."

Katherine studied Beth, thinking how good she would be at helping authors realize their dreams.

Brittany finished her coffee and tidied up the table. "You know, that sounds fascinating. I'm particularly interested in helping women entrepreneurs. Let me think about it and I'll get back to you soon."

Katherine chimed in. "We have that in common, too. In addition to my university teaching and research, I volunteer with an incubator in D.C. I help women write better business plans. It's very rewarding to see these women get funding and launch their businesses successfully."

Brittany picked up her trash. "Thank you for inviting me.

It's been great meeting you. And hopefully, we'll run into each other again – although not literally this time."

Beth glanced at Katherine who nodded. "There are a few women who get together Sunday evenings for a glass of wine — or two — at different restaurants in Rehoboth to talk about books and other important topics — like where to find the best scones." She laughed. "If I do say so myself, we're an interesting group. A few of us have started our own businesses, and the others are successful businesswomen. Would you be interested in joining us on Sunday?"

Beth finished off her coffee and continued. "This Sunday we're going to the Back Porch. They set aside their back room so we can get as rowdy as we want." Beth grinned at Brittany and Katherine. "Actually, we don't usually get very rowdy, but it's possible."

Brittany hesitated. "If you're sure it wouldn't be a problem...I've missed the women I worked with. I'd love to join you. What time?"

Beth checked her phone. "6:00. They close at 7:00 but they let us stay later while they clean up around us."

"Great. See you there."

# Chapter Thirty-Nine

Katherine threw on one dress and scrutinized the mirror. *Nope, I look like a 1950s schoolteacher. And it's hanging like a sack on me. All this walking and biking seems to be making a difference.*

She tore into her pathetic closet, the metal hangers screeching on the closet rod, as she rejected every dress she had. *I didn't expect to be going out to dinner. I didn't bring that many dressy clothes and what I did bring I don't like anymore. I need some help.* She picked up her cell phone, scanned the contacts, and made the emergency call.

"Sandy, are you busy right now?"

"No, it's not too busy in the shop at the moment. What can I do for you?"

"I'm going out to dinner tomorrow night, and I don't have anything to wear."

"Well, come on in. I'm sure I can find something perfect for you."

Katherine racewalked the few blocks to the Lookin' Good boutique and threw open the door into the welcoming coolness.

The shop was a vision of sea blues, mint greens, soft violets, gray pinks — the colors of the beach. Katherine had looked longingly in the windows every time she passed by on her way to Browseabout but had never felt comfortable going in. She was sure they wouldn't have anything in her size.

Sandy had urged her to come in "to take a look" but Katherine had never had the confidence to take her up on the offer. Now she was desperate. She looked around wildly for Sandy who came out of the back with her arms full.

"I pulled a few things that I think are going to look fabulous on you. With your lovely pink complexion and green eyes, I think we're going to focus on the greens, violets, creams. I want you to try these."

Sandy directed Katherine to the dressing room. "There's no one else in the store right now. We have the place to ourselves so we can play." She hung the outfits around the room on the hooks and over the door.

Katherine's eyes widened as she reviewed the selections. "I can't wear that! The neckline is down to there! And that one is way too fitted — I'll look like a sausage in that. And I've never worn anything in either of those colors. Most of my wardrobe is black and navy blue — you know, professional colors."

"Come on. Just trust me. Try them on. If you don't like them, I'll find something else." Sandy closed the fitting room door softly. "Come out when you've got the first one on. I want to see all of them."

Katherine closed the door to the dressing room with a sigh. *This was a bad idea. I should go. I could wear my favorite black pants and a nice white blouse.*

"How's it going in there? Need any help?" Sandy called through the door.

Katherine, startled, reached for the first dress, a mint green jewel neck sheath with elbow length sleeves and a draped shoulder panel that graced the waistline. The soft jersey fabric felt cool as it slid over Katherine's shoulders. Instead of clinging, it skimmed over her curves. Katherine, stunned, flung open the dressing room door.

"How did you do that? How did you pick something that fits and actually looks good? I never would have pulled this off the rack if I were shopping alone."

Sandy smiled smugly. "I've been doing this for years and sometimes when I meet someone, I can picture them in a dress I have in the shop." She turned Katherine around and examined her from all sides. "This is very good, but I want to see the others before I make a recommendation."

Katherine cast one last admiring glance in the mirror before she turned back to the dressing room. "Okay, but I don't see how you're going to top this."

She carefully hung up the dress, caressing the jersey, and plucked the next dress off the hook. She slipped the soft pink dress over her head and waited until it settled down. She zipped the zipper before she turned around to the mirror, wanting to get the whole effect.

*Huh, now what? I love this one, too!* With a slight V-neck and tapered waist with a faux tie front detail, this dress accentuated her hourglass shape. The slight gathering at the tummy hid the mommy bulge that no amount of exercise seemed to get rid of, even after all these years. The color set off her light tan.

"Come on out. I want to see, too." Sandy tapped at the dressing room door. "Oh yes, I thought that would be a good one for you. What do you think?"

"I think you're a magician, or my fairy godmother. Did you wave your magic wand over these dresses before I came in? I thought there wouldn't be anything in my size in this shop. The models in the windows are pretty intimidating — thin and angular — which I'm not." Katherine turned this way and that way. She stood on her tiptoes, imagining what the dress would look like with a little heel.

"You're selling yourself short. You have a lovely figure. And if I can be honest, I think you've been hiding in your old clothes. They may have been right for a professor, but 'you're not in Kansas, Dorothy.' Don't you think it's time to let the new Katherine out to shine?" Sandy chided her gently.

Katherine teared up. "You know, I let my ex do such a number on me. And I didn't even realize how much his comments and behaviors were taking a toll on my self-confidence. I don't remember the last time he ever complimented me or showed any affection. He was always quick to ask me why I was wearing that old thing or why didn't I exercise a little more or did I need that piece of cheesecake? He battered and battered me with his hurtful words, and I let him. Thank you for reminding me that I'm more than enough and for helping me see myself with different eyes." Katherine took another admiring look in the mirror. This pink dress was so lovely, and she felt pretty.

"It takes strength to do what you're doing now so don't beat yourself up. You can decide who you want to be and how you want to show that 'you' to the world. If you want to wear black and navy blue because you want to, then go for it. If you want to wear this pink dress or that green dress, go for that then. It's your choice."

Katherine hugged Sandy. "Despite my tears, I haven't had this much fun trying on dresses ever. Okay, Fairy Godmother, let's see what other magic you have up my, I mean, your sleeve."

She tried on a cream long sleeve linen jacket with fitted linen chop pants that she fell in love with. The jacket was hips friendly, middle friendly and looked perfect with the flat waisted ankle pants. Outfit after outfit, she was amazed at

Sandy's choices and soon began to panic because there were several things she liked!

The last dress — a simple shirtwaist in a pale lilac. Katherine was tired and almost decided not to try it on. The crisp cotton kissed her body as it slithered over her arms. She did up what seemed like a hundred tiny covered buttons and cinched the wide cloth belt tight around her waist. She flipped the collar up just a bit in front and then turned to the mirror. *Oh. My. Goodness.* She could hardly breathe. This was THE ONE.

Sandy called, "Last one. Let's have it."

Katherine opened the door and Sandy said, "I knew it. I knew it would be perfect. The others are great but this one looks fantastic on you."

Katherine gazed at the image in the mirror and wondered who that woman was. She looked vibrant and even beautiful. The fitted dress and cinched waist flattered her. The starched collar framed her face and drew attention to her eyes. The violet made her green eyes even greener.

"I'll take it," she breathed.

"Of course, you will! You would be crazy not to, and I can tell you're not crazy. But wait right here. I'll be right back." Sandy dashed away and came back with the perfect sandals and the right earrings that dangled just enough.

"Thank you. Thank you. You are a genius. And you know what, I'm going to take the pink dress and the cream jacket and pants, too. It's time for me to be happy with my choices."

"What's the occasion for dinner tomorrow? Going with anyone I know?" Sandy asked as she rang up Katherine's outfits.

"You might know him — he says he's lived here for a while and has always spent his summers here — his name is Richard," Katherine mumbled.

"You don't sound all that excited."

"I'm not really. I met him for coffee the other day and he insisted on taking me out to dinner. He seems nice enough. Well dressed. Successful. He does something with investments." Katherine continued. "I'm not really ready to date, but he seems like a good match." She stopped. "I'm more excited about wearing my new outfit. But which one should I wear!" She loved all her choices.

# Chapter Forty

"We're not quite open yet." Katherine heard a disembodied voice from somewhere in the darkness. "Oh, hey, Katherine. I couldn't see it was you."

Eyes adjusting, Katherine spotted Isabella behind the shiny stainless-steel bar flanked with backless chrome bar stools. She admired the sleek modern look — such a contrast with the more typical dark wood and picnic tables in other brewpubs.

"Hi, Isabella. I know I'm a little early, but I was out walking and thought I would stop in to say hi. Great place you have here. How long have you been in business?"

"Twelve years. And I think we've turned a corner from COVID. The pandemic set us back a bit, but we adapted. We sold a lot of beer to go — in growlers and cans. We were lucky we had our canning operations already established. We shifted our taproom people to the canning business. I didn't have to lay off anyone."

"You were lucky. Or smart. Or probably both." Katherine climbed up on the bar stool.

"It was bad for many of my peers across the country. Thank

heavens, it's getting better. At the last Craft Brewers Conference, the chief economist of the Brewers Association said there were about 650 new breweries opened in 2021 and only about 180 closings. That's not as many openings as previous years. Fewer closings in 2021 than in 2020. That's a good sign."

"Sounds like you're on top of the industry."

"I like to be aware of the trends. If you don't, your business is going to suffer."

Katherine reached for the bar menu. "Every time I walk by here in the evenings, it's packed. Looks like you're doing very well."

"You know I started this business very lean. I went door to door delivering my beers to the local restaurants. Jeff was a big supporter. He was one of the first to carry my beer."

At Katherine's raised eyebrows, Isabella shrugged. "Yeah, he took a chance on me and served my beers in his restaurants. It was a huge win for me."

"You're the second woman to tell me how much Jeff helped her get started," Katherine mused.

"You should talk to him sometime about his vision for small businesses. Have you talked with Cassandra? He helped her get started, too. She was having some trouble with zoning where she wanted to put her store. He worked with the City Council to get them to approve her plan."

"Huh. He's full of surprises," Katherine said thoughtfully. "He didn't see you as competition?"

"Not at all. We've never had a restaurant. Not my area of expertise. I've relied on rotating food trucks who park outside the tap room. That way I can support other small businesses in the area. Kind of paying it forward from Jeff."

"What a great idea!" Katherine exclaimed.

Isabella handed her the monthly calendar showing which

food trucks would be on which dates. "Customers like the variety. I make it an event with live music to match the truck. When the Backyard Ribs Truck is here, we have a country band. When the Jamaican Kitchen Truck is scheduled, we have reggae. It's always a party here."

Katherine studied the calendar. "That's fantastic. You don't have to carry the overhead of a restaurant. You meet your customers' needs. The food truck owners have a market for their food. It's a win-win-win. No wonder your parking lot is full every night."

Isabella smiled. "It works for us. And I get to do what I love — make beer."

"Is it too early to taste some of your beers?" Katherine asked hopefully.

"It's five o'clock somewhere. I'll set you up with our mini flight — six three-ounce tastes. Don't want you wobbling home." Isabella went behind the bar. "We've got fifteen beers on tap right now ranging from IPAs to porters to ales to stouts including a raspberry chocolate stout. They go from a 5.5% ABV to our big boy at 10.5% ABV. What's your pleasure?"

"Whew. I'm going to stay away from the 10.5% guy. Start me off with the IPAS and lighter ales and work me up to the raspberry chocolate stout."

Isabella turned back to the sleek chrome taps lining the wall behind her. Above her head were carefully labeled stainless steel barrels, each with their own temperature gauge, tubed to the taps below them. Isabella expertly poured the flight and lined them up on the flight board. Behind each glass, she placed the beer tasting notes. She handed Katherine the beer flight scoring sheet — appearance, aroma, taste, mouthful, finish.

"Okay, start tasting from left to right and tell me what you think."

"Thanks. How'd get into this business?" Katherine asked as she sipped the first sample.

Isabella laughed. "I was pretty much a newbie — tinkering around with making home brews — and working as an engineering manager for a major defense contractor. My skills are in the business and process side of the business. You've got to know your own strengths and how to complement those with other people who have the strengths you don't."

Katherine scored the first beer twenty out of twenty-five. It was a little too light for her taste. She moved on to the second sample.

"One of the best decisions I made was hiring Katrina as my brew master. I met her at the Richmond chapter meeting of the Pink Boots Society." Isabella preened. "She was quite the catch — an outstanding talent."

"Pink Boots?"

"Stylish, no? Teri Fahrendoft, one of the early innovators in the industry, founded the group to help more women get into the beer industry. 'Boots' are a nod to the safety boots brewery workers have to wear to protect their feet against boiling hot water, dangerous chemicals, slippery floors, and walkways — but we wear "pink" boots for women. It's a great networking and support group for us. How's the beer?"

"I loved number three — I can taste vanilla and coffee," Katherine gushed. "And I didn't expect to like the raspberry chocolate beer, but it's smooth and sweet. It's like drinking dessert."

Isabella smiled. "Just what we were hoping for. And the number three that you like? We partner with one of the local coffee roasters to use their Brazil Cerrado beans for flavor. The nutty, malty notes of the coffee blend well with the beer. You have a good palate. Want a job?"

Katherine chuckled. "Thanks, but I have enough on my plate. How about you? Is it just you and Katrina?"

"No, I've got an exceptional staff now which gives me time to work with other new brewery owners. I'm pretty involved with the Craft Brew Association." Isabella blushed. "I'm heading to the World Brewing Congress in August. I try to go every year."

"What's the blush for?" Katherine teased. "I don't usually blush when I talk about my English conferences."

"I've met some great people there." Isabella looked down at her shoes.

"People or person?"

"People and person, I guess. There's a guy, Samson. He owns a brewery in Portland, Oregon. We catch dinner every year." Isabella blushed even brighter red.

"Just dinner?" Katherine nudged. "Looks like it's an important dinner."

"Just dinner. But we have such a great time. We talk about everything related to business and everything else. If only he didn't live so far away..." She sighed. "It does get lonely sometimes."

"Have you ever been married?" Katherine asked.

"No. I've never had the time. And I'm going to be sixty next month so it's probably too late."

"Don't say that. Who knows what the future will bring? I have a friend from high school who got married for the first time when she was fifty-eight. She was like you — building her career was the most important thing. Then she met a fantastic guy, fell in love, and has been happily married since then. It's possible."

Isabella nodded skeptically.

Katherine stood up. "What do I owe you?"

"The first round is on the house." Isabella waved away Katherine's money. "I expect to see you in here more often."

"You got it. Thanks again. You've got an impressive business."

Jeff answered on the first ring. "Were you sitting on the phone?" Katherine teased.

"No, I was hoping you would call. Do you know how much I enjoy these calls?"

She could hear him wrestling around on his bed, sitting up and getting more comfortable. "Kind of like phone sex."

"What?!" Katherine exploded. "This is *not* like phone sex. Although I don't know what phone sex is since I've never done it, but I'm pretty sure this is not it!"

Jeff chuckled. "I love getting a rise out of you."

Katherine snorted.

"You're right," he continued. "It's not like phone sex. Although I'd be open to try if you're interested…"

"Oh, you. Why do I always fall for your tricks." Katherine pulled the comforter up higher to get warmer. A vision of Jeff spooning her in this too empty bed flashed before her eyes. Fanning herself, she thought, *Better not go there, but it sure felt good visualizing it.*

Jeff hesitated. "I'm hoping that's not all you're falling for."

Katherine was quiet for a moment. *I could be falling for a whole lot more than that.* "I've got a bone to pick with you."

"Now what have I done?" Jeff said, sounding amused.

"How come I have to hear about all the good stuff you do to help start-ups from everyone else but you?" Katherine turned off the bedside light. The full moon washed the room with a soft glow. "I talked to Isabella today and she told me about how much you helped her get her business started. And Susie Lincoln told me about the big break you gave her with your restaurants. They talk about you like you're a Superhero."

"Did I hear you turn off the light? Are you sitting there in the dark?"

She noticed how he deflected the question. "I'm not telling until you answer my question."

Jeff laughed. "It was the right thing to do, and it was good for my business. Susie does great construction work, and my restaurants needed remodeling. Isabella makes terrific beers, and my customers like them. It worked for all of us."

"You are one of the good guys, aren't you?" Katherine murmured.

"I keep trying to tell you that," Jeff whispered.

*I'm starting to believe you.*

# Chapter Forty-One

Katherine put the finishing touches on her lipstick and spritzed a light spray of her favorite perfume. She looked good and felt good. And confident. She wondered where Richard was taking her to dinner and hoped this new dress was appropriate. He hadn't given her any idea where they were going.

The doorbell rang insistently. Katherine hurried to the door. Instead of Richard, there stood Jeff, looking sexier than he should in his Grateful Dead T-shirt and jeans that caressed his legs. "What are you doing here, Jeff?"

"Wow! You look great! Are you going out?" His gaze trailed slowly from the tips of her newly highlighted hair down to the gentle swell of her breasts peeking out of the mostly demure V-neck of her dress to the tightly cinched waist to her freshly pedicured cherry red toes. "You look fantastic. How come you never look like that when we go out?"

Katherine flushed with pleasure at his appreciation. "Yes, I'm going out and my date should be here any second. And when have you taken me out other than to your bar and

Funland? I'm not going to a bar or Funland dressed like this. Again, what are you doing here?"

Jeff shifted from foot to foot. "Well, you mentioned that the back door was sticking. I thought I would take a look at it. And then I thought we could grab some sandwiches and a couple of beers and sit on the beach. But I can see this isn't a good time. I'll come back another day."

Katherine, surprised at how disappointed she was, replied, "Maybe tomorrow?"

"Can't tomorrow. I've got to be in Bethany working with my manager down there. We're redoing the menu and I have to give it the final approval." Jeff added, "How about the next night?"

Katherine nodded. "That works for me."

"Okay, I'll get someone to close for me, so I'll see you about 8:00 after the dinner rush." Jeff swaggered back to his dusty blue beat-up Jeep Wrangler.

*He sure does fill out his jeans nicely.* Katherine thought as she watched him reach his car.

Richard cruised up in his silver Porsche 911, the engine rumbling as he pulled smoothly to the curb. Jeff turned and took in the car and the man climbing gracefully out of driver's side. He turned back to Katherine, scowled, and started back to her door. Katherine shook her head. Jeff nodded and then pointed to his eyes and then pointed at Richard.

*Yes, I get it. He's got his eyes on Richard.*

Jeff flicked a glance at Richard as he strolled up the sidewalk, testosterone scenting the air as the two alphas circled their prey.

As Richard came up the front steps, he cast a disinterested look at Jeff. Turning to Katherine, he oozed, "You are lovelier beyond anything I could have imagined. These flowers pale in your beauty."

Even as Katherine heard the words, she thought that Jeff's comments and look touched her more. Richard's words were practiced — a script that probably was meant to sound sincere but delivered in such a way that Katherine felt he had probably used the same words many times before.

She took in his perfectly coiffed silver hair, the oh-so-proper gray and white seersucker suit, the perfect pocket square. He was a very handsome man. He would fit right into her life at the university — distinguished lawyer, well-traveled, well-read, polite, charming. Her university friends and McLean neighbors would no doubt see him as a perfect match for her.

Katherine leaned in to take the flowers from Richard. He thought she was leaning in for a kiss or a hug. There was an awkward moment when he got closer and she started backing away.

"Thank you for the lovely flowers. Let me put them in some water and grab my purse. Come in for a second."

Richard glanced around. "This is very lived-in, isn't it?" Katherine could see the house through his eyes. It looked pretty dilapidated. The colorful rugs and pillows couldn't hide the fact that it needed a coat of paint.

Katherine returned from the kitchen with her bag and a light wrap.

"That is a beautiful dress and will be perfect for where we're going."

"Where are we going?" she asked, flipping on the porch light, and locking the door.

"It's still a surprise. Shall we go?" he said smoothly.

He held out his arm and after a moment, she slipped her arm through his. He escorted her carefully to the car and opened the door.

Katherine glanced to where the Jeep had been parked. *Richard and Jeff couldn't be more different.*

After a short ride, they arrived at the Lewes Yacht Club, a gorgeous white sprawling structure with floor to ceiling vaulted windows and a welcoming porch surrounding the front leading to an expansive deck in the back. The valet rushed to open Katherine's door and greeted Richard familiarly. He was clearly a regular.

"Thanks, Barry. I know you'll take good care of my car. We're here for dinner and drinks. I won't need it for a few hours."

They climbed the big wooden stairs to the porch and followed it around to the dining room door.

"Is this a members only restaurant? I've never heard anyone recommend it before."

"Yes, membership in the club is required. My parents were members here for many years. I keep the membership up even though I don't do any boating anymore. The chef is a friend of mine. He's very talented and, of course, uses the freshest ingredients. You do like seafood, I hope?"

"Most definitely. You must come here often. The valet seemed to know you quite well."

"I get here about twice a month, sometimes more often than that. I've even brought clients here if they want to make the trip from Wilmington and spend the weekend here."

They entered the hushed dining room and were greeted by the hostess. "Good evening, Mr. Ferry. Your table is ready." She led them to a table by the window overlooking the bay. Sailboats bobbed merrily in the early evening sun while the power boats raced into the marina.

The vaulted ceilings were softened by the lazy ceiling fans. The slate blue walls made it feel like they were almost sitting in the water. The tables draped with pristine white tablecloths that hung to the floor were spaciously situated and separated by plants and low bookcases. Each table felt like a private room.

Wicker chairs with tropical patterned cushions brought a touch of color to the room. Flickering candles on every table complemented the setting sun, bathing everything in a soft golden light.

"Mr. Ferry, so nice to see you again. It's a lovely evening, isn't it? I'll be taking care of you tonight."

Richard greeted the waitress with a smile and said, "Jan, nice to see you again." He turned to Katherine. "Jan is my favorite waitress. I always request her section because I know she'll take excellent care of us." Shifting his focus back to Jan, he introduced Katherine. "This is my very special friend, Katherine. It's her first visit here and I hope it will be one of many."

Katherine ducked her head, then looked up at Jan. "This is such a lovely room. I'm sure the food will be wonderful."

"Yes, our chef is quite good. Would you like to order a drink before looking at the menu?"

Richard interrupted. "Yes, we'll both have Kir Royales."

"Kir Royale?" Katherine raised an eyebrow.

"Champagne and crème de cassis. Their signature touch is the raspberry at the bottom of the flute. I thought we should have something celebratory."

Katherine said, "It sounds delicious although I'm not sure what we're celebrating."

"Our first date," Richard replied smoothly.

After their drinks were served, Richard turned to Katherine. "Now, tell me something I don't know about you yet. Why did you choose English for your PhD?"

"It was an easy choice, really. Since I was a child I have loved to read. And write. I was forever writing stories about my pets, my friends, imaginary places — anything and everything. And when I wasn't writing, I was reading. We couldn't afford many books, but we took lots of trips to the library."

Richard's eyes glazed over.

"I would take out all the books I could on my card, and sometimes convince my mother to take out a couple more on her card. Then I would squirrel away in whatever quiet cozy nook I could find and read and read." Katherine watched him scan the room. When she paused, he turned back to her, and seemed to process what she had said.

"Didn't you want to go outside and play?" He looked perplexed. "I never wanted to be in the house if I could be outside. I read my schoolbooks and textbooks but never bothered reading anything else."

She looked askance at him, wondering how it was even possible that he only read the bare minimum. "Oh, the places I've gone reading. Paris. China. California. I was fascinated by other people and places. I got plenty of outdoor time — I was reading outdoors."

Richard signaled the waitress for menus. "I still don't read much. Never had the time for it, nor the interest. I'd rather travel to those places than read about them."

Katherine said, "I love to travel, too, but I learn so much from reading."

Richard looked skeptical. "I don't see how reading can take the place of the real thing."

*I can't imagine not wanting to read,* Katherine thought.

"You said you also like to write?" Richard asked. "What do you write? Reports? Articles for magazines or the newspaper? Are you...like a journalist?"

Katherine explained. "No, not a journalist. As an English professor, I have to do research and publish my findings or interpretations of the literature. I've had several scholarly articles and a couple of books published."

With an unimpressed expression on his face, he asked, "Do you make money on your books?"

"Most academics don't make money on their books. It's not the point. We write books because we have something to share. And because it's required for tenure and promotion."

"You don't make any money on your books?" Richard was clearly mystified. "That seems like a waste of time."

Katherine composed her features to conceal her dismay, but she was very disappointed in Richard's attitude. "Not everything is about making money." He raised his eyebrows at that.

Realizing they had very different value systems, Katherine said, "I've also done some creative writing — short stories, poetry. But I've gotten away from it. Between the teaching, research, administrative stuff, as well as taking care of my family, my creative writing has gone by the wayside. I'm hoping that the time I have here will rekindle my writing energy."

Richard picked up the menu. "Would you like to order now?" He signaled Jan they were ready.

Disappointed that he didn't ask her more about her writing, Katherine responded, "I'm going to have the special — the grilled halibut, Moroccan sweet potato stack with French green beans, sounds perfect."

"I like a woman who knows her own mind. I'll have the blackened sea bass and Carolina grits. We'll have a bottle of the Stags' Leap Viognier." He looked pleased with his choice. "You'll like how crisp and complex this wine is — citrus, stone fruit, lemon, and a touch of white pepper."

Katherine was a little irritated that Richard had ordered without consulting her again. First the Kir Royale and now the wine. Her ex always did the same thing. She did know her own mind — and she would have preferred a sauvignon blanc.

Drawing on her good upbringing, she attempted to engage in small talk. "Do you see your children very often?"

"No, their mother had custody of them while they were in

school. I saw them on the weekends and some holidays, but we didn't stay very close. How about you?" He caught the eye of every new arrival in the dining room, making sure he was noticed.

Irritation rising, Katherine tried again. "I usually see Vanessa every week for brunch on Saturday or dinner one night during the week when I'm in D.C. Since I've been here, she's been up for a couple of weekends, and we talk every other day." Richard waved to a very stylish couple and turned to check out the bar to see who else was there.

Katherine raised her voice to get his attention. "I don't see my son as often as I'd like since they're in Atlanta, but we talk once or twice a week while he's driving to or from work. They're coming up the end of next month to spend a week with me. I can't wait to see my grandbaby. I love playing with him and taking care of him. I always send my son and daughter-in-law out to dinner when they visit so the baby and I can play."

"No grandchildren for me, thank heavens! I'm too young to be a grandparent," Richard exclaimed.

Katherine scrutinized him thoughtfully. Lucas, her only grandchild thus far, was the joy of her life. She was looking forward to more grandchildren if that was in the cards for Anthony and Sonja, and maybe Vanessa and Curt sometime in the future.

Richard seemed to realize that he was neglecting her and turned his high-beamed smile on her. "How's everything going with your divorce?" he asked casually. "You know my offer still stands. If you want me to steer you toward some great, risk-free investments, I'd be happy to do that."

Katherine regarded him in surprise. *Where had that come from?* She decided to quiz him. "What kind of investments? What kind of returns are you getting?"

Richard launched into a detailed discussion of the

exorbitant returns he earned for his clients, emphasizing that he only allowed a select few to get in on these very profitable ventures. He stressed how satisfied his clients were.

"Sounds very intriguing. Could I talk with some of your clients? To get a better understanding of how things work? My soon to be ex-husband managed our portfolio so I'm a little naïve about this."

Richard looked like he was going to respond but Jan arrived with their dinners, interrupting the conversation. Katherine's stomach growled in appreciation. Embarrassed, she said, "I guess I'm hungry and this smells divine." She was even more mortified when she looked up and caught Richard scanning the room to see if the noise had attracted anyone else's attention.

They finished their dinners, chatting about their favorite places to travel — Katherine loved Paris and London and all places European while Richard raved about his travels to Japan and Singapore and all places Asian. When asked what her favorite movie was, Katherine responded, *Sabrina* and if she was feeling silly, *Pitch Perfect*. Richard had never seen either of those movies — his favorites were *Bridge Over the River Kwai* and *The Longest Day*, neither of which Katherine had ever seen. They discovered their tastes in music were quite different, too. They did find they had something in common — they both loved well-prepared food.

"Tell Chef Eric that his dinners were superb as usual," Richard commanded Jan. "I'd like some decaf coffee. Katherine? Dessert or coffee?"

Katherine was hoping for a piece of the key lime pie she had seen on the menu, but decided to pass on that since Richard was not having dessert. "I'll have coffee as well, regular, black."

Slowly stirring his coffee that he loaded with cream and two sugars, Richard gazed into Katherine's eyes. "Katherine, I have to tell you how much I've enjoyed this dinner. And I am very interested in you and getting to know you even better. I'm curious about how you're feeling."

Katherine sipped her coffee before asking, "I meant to ask you earlier…when we were trying to set up this dinner, you said you were going to be out of town the weekend we were contemplating," Katherine said. "But I'm pretty sure I saw you near the gazebo that Saturday night." She waited while he formed his answer.

"What weekend was that?" Richard stalled.

Katherine gave him the date.

"Oh, that's right. I *was* going out of town, but then a business associate and his wife showed up unexpectedly. I cancelled my plans to go to Wilmington and stayed here to entertain them. That happens to me all the time since I have extra bedrooms in my house."

He paused. "I give my friends an open invitation to come see me. Most of the time it works out, but sometimes it makes me change my plans." He gazed at Katherine so sincerely.

*If he was with 'friends,' I didn't see 'them,' only a woman. And she and Richard were awfully chummy,* Katherine thought. *I wonder where the husband was if there was one.*

Katherine looked across the dining room and realized they were alone in the big room except for the waitstaff. She paused, trying to collect her thoughts, realizing that she was even less sure that she wanted to spend time with him. His explanation was plausible, but it didn't sit quite right with her. He was too quick and too glib. She couldn't tell whether he was lying. And that whole business with the investments made her nervous, especially after what Jeff overheard.

She "ought" to be interested in him. He was all the right things — considerate, nice looking, with a steady job, well-traveled even if he traveled to places she wasn't that interested in. And besides the uneasiness she felt about him, there was no tingle, no electricity. Jeff's face flashed in front of her — there was electricity there.

"Richard, you are a very nice man and I've had a nice time tonight. I'm not sure we have that much in common."

"I think we could develop that. I'm ready to try." He looked so earnest.

"Let me think about it." Katherine hedged. "I think we should let Jan and the rest of the staff go home. We've kept them here long enough."

"Of course. Let me sign the check."

# Chapter Forty-Two

Getting in her 10,000 steps before it got too hot, Katherine loved looking at the ocean when the sun was coming up. It never failed to lift her spirits to see the sun come peaking over the horizon, turning the sky a dusty rose first, gradually lightening into brilliant pinks and oranges, until the sun burst forth in a blazing yellow ball. Except for the gulls and the waves slapping the beach, it was quiet.

She spotted Brittany sitting on one of the white wooden benches that dotted the boardwalk. "Good morning. You're up early."

Brittany looked up from her knitting. "This is my favorite time to knit. I love to sit out here and watch the sunrise."

Katherine exclaimed over the piece Brittany was working on. "Oh, that is beautiful! I love that yarn." She plopped down on the bench beside Brittany and mopped her forehead. "Tell me about your knitting while I take a rest."

"Thank you. This is Akari yarn — it's a blend of silk and cotton. The silk adds this beautiful sheen that makes it shimmer. I'm making a shawl for my friend, Kristen. She'll be able to use it all year round."

She noticed Katherine panting. "Do you need some water? I have an extra bottle here."

"Thanks. I have some. Beth appointed herself my get-in-shape coach this summer. She made me get this hydration waist belt. Now I can carry my water bottle hands-free." She drew her water bottle from the small of her back. "Don't tell Beth — she'll gloat since I told her that I didn't need it. But it's actually pretty comfortable and a lot easier than holding my water bottle in a football hold like I used to. Now that I'm walking a lot more, I'm glad I have it."

"I'm very impressed with you. After the year that you've had, you've picked yourself up." Brittany watched Katherine chug the entire water bottle.

Wiping her lips and mopping her face on her T-shirt, Katherine said, "Thanks. I think it's partly being here at the ocean. I love being outside and walking. But I think the most important thing is the support I'm getting from Beth and the others. They always seem to know when I need a little boost. Have you always been a knitter?"

Brittany shook her head. "I did some knitting as a child, but I took it up again after my husband died. I needed something to help me deal with the grief." Her eyes filled with tears, and she brushed them away impatiently.

Katherine patted her arm. "I'm so sorry."

Brittany gathered herself. "My grandmother taught me how to knit when I was about ten years old. She lived in Wisconsin and every summer I would spend two or three weeks with her. She started me on simple squares, teaching me different stitches." She smiled. "I made piles of misshapen samplers from her leftover yarns. I can't believe my mother gave them to my teachers as Christmas gifts."

Katherine touched the shawl, fingering the soft yarn in the intricate pattern. "Well, you've certainly come a long way by the looks of this."

Brittany held up the mostly finished shawl. "I did get better. Grandma never lost patience with me. We practiced every summer on her yarn scraps until I finally got the hang of it. Then she let me pick out my own yarn at her favorite yarn store in Verona, Wisconsin. I loved going there with my grandmother. It was the highlight of my summer."

"What was special about it?" Katherine asked.

"The shop was in an old Victorian house. The front room was crammed with mismatched wooden tables and chairs. The two side rooms housed an amazing collection of yarns, needles, patterns. You could find anything you needed there. And they offered a full class schedule — beginning knitting, mitten making, brioche knitting — and knit-ins where everyone brought their own project to work on in the company of others." Brittany picked up her needles and started knitting.

"That sounds like fun. I wish there were a place like that here. I'd love to take a knitting class."

"Grandma got a cup of coffee — I loved the smell. When I smell coffee now, it always takes me back to the Sow's Ear, the shop in Verona. She treated herself to one of their fresh-baked muffins. I had chocolate milk, and toast and jam." Brittany looked off into her memories, smiling slightly, as she relived those magic moments. "Groups of knitters would meet, drink coffee, and knit. Other people would just come for the coffee and sit and read the well-thumbed newspapers that were lying on the tables for anyone's use. It was such a warm and comforting place."

Katherine nodded. "Isn't it interesting how some places make you feel at home? I feel that way when I'm at Browseabout Books."

Brittany reminisced. "After we had our treat, we would spend an hour or so choosing our next project, admiring the variety of yarns, cotton, wool, blends. It was a visual delight to browse the jam-packed rooms." She sighed. "I'd love to find a place like the Sow's Ear here. I've looked in the area. There's a nice yarn store in Bethany Beach and another one much further away in Cape May — you have to take the ferry from Lewes to get there. Neither of them has both the yarn and café. And that's what made the Sow's Ear special."

Katherine contemplated Brittany. "You know, there may be an opportunity for you. You glow when you talk about the Sow's Ear. You've said you're kind of at loose ends right now. Maybe you should think about creating your own café and yarn store here."

Brittany looked dumbstruck. "Who? Me? I don't know anything about running something like that." She paused. "But it's an interesting idea."

# Chapter Forty-Three

Katherine waited anxiously for Jeff to arrive. She smoothed her hands down her Bermuda shorts and sleeveless T-shirt and hoped they were appropriate for whatever he had planned. Her stomach churned — *was this the right thing to do? Was she really going on another date with Jeff?* Yes, she had been on a couple of dates with Richard, but he didn't excite her like Jeff did. She glanced at the clock again. *He should be here by now.*

She checked the mirror again and was pleased that her new haircut was behaving itself. Her arms were more toned, probably from lifting boxes of books at Browseabout. She liked getting her exercise naturally instead of at a gym, especially Ashleigh's gym. She wouldn't have been surprised if Ashleigh dropped a weight on her toes if she knew that Katherine was going on another date with Jeff.

Katherine paced back to the bedroom. *Maybe the other shirt would be better?* she thought, observing the chaos of clothes on the bed. *No, leave it. Why are you stressing out?*

The doorbell! Katherine scampered back to the door and

then stopped to take a deep breath and wipe her sweaty hands on her pants.

"Come in!" Katherine welcomed Jeff with a tentative smile. "I wasn't sure what to wear. Is this okay?"

Jeff looked down at his black board shorts that clung to his long lean legs. Katherine tracked up his shorts to the sleeveless shirt that molded his pecs and abs. His strong tattooed arms were lightly tanned. She met his eyes and flushed. He grinned.

"Like what you see?" He laughed. "You look great! And perfect for where we're going," he said. "Let me see your shoes."

Katherine held up one rubber-soled sandal. "They're comfortable," she said apologetically.

"They're just right. Are you ready? Do you have sunscreen with you?"

Katherine looked over Jeff's shoulder, relieved to see the Jeep. "Good. I was afraid you brought your motorcycle."

Katherine grabbed her sunhat and her bag loaded with sunscreen, a towel, and her swimsuit as Jeff had requested, but she was pretty sure she wasn't going to be wearing her swimsuit in front of him, not with her "mature" body. She was in better shape than she had been for years, but her body wouldn't compete with the little beach bunnies. Or doctoral students, she thought grimly.

"I'll get you on my bike sometime, but not today," Jeff promised.

He helped her into the SUV and threw her bag in the back seat. "Buckle up — it's going to be a bumpy ride." Katherine panicked and snapped her seatbelt in place and grabbed the door handle for stability. "Just kidding. We'll be on a well-paved four-lane road all the way to Fenwick Island."

"What are we doing in Fenwick Island?" Katherine asked.

"You'll see," he said as he politely drove the speed limit of twenty-five through Dewey. "I got too many tickets when I was a teenager in Dewey. I drive the speed limit now."

Katherine relaxed her grip on the door handle. "How did you get the whole day off?" she asked.

"Mondays are our slow day. I've got it covered," he responded. "Okay, are you going to guess what we're doing?"

"Probably not hang-gliding since you told me to bring a swimsuit. And probably not dining in a five-star restaurant since we're dressed pretty casually," Katherine guessed.

"Good guesses and I'll store them away for later dates," Jeff commented. "Assuming there are later dates..."

"We'll see how this one goes," Katherine said demurely. "Are we going rock-climbing?"

"Well, aren't you the adventurer?" Jeff regarded her with admiration. "Nothing that daredevilry."

Jeff turned into Shark's Cove Marina and Watersports with a huge billboard featuring parasailing and wave runners among other water sports. "We're not going parasailing, are we?" Katherine shrieked.

Jeff laughed at Katherine's horrified expression. "Not today. We're doing something tamer."

He parked by the office and came back in a minute with a key on a float. "Come on, grab your stuff. I'll get the cooler and my bag."

Katherine apprehensively followed him down the dock looking anxiously at the wave runners and paddle boards. Finally, Jeff stopped at the end of the dock in front of a gleaming white pontoon boat.

"Here it is. Your chariot for the day."

Katherine said, "We're going on a pontoon boat. Just the two of us? Can you manage this by yourself? I've never been on a pontoon boat. Are you sure they're safe? Are we going out on the ocean?" she chattered on.

"Whoa. Whoa. Whoa. Yes, they're safe. Yes, I can handle it myself. No, we're not going out on the ocean. We're going to tootle around the bay," Jeff assured her. "Take a deep breath and relax. You're going to love it. Come on, let me help you on the boat. See the nice chair there under the canopy? That's for you."

Jeff stowed the cooler under the bench seat and then turned to help Katherine onto the boat. He handed her a life jacket. "You can wear this if you'll be more comfortable. But trust me, this boat is safe and I'm as careful a driver on the water as I am on land."

Katherine thought about it and realized that for some reason, she did trust Jeff. She shook her head and settled into her chair. Jeff took the captain's chair, did the pre-cruise check list, untied the lines, and eased the boat out into Assawoman Bay.

The weather couldn't have been more perfect — low seventies with a hint of a breeze. And at 9:00 in the morning, the sun didn't beat down too hot. Later the canopy would be a welcome relief. Katherine slathered her arms and face with sunscreen and then turned her attention to her legs.

As she stroked her legs from toes to thighs, Katherine felt Jeff's eyes following her motions. She glanced up as she finished and caught Jeff's smoldering look. She dropped the sunscreen. As they both reached for it, their hands touched, and she felt the shock of attraction. She could see that Jeff felt it, too.

"Oh sorry," she stammered. "I don't know why I'm so clumsy."

Jeff held her hand a moment more. He didn't say anything as he kept her warm, smooth hand in his. She offered him the sunscreen.

Releasing her hand, he took a deep breath. "Thanks, but I

lathered up before I came over." She was surprised at how much she missed his touch.

He handed her the map and pointed out their route. "We're going to motor down to the Isle of Wight and drop anchor offshore. We'll have lunch there. If you want something to drink now, I've got water and lemonade in the cooler."

She helped herself to a lemonade and surveyed the boat. *It looks pretty seaworthy.* "Do you do this a lot? Take a pontoon boat out?"

"No, actually, you're the first person I've done this with." Katherine caught the significance of that. "I haven't done much dating since my divorce."

"What happened with your marriage?" Katherine asked.

"When we got married, I was working like a dog to get the restaurants going. I wasn't around as much as she needed. And when we had the baby..."

"You have a child?" Katherine exclaimed.

"Yes, I told you about her when we were walking on the boardwalk."

"Oh, that's right. I remember now. How old is she again?"

"She's sixteen and quite the handful. She'll be spending the last month of the summer with me, working in the restaurant, of course. Right now, she's taking two courses at the community college in Newark. I usually go up there every Monday to see her."

"That's why I never see you around on Mondays. How come you're not there today?"

"Have you been looking for me?" Jeff teased.

Katherine swatted his arm. "Of course not. I noticed that you weren't around."

"Uh huh." Jeff carefully motored down the bay, giving a wide berth to the kayaks and other pontoons. They were moving at a nice, sedate pace.

Katherine relaxed and waved to the other boaters. "Why not today?"

"One of her older cousins got married so she and her mom went to Massachusetts for the wedding. They're coming back today." Jeff concentrated on his steering.

"Do you get along with your ex-wife?" Katherine asked, wondering if she and Stan would ever be civil with each other again.

"It was rough in the beginning. She was pretty unhappy with me for working all the time. But she's remarried now and has another child. We've resolved our differences for Chelsea's sake." He pointed to the cooler and mouthed "water."

Katherine carefully stood up and crossed to the cooler. Holding on to the railing and then the benches, she made her way back to Jeff. "Why is Chelsea a handful?"

"Because she's a teenager? She's not that bad—a lot of eye-rolling and 'oh Dad.' I don't think we even speak the same language."

Katherine laughed. "I remember those days with Vanessa. Don't worry, it'll pass."

"And she thinks she's old enough to date, but she's not," he said emphatically.

"Sixteen? Of course she wants to date." A rogue wake caught the pontoon and tilted Katherine right into Jeff's arms. He tightened his hold and brushed a light kiss on her neck. She shivered with pleasure.

"Nope, not until she's thirty-five," he swore. Katherine chuckled and reluctantly moved back to her seat.

They chugged slowly down the bay, taking their time, admiring the long stretches of marsh, broken by an occasional tall pine tree. River otters swam determinedly across the bay, with a clear destination in mind that Katherine and Jeff couldn't see. When they reached the Isle of Wight, Jeff dropped the anchor. He hauled the cooler out from the bench seat and started to lay out lunch — a fruit parfait, some prosciutto and cantaloupe, a plate of cheese and crackers. He pulled two bamboo plates and checkered cloth napkins from the side pocket.

"Wow, I'm impressed! " Katherine said, thinking about Richard's fancy dinner at the yacht club, and preferring this simpler, but more intimate meal.

"I aim to please. And there's still dessert to come. Dig in." They settled into a comfortable togetherness, enjoying the food and delightful day. Katherine occasionally glanced at Jeff and shook her head. Finally, he asked, "What are you thinking?"

"I can't figure you out. You send out this hard, bad boy vibe with your tatts and your leathers, but you're really a pussycat. You help so many people." She paused. "And look at this — this whole day has been so thoughtful. And you're so much fun."

"You need to stop judging this book by its cover. Just because I don't look like all your colleagues in D.C..."

"I know. I know. I'm ashamed I'm so shallow."

"You're not shallow. You're waking up." Jeff sat up quickly.

"Look! Look over there. Do you see the great blue heron?" Jeff asked. "This island attracts both the great blue herons and the smaller green herons. They're hunting for fish. Did you see that? He got one."

They sat quietly watching the birds stalk majestically along the shore, their long legs hardly disturbing the water. A sudden noise started the heron, and he lifted his massive wings and soared his prehistoric body out further into the marsh.

"I love this. Thank you for bringing me here. It's peaceful and calm." Katherine touched Jeff's arm.

He reached over and covered her hand with his. "It's my pleasure. We'll come back in the winter when you can hear the loons laughing."

The wind picked up and the sun went behind a cloud. "We'd better head back. I don't think there's a storm coming in, but better safe than sorry."

Katherine packed up the remains of lunch and Jeff pulled the anchor. She moved to sit beside him. He reached over for her hand to help her settle. She didn't realize until they reached the marina that they were still holding hands.

The steady downpour started as they pulled out on Route 1 from the marina. The windshield wipers rhythmically kept time with the smooth jazz softly playing. The light whitecap surf appeared through the dunes on the right and the bay marsh grass swayed gently on the left. Before she knew it, the striking blue Indian River Inlet Bridge rose up in the storm-darkened sky.

Hating to destroy the peaceful ride, Katherine mused, "I've always wondered why this bridge has blue lights. It's beautiful, but I've never seen another like it."

"It's for the bats."

"Bats?"

"Yeah, bats. Bats hunt at night. The blue light doesn't disorient them. Other colors do. So this bridge is blue."

"Huh. I thought it might have something to do with Delaware's state bird — the Blue Hen."

Jeff chuckled. "Most people think that but it's really for the bats."

Katherine settled back in her warm seat as Jeff slowed to the Dewey speed limit. The streets were deserted in the rain. The beach toys forlornly standing at attention until the next sunny day.

Jeff tapped her gently when they reached her house. "Wake up, sleepyhead."

"Oh, sorry. The sun. The rain. I guess I dozed off. I hope I didn't snore or drool." Katherine furtively swiped her chin.

"No snoring or drooling."

He walked her to the door and quickly stopped. "Wait! You didn't get dessert!" He dashed back to the SUV and came rushing back dodging the puddles. "It's a good thing we got back when we did. I think we're in for a lot more rain. That's the thing about the weather here. It can change on a dime."

"Do you want to come in?" Katherine held the door open.

"I'd like to, but I can't. I'm going to give Chelsea a call and see how her weekend went. I need to find out when she's coming in. This is for you."

"What is it?"

"Dessert — chocolate mousse pie with an Oreo crust."

"Oh, my goodness! Don't you want to share?" Katherine swooned with delight at the decadent treat.

"Nope, all for you."

"You sure know the way to a girl's heart."

"I'm trying."

# Chapter Forty-Four

Katherine rolled her shoulders to get the tension out of her neck, but it didn't help. She switched the phone to the other hand.

"Stan, we've already been over this. Our lawyers have been over this. Why do you want to change the divorce terms now? The divorce is supposed to be final the end of next month."

Katherine tried taking a deep breath and letting it out slowly. She rubbed her forehead. "You insisted that I keep the house since you didn't want to disrupt me and that it was the kids' childhood home, even though neither of them has lived in the house for many years. Now you want to buy me out so you can live in the house?"

Stan hemmed and hawed. "Well, I know that you thought the house was too big for you and that you would probably sell it anyway."

"But you didn't want to have anything to do with the house! I thought you and Chrissy were happy with your condo in Georgetown or the Watergate or someplace downtown."

"We've been thinking that we'd like a place with a little

more space. Chrissy likes the neighborhood and there are good schools there."

"Schools? Why would she be concerned with schools?" she puzzled. "Oh, don't tell me she's pregnant?"

"We just found out. We haven't told anyone yet since the divorce isn't final. But Chrissy thinks we should keep the house and buy you out. We can raise our family there. And besides," he wheedled, "you don't want to be saddled with that big old house, do you?"

Katherine laughed humorlessly. "This is rich. You're sixty-three years old, expecting a baby, and you're not even married yet. And did you tell Chrissy how little you were around when our kids were growing up? I hope she's prepared to put her career on hold while you keep building yours."

"It's not going to be like that. I'm committed to being a real partner in raising this baby."

Katherine interrupted, "Well, I'll believe that when I see it. Have you told Vanessa and Anthony yet?"

"No, I was hoping you might do that. You have a much better relationship with them than I do," Stan whined.

"Oh. No. This is your mess. You tell them."

Stan's silence was palpable. He finally said, "I don't know what's gotten into you. You used to be much nicer and would do anything to make the kids happy."

"I still will do everything I can for our kids, but I'm not going to do your dirty work anymore."

"Fine. What about the house? I'll give you a very generous offer." He named a ridiculously low amount.

"You have got to be kidding me? Do you think I'm stupid? I've already talked with a real estate agent to get an idea of the market. We could sell the house for almost twice that amount. Since the current divorce document says that I get the house, you'd better rethink that offer before I'll even consider it. And we'll need to talk about who is going to cover all the additional legal fees because you're changing the agreement just as the papers are about to be filed."

Stan blustered, "I don't think you're being reasonable. And if you think I'm going to pay your legal fees..."

Katherine said sternly, "Stan, I'm not the milquetoast woman you ditched. I now realize how much you undermined my capabilities and self-confidence since we got married. You are not going to use me the way you did for our married life. If you want to reopen negotiations, be prepared to be reasonable and fair because I won't be walked all over anymore."

Stan sputtered and then slammed the phone down without a word.

~

"I'm sorry to keep calling you like this." Katherine dangled her feet in the little pool.

"How many times do I have to tell you?" Jeff said. "Call anytime. You know I love talking to you."

"It's a wonder that we haven't run out of things to talk about. How many hours have we spent talking on the phone like this or talking while we're walking?" Katherine paused. "I like talking with you."

Since their trip on the pontoon boat, they had talked almost every day — sometimes during their now almost regular morning walk and other times like this — at night before bed. A day didn't feel complete unless she talked to him.

"I like talking with you, too. Now, what's up?" Jeff asked. "Not that I mind, but we've already talked twice today."

"Stan called today. I found out why he wants the house." She struggled to keep the tears at bay. "His girlfriend is pregnant and now she wants to move into my house."

"Ahh, honey. That sucks. Do you want me to come over?"

"No, it's late and I have to open Browseabout tomorrow." She covered her shoulders with a beach towel to ward off the chilly ocean breeze. "I don't know why it bothers me so much."

"Do you still have feelings for him?" Jeff asked quietly. "Finding out that he's having a child with someone else has to be hard."

"He pretty much killed all my feelings for him." Katherine hesitated. "It feels like she's taking over my life — first, she takes my husband, then she takes my roles as the mother of his children and his wife, and now she wants my house, too? It doesn't seem fair."

"For what it's worth, I think your almost ex-husband is an idiot," Jeff said. "Why he would let such a beautiful, smart, sexy, interesting woman like you get away is proof that he's an idiot."

Katherine wiped her nose. "You always seem to know the right thing to say. Would you mind repeating that?"

"For what it's worth, I think your almost ex-husband is an idiot."

"Not that part — the 'beautiful, smart, sexy, interesting' part?"

"Listen — I'll tell you that every day. Because it's the truth. You are the most beautiful, kind, smart, loving, sexy, fascinating, gorgeous, intelligent..."

Katherine laughed. "I'll pay you a dollar to keep going."

"That's better. I like to hear you laughing," he said. "I know it's hard to believe sometimes, but you're going to be better off without him."

When she didn't respond, he went on. "What are you going to do about the house?"

She took a deep breath. "I've already called Shawna. I'm not going to fight him on the house, but I am going to make sure

I get a fair settlement. He made a ridiculous lowball offer — I told him that, too. But that house is part of Vanessa's and Anthony's inheritance. I don't want them shortchanged."

"You need to make sure you're taken care of as well."

"Between my retirement accounts and the money my parents left me from the sale of their business, as well as my salary, I'll be okay."

"Are you feeling better now?" Jeff asked.

"Thank you. I can always count on you, can't I?" Katherine reflected on how often he was kind and supportive. "Time to hit the sack. Early start for work tomorrow."

"Want some company? I could be there in five minutes," Jeff teased.

"In your dreams, buddy."

"Yes, you are." Jeff gently disconnected the call.

# Chapter Forty-Five

Brittany reached for the door to the Back Porch just as Katherine rushed up out of breath. "Oh good, I'm glad I'm not the last one here. And now I can introduce you to the rest of the group." Katherine paused to catch her breath. "Did you have trouble finding this place? It's hidden down this little alleyway."

Brittany pulled the screen door open and pushed on the big oak door. "No, I've eaten here a couple of times. Not as often as I'd like – no time when I was running back and forth to Wilmington selling the house and it's closed for the season from November to April."

As Katherine's eyes adjusted from the brilliant early evening sun to the cool dimly lit room, she looked for someone to help them.

"Can I help you?"

Katherine surveyed the massive wooden bar lined with sparkling glasses and stocked with a wide assortment of liquors, trying to locate where the voice had come from. Turning almost completely around, in the shadows by the front door she spotted a 6oish-year-old guy smiling at them.

"Roger, how are you? I haven't seen you since last season." She reached out to give him a hug. He was very Italian looking, dark, almost black, hair with a little bit of gray at the temples, strong chin, high cheek bones. His gleaming white turtleneck with a blue brocade vest set off his olive complexion.

"Good. Good. How have you been?"

"I'm getting better – long story we won't go into now." Pulling Brittany forward, she said, "This is my new friend, Brittany. We ran into her by Star Colony – or rather, she ran into Beth and me. She's joining our books and wine club tonight. Is Beth here already?"

"Yes, she's in the back by the double wooden doors." He turned to Brittany, his chocolate brown eyes widening in appreciation at her bold orange and lime green floral dress and orange high-heeled sandals. Her shoulders were lightly covered with an orange delicate lace knit shawl, affording him tantalizing peeks at her bare shoulders. He smiled broadly, and said in a warm baritone voice, "I'm very happy to meet you."

Brittany clasped his hand in hers and said breathlessly, "No, I'm very happy to meet you."

Katherine watched the exchange with interest. The air was sizzling with sexual tension. She had never seen Roger react this way before. "Ahem...did the group already order?"

Roger didn't take his eyes off Brittany. "Would you like something to drink? Take a look at the wine list? It's on the bar."

"Thanks." Katherine laughed and scanned the wine list quickly. "I'll have the Juggernaut cabernet sauvignon."

Still holding Brittany's hand, he said seductively, "And what would you like?"

She drew in a deep breath and gazed brazenly at him. "What do you like?"

"I like what I see." He reluctantly released her hand. "For you to drink, I'd recommend a big, full-bodied Chateauneuf-Du-Pape. It would suit you."

Katherine fanned herself. "Okay, you two. Do your flirting on your own time. Beth and the others are waiting for us."

With one last long look at Roger, Brittany followed her through the enclosed patio. All the tables were still filled with diners lingering over their desserts. Katherine's mouth watered at the chocolate cheesecake. They dodged a couple of tables being served Back Porch's signature coffee flamed at tableside. Brittany commented to Katherine that it was a wonder the waitstaff didn't set their sleeves on fire. Winding their way through the back dining room, they finally saw Beth and the other women.

"Katherine, we were just wondering where you were," Beth said. "I'm glad you made it, Brittany. Let me introduce you to everyone."

"This is Isabella — she's the owner of the best brewpub in Rehoboth. Well, it's so much bigger than a brewpub now — she distributes to several states and even some countries."

Isabella raised her glass of red wine. "Welcome."

Beth continued, "Next to her is Cassandra. If you ever need a bike or need your bike repaired or some fabulous biking clothes, head to her store. She's the owner of Bikes for Life. She serves all people, but she has one of the most extensive collections of woman-specific bikes, clothing, accessories." A trim, short-haired blonde reached across the table to shake Brittany's hand.

"This is Michelle."

Brittany interrupted Beth. "Yes, I know Michelle. She's the one who helped me find my condo. Nice to see you again."

"Nice to see you. I hope the condo is working well for you." The group watched as Michelle stepped into her real estate agent role.

"I love it and now that everything is finally settled in Wilmington, I'll be enjoying it more." Brittany slid into the empty chair next to Beth.

"Brittany moved here a couple of years ago from Wilmington," Beth told the others. "Katherine and I bumped into her, literally, the other morning when we were walking. She was chasing the dolphins trying to get their pictures." They all smiled knowingly – they had done the same thing themselves.

Isabella said, "What made you move to Rehoboth?"

Brittany sighed. "My husband passed away just after he retired. I was at loose ends so after a year or so, I decided to sell our house, retire, and move here. It's been a long slog and I'm still not sure what I want to do next. "

"I'm very sorry to hear about your husband. What kind of work did you do?" Cassandra asked.

"I was in advertising."

Cassandra sat up quickly and leaned across the table to Brittany. "Really? Do you ever do any consulting? I was talking to my partner the other day and told her that we needed to up our game."

"You're the second one in the last few days that has asked me about consulting." She glanced at Beth. "I'm thinking about it and I'm not sure I want to get back into advertising full-time. My real dream is to have my own coffee and yarn shop. I know...not very sexy or glamorous, but I've done glamorous and I'm ready for a change. However, I wouldn't mind taking a look at your advertising strategy sometime and see what I might be able to help you with."

Beth interjected. "Hey. I've got first dibs. I found her first — or rather, she found us when she bumped into us."

Isabella chimed in. "I like the idea of a yarn store in town. The closest one I know is about fifteen miles away. I did a little knitting when I was younger. It was supposed to be relaxing but I never got good enough to stop dropping stitches or adding stiches where I wasn't supposed to. Maybe you could offer classes?"

"Whoa! Wait!" Brittany chuckled. "Let's not get too far ahead of ourselves. I'm muddling the thought around."

Roger came by the table. "I sent the waitress home since her section is clear and it's almost time to close. If you want another glass of wine, let me know now." Roger glanced at Brittany who winked. When he licked his lips, she flushed.

"I'll take another glass of the Chateauneuf-Du-Pape. You're right, it does suit me."

Isabella watched as Roger and Brittany sizzled. She broke in, "I'll have another, too, if you guys are done."

"What?" Roger chuckled. "Just getting the lady a glass of wine. Cassandra, Beth, Katherine — do you want another, too?"

After Roger left, Brittany turned to Isabella. "What's with Roger? Has he worked here long? I haven't seen him the other times I've been in."

"Roger winters in the Keys while the Back Porch is closed. He's been working here for the past four to five years. His wife died some time ago — sudden heart attack. He sold his accounting business — said he had other things he wanted to do — and moved here. He helped me set up my books when I started my brewpub."

Brittany looked puzzled. "Being a bartender sounds like a big step away from his previous life."

"He likes being a bartender. He gets to meet interesting

people here. And spend his winters fishing in the Keys. Not a bad life."

"He's not remarried or in a relationship?"

Isabella looked at Brittany speculatively. "No, as far as I know, you're the first woman who has piqued his attention. I haven't seen him flirt with anyone else but you."

Beth tapped her glass. "Who finished reading the book?"

"I'm on auto-buy when it comes to Susan Mallory's books — I don't even have to read the back cover," Cassandra exclaimed. "And this one, *The Boardwalk Bookshop*, is already one of my favorites."

Michelle paged through her copy. "The women reminded me of us. I loved the way they supported each other and helped each other succeed."

They argued about which woman had grown the most by the end of the book. Michelle thought it was Bree, but Isabella disagreed and believed that Mikki had made the most strides. Of the three main male characters, they all liked Harding, but thought he pushed Bree too hard at first. Michelle identified most with Mikki — she also had an ex-husband with whom she had a civil relationship. She confessed that she was afraid she was never going to "move on" because of that.

Katherine noticed Brittany listening raptly as the women vigorously defended their positions, mocking and teasing each other over unpopular statements like Isabella's support of Seth.

"Not everyone wants to get married, or has to be married, to be in a committed relationship," Isabella said.

Brittany piped up. "But it sounds like Seth was a real weasel for not proposing to Ashley after being together for eight years."

Roger finally came in and told them everyone else had gone home. "From what I could hear, you seemed to be having a great time. I'm sorry to have to break it up but I need to go home and get my beauty sleep." He glanced at Brittany who was watching him like he was crème brulée.

Beth spoke up. "Thanks, Roger, for letting us hang out here." She drained her wine glass. "One last thing about the book. I loved that the three women celebrated the end of each week with champagne on the beach. Don't you think we should try that?"

Katerine gushed. "I love that idea! Let's do it for our next meeting."

# Chapter Forty-Six

Katherine reread the last paragraph on the half-filled screen. *Not bad.* She finally felt like she was creating again. It had been such a long time. She used to write "stories" all the time when she was growing up. All through high school and college. But somehow her creative writing had slipped away. *No regrets. But I'm glad to be back at it.*

The Rehoboth Beach Writers Guild weekly Freewrites had been liberating. One week the prompt focused on "writing with all senses" — touch, smell, hear, taste, and see. They did a field trip to the boardwalk — she felt the hot afternoon sun burning her bare arms. She felt the ridges between the boards on the boardwalk as her flip-flops struck the boards.

Passing by Grotto's Pizza, she smelled garlic and tomato and oregano pizza. The smell of Thrasher's French fries clashed with coconut scented suntan lotion. One young man who passed by her clearly had forgotten his deodorant.

She heard gulls and children crying, teenagers giggling and chatting nonstop, parents yelling "Come back here" to their fleet-footed wily three-year-olds.

She stopped and sampled banana then licorice then watermelon taffy from Dolle's. The cloying sweetness of the banana, the pungent sharpness of the licorice, the soft freshness of the watermelon. The tastes rolled around her mouth.

The boardwalk was swarming with moms and dads herding their slightly sunburned, cranky children away from the beach. And gaggles of giggling girls, staying three or four feet from their parents, pretending not to notice the crew of teen boys strutting beside them.

The sharp blue sky, the dark green and blue water topped with white caps, the rainbow of beach umbrellas dotting the sand so thickly it was hard to see the sand. The brown and white and tan and red oiled bodies catching the rays to just the right doneness.

Just being here had awakened her senses and reengaged her writing muse.

Perhaps the best advice the Writers Guild gave her — sit down and write every day. Every single day. It didn't matter what she wrote — write every day. She could write to a prompt. Or she could write a piece of the story. Or pick a word randomly from the dictionary and write a scene around that word. It didn't matter what she wrote. It was about building her writing muscle by using it every day — kind of like her training for the Wild Goose Chase bicycle ride. Little by little her riding endurance and skill got stronger. Between Freewrites and the writing every day, Katherine was pleased that her pile of stories and essays was growing.

She glanced around the serene leaf-sheltered patio overflowing with red and pink impatiens framed with purple cone flowers, giant ostrich ferns, and variegated Hostas. The sun peeped through the crape myrtle tree, breaking the dim light with spotlights on the pool. The stone fountain murmured an alto accompaniment to the staccato cheeps of sparrows nesting in the trees and the long oboe notes of the gulls flying overhead. The sounds soothed her, and the shadowed warmth on the patio blocked the increasingly cool breezes of early fall. Bare feet were still okay, but the light sweater and long cotton pants felt good.

This time in Rehoboth had been good for her. She thought about the last conversation she'd had with Stan and knew she had come a long way from the wounded woman she was when she arrived here in May. He didn't rattle her anymore. She didn't let him have that power over her. Back in May, she had been hurt, betrayed — her self-esteem was in the dumps, thanks to Stan's relentless attacks on her appearance, her behavior— nothing was good enough. *She* wasn't "good enough." Thanks to her friends here, and she had to admit it, Jeff, she knew she was more than enough.

She chuckled when she thought of the baby steps she took when she first got here. Standing up to Anthony and telling him she didn't need him to take her under his wing. Making the decision all by herself to stay in Rehoboth for her sabbatical. With Michelle's help, renting her own place — that met her needs alone, not worrying about whether Stan would like it or not.

It had been hard to trust her own judgement. When Stan first asked for the divorce, she blamed herself for choosing a bad mate. But she realized that she had made a good decision at the time. When she married him, it was for all the right reasons. – she loved him and thought they were well-suited. And they created wonderful children. And she had loved her life as their mother. Her judgement hadn't been flawed. It hadn't been wrong until Stan took up with Chrissy. He was not the man she married.

She reviewed where she was now. Living in a place she loved. Hanging out with a great group of women — great friends who had been so supportive. Working in a bookstore for fun. She loved helping people find the right book and bringing in authors to tell their stories and share their writing. And writing — her collection of short stories kept growing.

And Jeff. Their back-and-forth dance. She had not liked him at all when they met the first two — or was it three — times. Rude! Arrogant! She remembered her first reaction to him as a bartender — ponytail, black T-shirt showing off tattoo sleeves. Yes, he was good looking. Yes, he had rich chocolate eyes. But he was a jerk and not at all her type.

But the stories Beth and the other women told Katherine about Jeff didn't jive with her first impressions. He was incredibly supportive of the women starting businesses, gladly sharing his expertise and contacts, and giving the new entrepreneurs a chance that helped them launch their businesses.

And he cared so much for his staff. She loved the way he took care of Joyce when she had to go on bedrest for the last month of her pregnancy, and Jerry when his dad needed him. His staff had good healthcare benefits and tuition benefits. There was such a soft side to him that wasn't visible at first.

But he could be so darn irritating.

Sighing, Katherine settled her fingers on the keyboard and started to write. *I'll figure him out later.*

# Chapter Forty-Seven

Richard drove slowly into his driveway, noting with approval that the subtle cues that his place was undisturbed were still in place. The Welcome to the Beach sign on the screen door hung square — a clear indication that no one had opened the screen door. He had rigged the sign with a fine thread that snapped if anyone opened the door — the sign would not hang straight if the door had been opened. The white powdered chalk he sprinkled on the sidewalk and front porch was unmarred by footprints. He checked to see if the latch to the backyard gate was still in the locked, upright position.

The waist-high boxwood hugged the house walls, creating a solid green moat that made it impossible to peek in the windows. The sign and chalk, unremarkable to the casual observer, satisfied his need for early warning signs of snooping. The landscaping masked the hidden motion detectors and cameras that made up the real security system. There were so many disgruntled investors that he wouldn't put it past them to hire a private eye to see what they could dig up, so he had to take precautions. He might be a bit paranoid but when you had cheated as many people as he had, he couldn't be too careful. He had already reinvented himself once with a new name and identity. His go-bag was always packed and ready.

Katherine wouldn't notice a thing. He was taking a risk inviting her to dinner, but he needed to move this relationship along.

*I need her money. I've got too many people breathing down my neck.*

The house had that slightly neglected look that many old beach houses have — faded white shutters, salt-dulled hinges, weathered to flat slate-gray wood shakes. It looked no different than any of the summer cottages in North Rehoboth, the older neighborhood that bumped up against Lewes. He had deliberately kept the façade of the house as it was when he bought it, with only the most minimal maintenance, to keep it consistent with the neighborhood.

He had lied to Katherine when he told her he had inherited his parents' house. In reality, he had chosen this house and street carefully. The street ran straight in and out and dead-ended into three cottages on the waterfront, making it easy to see anyone coming down the street. His two neighbors were summer people who spent two weeks every August in their cottages and otherwise did weekly rentals during the season. No neighborhood get-togethers. No nosy neighbors at all. He didn't want anyone getting into his business.

He stepped out to open the garage door, the briny, fishy breeze rushing in to displace the metallic air-conditioned air in the car. Tapping in the code, he heard the alarm disengage. He raised the door and surveyed the garage. The second alarm light by the door burned bright red. His eyes flicked to the Harley. It was precision tuned and ready to go whenever he needed it. Satisfied that nothing was out of place, he eased the Porsche into its spot and closed the garage door.

He pressed his eyes to the security panel and waited for the green scan to be completed. The steel reinforced door clicked open, and he stepped into his real house. Unknown to any outsiders, he had gutted the house and created his personal fortress and oasis.

Carefully removing his Top Siders and lining them up precisely in the closet, the cold slate felt good on his bare feet. He crossed to his Fabio & Co Adriano white Italian leather sofa and dropped his keys on the Alaric glass coffee table. Picking up the iPad controller, he raised the shades on the two-story great room floor-to-ceiling windows and gazed out on his backyard with his massive private deck and infinity lap pool.

Soldiers of densely planted Nellie Stevens Holly with year-round impenetrable spikey leaves stood guard along the property lines almost down to the beach. Blocking his view of the ocean, boulder-sized planters spaced every couple of feet effectively stopped any vehicle from crashing into the house from the water. Short of constructing a twelve-foot wall around the property, the holly and planters served as a very effective barrier. *I just can't be too careful.*

It was cool enough that he turned on the stone firepit and set the fan to blow the warmed air to the pair of white wicker chaise lounges. The vibrant red cushions against the sleek white wicker glowed in the setting sun's rays.

*First things first. I need some wine to help me get through this night.*

The door to the left of the Sub-Zero refrigerator opened into his custom-built wine cabinets. It had been worth it to fly in a master craftsman from France to build this and to pay him extremely well to keep his mouth shut. Of course, it helped that they had worked jobs together and he knew what would happen if he didn't keep his private business private. The wine cabinets were works of art — solid mahogany walls, super-insulated, argon-filled, low emissive, tempered glass panels, and a commercially rated temperature control system with multiple temperate zones suitable for reds (55°–65°) and whites (45°–55°).

He knew what he wanted and reached directly for the 1983 Petrus. He could already taste the beautiful flavors of black figs, dark chocolate, and plums. He set the bottle down gently on the black Carrara marble counter in the kitchen and reached for the decanter and the Durand corkscrew. He sliced the foil off carefully and worked the cork slowly out of the bottle. One sniff of the cork and his taste buds came alive. Yes, he could smell the figs and the chocolate, and he was also picking up a bit of spicy vanilla. Pouring slowly, but steadily, with the lit candle behind the neck of the bottle, he relished the sight of the wine flowing down the side of the decanter.

When he reached the bottom half of the bottle, he poured even more slowly to ensure the sediment stayed in the bottle. *I'll let this breathe for some time while I get the steak ready to grill. It's kind of a shame to waste this bottle on Katherine since she has no taste, but I'll enjoy it.*

Katherine was nice enough, but pedestrian, with her mousy brown hair and slightly chubby physique. He favored more exotic, more worldly women. But right now he needed someone like Katherine to give him the appearance of stability and normalcy. More importantly, he needed her funds to offset the bad investments he'd made. The other investors were clamoring for their returns, and he couldn't stall them much longer. He was sure he could get her to let him manage her money — she was gullible. Look at the way her ex controlled her. She's lucky that she had her inheritance tied up so the ex couldn't touch it, but he knew how to get around that. And she has that monster house in McLean — it's got to be worth several million.

*I'm sure I can get her to sell that, too.*

# Chapter Forty-Eight

When the doorbell chimed, Richard hurried to greet Katherine. "Did you have any trouble finding the house? I still wish you had let me pick you up," he said as he drew her in lightly and kissed both cheeks European style. He had to be careful not to scare her — she was still skittish and distant even after that great dinner they shared in Lewes. He thought she would have warmed up to him after that investment. "You look lovely as usual. I'm so glad you came."

Katherine thrust a small bouquet of flowers at him. "I wanted to bring you something. Normally I would have brought some wine, but after our discussion last time about your collection, I thought it would be like bringing coals to Newcastle."

Richard eyed the pathetic bunch of carnations and roses and gushed, "How thoughtful of you. No one ever brings me flowers." He stepped aside to lead Katherine into the living room.

"Wow! You could never tell from the outside that it looks

like this on the inside. It's kind of deceptive. Did you do all this or did your parents do it?"

Richard puffed up with pride. "They started some of the renovations, but I took over when they passed. Come on in, let me show you around."

He led Katherine through the foyer to the great room. She stopped short as she gazed around the room, taking in the huge Jackson Pollack over the fireplace, the white leather sofa, the chrome and glass triangular coffee table. "It looks like something out of *Architectural Digest!* I'm almost afraid to sit anywhere."

Richard rolled his eyes behind her. "Don't be silly. Come on, let me pour you some wine and we can head out to the patio." He turned into the kitchen. "I hope you like this red." *She'd better, given how expensive the Petrus is.*

Katherine followed Richard out to the patio, commenting on the exquisitely set dining room table with its shiny silver square pillar candlesticks, the low floral arrangement of cymbidium orchids, some other kind of orange flower that looked like an artichoke, sea grass, and twigs.

"What a lovely pool." Katherine glanced uneasily at the dense holly hedge and intimidating planters. "It's a shame you can't see the ocean from your deck. You seem pretty cut off from the rest of the world here. Do you have any neighbors?"

"I like my privacy. I do have neighbors, but I don't think they're here very often. They rent it out a few weeks during the season, but I've never met any of them." He helped Katherine into the chaise lounge. "Have you had a Petrus before?"

"No, I've heard of it, but never had a glass."

He smiled smugly. "I picked up this 1983 Petrus a couple of years ago for about $5,000. Now it's worth about $7,500." He handed her a delicate crystal glass.

Katherine nearly dropped the glass. "Oh my. I've had

expensive wines before but nothing like this. This little glass is about a $1,000! I'm not sure my palette is sophisticated enough to appreciate it."

"Nonsense," Richard assured her, thinking again that this was a waste of a great wine. "It's just wine and I want tonight to be very special for you." He leaned in to stroke her arm.

Not comfortable with his intentions, Katherine sat back and sloshed wine on the white linen cushion. Mortified, she watched the wine stain blooming across the seat. "Oh dear, I'm so sorry."

Richard leapt up, irritation showing briefly on his face, which he quickly replaced with an indulgent smile. "Let me get something to mop that up. And I think the coals are ready. I'll put the steaks on."

He strode into the house, shaking his head and scowling. *Remember the goal. Get her to let you 'invest' her money for her — maybe even marry her and then divorce her in a year or so. I just have to put up with her for a couple of years.*

He made short work of grilling the steaks and served them with the lobster mashed potatoes and truffle butter sauteed wild mushrooms he special-ordered from the best steakhouse in Wilmington.

Katherine grew more relaxed as she told him about the writing she was doing. He pretended to be interested, nodding, and commenting in all the right places. As he was clearing their plates and serving the chocolate praline mousse with toasted marshmallow ice cream, he stopped short at her comment. "What did you say about the house?"

"Stan is renegotiating the divorce settlement. It seems that he wants to buy out my half of the house so he and his pregnant girlfriend can live in it."

*That will never do. Then she'll only get half of what that house is worth.* Richard fumed as he topped off her decaf coffee.

Keeping his tone even, he asked, "What do you think of that? Weren't you planning on selling it and investing that money for your retirement?"

"I was, but I'm tired of fighting with Stan about it. I think I can retire very well on what my share will be. And I don't plan to retire for several years yet." Katherine licked the mousse off her spoon like an ice cream cone.

*Good grief. That's not how you're supposed to eat. Terrible manners. Well, at least I should get some points from her for the great dessert.*

Richard interrupted, "I wish you'd let me help you with your financial planning. You know that's what I do for a living. My clients are very happy with their investments." *Well, most of them anyway.* "It seems like your husband – ex-husband – is taking advantage of you again. Would you like me to talk with your lawyer? You deserve the best possible financial outcome from this divorce." He patted her arm as if she were a child.

Katherine shook his hand off and bristled, "No, I think I'm doing fine. Letting Stan buy me out is the right plan. We just have to agree on the payout. My lawyer has that under control – she's making sure I'm being treated fairly. And Stan has to pay for the additional legal fees since he's changing the terms of the divorce. I'm not letting him take advantage of me anymore."

*Shit!* Richard backed off, realizing Katherine's hackles were up. "Of course, I know you can handle yourself. I didn't mean to imply that you couldn't. I was offering to give you some free financial planning services since I care about you."

Katherine refused to be placated. "Thanks for a lovely dinner. It's probably time for me to take off." She rose from the table and went to pick up her purse and wrap. "Your house is beautiful. I never would have guessed from the street it looked like this inside."

"Don't go," he murmured, putting his arms around her. "I was hoping that we could take our relationship to the next level tonight. You know how much I want you."

Katherine quickly reached for the door. "I don't think that's a good idea. We don't seem to be on the same page."

*Damn, damn, damn.* He struggled to control his anger. "I'm sorry I upset you. Would you let me try to make it up to you next week? Could I take you to dinner next Saturday?"

"Let me think about it. Good night, Richard. Thanks again for dinner."

# Chapter Forty-Nine

Katherine listened as the neighboring table raved about their crab cakes and the pan-seared scallops. It was easy to see why Salt Air was named the Best Rehoboth Beach Restaurant in 2020 and the Best Restaurant in Delaware in 2018. She scanned their extensive wine list and selected the Unshackled Sauvignon Blanc from the Prisoner Wine Co in Paso Robles, California. Prisoner Wine was one of her Uncle Phil's favorites. After he introduced it to her, she loved it, too.

Since she was a little early for the women and wine group, she relaxed and admired the wine collection lining one wall. The group seated in that secluded room looked happy and satisfied as they finished their desserts. She noticed the clever art that adorned the walls, especially the full-face cow that watched with her liquid brown eyes. The room was a mix of modern and rustic — polished concrete floors paired with gold and orange silk leaf garlands framing the mirrors.

Beth came rushing in. "Sorry. I had to close the bookstore tonight — I got caught up in counting the cash drawer and all that."

"No worries. I know how that goes. Yesterday I didn't get out of there for over an hour after we closed. And you're not even the last one here. The rest of the gang just came in the door." Katherine waved at Isabella and Cassandra to get their attention. Brittany and Michelle spotted her and headed for the table.

"Whew! What a day!" Cassandra moaned. "I think everyone and their mother wanted to rent bikes. As soon as I got them in, there was someone waiting to take them out. I probably could have rented another couple of dozen if I'd had them."

"Tell me about it," Isabella piped up. "When it's hot like this, everybody wants to drink beer. I'm not complaining — we make most of our profit during the season — but I had to step in and pour beer to keep up. My feet are killing me."

"You know it's your own fault — if you didn't have such great businesses, you wouldn't be so busy," Katherine teased. "You all are such great success stories. I hope you're sharing your secrets to success with other entrepreneurs."

Beth interjected, "You know that's one of the biggest stumbling blocks for entrepreneurs, especially female entrepreneurs — they don't have mentors and advisors. I was reading last week that almost 50% of female entrepreneurs don't have a support group that can mentor them."

"That's why the Pink Boots was started back in 1997 — to help women get involved in the beer industry and to support them. It's a national organization and I've learned a lot from them. But I've also learned a lot from you all — it's nice to have a local support group," Isabella said.

After the waitress took their drink orders, Cassandra remarked, "We've got the National Bicycle Retailers Association, and they offer great programs. And I'm with Isabella — I learn a lot from Beth and Isabella and Michelle.

And don't forget some of the guys, like Jeff. He's always willing to share his experience and expertise." She added, "Katherine, haven't you helped a number of start-ups? Don't you review business plans or something?"

"I do. You know what's interesting? I'm seeing more and more business plans from older women. I looked it up the other day and the number of women over the age of fifty starting new businesses has risen steadily over the past few years. And they are often more successful than younger entrepreneurs."

Beth asked, "Why do you think that is?"

Katherine accepted her glass of wine before continuing. "For one thing, midlife and older women understand their own market best. One very successful entrepreneur, Sonsoles Gonzalez, who, after twenty-five years working for Procter & Gamble and L'Oréal, founded the hair product company, Better Not Younger. She was in her fifties and was looking for products that worked with her changing hair and couldn't find anything. She connected with an MIT chemist who developed the formulas that replace the nutrients that thinner, more brittle, hair needs."

Michelle said, "That makes sense. I've noticed those changes in my hair and nothing I've tried to add volume seems to work." The others looked at her perfectly styled hair and shook their heads. She went on. "And I think I have a good handle on what boomers and Gen X clients are looking for in real estate. I see a lot more clients looking for a primary bedroom on the main floor so they can live on one floor — important for aging in place. I know I'm happy that I don't have to run up and down the stairs all the time to get to the bedroom."

Katherine picked up the menu. "I think another reason why older entrepreneurs are successful is that they are committed to making a difference. And research shows that customers are four to six times more likely to buy from a business with a clear purpose that's consistent with the consumers' values. I know I shop that way — I support businesses that have values the same as mine — that's why I'm a big supporter of independent bookstores."

"Hear! Hear! I'm for that!" Beth lifted her glass to the group. "Independent bookstores need all the support we can get."

Katherine grinned at Beth. "And that's why I love working at Browseabout — it feeds my book habit and I get paid...well, I get paid a little." She elbowed Beth playfully. "Seriously, the money is not why I'm working at Browseabout. I've made a number of new friends and it's a pleasure helping people find the right book."

"That's very interesting about Sonsoles. Is she an anomaly or are there other over-fifty female entrepreneurs?" Brittany asked.

"Besides my anecdotal evidence from the business plans I've reviewed, there are a couple that I've followed. Julie Wainwright founded The RealReal, the online luxury consignment retailer, at age fifty-three. It's worth more than $1 billion." Isabella whistled in appreciation.

Katherine continued, "And Vicki Vasques, founder of Tribal Tech, was sixty-two when she started the company. Her company has won all kinds of awards from *Financial Times* — one of the fastest growing companies in the Americas — and *Inc.* Magazine — Fastest Growing Private Companies Hall of Fame. She is a force of nature."

"Very impressive. But what about me?" Brittany asked. "I want to open a little knitting and coffee shop."

"You would be in good company. In 2021, almost 50% of new businesses were founded by women. And according to the Census Bureau, women-owned businesses made up 21.4% of all U.S. businesses. And you know what kind of businesses women start?" Katherine knew she was lecturing, but she was so passionate about this, she couldn't help it.

"What?" asked Brittany.

"Retail. Consulting. Software. Services. You would be right in the mainstream. And to take us back to where we started — most female entrepreneurs wish they had a mentor. You've got a tableful of mentors right here!" Katherine waved her arms to include the women seated around the table.

Brittany said thoughtfully, "You know, you're right. But all this thinking has made me hungry. Do you think the kitchen is still open? I could use some of their cucumber melon bruschetta. Anyone want to join me?"

"I'll share the crab and spinach dip if you'll share your bruschetta," Isabella offered.

"Deal."

After devouring the small plates and appetizers, they sat quietly sipping their wine before discussing the book of the night. Brittany cleared her throat to get their attention. "Before we talk about Susan Wigg's book, I just have to say how much I enjoyed the discussion last time about Mallory's book. The conversation about Bree, Mikki, and Ashley was so inspiring that I had to get my own copy of the book and read it. I loved how they found a way to make all their dreams come true by working together."

Beth agreed. "I think it was Michelle who said that these three women reminded her of us. Creative. Determined. Supportive. I know I feel like I could do anything with you behind me." She continued. "I didn't deliberately pick Susan Wigg's *The Lost and Found Bookshop* for our book this week — I just happen to like books about bookstores."

"*Riiight*," Michelle drawled. "Just like I don't automatically turn to the real estate section of the newspaper." She smiled. "It's a good thing we all like booksellers."

Isabella took over the conversation to say how much she loved Natalie's grandfather — he was her favorite character in the book. Michelle was partial to Dorothy, the precocious ten-year-old who read books with Natalie while her dad, Peach, did necessary repairs on the neglected building.

"I loved all the books that were mentioned in the book," Cassandra piped up. "I started making a list and was pleased that I had read quite a few of them."

Michelle wondered about Natalie's mom's gift of being able to find exactly the right book for what a customer needed to read. "I've read a couple of other books where the owner of the shop had the same ability. Beth, do you think that's real? Do you have the gift?"

Beth looked out the window thoughtfully. "I think it comes down to asking the right questions and then listening carefully. And reading a lot. When a customer comes in, I ask them what they're looking for. Sometimes they know what they need. Other times I have to probe a little and read between the lines. It's very satisfying when they come back and tell me the book really hit the spot."

They chattered on about all the tactics that Natalie used to save the bookstore and whether she should just have sold the bookstore in the first place. Cassandra said she knew that Natalie couldn't turn her back on her inheritance. She was the most sentimental of the group.

As the restaurant emptied, they wrapped up the conversation. Out on the street, Katherine turned to Beth. "Great choice tonight. How can you not like a book about books? I'll be looking forward to your next selection."

# Chapter Fifty

Michelle met Katherine at the coffee shop across the street from Browseabout. "Hey, Katherine, thanks for meeting me. Did you order anything yet? Can I get you something?"

Katherine surveyed the chalkboard menu. "It's hot enough already. I think I'd like to try a cold brew, black. Let me give you some money."

"No, my treat this time. I made you get up extra early." Michelle grabbed her purse and followed a young family into the shop.

"Sorry that took so long." Michelle came back with the cold brew, a frothy something or other, and two chocolate chip scones. "The little kids couldn't decide what kind of ice cream they wanted. The apples didn't fall far from the tree — the dad couldn't make up his mind between a caramel macchiato or a cappuccino."

Katherine raised a brow at Michelle's frou-frou drink. "What's that you're drinking? It looks like a milkshake."

"It might as well be. It's a chocolate chip caramel cream

cold brew — it probably has more calories than a milkshake." Michelle shrugged. "What can I say? I got you a scone — chocolate chip, of course."

"Is this stress eating? It's not like you to go so heavy on the sweets." Concerned, Katherine examined Michelle. "Is everything okay?"

Michelle was quiet for a moment. "Let me get this over with. Didn't you tell us that Richard inherited his house from his parents?"

"Yes, why?" Katherine nibbled a corner of the scone and hummed with pleasure.

Michelle grimaced. "Well, the other night when you were talking about your dinner at Richard's house and going on about where he lived, there was something bugging me about that house. I checked with Sheila in my office, and she said she sold that house to Richard about five years ago."

Stunned, Katherine shook her head. "I'm sure he told me that he and his sister inherited the house when his parents passed. He bought his sister out since she lived in California and wouldn't get much use of it. What a liar!"

She slammed her cup down on the table, sloshing the cold brew everywhere. "Come to think of it, the other night at dinner, I asked him how his sister was doing, and he said he didn't have a sister," Katherine ranted. "I thought I had misunderstood or misheard him."

Michelle sipped her cold brew concoction. "Wow! Is that sweet! I think my pancreas just turned over. Hang on a second." Michelle went back to the counter and returned a few minutes later with a regular black iced coffee. "I can't drink that thing." She pushed the offending cup away.

She checked to see if anyone was eavesdropping. "He told Sheila that he didn't have any family except an ex-wife and a couple of kids. Sheila said that Richard was anxious to move to

Rehoboth. He bugged her every day for a couple of months to see if anything new was on the market that met his requirements. She said he was very specific about what he wanted — isolated, not very many neighbors, on a dead-end street. She thought he was a little paranoid."

Her usual stress reaction, Katherine's foot was jiggling so fast the table was rocking. "That describes his house perfectly. I even commented on how cut off he was. It was almost like he was hiding or something," Katherine said. "And the inside was quite different from the outside. The outside looked like every other cute little cottage in the area. But inside was all modern — I don't think there was a single original wall left. And it was like a fortress — I'm pretty sure he had an eye scan identifier on the back door. I saw it when we came in from the patio."

Katherine grew more agitated. *Why would he go to such lengths? Who is he hiding from? I thought that house was strange. Now I know it was.*

Michelle smiled at the disheveled new mom who settled the baby carrier on the table with a thump. The baby, who couldn't have been more than a couple of months old, started to fuss. "Sheila told me the owners of that house decided to move closer to their grandchildren. They lived in that house forever and Sheila has known the family for years. She even went to high school with the daughter. That's one reason she got the listing and how she knew it was coming on the market."

Katherine replayed every interaction she had with Richard. *I should have listened to my gut when I met him at the parking office. There was something off about him.*

Michelle continued, "As soon as she learned they were selling the house, she called Richard. He was so excited. He didn't even want her to list it, but she had to. The first day the house was on the market, Richard made an offer that was significantly over full price. Of course, the owners accepted it right away. That's why I remembered it — it was a huge commission for her."

Even more distressed, Katherine said, "Why would he lie about this?"

"I don't know, but Sheila said he told her he was managing a huge portfolio for one of his clients and he had done well on the investments. She remembered that he said he had a couple of new clients that were going to be big payoffs. He even asked her if she wanted to invest with him — it was a sure thing — and now that she had that nice commission, he could double her money quickly. When she told him she wasn't interested, he got pretty nasty and said she would always be a small potatoes real estate salesman," Michelle said angrily. "I wish she had told me about this when it happened. Nobody treats my people that way."

*He kept bringing up how he'd like to 'help' me with my investments. It irritated me. I don't need his help. But he was pretty pushy about it.*

"But why would he tell me that he inherited the house? I don't get it. What's his agenda?" Normally she wouldn't be bothered by the screaming baby next to them but today the poor thing just added to her headache. Her face flushing bright red, Katherine rubbed her forehead.

Michelle touched her arm. "Are you okay? I'm so sorry." She got Katherine a glass of water and offered an aspirin. "I didn't want to be the bearer of bad news, but I thought you needed to know this. There's something that's not right going on. You should be careful with this guy."

"You're the second person who warned me about him," Katherine seethed. "I should have listened to Jeff." She stood up abruptly. "Thanks, Michelle. I appreciate you telling me this. I've got to run to work now, but you can be sure I'll be calling Richard to find out why he's been lying to me."

# Chapter Fifty-One

"Richard. This is Katherine." Still steaming about Michelle's revelations, Katherine slammed the house door and threw her keys on the table. Stewing all day, she was ready to let him have it.

"Katherine, I'm so glad to hear from you. I didn't like the way we left things the other night." Richard oozed warmth and charm. To Katherine's ears, it sounded so fake. *I should have trusted my instincts.* "Would you like to get together for a drink? I want to apologize properly."

Barely concealing her anger, Katherine challenged him. "This isn't a social call. Why did you lie to me? You didn't inherit your house — you bought it!"

"Wait a minute. Where did you hear that?" Richard exploded. "I bet it was that bitchy real estate agent. She wanted in on one of my investments, but I wouldn't let her because she couldn't meet the minimum investment requirement."

Katherine held the phone away and just stared at it. *I can't believe it. He's attacking the real estate agent.* "Richard, did you or did you not buy that house?"

He backpedaled. "Please forgive my outburst. I shouldn't have stooped to her level and called her that name. I hate it when people are so petty when I don't let them share in my success."

*Unbelievable. That's not true.* Michelle told her that Sheila had turned down Richard's offer. She paced the kitchen, growing even more angry. "It doesn't matter who I heard it from. You told me you inherited the house. Is that true or not?"

"Katherine, Katherine — perhaps I wasn't clear when we were talking about my house. When my parents passed, my sister and I got a huge inheritance from their estate since I was managing their investments. I used my inheritance to buy this house."

*Do you think I'm stupid! I know what you told me. Don't you tell me that I didn't understand what you said.* Katherine raged. She put the phone on speaker and opened the refrigerator. *I need wine to deal with this.*

He went on. "It was so important to be here where we had spent many happy times together as a family. . ."

"Did you really come here with your family?" she interrupted, slamming the refrigerator door so hard the box of crackers stored on top crashed to the floor.

"Of course I did." *I don't believe him.* He kept laying it on thick. "My happiest memories are here in Rehoboth — both with my family and the new ones I'm making with you."

She interrupted. "I thought you told me you bought out your sister? Do you even have a sister?" She paced to the patio door back to the kitchen back to the patio door. She sat down on the sofa, her foot jiggling a mile a minute.

"My sister used her inheritance to buy beach front property in Oregon."

Katherine pounced on that statement. "You told me she lived in California."

Richard stammered. "She moved to Oregon last month."

Katherine didn't say anything. *Fool me once, shame on you. Fool me twice, shame on me. Well, you a$$hole, you're not going to fool me twice.*

"You do believe me, Katherine, don't you? I would never lie to you. I know how much Stan hurt you with his lies." Richard lied smoothly. Katherine knew he was a chronic liar.

"No. I don't believe you. I'm not sure what your game is, but I'm not going to be a part of it. Goodbye, Richard. Don't call me ever again." To be sure he couldn't contact her again, she blocked his number.

Katherine paced back and forth on the patio, waiting impatiently for Jeff to answer his phone.

"You were right."

"Hello to you, too," Jeff laughed. "I like being right. What was I right about this time?"

Seriously, Katherine said, "You were right when you told me to be careful of Richard. I still don't like it that you 'told' me to be careful, but you were right." Katherine drew in a deep breath, breathed out slowly, and tried to calm her racing heart. "He's a lying scumbag. And he probably *was* trying to scam me. Thank heavens, he didn't get his grubby paws on my money."

"Whoa. What happened?" Jeff's voice rose in anger.

"I found out from Michelle today that he's been telling me a pack of lies. He didn't inherit his house here. He bought it five years ago. He may or may not have a sister who lives in California or Oregon or who knows where. I don't think I should believe a thing he told me. I'm not even sure Richard is his real name."

"Son of a . . ." Jeff erupted.

Jeff's anger soothed her. She sat down heavily on the chaise lounge, exhausted from the emotional roller coaster she had been riding since Michelle's coffee meeting. She told him about the extraordinary security measures that Richard had at his house. "It struck me as odd when I saw them."

"That is weird. It sounds like he's paranoid. You know the old saying — something like 'you're not paranoid if someone is after you.' Maybe he's got some bad people looking for him."

"It wouldn't surprise me given what a jerk he is," Katherine sputtered. "And to think I wasted my favorite new dress on him."

Jeff's voice dropped an octave as he murmured, "Lucky for me I got to see that beautiful you in your lovely dress for a few minutes. It wasn't wasted on me."

Katherine flushed remembering the way Jeff had checked her out.

"I've got an idea. Let me take you out Monday night. Wear that dress and we'll make some better new memories." Jeff growled, "I'd like to see more of that dress—both with you in it, or better yet, with you out of it."

"You are incorrigible," Katherine laughed. "But I like the idea of cleansing any bit of Richard away."

"I think you're beginning to like me a little," Jeff teased.

*I think I'm beginning to like you a lot,* Katherine thought.

# Chapter Fifty-Two

"It's about time we had our group meet here," Katherine said to Isabella. "You make the best beer, and we should support your business. And this loft is such a great place for us to talk."

Katherine could hear the buzz and laughter downstairs, but the loft was surprisingly quiet. Rather than the tables and stools Isabella used downstairs, the loft was furnished with burgundy brushed corduroy easy chairs and loveseats clustered around coffee tables. The hanging diffused globe pendant lights lit the loft softly, giving a feeling of a cozy lounge or library. The railing was lined with bushy palm trees and old wooden bourbon barrels that Isabella used to age her imperial stouts but were now being used as a sound barrier from the chatter below.

Isabella sank into the loveseat and pushed the plump pillow onto the floor. "I wanted to create a different feel up here — something more intimate and relaxed — a place where you can sit and have a conversation and a beer. We meet here about every three months. We like to spread our business around."

Katherine greeted the rest of the group and looked with

interest at the smartly dressed newcomer. "Hey Beth. How's it going? Cassandra, is Penny joining us tonight? Brittany, how are you? Michelle, has work slowed down with you?"

"Katherine, let me introduce you to Stella. She's a regular but for a variety of reasons, she hasn't been able to make the last few months. She's vice president at the bank — a loan officer who specializes in small business loans." Stella shook Katherine's hand.

"Stella, Katherine is here on sabbatical," Beth said to the new woman. "She teaches in Washington, D.C. Unfortunately, she has to go back in a couple of months when her sabbatical is over in January."

Beth continued the introductions. "Stella, I don't think you know Brittany either. She moved here from Wilmington a couple of years ago, but she didn't join the group until we literally bumped into each other a few months ago." Beth grinned at Brittany.

"A pleasure to meet you both. I've missed this group and I'm sorry I haven't been able to make our get-togethers. I had a temporary assignment down in Dover helping set up another branch. I'm glad to be back — you all have been my lifelines," Stella said emotionally.

She turned to Brittany and Katherine. "I was diagnosed with breast cancer a year and a half ago. These wonderful women took such great care of me — drove me to chemo when my husband couldn't do it, brought me enough casseroles that we didn't have cook hardly at all — even breakfast casseroles. Who brings breakfast casseroles? That was so smart. And they sat with me and played board games or sat with me when I was so sick, and I didn't want to do anything. I don't know what I would have done without them."

Cassandra reached over and hugged Stella. "We're glad you're back. And we would bring you more casseroles if you needed them." She smiled. "But we're glad you're in remission and don't need them anymore. We'll bring them for fun now." Isabella and Michelle nodded.

"That's a great idea. Let's have a casserole celebration — you've been cancer free for a whole year now," Michelle said. "Let's do it before Thanksgiving."

"I'm happy to host it at our house," Cassandra offered. "Michelle, I'll give you a call to talk details."

Isabella piped up. "Okay, who wants to try our new seasonal beer? We've got a pumpkin beer and a wet hop beer."

"What's a wet hop beer?" Brittany asked.

"It's a beer that's made with the hops that are harvested at the end of August and used within twenty-four hours. They're still full of moisture. Almost every other beer is made from dried hops. The flavor is quite different — earthy, citrusy, and a little floral. It's like the difference between fresh herbs versus dried herbs. You know how fresh cilantro tastes different than dried cilantro. It's available for a short time and it's only on draft," Isabella explained.

"Huh. I've never had one before. I'll try it," Brittany said. Choruses of "me, too" went around the chairs.

"I'll try the pumpkin beer later. It doesn't have pumpkin in it, does it?" Brittany asked.

"No, the flavor is from the spices we add like nutmeg, cinnamon, and ginger," Isabella said.

Isabella asked the waitress who had been waiting patiently for their order to bring a wet hop pitcher and some glasses.

Turning back to the group, she said, "The Tex-Mex Food Truck is here tonight. Anyone want some nachos? Or wings? Or jalapeño poppers?"

"Nachos for me."

"Poppers."

"Wings."

"Wings for me, too. And poppers," Beth said. "What? I didn't have any lunch today."

Isabella laughed and turned back to Becky. "Would you mind running out to the food truck for me? I know it's not your regular duty, but I'll tip really, really well. Bring two orders of the wings and the poppers, and a large nacho with everything."

"You got it, boss."

"And bring lots of napkins. This isn't the neatest bunch."

Michelle leaned over the coffee table to Brittany. "Hey, wanted to let you know there's a retail space coming open in one of the mews downtown. It's across from a coffee and ice cream shop that closed a while ago and is being converted into an art gallery. It's not a big space, but it might be perfect for you."

"I haven't done much more thinking about my knit and sip store, but I'm interested in learning more about this space," Brittany said.

"What kind of business are you talking about?" Stella asked, leaning in to hear better.

"I've always wanted to have a yarn store and coffee shop like the one that I went to with my grandmother in Wisconsin. It was such a warm and inviting place — they sold the most beautiful yarn and gave knitting and crocheting classes. And they had a small café — six or eight tables — where they had the best coffee and tea and muffins. Mmmm, makes my mouth water to think about them." Brittany continued, "But I haven't run any of the numbers and I haven't written a business plan."

"I can help you with that," Katherine said. "You know that's my side hustle in D.C. Outside my university work, I work for an organization that reviews business plans for entrepreneurs who are applying for loans."

"And I can help, too," Stella said. "I do small business loans at the bank. I have to review business plans."

Cassandra piped up, "I can help you with the business licenses."

"I have an in with the Chamber of Commerce," Isabella contributed.

"And Cassandra and I have been involved in retail sales for years. We can help with inventory and sales systems," Beth said.

"You all would do that?" Brittany asked.

"Of course. You're one of us now. We help our friends," Beth said. "And we want to support other women entrepreneurs."

"It's always felt like a pipe dream, having my own shop, but maybe with all your help, I could make it happen," Brittany said. "You know, with all the experience and expertise you all have, and your willingness to help, you should form a group to help other women entrepreneurs. You're all so savvy." She continued, "I know! You could call yourselves 'The Savvys.' You could help female entrepreneurs realize their dreams."

They sat quietly weighing the idea. Katherine spoke first, "You know, that's an interesting idea. I think it would meet the needs of women I've talked to who want to run their own businesses. We have all the basic business functions covered. Don't forget Brittany has advertising experience."

"I mentor other women in the brewery business. The work I do at the national level is education and awareness about the opportunities in the brewery business in general and for female entrepreneurs specifically," Isabella said.

"Penny and I have done the same thing for other women who want to open their own bike shops," Cassandra shared.

They turned quiet again.

"The Savvys," Beth said. "I like it. I think we could do a lot of good for women. I think we all want to give back since we've been fortunate in our lives."

Michelle said, "Maybe you could think of Brittany as your first 'client?' Help her get her business off the ground. I don't mean to rush you, Brittany, but this could be the nudge you've needed to get your bearings and start moving forward."

Beth asked, "Brittany, are you willing to be our guinea pig?"

"Hell, yeah! I can't think of a better group of mentors — and friends!"

# Chapter Fifty-Three

Katherine looked around anxiously for Cassandra and Penny. It was still drizzling, and the roads were wet from last night's rain. The paved roads wouldn't be too bad, but the packed dirt trails might be dicey. *Thank heavens Cassandra had dragged me out on those rainy days in Rehoboth so I would be prepared for this.* If it turned into a downpour, Katherine had a rolled-up rain shirt in her backpack. Her helmet kept the water out of her eyes and the rain shirt would keep her warm and dryish. It was supposed to stop raining by noon, but the wind was going to pick up. Good for drying the roads, but not so good if it was a headwind.

She was early for the Wild Goose Chase Bicycle Ride, but she wanted to have plenty of time to do the last-minute bike check and get mentally prepared for the ride. Women called out greetings — "hello" and "how have you been since last year?" — as old friends renewed friendships from other years or rides. Katherine recognized a few of them from yesterday's basic bicycle maintenance class. What a great refresher that was—always good to be reminded about how to avoid flat tires, and if you get one, what's the best way to fix it. Katherine patted her backpack with her puncture kit, spare inner tube, and multipurpose tool for any adjustments she might have to make on the course. She thanked Cassandra mentally for drilling her on bike repairs.

A kaleidoscope of jerseys of all colors and patterns that shrank and grew as women joined or separated from the clusters of women prepping for the ride assaulted Katherine's eyes. A group of women wearing T-shirts emblazoned with "biker chick" and a picture of a baby chicken tickled Katherine and she giggled out loud. Katherine spotted Penny over the top of the crowd and waved. As the crowd shifted, she saw Cassandra right behind her.

"Hey, I'm glad to see you. I don't know why I'm nervous. I've been doing the training. I even did an eighteen-mile ride two weekends ago. I know I can do this," Katherine said to Cassandra.

"You've got this. It's normal to feel the way you are," Cassandra reassured her. "You know Penny and I are going to stay with you until you're comfortable."

"I don't want to hold you back."

"Don't worry — this ride is not about "competing" — it's about "completing." It's all about doing it and proving to yourself you can do it," Cassandra continued. "You'll see. Some women make it an all-day affair — stopping whenever they want to for a rest or to take out their binoculars to see what birds they can spot. You know there's more than 250 species of birds in this refuge?"

"Yes, I know. Jeff and I spent the day here a few weeks ago. I wanted to get the lay of the land. We saw eagles, osprey, geese, and birds that I don't know the names of. We did a little hiking, but mostly just drove the course. I loved how flat it is."

Katherine smiled. "I know hills are my friends, but for this ride, I could use fewer 'friends.'" She grinned.

"That was smart to check out the course. Now it's not going to be a surprise today."

"You taught me well. And I was impressed by how much I knew in yesterday's bicycle maintenance class, thanks to your training."

"Well, I'm impressed with how good a student you are and how dedicated you've been in your training."

Penny teased, "If this mutual admiration society is over, they're beginning to line up."

The trio walked their bikes over to the start line. "We're not going to start at the head of the line. There are some women here who are interested in their time. We'll let them get ahead of us. We'll start in the middle of the line on the outside. The key is to not get in anyone else's way," Cassandra reminded Katherine. "Give yourself space to ride and enjoy it."

When the starter's gun sounded, Katherine waited until the line began to spread out and then pedaled slowly to get into the rhythm. Cassandra and Penny were ahead of her. A determined woman on her right glanced once her way, gave a grim smile, and then focused on her pedaling.

Out of the corner of her eye, Katherine caught a glimpse of Jeff as he waved from the other side of the starting line. "Go, Katherine!" he yelled.

Katherine blushed and ducked her head. Jeff had been a great cheerleader over the past few months. He had even dragged his old fat tire bike out of storage so he could do leisurely rides with her. They cruised the streets in North Rehoboth toward Cape Henlopen State Park where President Biden had a beach home. When he was in residence with his children and grandchildren, the Secret Service limited their access to the area, but there were plenty of streets to ride on and admire the towering crape myrtle trees, the lush bunches of tiger lilies, and the dense carpet of ferns.

They played a game, making up stories about the people who lived in the houses. Who lived behind the tall, gated fence in the Georgian brick house? Or how about the brightly painted yellow house with the lawn scattered with modern metal sculptures? And Katherine's personal favorite — the low-slung weathered wood one-story home that took up a whole block, framed on one end with a fantastic wooden playground in the shape of a whale, and on the other end with a Japanese garden.

The line of bicyclists lengthened and stretched to almost single file with a few side-by-side riders. Cassandra looked back over her shoulder and Katherine gave her a thumbs up and waved her on ahead. Cassandra nodded and she and Penny picked up speed, leaving Katherine content to take the ride at her own pace. She and the determined woman leapfrogged each other as one or the other got a burst of speed. It almost felt choreographed as if they were riding together in a beautiful bicycle ballet. It was nice to have someone to ride with even if they weren't together.

The salt marsh smelled fresh and a little salty. The rain had washed down the usually rotten egg odor that marshes often smelled of. The road was closed for the ride for a couple of hours — after that, Katherine would have to watch out for traffic. She was glad she had experience dodging cars on narrow Rehoboth roads with shallow shoulders.

The road was banked on either side with inlets of gray water reflecting the cloudy rainy skies. The marsh grass sharply defined the water. *I wonder why the marsh grass lines are so precise — it looks like someone came through with a lawn edger.* She could see trees far off in the distance, but between her and the trees, there was nothing but flat. She coasted a bit as she approached the first rest stop, buzzing with volunteers but not too many riders. This early in the ride most people didn't need the granola bars, bananas, water, or orange juice. They cruised on by.

Four miles down, sixteen more to go. Katherine was impressed with the participants who were planning on doing thirty-nine or even sixty-three miles! *That's a goal for another year — sixty-three miles.*

She thought back to July when she got her bike. She took it out the first weekend and it felt so good she rode five miles. And then she paid for it. She could hardly walk to work the next day — her calves and thighs were killing her. She knew better but it felt liberating to sail along the roads, turning right when she wanted to, left if she felt like it — just doing what she wanted to do. Beth laughed when she told her what she had done over the weekend. "Such a rookie move, Katherine."

*At least I learned.* Katherine rested that week and then on Saturday she went for a two-mile ride after she stretched and warmed up. By the beginning of August, she was up to a comfortable four-mile ride. Then she posted the eight-week training plan that Cassandra had given her on the refrigerator and followed it religiously. Every Tuesday she did a "speed ride" for fifteen to twenty-five minutes, pedaling as fast as she could until her legs burned so badly, she wanted to scream. She sweet-talked the night manager at one of the hotels to let her dangle her legs first in the pool and then in the whirlpool. She sighed, thinking of the relief.

Then Thursdays she did a "steady ride" starting with two intervals and working up to four — pushing for fifteen — thirty minutes, then pedaling leisurely to get her heart rate down to normal. For the first two weeks, she could only do one interval.

Jeff had given her a sheet of gold stars to mark her progress.

Katherine proudly awarded herself a gold star when she did four 30-minute intervals.

She grinned when she thought about Jeff. He started humming the theme song from "Rocky" every time he saw her. He was often waiting for her with a nice cold bottle of water and an energy bite that he made himself with oatmeal, peanut butter, flax seed, and honey.

Katherine wasn't sure if she was prouder of the Thursday intervals or the long rides on Sunday mornings early. Since she had to open Browseabout at 8:00, Katherine did her long rides first starting at 6:00AM, and then moving them to 5:00AM when the distance got longer. She so appreciated the bike club that included her in their early rides. It was a little spooky riding the streets before dawn by herself the first few weeks.

When Cassandra had mentioned the bike club, Katherine called them right away and found a steady group of five riders of varying abilities who were happy to have her join them. She wished some of them were here with her now, but they had other rides they were doing, or they weren't available this weekend.

*At least Cassandra and Penny are here if I fall and break my leg,* Katherine thought, and then quickly pushed that thought from her head. *Don't send that intention out into the universe! I'm not going to break my leg. Take that, Universe.*

Katherine barely noticed when they left the road and turned onto the two-track dirt road. The rain had stopped some time ago and the wind was trying to dry the dirt without much success. She slowed down and dodged the muddiest holes and rode on the edge of the path where it bordered the grass and was a little less muddy. The sun was peeking around the clouds, making the waters sparkle blue and the marsh grass greener.

The determined woman was right behind Katherine and

struggling. Katherine signaled her to pull over and rest for a minute, but she shook her head 'no' and kept pedaling. With a thumbs up, Katherine pushed on until she came to the next rest stop, the halfway point. Deciding to set a good example, Katherine stopped to get water and a banana. She was pleased when the determined woman pulled over beside her.

"How are you doing? I'm Katherine, by the way."

"I'm Jenna. Whew." She stepped off her bike and wobbled a bit. "I love seeing the ten-mile sign! I told myself I wasn't going to stop until I made it here." Katherine reached out to steady her. "I'm good. Just a little crampy and achy. I need to do a little stretching."

Katherine watched as Jenna grabbed a bottle of water and walked off a bit to put her leg up on a bench, stretching out her hamstrings one at a time. Then she did some calf stretches and touched her toes. Katherine went over to the volunteer table to grab a banana and a peanut butter graham cracker. *These are so delicious. Just what I need for a little extra energy.*

Jenna approached Katherine. "Thanks for hanging out and waiting for me. I don't know anyone else on the ride, but when I saw the ad in the paper in early September, I decided I wanted to do it. Protecting the environment is very important to me. Doing the ride kills two birds with one stone – I get exercise *and* support a good cause. You know, they've raised over $175,000 to support this Blackwater Wildlife Refuge."

"Yes, I know. My friend and I came down here earlier and did the birding tour that starts in Cambridge, Maryland. Did you see the pair of eagles sitting in the tree a few minutes ago?" Jenna nodded as Katherine continued, "The guide told us how important the Blackwater Refuge is. It has one of the largest breeding populations of American bald eagles on the East Coast. And I didn't know anything about it until I signed up for the Wild Goose Chase." Katherine checked her bike tires and strapped on her helmet.

"Don't you love the play on words, 'Wild Goose Chase?' It just tickles me," Jenna laughed. "Most people think it's about the dictionary definition — something like a pointless pursuit of something — but it's about the fact that Blackwater Wildlife Refuge is one of the primary wintering places for Canada geese! Get it? 'Wild goose chase'?" Jenna continued to chuckle.

Katherine laughed, too. "I'm an English professor. I love word play." She grabbed another package of peanut butter graham crackers and thanked the volunteers for being there. She turned back to Jenna. "I'm ready to head out. Are you?"

"Yes, thanks. Do you mind if we ride together for the rest of the trip? I didn't train as well as I should have so I'd like to know someone is keeping an eye on me."

Katherine thought about how far she had come over the summer when she was the one being taken care of. "Of course. We'll keep leapfrogging each other. You know that's what the geese do when they're migrating. One takes the lead and when she's tired, she falls to the back of the vee, and the next one leads so the other can rest. They can actually fly further when they take turns being the leader."

"Smart geese. We should learn from them."

Katherine, refreshed and relaxed, climbed back on her bike. She and Jenna rode together until they stopped at the Harriet Tubman Underground Railroad National Monument.

"It's amazing that this tiny, illiterate woman saved so many people. She was courage personified," Katherine said. "You know her birthplace isn't too far from here and we're going to go by her childhood home. I feel like I'm walking on sacred ground when I think about how much she sacrificed and how courageous she was." Katherine looked across the open fields lined with a thin wall of trees. "She took such huge risks."

"I studied Harriet Tubman in college. She made nineteen trips to help people escape slavery — and saved over 300 people. And she supported women's right to vote. She was such an inspiring woman," Jenna read the roadside marker. "The Moses of Her People."

Katherine and Jenna quietly resumed their ride, both lost in thought at the courage of Harriet Tubman.

Crossing the nineteenth mile marker, Jenna and Katherine were surprised to see the road lined with people waving signs, blowing horns, and clanging bells. With a renewed burst of energy, they pushed through the last mile, crossing the finish line side by side, smiling broadly.

Cassandra and Penny were waiting for Katherine and came forward to slip her finisher's medal over her head. "You did it!"

"We did it!" She introduced Jenna to Penny and Cassandra. "We didn't start out to do this together, but it was much better to have Jenna's support and companionship. I could have done it alone, but this was better."

Jenna nodded. "It made it much more special."

They walked their bikes by the other finishers, some exuberant with success, others hobbling with cramps or sore muscles. *I did it.* Katherine was so proud of her accomplishment — the medal meant more than just completing this race. It marked a real milestone in her growth. When she started this journey, she wasn't sure she could complete it. *I stuck with it and look what I did!*

Cassandra and Penny waved at some old friends. "Great job, Katherine. And you, too, Jenna. Stop by our store sometime for a free coffee."

"I'll do that." Jenna turned to Katherine. "Thanks again for letting me tag along. The hot tub and some Advil are calling my name."

Cassandra put her helmet back on. "We're headed out with

some of the ride organizers for lunch. Do you want to come along, Katherine?"

Katherine looked around. "No thanks, I saw Jeff just as we crossed the finish line. He said he was going to meet me by the medical tent."

Jeff burst around the corner and grabbed Katherine. Swinging her around in the air, he said, "You did it! Way to go!" Then he kissed her soundly.

Katherine melted into him and felt his arms tighten around her. She backstepped until she was between the snack tent and the medical tent. Running his tongue around her lips, he danced in and out of her mouth. He moved his lips down her neck, licking the sweat away and nibbling his way to her ear. Katherine moaned and pulled his lips back to hers.

He murmured, "You taste good."

"If you like the taste of sweat." She drew him closer.

"I *love* the taste of sweat. Are you sweaty all over?" He pulled her tighter against him, letting her know how excited he was.

Katherine groaned. "We have to stop. We're barely hidden. We should go home."

Jeff paused his caresses. "What should we do when we get home?"

Katherine said, "Pick up where we left off."

# Chapter Fifty-Four

Jeff backed Katherine up against the front door. "You shouldn't have been doing that all the way home from Blackwater."

"What? I was stroking your thigh," Katherine panted.

"That wasn't my thigh." Jeff dragged her up against him. "Where's the key?"

Katherine wiggled around, rubbing his very impressive arousal, and pulled the house key from her front pocket. Jeff let go with one arm and managed to open the door. He moaned. "I've been thinking about this for a long time. Are you sure?"

Katherine backed into the house, pulling Jeff tight. She kissed him, licking his lips, thrusting her tongue in and out, sucking on his lower lip. "I'm sure."

He led her back to the shower. "You told me you were sweaty. I think we should shower, don't you?" He kissed his way down her front, stopping to nuzzle all her sensitive parts. *I love the way he makes me feel – so loved. Cherished.*

Slowly he pushed her jacket off and dropped it to the floor. Katherine arched her back, seeking as much contact as possible.

Jeff nipped at her neck and slipped his hands under her jersey, inching it up over her head. His hands were slightly rough like a cat's tongue as he grasped her firmly around the waist, his thumbs stroking her skin in lazy circles. He slowly worked his way over every rib, stroking her skin until she burned.

"Too tight. This sports bra is too tight. I need to feel you." Jeff tugged the zipper.

Katherine raised her hands to cover her chest. "This is a sixty-one-year-old body. It's a roadmap of my life – childbirth, age, neglect."

Jeff pulled her hands away. "It's beautiful. I love it. Don't cover it up." He held her away. She watched his eyes darken as he swept his gaze down her body.

"Jeff, you're driving me crazy." Katherine rested her forehead on his. "I haven't felt this way in so long. You make me feel so desirable."

"You are desirable. I've desired you for months. And you can feel how much I desire you now." He placed her hand on his arousal. She raised her eyes to his, knowing her eyes reflected the same passion.

She tugged at his shirt, running her hands up his abs, twining her fingers through his furry chest. Lifting his shirt, she licked his belly button. "You're kind of salty, too. Maybe we should try out that shower of yours?"

Jeff hooked his thumbs in her bike shorts and rolled them down to the floor. Running his hands up her thighs, he stopped at her bikini bottoms before ripping them off. "I owe you some new ones."

Katherine gasped. "I'll hold you to that."

"Darlin', you can hold me to whatever you want."

"Jeff, take off your pants. Take off everything."

Flinging his clothes everywhere, he lifted Katherine and carried her into the shower.

"Ohhh, too cold."

"Hold on. I'll warm you up." Jeff grabbed the soap and lathered Katherine from top to bottom. He tightened his grasp, pulling her closer. "Sharing is caring. Don't you want to save the planet?" He pressed his body to hers. "Share the soap and water?"

Katherine wrapped her arms around him. Swaying slowly back and forth. His hairy chest against her bare skin created such a delicious friction. Jeff groaned softly.

"You know, I think I'm clean enough. I think it's time to get out." Jeff stepped out of the shower, keeping Katherine close to him. Throwing a towel over his back, he grabbed a soft white towel and dried her carefully. He backed her to the king-sized bed and laid her gently down.

He looked down at her with wonder. "How can I be so lucky? You are beautiful. And strong. And sexy."

Katherine reached up and pulled him in for a kiss. She traced the tattoo crossing his left shoulder and running down his arm. "I haven't been with anyone for over a year. And when Stan told me about his affair, I got tested. I'm clean."

"I am, too."

"Well, we don't have to worry about birth control either," Katherine whispered. "You know what that means? No raincoats."

Jeff chuckled at her old-fashioned term for condoms. "Another bonus to making love at our age."

Jeff licked her lips and settled deeper between her thighs. His weight felt right. Katherine rubbed impatiently against him. "Don't you think it's time you collected your bonus?" She captured his mouth and kissed him with such intensity he felt his control slipping.

He grit his teeth. "God, I feel like a teenager. This first time I may not last long."

Katherine responded by tightening around him. "Let's go together. And then take our time the next time."

They lay there spent, skin to skin. *How could it have been so perfect?* Even though it was their first time, they fit together. Katherine felt like she had been waiting for him her whole life. She was filled with joy that she could feel this way and that he seemed to feel the same way. She sighed. Jeff raised himself up on one elbow. "Are you okay?"

"Nope. Not okay. I'm great!" Energy coursing through her body, she felt like she was waking up after years of drifting in and out of light sleep. Feelings she had forgotten surged through her, feelings she didn't expect to have again at this point in her life.

Jeff rolled over pulling Katherine on top of him. He reached up, framing her face with his hands. "I've dreamed about doing this. But my dreams weren't half as good as this was. You are so special."

He gathered her in his arms. "I need a little rest. And then can I have seconds?"

# Chapter Fifty-Five

"Vanessa, I'm good. I appreciate you worrying about me, but I'm getting better and stronger." Katherine hugged Vanessa. "I love my little house here. It gives me such joy to sit here in the backyard and listen to the fountain and dip my toes in the pool."

Vanessa scooted her chair closer to her mom. "I'm glad, Mom, and you are looking very healthy and vibrant. And you've done a great job making this place your own even though you're renting. I love the rugs and the art and the flowers. I never knew you liked flowers so much."

"It's all the walking and bike riding. You know I did that Wild Goose Chase earlier this month. A twenty-mile ride. And I wasn't even that tired at the end," Katherine boasted.

She looked around the garden. "I've always loved flowers. And gardening. Most of the flowers in the house came from the garden I planted on the other side of the house."

She had introduced more flowering plants — the night blooming jasmine scented the air deliciously. The cinnamon spicy smell of the bright pink dianthus tempered the sweetness of the jasmine. And the lowly petunias exuded their strong vanilla smell in the dark, hoping to attract the night flying pollinators. She could make out the new dark rose crape myrtle she planted in the far corner lit by a small solar light.

"I don't think I ever knew that about you — I took the flowers for granted and thought you picked them up at the grocery store. My bad. I should have been more observant." Vanessa admired the lush hostas and flowers, illuminated with downward facing bell-shaped solar lights.

Katherine patted Vanessa's arm. "No 'shoulding' allowed. You know what Shawna always says..."

Vanessa laughed. "Stop 'shoulding' on yourself."

"It's easy to second guess ourselves or play the 'if only I had...' game, but it does us no good," Katherine continued. "I've had to work on that myself. 'If only I had been thinner...' 'If only I had been as smart as your father...' 'If only, if only, if only.' 'I should have exercised more.' 'I should have...' But that's taking all the responsibility of my marriage breakup on myself. And I'll acknowledge that I played a role in the demise of my marriage."

"Really, Mom? Did you make Dad have an affair?" Vanessa interrupted vehemently. "I think not."

"No, not that," Katherine mused. "But perhaps if I had been more exciting... No, there I go again." Katherine stopped. "I am enough. I am the right size. I am very smart. I am interesting."

"Good for you, Mom," Vanessa complimented her mom. "You are all those things and more. I hope you believe it."

"I do on most days," Katherine stated. "And the people I've met here and my real friends back in Washington remind me every day to count my accomplishments and appreciate who I am."

Vanessa helped herself to another half-sandwich. "I'm

happy that you're not sitting around waiting for Dad to come back."

"Come on, Vanessa. You should know me better than that by now. I'll admit I had some pretty low times — it was a lot to lose when your dad asked for the divorce. I had a different future planned out that included him. Now I'm creating a new future. I'm pretty excited about it."

"Does it have anything to do with this guy you've been seeing? Am I going to meet him soon?" Vanessa teased.

Katherine blushed a little. "Not entirely. We're not talking about the future. We're enjoying the present." Looking defiant, she said, "And yes, you'll meet him at Thanksgiving. He's cooking dinner for all of us and the rest of our friends here who aren't traveling."

"What's *your* plan for the future?" Vanessa asked.

"First off, I want to recover my *joie de vivre*. Before I was married, and even after I was married, I was more dream driven." Katherine shrugged. "Your mother was not really a wild woman, but she was — I was — much bolder than I've been over the last few years."

She paused to take a sip of iced tea. "You know I spent a year in Paris between my undergraduate degree and my masters. I swore I'd spend more time there, writing and living. Somehow that got away from me."

Concerned, Vanessa asked, "Is it because you had Anthony and me?"

"No, you're the best parts of my marriage. I wouldn't trade you two for anything," Katherine assured her. "I didn't make time for my dreams. I let everything else take up my time, including putting your father's needs ahead of mine. Now I'm realizing I have to take time for myself. It makes me a happier, better person."

Vanessa murmured, "I can see how easy it would be to be

caught up in activities. Curt and I talk about this — that we want to support each other but we have to take care that we don't get swallowed up and forget about our individual needs."

Katherine picked up a notebook from the coffee table. "I started my list of dreams. Things I want to do or have. Not a bucket list. I hate the idea of a bucket list. Who wants to finish your bucket list and kick off? Not me."

Vanessa laughed. "You know that's not what they mean by a bucket list — you're not going to kick the bucket when you finish it."

"I'm not taking any chances." Katherine flipped through the pages. "I'm calling mine a List of Dreams. I learned about this from this time management — actually, a life management — guru, Laura Vanderkam. It's a list of whatever I would do if I could do anything I want. That's what I'm beginning to appreciate. I *can* do whatever I want to do. It's totally terrifying and exhilarating at the same time."

"You're not going to go join a commune or something? Go totally off the grid?" Vanessa teased.

"No, nothing quite that radical. But I am going to shake things up a bit. Don't worry — I'll still be there for you and Anthony whenever you need me — which isn't as often or as much as it used to be since you're all grown up."

"We'll always need you, Mom, no matter how old we are. " She hugged her mom.

"I know. But it's different. You're heading off to Ethiopia soon. And Anthony is happily married with a new baby in Atlanta. You both need me differently than you used to. And that's how it should be."

"What are you going to do?" Puzzled, Vanessa studied her mother. "Don't they say to not make any drastic changes for a year after you divorce? Don't rush into anything or do something impulsive?"

"Yes, it's true they say to be careful about making big life changes right now. But this divorce has been a big wake-up call." Katherine shifted so she could look Vanessa in the eye. "The time I've spent here — walking on the beach, riding my bike, even working in the bookstore — has given me the opportunity to think about what I want. How I want to spend my time. What kind of adventures I want. What changes I want. It's kind of a blank slate at the moment, so that's a little intimidating, but I'm determined to create an interesting, fulfilling life for myself."

Vanessa poured her mom some more iced tea. "Are you going to quit your teaching job?"

"No, I don't think so. Not right away anyway. I owe them a semester for my sabbatical. I wouldn't leave them, and more particularly, my students, in a lurch," Katherine stated firmly. "Besides, I love what I do at the university — I'll always be a teacher at heart. But I may try to redefine my role a little, or I might think about getting a visiting position at another university for a change. There's always Paris — I could teach there possibly."

Vanessa looked surprised. "Would you actually move to Paris?"

"It would be closer to you in Africa," Katherine teased. "I'm not rushing into anything. But it's on my list of dreams, so maybe. I'm trying to imagine all the possibilities."

"I'm proud of you, Mom."

"Thanks, honey. I'm proud of me, too."

Katherine waited until Vanessa said goodnight and closed her bedroom door. She crept quietly back out to the patio, feeling a little like a teenager sneaking out in the middle of the night to meet her boyfriend. The phone barely rang before Jeff picked up.

"Hey, how's it going with Vanessa?"

"It's going great. I'm going to miss her when she leaves in February," Katherine said, her voice tinged with sadness. "We've always been close. I think these last few months we've gotten closer as adults. Always mother and daughter, but now we're better…" Even though Jeff couldn't see her, she made air quotes. "Friends? Does that make sense?" Katherine settled back into the chaise lounge and admired the millions of stars overhead.

"It does." She heard Jeff open the refrigerator and then the pop top of a beer. "I'm looking forward to that day with Chelsea — if it ever comes."

"It'll come. She's a teenager now. I think Vanessa hated me from the day she turned thirteen until she was twenty-two. We had our good days for sure, but all those tears when I wouldn't let her wear a shirt that showed her belly button to school." Katherine chuckled. "She was sure I was ruining her life."

"I've heard that already." Jeff laughed. "I 'ruined her life' when I vetoed the tongue piercing. When I wouldn't let her go to a boy/girl party when she was thirteen — at a friend's house whose parents were going to be out of town." Jeff snorted. "Does she think that I was never a thirteen-year-old boy? I know what was on my mind."

"I don't miss that teenage drama. But I miss the moments of sweetness — when she asked me — just me — to go prom dress shopping with her." She laughed. "Although as I think about it, it was kind of a back-handed compliment. She told me that for an 'older woman' I had good taste."

Katherine and Jeff both were quiet for a moment.

Jeff broke the comfortable silence. "Well, I think you have great taste. You're hanging out with me, aren't you?"

"You always make me smile. I don't think I've smiled as much in a long, long time. Since I've been 'hanging out with' you, my cheeks are tired from smiling." Katherine paused. "Thank you."

"Thank you for what?" Jeff asked.

"Thank you for helping me find my smile again. And for finding me interesting and smart and talking to me until all hours of the night." She caught her breath. "And for kissing me. And for making me feel things that I haven't felt in a long time."

"Believe me when I say, it's my pleasure," Jeff murmured. "Speaking of pleasure, how long is Vanessa staying?"

Katherine purred, "She has to go back the day after tomorrow, Tuesday. Two more days."

"That long," Jeff groaned. "I mean, that's great." He whispered, "What are you doing Tuesday night?"

"I was hoping for some more pleasure...with you."

"I'll be counting the hours."

# Chapter Fifty-Six

Katherine checked the outside lights for the hundredth time. They were still on from the last time she checked five minutes ago.

"They should have been here by now," she fretted.

"Stop worrying," Jeff soothed her. "Vanessa texted when she and Curt collected them at the Baltimore airport. It's an almost three-hour drive from there on a good day and since it's the day before Thanksgiving, it will probably be longer."

"Yes, I know. But it's been three and a half hours," Katherine muttered anxiously.

"Vanessa said they may have to stop to let Lucas stretch his legs since he was sitting so long on the plane even if it was a direct flight from Atlanta. All that time in his car seat has to be tough on the little guy," Jeff consoled her. "Come here." He held out his arms. Katherine went into them willingly and marveled again at how good he felt. She nestled deeper and buried her nose in his neck. "Why are you anxious?"

"I'm glad you met Vanessa and Curt last month when they came for the weekend. They accepted you fine. I wish I weren't nervous about how Anthony is going to react to you. Even though he's resigned to the fact that his dad and I are not together, he can't think about his mother dating. Or worse yet, kissing!" Katherine disengaged from Jeff and started to pace. "I can't even imagine what he would think if he knew we were sleeping together."

Jeff grabbed her on her next pass and pulled her close. He nibbled on her neck, working his way up to her ear, a particularly sensitive part that always made her want more. She lifted her lips to his. He teased her with a soft kiss and then ran his tongue along her lips, pressing his lean body against her. She ran her hands down his back, melding her body to his. He pushed back on her gently and rested his forehead on top of her head. "You keep doing that and we'll both be embarrassed when they show up."

Katherine giggled. "Wouldn't that frost Anthony's cake?"

"We might not want to beard the lion so directly," Jeff deadpanned. "Let's give him a chance to like me before he decks me for messing with his mother."

"It did take me a while to warm up to you." Katherine stepped back. "But you're probably right. We should be a little more circumspect. Are you okay with not staying here tonight? Your toothbrush is missing in the bathroom."

"I'd much rather be staying with you, but I don't think we should push it. And besides, I've got a lot to do before Thanksgiving dinner tomorrow. I'll be up very early." Jeff nuzzled her neck and pulled her closer.

Car lights flashed across the living room ceiling. Jeff and Katherine sprang apart, and Katherine rushed to open the door. "They're here!"

"I'm happy to see you all." Katherine smiled from ear to ear as she first hugged Vanessa and then turned to release Lucas from his car seat. "Come to Gamma, you sweet thing! I bet you're tired of sitting in that car seat." Lucas grinned a toothy smile, showing off his two front teeth.

"Hang on, Mom. Let me have a hug first and then I'll take him out." Hugging his mom, he spotted the guy standing behind her and scowled. "And you are?"

"Anthony, this is Jeff. I've told you about him. I'm renting this house from him and he's cooking Thanksgiving dinner for us tomorrow." Jeff held out his hand. Anthony, dressed in khakis and a blue dress shirt, took in Jeff's jeans, the Rolling Stones T-shirt, and the ponytail, hesitated and then gave his hand a brief shake.

"Katherine, it's good to see you," Sonja interjected. "Let's get this boy out of his seat and take him inside so he can walk around."

"He's walking now?" Katherine exclaimed as she gave Sonja a hug.

"He's starting. He mostly cruises around the furniture," Sonja replied. "But he's getting faster every day."

"We've got the baby fence all set up in the living room like you asked." The baby gates were designed to keep Lucas away from the fireplace and out of the kitchen while providing him with a total "yes" environment. Katherine had done that with Vanessa and Anthony when they were babies so she didn't have to constantly tell them "no." As long as they were in the safe zone, they could do anything they wanted.

Sonja smiled gratefully. "Thank you. We can keep him corralled."

Katherine hugged Curt. "Hey, Curt, good to see you again. Thanks for renting the van so you could all come together. How was the drive?"

"Not a problem. Traffic was light once we got across the Bay Bridge in Annapolis," Curt explained. "That bridge is always a nightmare on holidays and in the summer."

"Can I give you a hand with the luggage?" Jeff asked.

"I've got it," said Anthony, not very graciously. Sonja gave him a look as if to say behave yourself. "Sure. That would be great."

"Jeff, Anthony and family are in the bedroom next to me. Curt and Vanessa are in the one I use as my office. No work for me while you guys are here," Katherine instructed.

Sonja stepped over the baby fence and sank down on the sofa. "Why is flying so hard? Especially with a baby! Thank god, we had a direct flight. Lucas slept for a few minutes, but he was mostly too busy entertaining our seatmate by grabbing everything he could reach off her tray table."

"Okay, it's your turn to relax. I've got the baby for a while," Katherine crawled around the floor with Lucas, watching as he explored his new environment. Everything was fascinating to him. She rescued a ceramic coaster from him. *Not completely babyproofed I see. I missed that.* She looked around the room for another other potential hazards.

Lucas cruised along the sofa, made the transition to the loveseat, and plopped down by the basket of board books. One more benefit Katherine got from Browseabout since she started working there — although with as much as she spent on books, they should have paid her in books. He grabbed *Goodnight Moon*, crawled over to Katherine, and clambered into her lap. "Boo."

"Boo to you, too," Katherine replied.

"That's 'book' — his favorite word, and his only word so far," Sonja laughed. "He wants you to read it to him. But I'll warn you — he'll want you to read it to him over and over. We sometimes have to hide that book so he'll ask to read a different one. There's a limit on how many times you can read 'goodnight to the old lady whispering hush.'"

"Got it." Katherine settled Lucas and opened the book.

"Before I start this, would you like some wine? And some cheese and crackers?"

Vanessa and Sonja both murmured their interest.

"Jeff, would you open the wine and set out those platters we made earlier?" Katherine called as Jeff came into the room, followed by Anthony and Curt.

"Would you like some wine?" Jeff looked at the two men. "We have a chardonnay and a merlot."

Anthony stared at Jeff and then at his mom, clearly bothered by Jeff's familiarity with his mom's kitchen and wine selection.

"I'd like the merlot," Curt responded. "I'll help you."

Anthony stepped over the baby fence and sat down next to Sonja. "I'll have the chardonnay."

"Sonja? Vanessa?" Jeff asked.

"Chardonnay for me," Sonja replied.

"Me, too," Vanessa took a seat on the loveseat and patted the cushion next to her for Curt. "I wasn't even driving and I'm stressed out."

"You know what I want." Katherine smiled.

Anthony's eyebrows shot up to his hairline. Katherine watched Sonja give him a warning pat on his leg, and a look suggesting he should calm down.

Jeff and Curt delivered the wine and cheese platters. For a moment, the only sound was Katherine reading to Lucas. "Goodnight, mittens. Goodnight, kittens."

Jeff sat down on the floor with Katherine. "I read that book to my daughter all the time."

"You have a daughter? How old is she? Are you married?" Anthony began his cross-examination.

"Anthony!" Katherine exclaimed crossly. "What are you doing?"

"Just trying to get to know your friend."

"It's okay, Katherine." Jeff turned to Anthony. "I'm divorced — I have been for ten years. My daughter is sixteen. She lives in Wilmington with her mother and stepfather. She spends some holidays with me and usually spends all summer with me except last summer when she took college classes at the community college. She spent last August with me, working in the restaurant. I go see her in Wilmington almost every Monday." Almost as an afterthought, he added. "And she and your mother have enjoyed getting to know each other. We've had lunch and dinners together many times."

Anthony checked with his mother to see if this was true. Katherine nodded without hesitation.

Jeff continued calmly. "I'm financially stable. I own several restaurants and this house. Your mother and I are good friends, very good friends, and possibly moving toward more than friends, but that's up to your mother."

Anthony blustered, "Of course it's up to Mom. I was surprised about to learn about your daughter."

Jeff unconsciously tugged on his ponytail, a habit that Katherine recognized as a sign of irritation. "You'll meet her tomorrow. Her mom is bringing her down in the morning. That is, if you're still coming to dinner?"

Katherine watched the two alpha men. Fluffing their feathers to appear bigger. Broadening their stance to look more intimidating. *Who was going to rule the roost? This is silly.*

"Okay, you two banty roosters. There's more than enough testosterone in the room. We're all going to have hairy chests at this rate," Katherine scolded.

"Anthony, I think this baby is getting sleepy." She gathered the tired baby in for a hug. "I set up the porta crib in your room. I borrowed the bath stuff from another grandmother and that's in your bathroom."

Anthony picked up the drooping baby and nodded to his mother. "Thanks."

"Vanessa and Curt, you can help me set out the rest of the food. We'll eat dinner after Lucas is in bed."

"And that's my cue to take off. I've still got a lot to do before you all come over for dinner tomorrow." Jeff rose and held out a hand to Katherine. "Walk me to the door?"

"I'm sorry about that," Jeff murmured. "I know Anthony is being protective of you. I shouldn't have responded to him like that."

"No, I'm sorry he behaved that way." Katherine shook her head. "I'll talk to him."

"Let's see how it goes tomorrow. Enjoy your time with your family. I'll see you tomorrow." Jeff lightly kissed her lips.

Katherine pulled him in. "Something more than very good friends, huh?"

"Only if you want to."

Katherine kissed him. "I already want to."

Katherine whispered, "I miss you."

"I miss you, too," Jeff whispered back. "I like sleeping with you. Not that we do that much sleeping. I like having you wrap yourself around me. Why are we whispering?"

Katherine laughed softly. "I feel like a teenager with you — sneaking around, making phone calls with the covers over my head." She wrapped the blanket more tightly around her. The patio sheltered her from the November winds, but the air was still cool.

"You have the covers over your head when you call me?" Jeff chuckled.

"Of course not, silly. But I snuck out to the patio to call you, dragging the quilt off my bed to stay warm. I didn't want Anthony to eavesdrop. How thick are the walls between the bedrooms?" She glanced at the patio door checking to see if Anthony had followed her.

"I don't know. I've never had to worry about that."

"I don't know why I'm so anxious." She paused. "Good grief. I'm a grown woman. I'm not embarrassed by us. I'm not going to let Anthony dictate how I live my life."

"It's going to be okay. How many people don't like me once they know me?" Jeff laughed. "He'll fall for my charm. Or he'll fall for my turkey and dressing."

"Do you have a big enough bucket for that ego of yours?" she teased.

"It's a burden for sure," Jeff said. "But I'm man enough to do it."

"I would say — you're enough of a man for me."

# Chapter Fifty-Seven

Jeff surveyed the restaurant with satisfaction. After closing last night, Tim and Jerry helped him push the tables together to make a small square. It wasn't ideal, but everyone would have at least three or four people to talk to, especially if he put the highchairs in the middle of two of the sides. The babies didn't need to talk to anyone besides mom and dad.

The tables were draped with long white tablecloths. In the center of the square, a low wooden tray rested on a burlap square. The tray was filled with a mix of orange and white pumpkins, artichokes, cabbage "roses" in purple and white, surrounded by green and white gooseneck gourds set off by Bosc pears and Pink Lady apples. The spaces between the produce were filled with yellow and rust chrysanthemums and short sheaves of wheat. Small votive candles were scattered randomly around the centerpiece. Jeff admired how it filled in the space but didn't obstruct anyone's view across the table. He hated centerpieces where he had to bob and weave to see who was seated across from him.

Aromas drifting from the kitchen tickled his nose. His stomach growled—there had been no time for lunch today. He needed some kind of snack before everyone showed up at five o'clock. Tim was rumbling around in the kitchen tending the turkeys which had been on since early this morning. Maybe he had something Jeff could snack on.

Tim was the only one in the kitchen. The rest of the staff was home enjoying their own Thanksgiving dinners. Jeff always closed the restaurant on Thanksgiving so his staff could enjoy dinner with their families. Jeff insisted that Tim join them for dinner in return for helping with the cooking. He didn't want Tim to work on Thanksgiving, but Tim assured him cooking Thanksgiving dinner was not work if he was cooking for friends. It was like cooking for his family and since he wasn't going home this Thanksgiving, this was his 'family' dinner.

Roger, his bartender friend from the Back Porch, was in the same boat. He wasn't making the trip to Charlevoix, Michigan, his hometown, to see his family, so he agreed to tend the bar. Jeff was puzzled over Roger's interrogation about the guest list. He noticed that Roger lit up when he mentioned that Brittany would be here.

"It smells great in here!" Jeff exclaimed. "I need something to eat."

"How about a little mac and cheese? We always serve that at my house," Tim said. "There's a little extra I couldn't fit into the casserole dish I put in the oven. It's already cooked — I wanted to brown the top a bit."

"That sounds perfect. I don't want to eat too much because I know what's coming. I need something to take the edge off."

"What time are people showing up?"

"I expect them about 5:00, but a couple will be coming early to warm up what they're bringing. Cassandra is bringing

Penny's 'world class cornbread stuffing' — her words, not mine. She told me that we would be glad that she wasn't cooking. And Brittany is bringing roasted cauliflower with parmesan and panko crumble. Their casseroles need to go into the oven to reheat."

"Yum. I think we'll have plenty of food. You've made enough mashed potatoes to feed an army. And we have sweet potato casserole along with creamed pearl onions and the absolutely necessary green bean casserole. And don't forget about all the appetizers that Katherine is bringing."

"Right. She'll be here early, too, so she can set that up."

Tim scooped up a large bowl of mac and cheese and put it in front of Jeff. "How did it go last night? Meeting her son?"

Jeff tucked into the bowl with enthusiasm. "We got into it a bit — I didn't like the way he was grilling me. All the time we were bringing in the luggage, he was quizzing me about my background, where I went to school, my businesses. He all but asked me for my profit and loss statement. And I didn't like the way he was implying that Katherine couldn't take care of herself or make her own decisions."

"Is it going to be awkward today?" Tim wiped the counters until they were spotless. He was a stickler for a clean kitchen.

"I hope not. Katherine stepped in and smoothed the troubled waters last night. I understand that he's protective of his mom. I appreciate that, but he doesn't get to run her life." Jeff patted his tummy. "That hit the spot. I think I can make it until dinner now."

"Where did you seat him?" Tim picked up the seating chart.

"Next to Beth who is next to Katherine. I put Chelsea between Katherine and me since they got to know each other last summer. Curt and Vanessa are on my other side. We got along fine last month when they visited."

"Well, if I see anything brewing, I'll distract him with some of my mac and cheese."

Jeff handed Tim his empty bowl. "As good as this is, that should do the trick. I'm going to change out of my work clothes. I smell like I've been cooking all morning. Do you have everything under control for a half hour?"

"No problem. I'll change after you come back."

Jeff checked the buffet table one last time before his friends arrived. All the silver chaffing dishes were ready with sterno that had to be lit as things came out of the kitchen. It was a real advantage owning the restaurants and having all the buffet equipment he needed. He even had a carving station ready for the turkeys. Allison had done a wonderful job decorating the buffet and the tables this morning — it looked more like an elegant dining room than a beach pub. The Oriental folding screens she used to block the bar created an illusion of a small private room.

Katherine and Vanessa bustled through the door laden with charcuterie and cheese platters. "Jeff, Curt is double-parked outside. Could you run out and get the other two trays?"

Tim swooped in to relieve them of the trays while Jeff sidled up to Katherine. "You look lovely!" He nuzzled her neck and stole a quick kiss. He whistled at Katherine's burnt orange dress topped with a silk jacket of oranges, browns, and tans. The not-quite-modest sweetheart neckline gave him a peek of the smooth curve of her breasts and caused his heart to beat a little faster.

"Oh, go on with you." Katherine beamed. "Go help Curt."

"Okay. Okay. But you shouldn't be tempting me looking so darn good."

Chelsea came out of the kitchen carrying a platter of crackers. "Dad, where do you want this?"

"Hey, Chelsea, you remember Katherine?"

Chelsea noticed her dad's hand on Katherine's back and looked a little surprised. "Of course. We talked about where I wanted to go to college. You pointed me to some great resources to help me decide."

"Nice to see you again, Chelsea. That's a beautiful outfit you're wearing," Katherine added. "You have quite a sense of style."

"Thanks." Chelsea raised an eyebrow. "Dad? This tray? Where does it go?"

"Right over there where Tim put the other appetizers. I'm going to run out and help bring in the rest of the stuff." He glanced at the door. "I see Brittany and Cassandra came in with their contributions. Katherine, would you show them where to put their stuff in the kitchen?"

Katherine watched Jeff leave, thinking how sexy he looked in that outfit. His black pullover accentuated his muscular back. She turned to his daughter, catching her speculative look. Katherine sidestepped Chelsea's unasked question by bringing Vanessa into the conversation. "Chelsea, this is my daughter, Vanessa. She's with the State Department. She and Curt are going to Ethiopia for a three-year assignment," Katherine continued. "Chelsea, didn't you tell me you were interested in international politics? Maybe it would be interesting to chat with Vanessa about her career."

Vanessa tugged Chelsea's arm. "Come on, let's find something to drink and chat. I love talking about my career and I'm especially interested in talking to people who are thinking about a career in international politics."

"Happy Thanksgiving!" Katherine chirped at Brittany and Cassandra. "Where's Penny?"

"Aren't you the chipper one?" Brittany teased. "Cassandra and Penny were nice enough to pick me up. Penny dropped us off and then went to park the car. This needs to be reheated." She handed Katherine a covered casserole dish. Cassandra held out Penny's dressing.

"Right this way. Tim left the ovens on so we can reheat this while we have a few appetizers. We don't want to eat too much before we get to the main event."

"Oh my god, it smells delicious in here." Brittany paused. She peeked through the kitchen door. "Is that Roger from the Back Porch? You didn't tell me he was going to be here."

"He's a friend of Jeff's and he wasn't going home to Michigan for Thanksgiving so, of course, Jeff invited him. Is there a problem?"

"No. No problem." Brittany blushed.

She unpacked her casserole from its carrying case. "Where's your son and grandbaby? I can't wait to see him in person. We've seen so many pictures of Lucas that we all kind of feel like he's our grandchild, too. Imagine that! Six grandmothers — not even counting Sonja's mom. He's one lucky kid — good thing he's not spoiled."

"No, he's not spoiled, but he sure has me wrapped around his little finger. I think I read *Goodnight Moon* ten times last night," Katherine laughed. "Tim, here are two sides that need to be reheated."

"Good. Leave them right there. Head back to the dining room. Have a drink and an appetizer or two. I'll put these in after a little bit. Don't want them to dry out. Is everyone here?"

"I saw Beth come in. And Isabella. Joyce and her husband and their new baby are going to come a little later as are my son and his family. Both families thought that limiting the time the babies are in their highchairs would be better. They'll be here after the appetizers." Katherine paused. "I think that's everyone."

Jeff hustled into the kitchen. "There you are! Everyone else is here so let's get this party started. "

When they returned to the dining room, Jeff tapped on his glass to attract the group's attention and then pulled Roger forward. "Everyone, this is Roger, the world class bartender and sommelier from the Back Porch. He's agreed to help us out today in exchange for dinner." Jeff tapped Roger. "Over to you."

"Hi y'all. Happy Thanksgiving! I know most of you, but for those I don't know very well yet," he looked directly at Brittany, "I look forward to spending more time with you."

He took his place behind the mobile bar. "For your beverage pleasure today, we have red, white, or rosé wine, Isabella's seasonal and regular beers, soft drinks, and water. Step right up and let me know what you'd like. I also see some fantastic appetizers over there that Katherine brought in. Who's first?"

Katherine cut in. "Just be warned that Jeff and Tim have been cooking all night and all morning. And I saw the dishes that Cassandra and Brittany brought in. Pace yourselves."

As the rest of the folks mingled and munched, Tim and Jeff started bringing out dinner.

"Dad, can I help?" Chelsea joined them in the kitchen.

"Of course, would you take this bread platter out? Isabella made these delicious dinner rolls. I know. I sampled one earlier today."

Soon the buffet was groaning with fried onion topped green bean casserole, sweet potato casserole, a mountain of mashed potatoes, Brittany's cauliflower dish, and Penny's cornbread stuffing. Jeff provided his famous dressing with figs and apples. Tim finished off the spread with the creamed pearl onions.

"Wait, don't forget Mom's famous cranberry and orange sauce." Chelsea rushed back to the kitchen.

"No way. I love how we've all brought something that represents each family's favorite," Jeff replied, placing the cranberry sauce where it couldn't be missed.

As Tim was bringing the first turkey to the carving station, Anthony, Sonja, and Lucas came in followed closely by Joyce, her husband, Will, and their seven-month-old daughter, Sarah.

Katherine rushed to take Lucas. "Hey, honey. How was your nap?" She smiled at Anthony and Sonja. "Did he go down okay?"

"He did—he took a long nap. Gave us time to relax, too, which we badly needed," Sonja said, looking pointedly at Anthony. "Some of us in particular needed to cool down and put things in perspective." Sonja took Lucas back and wandered over to talk to Vanessa.

"I'm sorry, Mom. I should have been nicer to Jeff last night. You know I just want you to be happy."

"I know that, Anthony. And I love you for caring so much. But I let your father run my life for too long so I'm going to run it now. I may make some mistakes, but they'll be my mistakes which I'll learn from. I got a good lesson with Richard, thank heavens, before he could do any real damage."

Anthony started to interrupt.

"I don't think Jeff is a mistake. And we're taking it slow. He's good for me. He doesn't crowd me. He's been very supportive over the last few months."

Anthony shook his head in bewilderment. "He doesn't look like your type. He's got tattoos and a ponytail, for god's sake. He's nothing like Dad."

"Thank heavens for that," Katherine stole a look at Jeff and smiled. He was dressed up today – black long-sleeved collared pullover with black tailored chinos. "I'll admit I judged Jeff by the way he looked at first. And he was also under stress when I first met him — understaffed, opening another restaurant. He wasn't his best self. But as I got to know him, I found out what a sensitive and smart and loving guy he is."

"Where do you think it's going?" Anthony looked at Jeff and shook his head. "I'll take your word on that."

"I don't know. We've been having a great time this fall. And I like being with him. We talk all the time. And laugh? He makes me laugh every day," Katherine said.

Anthony brows creased with concern. "You're only here for a short time. Isn't it risky to get involved with someone?"

"I know I have to go back to D.C. in January for next semester. I don't know what the future will bring. And I'm being careful not to lose myself now that I've found her again."

Puzzled, Anthony lifted an eyebrow. "What do you mean — 'lose' yourself? I always thought you were the most put-together person I knew."

"Thanks, Anthony. But sometimes the outer person isn't the same as the inner person. It wasn't completely a mask — more like a role that I played and wanted to play. And I don't think I even realized how much I was letting your father dictate our lives. I was content. I was happy taking care of you and Vanessa. I liked our life." She paused. "But when your father asked for the divorce, I realized there were parts of me that had been buried. It took me a while but now I view this as an opportunity to go back to who I was before, and move forward toward who I want to be now and in the future. It's scary."

Anthony put his arms around his mom. "I do want you to be happy. And if Jeff is part of that happiness, I'll try to do better in accepting him."

"Thanks, Anthony. That's all I'm asking — that you try — and that you trust me to know what's good for me."

Jeff called the group back to the center of the room. Conversations dwindled and all eyes focused on him. "Chelsea, come join me." He put his arm around her. "And Katherine, would you come here, too?"

She glanced at Vanessa and Anthony who both nodded. She smiled at Chelsea who smiled back. Jeff took her hand when she reached his side.

"I'm going to say a few words and then we'll dig into dinner." He yelled into the kitchen, "Tim, come out here!"

Tim rushed out, untying his apron, and took his place in the crowd.

"'The family we choose' — I read that was one way to define 'friend.' I'm thankful for each and every one of you, my family, Chelsea, and you, my friends. I'm grateful to have you in my life." Jeff hugged Chelsea and squeezed Katherine's hand.

"George Bernard Shaw once wrote, 'There is no love sincerer than the love of food,'" he continued. "As a restaurateur, I'm glad people love food." Everyone laughed. "I'm so grateful we could be together today to share this good food with good friends."

Katherine said, "Think back to the first Thanksgiving — the Pilgrims survived very trying times — and celebrated the first harvest as a tribute to their strength and persistence. It has been a trying year for some of us."

She glanced at Vanessa and Anthony. "And it's been a joyful year with the addition of Lucas and Curt. As we each look back on this year, I hope your gratitude list is long, that you have many reasons to be thankful this year."

Chelsea piped up. "I, for one, am grateful to have all this great food to eat. When are we going to start?"

As everyone laughed, Anthony stepped forward. "I'm

grateful for the warm welcome we've received from you all and I'm looking forward to getting to know you all better." He nodded to Jeff. "And now I'm with Chelsea, let's eat!"

# Chapter Fifty-Eight

The conference room at the Rehoboth Convention Center was packed. When JoAnn Winters, the president of the Chamber of Commerce, asked the Savvys to do a panel on starting a business, she told them there might be a small audience since it was three weeks before Christmas. But this was standing room only and the facilities people were quickly adding more chairs in the back of the room. Since Beth, Isabella, and Cassandra were well known in the community and active with the Chamber, they attracted a big crowd. Katherine quickly counted the chairs and rows and came up with about seventy-five people! No one realized that this topic would be so popular.

Michelle rushed in and joined the group on the riser in the front of the room. "Sorry I'm late. I was signing a contract on a warehouse for a new business."

Cassandra took in Michelle's daffodil yellow dotted jacquard knit jacket over a solid yellow pencil skirt. "How do you always look perfect even when you're rushing around? Not a hair out of place. Everything coordinated. Even your shoes are perfect." She looked down at her own black jeans and red sweater. "Could you come dress me some morning? I want to look as good as you."

Michelle laughed. "You would have a hard time riding a bicycle in this getup. I think you look great the way you are."

Katherine put up her hand. "How about me? I don't have to ride a bicycle so I want to look like you."

"Would you look at this crowd?" Isabella twisted a curl around and around her finger. "I don't think I can do this."

"You'll be fine," Beth assured her. "You've been an amazing success and they want to hear how you did it. Just be yourself."

Isabella didn't look convinced. "Yeah, but my success is with my brewery. Unless all these people are starting their own breweries. And I hope not! I'm not sure how my story can help them."

"If all these people are starting breweries, we're going to be in trouble." Cassandra patted Isabella's arm. "Your story is important. Remember how you felt when you got started? Remember how uncertain and vulnerable you were? That's what they're feeling right now. You can help them have more confidence and believe they can do it, too."

"It looks like we're getting ready to start." Katherine took a seat at the table. "I'm glad we each have a microphone. We won't have to pass it back and forth."

The Savvys sat in the order they would be giving their remarks. Isabella fidgeted in her chair. Michelle offered her a butterscotch life saver to calm her down. Stella held out her hand for one, too.

President Winters tapped her microphone to get everyone's attention. "Hello. Could everyone please take a seat? So we can see how many more chairs we need? If you don't have a seat yet, just hang on." She looked around the room. "Okay, good, I think we've got everyone taken care of now."

JoAnn put on her reading glasses and studied her notes. She smiled broadly. "I want to thank you all for coming to our panel on starting your own business. From the looks of the crowd, I would say there are a lot of you thinking about starting your own business." Scattered applause and a few calls of "You've got that right" filled the room.

Her voice grew more animated as she warmed to the topic. "Small businesses are very important in our state. We currently have almost 28,000 small businesses. Last year, small businesses generated almost $14 billion in wages and made up almost 60% of the state's workforce. The Chamber of Commerce is committed to supporting small businesses in several ways—education, resources, mentoring, networking, promoting. Please be sure to pick up one of our brochures in the back of the room so you can see all the ways we can help you succeed."

She waited while some latecomers looked for seats. "There are a couple of chairs up here in the front row. It's not like church where you want to sit in the back so you can nap."

The group chuckled and the back row looked sheepish. "We took our naps early so we could pay attention tonight," someone called out.

"I'm pleased to introduce our panel for tonight." JoAnn gestured to the table of women. "Beth Standish from Browseabout Books is going to talk about working with the Chamber as well as some of the other organizations who provide small business assistance." Beth waved to the crowd. "She's also going to talk about how this group of women got together and why they're called *The Savvys*."

JoAnn flipped to the next note card. "A relative newcomer to our community — she's been here seven months and unfortunately, she'll only be here another month unless we can persuade her to stay." She looked pointedly at Jeff. "Katherine

Lewis will walk us through a successful business plan. She's been involved with reviewing plans at a Washington D.C. incubator for several years. She knows what works. And what doesn't." Katherine smiled and nodded.

"Cassandra Stonehill hardly needs an introduction. Her business, Bikes for Life, was featured as one of our success stories, and she was honored as our Entrepreneur of the Year a couple of years ago." Cassandra blushed as red as her sweater and looked down at her notebook. "She is going to talk about finding your target market and differentiating your business."

"I'm sure most of you have visited the Gallina Azul Brewery?" Appreciative murmurs went around the room. "Isabella Ramirez is the founder of the brewery. She's built a very successful business and is one of the few Latina-owned breweries in the state, maybe even the country."

"Did you bring any samples?" a guy in the back row called.

Isabella laughed. "No, but if you stick it out to the end, I'll be handing out discount coupons on your next beer."

Michelle teased. "Hey, not fair. I don't have any coupons for properties." Isabella shrugged and winked at the audience. She seemed to have forgotten her nerves.

JoAnn continued her introduction. "Isabella is going to talk about permits and licenses you might need. She's also going to talk about staffing and managing your growth." Isabella raised her hands high in a "Raise the Roof" pose.

"Another relative newcomer — Brittany Spencer. She moved here from Wilmington about two years ago when she decided she'd had enough of the big corporate world. She was a partner in the largest advertising firm in Wilmington—her specialty was creating strategic advertising plans." Brittany waved to the crowd. "She's going to talk about telling your story so your customers can find you."

JoAnn pointed to the next woman on the riser. "You have

no doubt seen Michelle's billboards coming into Rehoboth. Michelle Schneider is one of our most successful real estate agents. She works with both residential and commercial clients. Location, location, location! Michelle is going to share her experience in finding the right location for your business." Michelle rose slightly and flashed her beautiful smile.

"Last, and certainly not the least, is Stella Norton. She is a vice president at the bank in charge of small business loans. She's going to talk with us about securing funding for your plans — from the bank and other sources. Let's give them a warm round of applause." JoAnn led the enthusiastic applause.

Beth turned on her microphone. "Thank you, JoAnn, and thank all of you for coming out tonight. We're a little overwhelmed by the turnout and very appreciative of your interest. We're going to spend the next fifty minutes talking with you, sharing our experiences, and hopefully, helping you not make the mistakes we've made. Because we *have* made mistakes. But thanks to our mentors, we were able to learn and grow."

Each member of the Savvys spoke for about seven minutes. As Beth started her talk, she passed out stacks of notecards and instructed the audience to jot down their questions as they came to them. At the end of evening, she asked the audience to add their email addresses to the cards and hand in their questions if they hadn't been answered. She promised that they would respond with the answers as soon as possible.

President Winters finally closed the meeting after two hours even though there were still people lingering to talk to the Savvys. She shooed the last ones out and closed the door.

Turning to the Savvys, she said, "That was great! I don't think I've seen that much interest in our meetings since we had the free happy hour when we opened the convention center."

Beth said, "I counted — we have fifty-four notecards here.

Questions we didn't answer. I'm going to take them home and see if I can see any patterns or common areas. Maybe we could answer them individually and also publish some Frequently Asked Questions on the Chamber's website."

"What a great idea," JoAnn gushed. She made a note in her planner to follow up with their web designer.

"I got a bunch of requests to review business plans — maybe fifteen or twenty," Katherine said.

"Oh, dear. Do you have time to do that?" JoAnn fretted. "I didn't intend for that to happen."

"It's okay. I can take a look at them," Katherine assured her. "If they're interested, and it makes sense after I read them, I may see if they want to meet as a group so I can give them overall feedback as well as specific feedback on their plans."

"I can help," Stella added. "That's part of what I do at the bank, too."

"Good. Let's set up some time to go over them together." Katherine pulled up her calendar. "I could meet Thursday after the bank closes." Stella checked her calendar and nodded.

"We seem to have struck a nerve here," Michelle chimed in. "I think we could help people realize their dream of owning their own business."

"You created some real momentum here," JoAnn replied. "Let's talk about how we can keep this ball rolling."

# Chapter Fifty-Nine

Katherine waved to Beth as she came in the café door. Beth dropped her umbrella in the stand by the door and shook her gray curls a little to get out the sneaky raindrops that came up under her umbrella.

"The rain is coming in every direction — down, sideways, up! I'm not sure the umbrella did much good," Beth commented. "This is what our early December weather is always like — we have cold rain. At least it's warm and toasty here. Have you ordered yet?"

Katherine shook her head. "No, I just got here, too. I'm trying to thaw my toes. That wind is bitter." She wrapped her sweater more closely around her. "I think I'm going to have hot tea and butternut squash soup. It feels like that kind of day."

Beth examined Katherine more closely. "That sounds good. But tell me what's going on? When you called me, it sounded like you have something on your mind that's troubling you." She paused. "You're not sick, are you? You're looking a little peaked. Are you feeling okay? Are you getting enough sleep? You've got dark circles under your eyes."

Katherine sighed. "I thought I did a better job with my makeup but clearly you saw right through it." She stopped and looked out the window at the blowing rain. The gloomy weather matched her mood. "Physically, I feel fine, but I haven't been sleeping well the last few nights."

The waiter interrupted her. "What would you like?" They both ordered hot tea and butternut squash soup along with a loaf of the homemade quinoa bread. It was one of the café's specialties.

"Why haven't you been sleeping?" Beth quizzed Katherine.

Katherine looked away. "It's Jeff. I don't know what to do with him."

"What do you mean, you 'don't know what to do with him'? I thought you guys were getting along great. At the Thanksgiving dinner, you looked pretty happy. And the way he was looking at you...well, I'd give a lot to have someone look at me that way." Beth nodded to the waiter when he dropped off their tea. "Could I have some lemon, please?"

Katherine desolately stirred her tea. "That's just it. We are getting along great. You know we've been spending time together. And I enjoy him. A lot."

She picked up her cup in both hands, trying to warm her hands. "He is so supportive of me. And not controlling. He occasionally gets a little overprotective which irritates me to no end, but when he realizes what he's doing, he apologizes and backs off."

Beth dipped her bread in the soup. "Jeff tries to parent and nurture everyone. I've had to tell him that I'm a grown-up a time or two. He gets very involved with the people he cares about and wants to make sure they're happy, if he has anything to do with it."

Katherine sipped her tea and grimaced. "I forgot to put

honey in my tea." She frowned. "It's not like me to be so distracted. It's all Jeff's fault."

Beth laughed. "How can that be Jeff's fault?"

"I think about him all day long. And I can't sleep at night because I'm worried about how much I care about him." Katherine nibbled on the bread crust and stirred her soup again.

"That's going to be cold if you don't start eating it." Beth referred to Katherine's soup. "You look like you've lost more weight. Eat some soup," she commanded. She waited until Katherine had taken a couple of bites. "Why is caring about Jeff a problem?"

"For one thing, I'm not officially divorced yet. And I won't be for a few months."

"Do you have any intentions to reconcile with Stan?" Beth asked pointedly. She emptied the tea pot into her cup and reached for another lemon.

"Heavens no!" Katherine said emphatically. "I have absolutely no interest in getting back together with Stan. That ship has sailed completely." She picked at the seeds on her piece of bread, piling them into a neat pile next to her plate.

"Okay, what else?" Beth asked as she scraped the bottom of her soup bowl.

"I head back to D.C. next month. And Jeff has to be here. I have to be there. I don't see how a long-distance relationship would work," Katherine moaned. "It's hopeless."

Beth raised both eyebrows. "Nothing is hopeless unless you don't want to try to make it work." She looked Katherine in the eye. "Is he worth it? How much do you care for him? How does he feel about you?"

Katherine put her head in her hands and mumbled, "He says he loves me."

"Pardon? I couldn't hear you." Beth leaned in.

"I said, he says he loves me." Katherine's voice bounced off the walls. Everyone in the café got quiet.

A voice in the back said, "Love is all you need, hon. You're lucky if you've got love."

Katherine, embarrassed, ducked her head and ate a spoonful of soup. "And I think I love him, too. But I'm scared."

Beth sat back. "I've known Jeff a long time. He's one of my very best friends. In all the years since he's been divorced, he has never said those words to anyone he's dated." She stopped. "What are you scared about?"

Katherine whispered, "I'm scared that I'm no good at relationships." Absentmindedly, she pushed the bread seeds on to the floor. "Look at Stan. I thought I was marrying him for life. And look at Richard. He seemed like a nice guy on the surface and then I find out he was trying to scam me."

Beth took Katherine's hands. "Look at me. Jeff is no Stan and he's definitely not a Richard. He's a good, decent guy, one you can trust."

"That's just it. I trust *him*, but I'm not sure I can trust myself yet. I know I've gotten stronger and more confident over the past few months. You and the other Savvys have helped me so much with your friendship and support." Katherine tried another bite of soup and grimaced. Beth was right — it was cold. "Maybe I'm feeling so vulnerable because I have to leave here and go back to D.C. I like the life I've built here. I love being with you and the rest of the gang. I don't think I've ever had such a great group of friends. You took me under your wing the first week I got here. Whenever I was feeling low, you all picked me right up."

"That's what friends are for. We're with you in the good times and bad." Beth patted Katherine's arm. "And you know we're still going to be your friends when you go back to D.C."

Katherine teared up. "How did I get so lucky?"

"Would you like me to clear your bowls?" the waiter asked.

"Way to break the mood," Katherine muttered.

Beth laughed. "Yes, you can clear the table. Put her soup in a to-go container so she can reheat it later. And could I please have another pot of hot water for more tea?"

The waiter made quick work of the table. "Back to Jeff. What do you want to happen with him?" Beth asked.

"I don't want to lose him." Katherine smiled softly. "We're good together. I love spending time with him. We talk all the time. He makes me laugh. He's tender and loving. He's funny and thoughtful—"

Beth interrupted. "That sounds like you're in love."

"But how's it going to work if we're in two different locations?" Katherine whined.

"I don't know," Beth said. "But I do know that you won't figure it out if you don't try. Let yourself be open to see where this is going. You're both smart people. See if there's a way to make it work."

"You're right," Katherine mused. "I need to trust myself and see what happens."

Katherine sat quietly on the screened back porch overlooking the little pool and the fountain. The fountain was turned off for the season, but the solar lights still illuminated the chrysanthemums and the struggling-to-hang-on roses. Against the chilly December air, Katherine tucked her feet under the knitted blue and green throw that Brittany gave her last week — an early Christmas and going-away present for when she had to go back home next semester.

Katherine stared at the throw. Brittany knew she had to go back. Beth knew she had to go back. She knew she had to go back. Katherine sighed. *I'm afraid that Jeff doesn't know it, or he's hoping that I don't have to. But I do.*

She turned and looked back into the softly lit, warm living room. So many memories. She marveled at how this place felt so much like home after seven months. She laughed out loud at the board game nights with the "girls" — who knew quiet Cassandra was that competitive? She chortled when she could pass a Draw Four card in Uno.

And the other nights of quiet conversation. She felt closer to these women than she had to any other group of friends. They had quickly accepted her, supported her, lifted her up when she was down. And it wasn't just one way. Katherine was glad that she could step in to help Beth at Browseabout. And they all provided support for Stella. *And baking bread together while we cleaned Stella's house was fun.*

Thanksgiving. After Anthony got over his "papa bear" manner, he and Jeff got along fine. Anthony was surprised at Jeff's financial successes with his restaurants and his investments. They swapped recommendations on great places to eat — Jeff knew most of the places Anthony named in Atlanta, but he steered him to some new ones — "If you liked that, you should try this one..." Before he left, Anthony was helping Jeff with a legal question that had plagued Jeff for a while.

This house was filled with laughter and love in a way that Katherine had not seen at the McLean house in a long time, even before Anthony and Vanessa moved out. *This is the kind of place I want to live in. I want to be in a happy home, one where people are comfortable and they want to come back, not a quiet, empty mausoleum.*

Katherine turned back to look at the darkening sky. The stars were beginning to come out. Jeff would be calling soon to see what she wanted to do tonight. He only missed the nights he went to Wilmington to see Chelsea. If Chelsea was in town, the three of them might spend one evening together. Katherine didn't want to butt in on their time together, but Chelsea seemed to enjoy their talks about writing and college. Katherine was surprised at how quickly she fit in with Chelsea and Jeff's life.

*If only this could go on forever,* Katherine fretted. *But it can't. I have to go back to Washington in January.*

*At least for a semester.* Katherine knew where that thought had come from. Beth had planted the seed that maybe there was a way. *But what was the way?* Katherine wrestled with the possibilities. Much as she cared for Jeff and much as she loved living here in Rehoboth, she was not going to rush into anything. Katherine didn't want to make another mistake. *But this doesn't feel like a mistake.* Katherine shook her head. *One step at a time.*

# Chapter Sixty

Katherine moped around the house. With a couple of weeks until Christmas, Jeff helped her decorate the tree the other night. Vanessa and Curt brought over some of Katherine's decorations from the McLean house — not the fancy designer stuff that Stan liked, but the ornaments that Katherine had collected from places they visited and that the kids had made. They laughed at the clothespin reindeer with the googly eyes that both kids made in second grade.

Vanessa told Curt about Katherine's bread dough ornaments that were so soft they crumbled when they tried to hang them. They hung the remnants anyway. Jeff insisted they have at least one strand of colored lights although Katherine was a white light person. The combination was surprisingly pretty. Katherine laughed again at Jeff's shocked face when she drew the line at flashing lights.

The house looked festive. She should have felt festive, but she was aware the clock was ticking. Only four weeks left — her sabbatical was almost over. *Where had the time gone?*

Her teaching schedule for next spring term — five courses

— was set. Two undergraduate classes and two graduate courses and one section of Business English that she taught on overload. Her syllabi were done. The bookstore had all the right materials on the shelves.

For her undergrads, she was teaching two courses she had taught for many semesters — American Literary Traditions and Creative Writing. There were multiple sections of the American Literary Traditions. The faculty coordinated to some extent to ensure they were consistent across the sections. The Creative Writing course was much more work since each student submitted several pieces of writing. But it was also much more interesting since the students brought their own unique perspectives to the topics.

The graduate seminars were very intellectually stimulating. Katherine varied the content considerably to keep it fresh for her and her students. This semester she was teaching a section on American Romance Literature: Melville, Emerson, and Dickinson, and another on Southern Literature: Antebellum Era. Both classes would keep Katherine on her toes to stay up with her students.

The Business English class wouldn't be a problem since the curriculum was prescribed by the Business School, and Katherine had been teaching it for years. *My parents would be proud of me for at least keeping a foot in the business world. They were such successful businesspeople — starting their own biotech firm in Newark, Delaware, before anyone was thinking about biotech.* Katherine knew they were disappointed when she decided to pursue her PhD in English. They thought, or hoped, that she would take over the business when they were ready to retire. She worked for the company for years, starting in high school and then summers during her whole college life, even during her doctoral program. But the company was not what excited her. She loved the academic life — the excitement of the students, the joy of teaching, getting lost in research. *Thank heavens, they finally accepted my decision.*

Katherine reflected back on Jeff's surprise when she told him she reviewed business plans both for the Business English class and for a women's business incubator. It was natural for her — she had reviewed her parents' business plan when they took their company public. And it was a good side gig when she was at Yale working on her PhD — she helped many women tighten up their business plans and successfully obtain the financing they needed to start their own businesses. There was nothing better than when one of the women she'd helped came bouncing back into the center with the news that the bank had supported her business plan and given her the funding she needed to launch her dream.

The D.C. incubator called every week to see when she was coming back to town. Katherine was looking forward to working with them again next semester.

Normally, Katherine would be anticipating the first day of the semester. Another beginning. Another opportunity to learn with her students. *So why not now?* Jeff's face flashed in front of her. *Yes, I know you're the problem. And I don't know what I'm going to do with you.*

# Chapter Sixty-One

Katherine noticed the young woman watching them. She was sitting by herself, shuffling papers, and punching numbers into her laptop, in a corner of the Christmas-decorated coffee house. At least, it had sort of a Charlie Brown Christmas tree in the corner, decked with paper coffee cups, stars made from stirrers, raw sugar packets strung as garland. Lights choreographed to the music flashed merrily and busily to Manheim Steamroller. She caught Katherine looking at her, flushed, and went back to her work.

"Earth to Katherine?" Isabella tugged at Katherine's ugly sweater. "We're supposed to be deciding who has the ugliest Christmas sweater. Yours is winning the most votes."

Katherine looked down at her red faux fur trimmed sweater, adorned with a Christmas tree shaped pear tree, outlined in tinsel and battery-powered blinking Christmas lights, decorated with a partridge, two turtle doves nesting at the top of the tree, three French hens pecking at peppermints on the bottom, and five gold rings. Two calling birds perched on each shoulder to complete the five days of Christmas.

"What? This is not ugly — it's a work of art." She grinned. "I was going to put the rest of the birds — the geese, the swans — on the back but I thought it might be uncomfortable."

Isabella looked down at her relatively tame red sweater, bearing a squirrel in a Santa hat tangled in a string of Christmas lights. "I'm definitely going to have to up my game next year if I want the trophy."

Katherine smiled at the young woman watching them wistfully. The Savvys were having a breakfast holiday party over coffee and scones at Rise Up Coffee. With Christmas just two weeks away, Beth and Cassandra could only meet very early in the morning since the local retailers had decided to open at 8:00. People were ramping up their shopping as the countdown to Christmas rushed by.

"Katherine wins the Ugly Sweater award. Here's her trophy!" Michelle handed Katherine a cracked mirror embellished with a blue ribbon. "I'm ready for presents. Anybody else?" she asked. Choruses of "me," "me, too" went around the table.

Stella said, "I'll start. I drew Isabella's name." She handed Isabella a huge gift bag overflowing with tissue paper.

"Hey, we put a dollar limit on our gifts. It looks like you went over," Isabella protested.

"No, I didn't. It's bulky stuff." Stella waved away her concerns. "Before you open it, let me tell you why you're getting these gifts."

She took Isabella's hands in hers. "You need to have more fun. You need to get out of the brewery. You work harder than anybody I know, and you've built a great business. It's time for you to enjoy your success."

"Awhh, that's not true. I have fun. I'm here with you, aren't I?" Isabella grumbled.

Stella scolded her. "Two hours a week of play isn't enough. Go ahead and open your gift."

Isabella dipped her hand into the bag and pulled out...a Slinky. And then a yoyo. Followed by a coloring book and crayons. Digging deeper she found a jump rope. Finally, she lifted out a butterfly-shaped kite with one hundred feet of string. "Ohhh, I've never had a kite before!"

Katherine saw the young woman laughing as Isabella emptied the bag.

"The guy at the Kite Loft said to stop by if you want some instructions," Stella told Isabella. "This is to get you started. At the bottom of the bag, there's a book about 101 fun things to do in Rehoboth. We're going to be quizzing you every month to see how many you've done."

Isabella let out a breath with a big whoosh. "I don't know about that. I have so much work to do."

Stella frowned. "Isabella, you know I had to confront my own mortality when I had breast cancer. I vowed that if I survived, I would live my life as fully as possible — not go crazy like bungee jumping off some cliff — but I wanted to try to have as few regrets as possible. Work will always be there — don't let it rob you of fun."

"I hear you, Stella. I love my gifts and I will try." Isabella gathered her gifts. "No, there is no try — I will have more fun."

"Brittany, this is for you." Cassandra handed Brittany a big box.

Brittany shook it and it sounded like coins rattling around. She lifted the lid and brought out a cash drawer stuffed with play paper money and real coins.

Cassandra explained, "I believe you're going to open your yarn and coffee shop. I thought you needed to learn how to count your cash." She grinned. "There's one real ten-dollar bill among all the play money. That's my first installment on all the coffee and yarn I'll be buying. And the coins were included to throw you off if you were a present shaker."

Brittany started counting the play money. "One, two, three... At this rate I'm not going to be able to pay my rent."

"Check under the tray." Cassandra stopped her. "There's a copy of the best book about managing cash flow for a small business."

"I'm next," Beth handed Cassandra a tie-sized box. "I drew your name."

Cassandra unwrapped it carefully and folded the paper neatly. She opened the box to find a scroll. She regarded Beth quizzically.

"Go ahead. Read it out loud," Beth instructed.

"This is a subscription to Raddish, a monthly cooking kit for children with easy-to-follow instructions." She giggled. "Have you been talking to Penny?"

Isabelle guffawed. "Oh man do you need that!"

"She told me that your sole cooking contribution is burned water." Unable to control her laughter, Beth continued. "She banned you from the kitchen, didn't she?"

Katherine nudged Beth, "I was happy when I heard that Penny did the Thanksgiving dressing." They all nodded knowingly having suffered through some of Cassandra's less than successful concoctions.

"Ha!" Cassandra snorted. "That's not my sole contribution. I can also burn toast."

"Raddish will take you back to the basics. And if a child can do it, I thought you should be able to learn."

"Very funny." Grinning sheepishly, Cassandra leaned over to whack Beth gently on the arm. "Seriously, I never learned how to cook as a child. This will give me the childhood I never had. Thank you. And more importantly, Penny thanks you."

"Michelle, you know we all hate you because you're always

so perfectly groomed and coordinated," Brittany teased. "Well, we don't really hate you, but I thought we should expand your wardrobe with a few new items." She handed Michelle her gift bag.

Michelle pulled out a pair of gently worn bib overalls with the Goodwill tag still attached, followed by a red and green plaid flannel shirt. To complete the ensemble, yellow, red, and blue floral garden clogs emerged next. Michelle shook her head, "Oh no, you won't catch me wearing these."

Brittany said, "Keep looking in the bag."

Michelle fished around in the bag and came out with a garden trowel and two packages of seeds — one for blue bonnets and the other for lettuce, and a twelve pack of peat pots. Finally, she found a certificate for soil from their local nursery.

"You always dress perfectly for every occasion. I thought you needed the right clothes for gardening." Brittany pointed to the seeds. "Gardening is good for you — it reduces stress and your blood pressure. You can start the seeds inside in the peat pots and then transplant them in the spring."

"I have been thinking about growing some herbs inside. Thank you." Michelle beamed at Brittany. "But you still won't see me in this hideous flannel shirt. I could be tempted by the flowery clogs however." She slipped off her boot and modeled the clogs.

"Beth, I'm sorry, but I think my gift is pretty boring compared to these." Katherine offered what looked like a Browseabout bag of books. "Similar to Stella's message to Isabella, you work so many hours you don't leave time for your own dreams. Here are some things I hope will inspire you."

Beth opened the bag and pulled out a Pinocchio-inspired children's book, *When You Wish Upon a Star*. A DVD, *The*

*Magic of Belle Isle.* And a copy of *Designing Your Life* workbook. She burst into tears.

Alarmed, Katherine said, "I'm sorry. I know they're not as funny or cool as the other gifts."

Beth wiped her nose. "No. No. They're great gifts. I feel so validated. You know I want to build my book-coaching business. These gifts show me that you believe I can do it. I'm so touched. Thank you." She started leafing through the workbook. "I've been eyeing this book for a long time. I can't wait to get started."

Michelle patted Beth's hand. "We all believe you can do it and we'll help however we can." She paused. "Stella, I drew your name. You are our Superhero."

Stella took the offered bag and peeked inside. Smiling, she pulled out her very own Wonder Woman Bracelets of Victory, followed by a Super Woman cape. At the bottom of the bag was a black sheer bag containing a Native American sun talisman on a thin leather thong.

"In Native American culture, the Sun has supernatural powers for healing and peace. It brings good luck and wards off any misfortune. I got it last summer when I visited New Mexico. I was looking for the right person to give it to. Giving it away increases its power." Michelle explained as she took the talisman out of the bag and dropped it over Stella's head.

"My turn." Isabella turned to Katherine. "I pulled your name. And I thought, what am I going to give this highly educated, professionally successful woman?" She handed Katherine a gift box.

Contrary to Cassandra's disciplined unwrapping, Katherine tore open the paper and threw it on the floor. Shaking the box, she wondered out loud, "I'm usually pretty good about guessing what my presents are, but this time, I can't figure it out."

The first thing she drew out was a huge old-fashioned hot water bottle. And then a bag of batteries. Puzzled, she turned to Isabella.

"I know that you have to go back to Washington soon so I thought the hot water bottle could keep you warm since Jeff won't be there."

Katherine flushed with embarrassment and felt the heat climb up her face.

Isabella continued, "And the batteries are for your you-know-what." Embarrassed, Katherine batted at Isabella.

Brittany whooped and clapped. "Way to end this with a bang, Isabella." She laughed. "Katherine, I didn't think anyone could blush that color."

They chatted about holiday plans for a few more minutes. Katherine noticed the young woman obviously eavesdropping. Beth finally stood up and said, "I've got to go open the store. Thank you everyone. I'm so glad we could do this. I've got a lot more holiday spirit now." With calls of "Merry Christmas" and "Happy Holidays" the group broke up and went on about their day.

Except for Katherine. She lingered until her friends were all gone, got a third cup of coffee, and approached the young woman. "Excuse me, do you mind if I join you? You looked like you wanted to speak to us, but we got involved with our holiday party. You couldn't get a word in edgewise."

"Of course!" She slid her papers to the side and closed her laptop. "I didn't want to intrude but I saw your presentation for the Chamber and I wanted to talk with you all. I'm Tammy Santos, by the way."

"Katherine Lewis. A pleasure to meet you."

Katherine studied the woman. She was not quite as young as Katherine thought initially — maybe late 30s to early 40s. Faint crinkles around the eyes gave away years of smiling. She had a ballet dancer's look — strong high cheekbones, willowy, graceful, tapered fingers, hair in a ballet bun.

Katherine indicated the papers and laptop. "You sure have been working hard while we were partying. What are you working on?"

Tammy said shyly, "My business plan." Then she rushed on. "I want to start my own Pilates studio. I've done my market research like you said and there are a few other studios — well, one real Pilates studio and some yoga and fitness centers that offer a few Pilates classes. But they don't do what I want to do."

"What sets your studio apart from the rest?"

Tammy didn't miss that Katherine said "your studio" like she believed it could be real.

Animated, Tammy said, "I've been teaching Pilates for fifteen years and I've taken increasingly specialized training to help my clients with neurological conditions, like Parkinson's Disease, Huntington's Disease, Multiple Sclerosis. Research shows that Pilates is more effective in creating increased muscle strength, especially in the lower body, better flexibility, reduced spasticity, and greatly decreases the risk of falls and injury. I've seen it help many of my clients."

She stopped. "I'm sorry. I could go on and on about this. The problem is that I can't help all the people I'd like to because there's not enough room or enough equipment at my current facility. I want to set up a studio that specializes in this kind of work."

Katherine couldn't help but be impressed with Tammy's enthusiasm and vision. "Where are you with your business plan? Have you run the numbers? Do you know how much you need in start-up costs and operating costs?"

"I've been trying to follow the outline you presented. I took pages of notes on all the Savvys." Tammy whipped out a notebook, fanning the pages so Katherine could see that in fact she had very detailed notes. "But this part is not my strength. I know Pilates. I don't know the business side."

"What's your timeline?"

"Is six months doable?" Tammy responded.

"That depends, but it's not impossible."

Katherine thought for a moment. "I have to run this by the rest of the group, but I'm pretty sure they would be on board with this. Would you be interested in being a Savvys' guinea pig? My friends, the Savvys, want to help entrepreneurs launch their businesses and help them be successful."

"Are you kidding? I would love that." Tammy frowned. "But how much would it cost? I've been saving all my money for the Pilates equipment and the space."

"One, you would be our first real client. We're learning on you. It wouldn't be right to charge you for our learning." Katherine sipped her coffee.

"Second, we've all been blessed and mentored ourselves. We want to pay it back, or pay it forward, or whichever direction that goes. Bottom line, no fee." Katherine laughed at Tammy's shocked expression.

"We would have some conditions — we'll be helping you, but you've got to do the work and you'll have to meet the deadlines we set. This is a commitment on both sides. Would you do that?" Katherine said firmly.

Eyes bright with excitement, Tammy all but shouted, "Oh yes! When can we start?"

"Here's my email address. Send me what you have, and I'll share it with the rest of the Savvys." Katherine stood up and shook Tammy's hand. "Let me know some times you have free next week — early mornings are best like this time. I'll try to set something up with at least some of the group so we can get started. Buckle your seatbelt — it's going to be a fast ride!"

# Chapter Sixty-Two

Katherine stubbed her toe as she dashed in from the patio to answer the phone.

"What are you doing? You sound out of breath like you were running." Jeff asked.

"I just came in from the backyard. We're supposed to have a frost tonight and I wanted to cover my, I mean, your rosebushes."

Jeff caught the possessive "my" and smiled. "Are you hungry? How does Grotto's pizza sound?"

"It sounds great, but I'm not dressed to go out and it'll be late by the time I cleaned up. I'll eat some popcorn or something for dinner."

Jeff chuckled. "Well, today's your lucky day. Open the front door."

"What...?" Katherine scurried to the door, quickly smoothing down her hair and tucking in her shirt. "Oh you — I look a wreck, but that pizza smells delicious so come in."

With one arm, Jeff pulled her toward him, sniffed her hair,

and nuzzled her neck. "Mmmmm — you smell even more delicious."

Katherine melted against him, molding her body to his, felt the smoldering heat that consumed her every time she saw him now. *I don't know what I'm going to do with you, but I sure do like the way you hold me.*

"Hey, you've already taken down the Christmas tree and all the decorations? It's not even New Year's Day. I always take everything down on Three Kings Day, January 6th. Why did you take it down so early? I loved celebrating Christmas with you." Jeff bombarded her with questions.

Katherine avoided his questions. "I've got some of Isabella's IPAs if that works for you. Or I could open a bottle of wine. Which do you prefer?"

Jeff backed Katherine up against the counter. "I'd prefer you."

She swatted him away. "I've been writing all day after I got back from my walk this morning. And then I was working in the garden. I haven't even taken a shower."

"I could use a shower, too. We should save water and take one together," Jeff teased.

She didn't meet his eyes. "Nope. Too hungry. Need to eat first."

Jeff waggled his eyebrows. "Well, that leaves open the possibility of a shower later."

Katherine laughed and dished up the pizza.

Pleasantly sated, they lounged by the firepit with the last of their beers. Katherine fidgeted, looking first into the fire and then at Jeff. Finally, Jeff said, "Okay. Out with it. What's going on?"

Katherine sighed. "You know my sabbatical is almost over. And I need to go back and get organized for classes. I've decided I'll go back right after New Year's. Will you prorate my rent for an extra week?"

Jeff regarded her with dismay. "Forget about the rent. I hope you see me as more than just your landlord." He frowned. "Why? Why do you have to go back? I'll even let you live here rent-free. You can keep writing. And we could keep seeing each other so we can figure out where this thing between us is going."

"Jeff, you know why I have to go back. I owe the university a semester at least for my sabbatical. And I need to get this divorce done once and for all. There are a multitude of tasks to complete with the house and the lawyers," Katherine rambled on.

Jeff inched away, stiff and unsmiling.

"And Vanessa and Curt are leaving around the end of February. We've got to clear the rest of her stuff out of the house and put it in storage somewhere since Stan and Chrissy are moving in as soon as the divorce is final. Which, by the way, is my number one priority, to be divorced. I'm so tired of Stan's shenanigans. I want it to be done."

Jeff scowled. "Isn't that why you've got that great lawyer? Isn't she supposed to be wrapping all this up? And how old is Vanessa? Can't she manage her own stuff?"

"You know you would do anything for Chelsea, and I'll do the same thing for Vanessa. This is hard on her — her father is having a baby with a woman who is a couple of years older than she is. And he's basically cleansing the whole house of everything that belongs to Vanessa and Anthony. She can hardly see straight she's so angry with her father," Katherine explained patiently.

"What about your lawyer? Can't she handle the divorce stuff?" Jeff whined.

"She can and she's doing most of it, but there are some things that I need to do in person." Katherine touched his arm. "Jeff, you know I care about you — so much more than I thought possible — but I have to do this. I have responsibilities at the university and the incubator that I can't drop."

He pulled her onto his lap. "But what about us?" He nuzzled Katherine's neck. "These last few months have been so great. How can you leave?"

Katherine moaned. "You know I can't think when you do that."

He sat up straight almost dumping Katherine on the ground. "How about this? You could stay here and commute to D.C. during the week. Go back early Tuesday morning and come back Thursday night after your classes! Didn't you tell me you had back-to-back classes on Tuesdays and Thursdays? That could work, couldn't it? Then—"

"Jeff," she interrupted. "Jeff," she said more forcefully.

He finally stopped talking. "Jeff, that is a lovely idea, but I don't just work on Tuesdays and Thursdays. I have commitments to the incubator on Monday and Wednesday evenings. And I have committee work for the department every other Friday. And faculty meetings. And department meetings." She ticked her obligations off on her fingers.

"And don't forget office hours — I'm contractually obligated to have six hours a week. And they're important to me because I learn a lot about my students when they come see me," she continued. "And none of this even considers the research I have to do. Contrary to what many people think, a faculty position is a full-time job." She tried to soften her tirade with a smile, but she was perturbed that Jeff seemed to be underestimating how hard she had to work.

He rubbed his eyes and drew Katherine back into his arms.

She sat stiffly, waiting for him to say something. "Katherine, I'm sorry. I know you have a full-time job and I know that you work hard. I'm going to miss you so much. I would do anything to get you to stay here with me. Is there an 'us' in your future?" He looked deeply into her eyes.

"I didn't expect you. And I didn't expect to fall for you. But the timing is off. I need to go back and straighten things out." She knew he was hurting and angry. But she had to do this — it was important to her.

Jeff's face hardened and his lips thinned. Angry now, Jeff said, "I'm sorry I didn't follow your timetable."

"Jeff, come on. You knew this day would come." Katherine pleaded with him to understand. "And neither one of us expected this kind of relationship at this time."

He growled, "You were clear when you told me earlier that you weren't looking for a relationship. I guess if you don't think there's a future for us that you were telling the truth. I know how important the truth is to you, Katherine. Here's some truth for you — I think you're a big ol' scaredy cat — just because Stan lied to you and hurt you, and then Richard almost tricked you with his Ponzi scheme. You're scared to make a commitment and scared to feel again."

Katherine's eyes filled with tears, but he refused to stop.

"I'll have Michelle draw up a daily and weekly rate for the house for January. You can decide when you'll leave and pay for those days. Strictly business." Jeff stormed over to grab his coat and keys.

"Jeff, don't be like this," Katherine cried. "Can't we enjoy the time I have left? What about New Year's Eve? We were going to spend it with the Savvys."

"That's not going to happen. I let myself fall for you and now you've made it clear that I was someone to pass time with until you went back to your 'real' life." He flung open the front door. Katherine could see the pain and fury in his eyes. He cast one final, angry look before slamming the front door behind him. Katherine sank back into the sofa and sobbed.

# Chapter Sixty-Three

Katherine glanced around the tiny house that had been her home for the last eight months. Her gaze lingered on the basket of shells that she and Jeff collected on their walks ambling along the shore. She would miss those quiet strolls hand in hand in the early morning before the crowds showed up. Even when the weather turned cold, they bundled up and raced the waves so their feet wouldn't get wet.

"He still hasn't called?" Beth asked quietly.

Katherine sighed and turned into the kitchen, checking the cabinets and drawers one last time to see if she had forgotten anything. Since Jeff rented the house furnished, she didn't have a lot to pack that was hers. She was leaving the seashell pattern pasta bowls and the flamingo margarita glasses. They were more in style for this house than for the McLean house or for her apartment wherever she ended up. She glanced at the living room where she and Jeff cuddled in front of the fire warmed by the soft beach-colored throws. She would leave those, too. Too many memories.

"No. Not since I told him I was going back to D.C. I've

called and texted him a couple of times, but he hasn't responded. I'm not even sure he's in town." Katherine morosely checked the bookshelves to make sure she hadn't missed any of her books.

"He can be so darn stubborn. He's my best guy friend and I don't understand why he's acting this way. I know he loves you. And he's smart enough to know that you have to go back to D.C. now." Beth shook her head. "I thought he would come to his senses by now."

Katherine swiped a tear from her eye. "He was so hurt and so angry." She murmured, "I don't think I led him on. He knew I was only here until January when my sabbatical time was over."

"He knew, Katherine," Beth said. "He didn't want to accept it. Once he started caring about you, he wanted a different future."

"Maybe he's right. Maybe I am afraid to make a commitment. Maybe I'm letting the past dictate my future." Katherine moaned. "But I have to go back to Washington now. I have an obligation to the university. To my students. I can't leave them in a lurch."

She wiped the tears from her cheek. "But I guess Jeff is done with me. No contact from him in over a week."

"Give him some time, Katherine," Beth advised. "I know it hurts now, but let's see where he is when he gets his head out of his—"

"Beth!"

"What?" She grinned. "I was going to say gets his head out of his armpit. You know — like flamingos tucking their heads under their wings? What did you think I was going to say?"

"Uh huh." Katherine smiled faintly. "Hey, thanks for spending New Year's Eve with me."

Beth replied. "It was fun, wasn't it? I'm not a big party goer.

I like to have a few friends over. Have a nice dinner. At ten o'clock watch a rerun of the ball falling in Times Square. A glass of champagne for an early New Year's. Everyone is home before the crazies are out on the road after the real midnight."

"Ten o'clock is midnight in Greenland so that counts," Katherine commented. "I wonder what their New Year's Eve traditions are?"

"Good idea. I'll figure that out for next year," Beth chuckled. "I had to laugh when Brittany and Michelle showed up in their jammies for the parade on New Year's Day."

"Brittany said she wanted to make the black-eyed peas. And Michelle had the grapes. Nothing better than watching the Rose Bowl Parade. One of these years I'm going to go work on a float, even if it's gluing sesame seeds on a flower stem. Maybe eating black-eyed peas and green grapes for luck will work this year." Katherine stared out the window at the hibernating garden. She would miss seeing the flowers in the spring she thought sadly. *I'm going to miss this place so much. And Beth and the rest – they're my new family.*

"Beth, how come you don't visit your family over the holidays? Or have them come here? They didn't stay away because I took up your time, did they?"

Beth hemmed and hawed. "No, of course not. I haven't spent the holidays with them for a long time."

"How come?" Katherine asked, puzzled.

"That's a story for another time. My family sided with my ex-fiancé when I left him standing at the altar. I was one of the original runaway brides," Beth said ruefully.

"What?! Why am I learning about this now — as I'm leaving?" Katherine exclaimed. "When was this? What happened? I'm sorry I've been so caught up in my own issues. I haven't been a good friend."

Beth reluctantly replied, "It's a long, long story that I don't like to think about, let alone talk about. Let's forget I mentioned it." She put on her jacket and grabbed her purse and keys. "Maybe we'll talk about it when I come see you."

Katherine hugged her friend. "Whenever, or if, you want to talk about it, I'm here. Lord knows, you sure let me talk your ear off about my troubles."

"We'll see. Like I said, I try not to dwell on the past. I've got enough to keep me occupied in the present and the future." Beth fidgeted and busily straightened up the note pad and pencils on the counter.

*There's clearly a story here. Shame on me for not finding out more about Beth's past. She always seemed so together.*

"Beth, I don't know how to thank you for all the support you've given me. I thought I was stronger after everything I've been through with Stan and Richard, but I guess not strong enough to deal with Jeff's rejection. You've been a lifesaver."

She held up the house keys. "You'll drop the keys off with Michelle? I've already written her a check for these few days in January." Beth nodded. "I've got a few things to put in the car. I'll leave the keys under the big blue flowerpot on the patio. Michelle said you could drop them off tomorrow sometime or anytime this week. I don't think Jeff is going to rent this place soon."

Beth put on her coat and was ready to rush off to open Browseabout when Katherine stopped her. "And I'm going to hold you to your promise to come visit me — I've got some great independent bookstores for you to visit."

Katherine wandered out to the back. Everything looked buttoned up and ready for winter. The roses were all covered to protect them from the ice and snow over the next few months. The water was turned off and the pipes drained. All the windows were shuttered. The thermostat turned down to fifty. The house was so quiet, closed, sad.

She took one last look around inside, checking all the closets and under the beds. She picked up the last box and locked the front door behind her. Stashing the box in her packed-to-the-gills car, she let herself into the patio and let the memories wash over her — sitting with Jeff in the chaise lounges, soaking with him in the little pool, laughing as they caught and released the fireflies, talking, always talking, and touching. *I'm sorry, Jeff. I didn't mean to hurt you.*

# Chapter Sixty-Four

Head down, shoulders slumped, Katherine walked back to her car. And collided with a big, solid, warm body. Jeff wrapped his arms around her and pulled her close.

Katherine stiffened and pushed him away. "What are you doing here?"

"I'm sorry, Katherine." Jeff tried to pull her back in.

She side-stepped around him and moved toward her car.

"Wait! Give me a moment, please. I know I've been a jerk for not calling or responding to your texts. The truth is..." He paused. "I'm the big ol' scaredy cat, not you."

She hesitated, wanting to hear what he had to say, but not ready to let him back in. She was too hurt. She reached for the door handle.

"When you told me you were going back to D.C., I got mad — not at you, but at me, because I felt so much for you, and I was mad that I let myself get hurt."

Katherine stopped and waited for him to go on.

"I know that wasn't the most mature response for a 60-year-old guy, but I don't have that much experience, and I kind of felt like a teenager with you so I reacted like a dumb kid."

She heard the anguish in his voice. Turning around, she found Jeff right at her heels. She touched his scruffy beard. He clearly hadn't shaved since he stormed out. Dark circles under his eyes.

"You did act like a dumb kid. And you said some hurtful things — some things that are probably true and others that I'm not so sure of." She poked him in the chest.

"What do you mean?"

"We'll get to that later. I don't think you're done apologizing yet," she said sternly.

"You're right. I'm so sorry, Katherine. I'm sorry I lost my temper. I was overwhelmed by my feelings and afraid." He paused. "I'm sorry I wasted the last few days in Rehoboth, especially New Year's Eve. I wanted to start the new year with you."

"I wanted that, too." She wrapped her arms around him. "I'm scared, too. I think we have something special. I'm scared that by going back to D.C. I'm going to miss out on something good. What if this is — you are — the best thing that is going to happen to me? And I'm leaving it behind."

"I'm not going anywhere. And I'm going to fight for us. No pressure, but I'm going to make sure you don't forget me." He tightened his hold on her.

Katherine tipped her head back to look him directly in the eye. "How could I forget about you? You've made me feel things I haven't felt in a long time. Who would have thought at my age that I could fall in love again?"

Smiling tenderly, Jeff said, "Love doesn't know 'age.' You know that. We're so good together and I want to build a life with you."

Katherine warned him. "I'm not ready yet. And I want to

go into a relationship with a clear mind and an open heart. My mind is still clouded with all the divorce stuff and while my heart is mending, I still have baggage to work through. Will you give me the time I need?"

He frowned slightly. "What does that look like? Are you saying you don't want to see me for a while? I was hoping that I could see you in Washington, and you'd come back here for some weekends."

"Hard as this is," she said, "I need a little space. When I'm with you, you distract me — in a good way, of course! But I don't want to use you as a crutch. I want to be strong enough to stand beside you as a real partner."

Disappointed, Jeff said, "No contact at all?"

"How about letters? Old fashioned letters. Some of my favorite books are collections of love letters like Nabokov's love letters to his wife, Vera. The letters won't be the same as our long conversations while we walked or when we sat by your pool, but sometimes, it's easier to put thoughts down on paper than to speak them out loud."

Katherine rested her head on his shoulder and buried her nose in his neck. He felt so good, so strong. She would miss him so much.

"When you're ready, you'll come back?" Jeff whimpered. "I'm so sorry I wasted the time we could have spent together. I should have come to my senses sooner. I'm such a fool."

Katherine pressed her lips to his. "You know, I think I love you."

"I'll take that. I think I love you, too." He kissed the tears that streamed down her face. "Just so you know, I've never written a letter on paper before, but I'll do it for you. Prepare to be overwhelmed with all the mail you'll be getting from me."

He kissed her thoroughly, taking her breath away. "Remember that too. There's more where that came from."

# Chapter Sixty-Five

Katherine rattled around the house. It was so quiet, too quiet. And too big. The kitchen, the family room, her bedroom, her office — she lived in just those four rooms. The rest of the house — the other bedrooms, the game room, the big living room — was dusty because she hardly ever went into those rooms. It was too much house for her. She missed Jeff's little bungalow. It was warm and cozy. She missed the patio and the screened-in porch where she got so much writing done. And she missed the bathroom. *I miss that shower. It was better than a spa..*

Shawna was still working with Stan's lawyers on the settlement. Katherine was fine with having the house go to Stan. She wasn't fine with how he continued to lowball how much he was going to pay for her half. He was arguing that since he had made more money than she did, he shouldn't have to pay her half of the value of the house since she hadn't "contributed" as much. Shawna wasn't going to let him get away with that. But if they couldn't come to an agreement soon, their new baby was going to be born before he was divorced.

Chrissy was evidently not happy about that. Shawna assured Katherine they were close — maybe it would be a done deal next week. Then she could think about moving into a smaller place.

Katherine sighed. Classes were going fine. But something was missing. She didn't feel the spark that she usually felt at the beginning of a new semester. Normally she was excited to meet the new classes and see what the students would write. She loved their creativity in her writing class and their analysis and perspectives in the literature classes. This semester the students seemed interesting, but she wasn't looking forward to the next few months.

*Admit it. You miss Jeff.*

She missed Jeff more than she expected. They had agreed that they would not see each other until she was ready to come back. True to his word, he sent letters and cards and more letters. Katherine laughed at some of the silly cards — the cat holding a computer mouse in its mouth, and the "I miss you a waffle lot" card. For not being a letter writer, his letters were filled with news, of course, but even more so with his thoughts about life and work and his feelings about her.

It wasn't just Jeff she missed. She missed the life she had created in Rehoboth. The Savvys — Beth, Michelle, Brittany, Cassandra, Stella, Isabella — were such good friends — laughing when she needed it, crying with her when she needed a shoulder, inspiring and motivating her, dragging her out on her bicycle at the crack of dawn to help her train for the Wild Goose Chase. She missed their wine happy hours and the book talks. Laughing out loud remembering Beth acting out The Carlton dance on a *Mind the Gap* challenge card, Katherine missed her friends so much. Yes, Shawna was here and she would always be a best friend, but the Savvys were special.

She liked her freedom there. She was comfortable riding

her bike just about anywhere. She felt safer there than she felt walking around campus. It was so freeing to be able to ride, or walk, alone without worrying too much as long as she paid attention.

Katherine missed her early morning and evening walks meandering along the shore or powerwalking on the boardwalk. She meditated on the morning walk. It was usually only the fishermen and the occasional walkers or joggers. She got to know many of them by sight, and a few by name, especially the ones with dogs. She didn't know what it was exactly, but she attracted all the dogs who demanded to have their ears rubbed or to toss their slobbery balls back into the water. People mostly stayed in their own worlds in the morning, no doubt relishing the quiet with only the sound of the surf breaking on the sand disturbing the peace, but the dogs didn't hesitate to draw her into their games.

She smiled thinking about her evening walks. Traffic was heavier in the evenings. The beach was crowded with serious joggers and walkers, intent on getting their 10,000 or 20,000 steps before the end of the day. The treasure seekers with their headphones and scoops failed to give way if they detected some metal. Katherine learned to give them a wide berth and stay out of their territory.

It was more hazardous, too, since she had to watch out for the sandcastle moats and the holes some child had created looking for China. Katherine always carried a plastic bag to collect the detritus from the sun worshipers — empty juice boxes, water bottles, pop tart wrappers. She stood the random sand mold or shovel upright in the sand hoping that the owner would happily retrieve it.

Pushing her happy memories aside, she realized there was still so much stuff to plow through. She was a thousand times stronger than when she first showed up in Rehoboth. She knew her own mind and she had a better sense of what she was capable of. She was proud of her accomplishments over the past nine months. Asserting her independence. Getting back into the best shape she'd been in. Stan had done the comic doubletake when he saw her at the first faculty meeting. After the meeting, he told her she looked like she had lost weight and then asked her why she hadn't done it when they were married. *What a pompous jerk. Eat your heart out.*

Since she had been back in D.C., she hadn't written anything. Whether it was because the divorce was front and center with Stan badgering her every other week to talk to her "damn lawyer" and force her to accept his offer on the house, or because she was back in this house and back teaching, she couldn't write a word. Her research draft was almost complete, but it sat on her screen unfinished. The last short story she had written was half done and Katherine had no clue how to end the story. The poor main character was dangling in the middle of her story arc.

She wandered back to the kitchen and flipped on the television. That was another thing she never did in Rehoboth, watch TV while she ate, but now she craved the company of the talking heads. At least there was someone to listen to, and occasionally talk back to. They never answered when she shouted her questions at the newscasters or the answers in the form of a question on Jeopardy.

*Maybe I should go to Rehoboth this weekend? No, I don't want to give Jeff the wrong idea. I'm not ready yet to take that next step.*

At least she would see the Savvys in a few weeks when they came to Vanessa and Curt's wedding. That's one good thing about this big house, she had plenty of room so everyone could stay here. Too bad the Savvys were only staying Sunday and Monday, but they all had businesses to run. At least they could stay Sunday night as well since most of the restaurants and retailers closed on Mondays during the winter season.

Katherine jumped when the phone shrilled. "Hey, Shawna, how are you?"

"Good. Good. I've got some great news for you. Stan has finally agreed to a reasonable payment on the condition he can move in on the first of March."

"Absolutely! That's great news, Shawna. I was sitting here thinking about how much I want to be out of this house."

"Do you think you can move that soon? That's only about five weeks."

"Vanessa and Curt's wedding is the middle of February. She's already been here to clear out her stuff and take it to her future in-laws. Anthony took whatever he wanted when they moved to Atlanta. I've been living in about four rooms, so it won't take me long to pack up. I realized how little I need when I lived in Rehoboth."

Katherine opened and closed the cupboard doors, assessing all that she would have to pack. "I'll have to rent a storage unit for our Christmas stuff and all the memorabilia I've saved. Can you believe I've got all the major projects the kids did from elementary school on? They probably won't ever want them, but maybe my grandson will want to see his daddy's work someday."

Shawna laughed. "Probably not, but you never know."

Katherine went on. "This will also force me to purge things that don't give me joy anymore. I'll definitely leave the hideous vase that Stan's mother gave us for a wedding present and the obscene ceramic elephant that she gave us two years ago for Christmas. I can't believe she spent good money on either of them." Katherine eyed the offending items.

"It's a good offer, Katherine. I had to squeeze him, but he finally caved when Chrissy started counting the weeks until her due date. It's going to be close, but I think you should be divorced by the middle to end of March. He's admitted to adultery which allowed us to file for the divorce immediately without a mandatory separation period. And you're covered anyway since you've been separated for over a year."

Katherine sniffled.

"Katherine, are you crying? I thought you would be happy."

"I am. But I'm sad, too. I never thought I would be divorced. I thought when I got married it would be happily ever after." She struggled to regain her composure. "Thank you, Shawna, for being a good friend and a great lawyer. You're the best."

Shawna said, "I'm glad we finally got Stan to be reasonable. You know I'd do anything to help you."

Katherine walked to the garage and gathered the moving boxes she had been collecting. "And now, I'm going to start packing and finding a new place to live."

# Chapter Sixty-Six

Katherine thanked Shawna for the celebratory champagne. "What would I have done without you? You are such a bulldog! Thanks for making sure that the divorce settlement was fair, and that Stan didn't take me to the cleaners."

"That's why you paid me the big bucks, or rather why Stan did after he changed his mind about giving you the house as part of the divorce." Shawna gloated. "And I wasn't named one of the best divorce lawyers in the metro area for nothing. It's a bonus that we've been friends since you moved into this house."

Shawna looked around at the hollow rooms of Katherine's, now Stan's, McLean mansion. Every bit of warmth and everything personal like pictures of Vanessa and Anthony were gone. It might as well have been a furniture showroom as lifeless and impersonal as it was.

"It's going to be weird not having you for a neighbor, but this house never fit you, you know? It was always a bit cold and, I don't know, too perfect." Shawna popped the champagne cork and poured them both a glass. "*Cin Cin.*" Shawna toasted Katherine.

"Thanks, I think," Katherine laughed. "When the kids were growing up here, I managed to keep the downstairs playroom and the kitchen homier. The rest of the house was Stan's showcase. He didn't like the kids in the formal living room or the dining room. Those rooms were for entertaining. And heaven forbid if they stepped foot in his study."

Katherine gazed out to the backyard to the infinity pool and patio with its professional landscaping. Daffodils bloomed profusely surrounded by the greening grass. The stone planters marking the corners of the pool overflowed with spring flowers – red, white, and pink tulips. The Kwanzan flowering cherry trees, with their deliciously scented double-pink blossoms, pruned to perfection, marched in equal rows along the patio. It was an exquisite design, but Shawna was right — it was a little too perfect, a little too manicured. It was all Stan.

*It didn't fit me. I'm more of a Monet's garden.* She remembered the garden she had in Rehoboth, brilliantly colored, a little wild and untamed, lush.

Shawna topped off Katherine's champagne. "At least you were able to hold Vanessa's wedding and reception here. I think it meant a lot to her. I'm sorry I had to miss it."

"I know, I wish you could have been there, too, but we didn't have much notice and you were already committed to your ski trip. When they decided to get married right before they went to Ethiopia, it got a little bit crazy." Katherine shrugged. "They had been talking about getting married, but I think when she found out that her dad was getting the house instead of me — she knew it would be her last chance to enjoy her childhood home. It moved up their timetable."

Shawna leafed through the wedding album. Katherine looked over her shoulder, remembering how perfect the wedding was. "Everything worked out. Even though they wanted a small ceremony, all the usual venues were booked since we didn't have the usual six months to a year that wedding planners say you need. It made sense to have it here. Anthony and his family flew up so he could walk her down the aisle that we created in the formal living room. And then we had a nice reception by the pool." She pointed to the blue and white striped tent. "Isn't that gorgeous? It was a good thing I rented the tent with heaters! It got pretty cold that evening."

"How did Stan react to not being involved with the wedding?" Shawna asked.

"What could he do? He wasn't very happy and, of course, blamed me for turning Vanessa against him. Vanessa made it very clear to him that she was still angry with him. And it's not like he's made any real effort to connect with her or Anthony. He insists that they have to accept Chrissy because she will be their stepmother." Katherine gagged a little.

"What on earth is he thinking? I'm so sorry for them and I feel sorry sometimes for Stan. How could he throw away his children? I don't know if he'll ever come to his senses, but he will regret this someday." Shawna pointed to a picture of Vanessa and Curt by the pool. "That's a beautiful picture of them."

Katherine nodded and then shook her head. "I don't understand him."

"Given how clueless he is, I'm surprised he didn't crash the wedding." Shawna held out her glass for more champagne. "I'm glad Vanessa and Curt put off their honeymoon to help you clear out their stuff."

"Yes, they and Anthony and Sonja stuck around after the wedding for a final walkthrough. Stan made it clear that he wanted the furniture and the furnishings, but he told them they could take things that had personal meaning for them if he approved the items," Katherine vented. "Unbelievable!"

She reached for a piece of brie. "That set both kids off. They weren't going to ask permission of their father for stuff they wanted. I went through the house with them and identified what they wanted. I sent the list to Stan's lawyer and told him these articles did not convey with the house. The nerve of that man."

Shawna shook her head at Stan's audacity. Closing the album, she changed the subject. "You've got a nice apartment — small — but what do you expect in Foggy Bottom? You're paying for the location, not the square footage. Do you think you'll like living there?"

"I hope so. I can walk to so many restaurants. And the Kennedy Center is a few blocks away. I'll probably go to the Millennium Stage there a couple of times a week. I can't believe the talent that I can see for free. The apartment is the right place for me at the moment. Is it my forever home? I doubt it." She finished her champagne. "After today, this house will be all Stan's. And I will be a lot wealthier."

"Did you find a financial planner that you like?" Shawna asked.

"I did. She's doing a great job, creating a portfolio for me with a reasonable amount of risk, but safe enough. Thanks to you, I have a nice sum that she's investing for me. And she's managing the funds that came from the sale of my parent's business," Katherine added. "That's another thing that I'm grateful to you for, advising me and my parents to have Stan sign an agreement that if Stan and I ever divorced those funds would not be part of the divorce proceedings. That was early in our marriage and divorce wasn't on his mind. He's kicking himself now."

Shawna smiled. "He's not as smart as he thinks he is." She

took her glass to the kitchen. "I have to go. I'm going to miss you, neighbor. It's been great having my best friend live next door to me. I know you're just across town, but it won't be the same as just popping over for a quick swim or glass of tea."

Katherine struggled to keep her voice steady. "I'm going to miss you, too. Promise me that you'll come see me in Foggy Bottom?"

"Of course, I will," Shawna said. "I'll even come visit you in your forever home wherever that turns out to be. Where do you think it's going to be?"

"I don't know for sure yet. You know how much I've missed Rehoboth and my life there." At Shawna's raised eyebrow, Katherine admitted, "And Jeff. I've missed Jeff. I admit it."

Katherine's thoughts turned to what she hoped would be a great solution. She was hopeful that it would come through. She wanted so much to be back in Rehoboth – for Jeff and the Savvys, and the whole life she had there.

"There are some other things I need to finalize here. I'm clearer about what's important to me so I'm finding ways to get what I need. My Foggy Bottom apartment is month-to-month so it's possible I could be back in Rehoboth by June."

"June?" Shawna asked. "Are you going for the summer?"

"No, if everything works out the way I'm hoping it will, I'll be there year-round."

Shawna looked puzzled. "There's a lot you're not telling me."

Katherine laughed. "Yes, there is, but I don't want to jinx it. As soon as I know, we'll have dinner and I'll tell you everything."

# Chapter Sixty-Seven

Katherine threw the pecan-crusted salmon into the oven and grabbed her demanding cell phone. Students had been calling all day for final advice on their projects that were due before spring break next week. Forwarding her office phone to her cell phone was a great idea. She could work on her research in her home office and still be accessible to students. But so many students had called that she had hardly any time to work on her own work. With a few minutes left in her office hours, she thought she could at least get dinner started.

"Hello. This is Professor Katherine Lewis." She reached for her cup of chamomile tea.

"Katherine, this is Stella."

"Hi, Stella. How's it going?" Katherine glanced at the clock. If a student beeped in, she could ask Stella to hold for a couple of minutes.

"Good. Good. How's the new apartment?"

Katherine looked around at her Foggy Bottom apartment. The walls were slate gray. The window treatments were steel gray. It was furnished with black furniture. Katherine had tried to brighten it up with art and pillows. It still wasn't warm and cozy. But it was convenient, and it had nice amenities like fast Wi-Fi, a pool, and an exercise room.

"It's fine."

"Hardly a glowing recommendation, 'fine.'" Stella chuckled.

Katherine laughed. "I suppose that's true. It's nice enough. I love how I can walk anywhere I want to go. It's just a little too modern for me. I miss the charm of Jeff's cottage in Rehoboth."

"I can see that. It was a special place. The backyard pool and fountain, the porch and patio — so peaceful."

Katherine flashed back to the hours she and Jeff spent talking with their feet dangling in the pool, listening to the gentle fountain, drinking wine or coffee. Flushing, she remembered their first kisses and the nights they spent together. She wondered what Jeff was doing right now.

"Katherine?"

"Oh, sorry, I got lost in thought there for a moment. What were you saying?" Katherine stammered.

"I was telling you that the Savvys have a potential new client," Stella continued. "Marcie, the founder of this business, approached me last week at the bank. She heard about the presentation we did for the Chamber of Commerce in December and wanted to know if we were taking on any new clients."

"That presentation was the best thing we could have done. It brought some very exciting female entrepreneurs out of the woodwork." Katherine checked the timer on the oven. She didn't want her dinner to burn. "What kind of business is Marcie interested in starting?"

"It's quite different than most of the businesses we've helped. Her business plan focuses on providing a software platform to help companies hire and manage remote workers around the country and the globe. She was the Vice President of People for a major technology company that has employees in several states as well as forty-five countries. She knows her stuff. Her target audience is medium-sized technology companies." Stella described the opportunity.

"This is a lot bigger than the companies we've dealt with so far." Katherine popped some leftover rice in the microwave and put the peas in the steamer on the stove.

"I ran it by the mayor and the president of the Chamber of Commerce, and they're very interested. This could be a big step in reducing our dependence on tourism." Stella shared how excited the Chamber was and how willing the mayor was to offer incentives to bring this business to Rehoboth.

Katherine asked, "Why is Marcie interested in the Rehoboth area?"

"She grew up here and she wants to return to the East Coast. She's been in the Seattle area for the last ten years." Stella rustled some papers. Katherine knew she was checking her notes. "And she likes the business climate in Delaware. Her proposal is to have a relatively small staff here at headquarters, maybe fifty-sixty people. But those would be new jobs for the area. The rest of her staff would be remote. She's laid out some pretty aggressive growth in her business plan. Do you want to take a look at it?"

Katherine sparked with excitement. "Absolutely. I've been thinking about how the Rehoboth area could supplement their current industries with some other kinds of businesses." She stopped. "What have the other Savvys said?"

"I mentioned it to Brittany and she's excited, too. You know she did global professional services strategy at her advertising firm in Wilmington?" Stella asked.

"Yes, I remember that. How about the others?"

"I wanted to run this by you two first. I'll send Marcie's

plan to the group and see if we can set up a meeting for early next week." Stella paused. "Marcie asked what we charge."

"Huh. Everything we've done so far has been pro bono because the businesses have been much more limited. This opportunity has the potential for an expensive contract. This could be our first paying client," Katherine said.

Stella concurred. "We need to talk about this as a group. This could be a much bigger time commitment than we've put in so far. If we go this way, some of us might have to consider doing this full-time."

"I'm sure Isabella and Cassandra would not be interested in that. They've got their own businesses to run. And Beth has her dream business that she wants to build," Hearing the oven timer, Katherine took her dinner out of the oven. The room filled with delicious aromas.

"I've gone as far as I can at the bank so I would entertain doing this full-time," Stella confided. "What about you? Would you be interested in doing this full-time? What's your status at the university?"

Katherine responded, "It's very appealing. Let's think about it and talk next week."

# Chapter Sixty-Eight

"Why did I let Vanessa sign me up for these dating apps?" Katherine wailed to Shawna. "I know they work for some people, but they're not working for me!"

"Why? What's the matter?" Shawna said calmly, reaching for another crispy shrimp egg roll. She loved visiting Katherine at her Foggy Bottom apartment. There were so many good Chinese restaurants that delivered here. "I can't decide which I like better—the crispy shrimp egg roll or the crab Rangoon. I think it's brilliant to just order appetizers. We can make our own small plates."

"Stop thinking about your stomach. I'm in a crisis here," Katherine whined. "First of all, I don't even want to do any dating," she said impatiently.

"You don't have to jump into a long-term relationship. You can go out for coffee or dinner." Shawna tried to placate her.

"I know. And you know I always go somewhere public first and let you know with whom and where I'm going. But the way Vanessa set up my profile, I've got all these men who keep 'liking' me and saying they want to see if we can develop a future together." Katherine harrumphed. "And then when I meet them, there's no way in hell I'd have a future with any of them."

Shawna laughed. "Why? What's the matter with them?"

"Oh, good grief. Some of the guys who 'like' me aren't even real. They have these fabulous profiles who look like great matches. They like to do what I like to do. They're interested in what I'm interested in. They always live in some romantic place that I've mentioned in my profile like France or Italy. It's such a perfect match, it's too good to be true."

"Sounds pretty good. What's the problem?" Shawna crunched on another crab Rangoon.

Katherine explained. "We text chat for a while and even talk on the phone. And then when I suggest a video chat, something always comes up and they can't make it. Ever. That's the first suspicious sign."

"Would you like another beer?" Shawna asked. "I don't know why I like beer with Chinese food better than wine."

Katherine shook her head. "The second indicator that there's trouble is when after two or three calls they start telling me how much they care about me. And how much they want to take the relationship to another level. How much they would love to come see me."

"Well, that sounds promising — they want to meet you in person and they're willing to fly here to do that." Shawna speared a pot sticker with her chopsticks.

"You might think so until they start hinting that they were 'just a little short of funds' right now so maybe we could split the cost of their plane ticket. Or could I pay for the whole thing, and they'll pay me back? And could I send them e-gift cards because that will be quicker because the fares are good right now? As if! Gift cards! That set off huge flashing red warning signs. AARP is always warning about that scam."

"Thank heavens you didn't fall for that." Shawna speared the last Rangoon and waved it at Katherine.

"Go ahead. I can't eat when I'm this upset."

Shawna quickly doused the Rangoon with soy sauce and gobbled it up in three bites.

Katherine looked askance at Shawna. "Did you not have lunch?"

Shawna sheepishly shook her head no. "Back to your story about the scammers. I'm glad you paid attention to AARP about the gift card scams. My sister-in-law missed the message and got taken to the cleaners to the tune of about $10,000 by a scammer. And she's well-educated. It goes to show it can happen to anyone."

Katherine nodded. "These guys are tricky. It would be easy to be scammed by them, especially when they seem to know all the right buttons to push. Promising love and romance when you're starving for it. Hitting you when you're vulnerable. And who wants to believe that people could be so dishonest!"

"Maybe it's because I'm a lawyer, but I'm suspicious of just about everyone," Shawna said. "Not you, of course." She grinned.

Katherine nibbled on the last egg roll. "I read a report by the Federal Trade Commission the other day that said romance scammers — that's what these guys, and they are mostly guys, are called — bilked people out of $547 million dollars in 2021! $547 million dollars! And that was up about 80% from 2020 so it's getting worse. And they mostly do it by getting people to send them gift cards," she ranted. "You have to be so careful."

"I can see how that would be scary." Shawna said, putting down her chopsticks. "I'm full. You've hardly eaten anything."

"Good thing I'm too upset to eat, considering you ate my share and yours," Katherine teased.

Shawna asked, "Are there any non-scammers that like you? What's up with them?"

"Everyone tries to present the most positive profile and pictures. Some of them post pictures of themselves twenty years earlier. When I meet them, they don't look anything like their pictures." Katherine took a big swig of her beer. She gathered their plates and put them in the sink. She put two fortune cookies in front of Shawna. "You choose which one you want."

Shawna pushed one toward Katherine and tore open the other. "What do they look like if they don't look like their pictures?"

Katherine wound up. "This one guy posted a picture of himself that made him look like he was about six feet three inches. When I met him, he was five feet two inches. I don't know how he did it. Some trick with the camera or the perspective or something. He was a good six inches shorter than me." She broke her fortune cookie. "And this other one had a full head of hair in his picture but he showed up bald as a billiard ball. I mean, I'm fine with bald heads so why post a picture of yourself with hair?"

"What picture did Vanessa post of you?" Shawna asked.

Katherine crumpled her fortune and tossed it into the trash. "She posted a picture of me right before the Wild Goose Chase – you know that bike ride I did. I looked pretty good if I do say so myself."

She moved to the sofa and turned on the living room light. Opening the window shades, she looked out at the people scurrying wherever they were going.

"But that's not the worst thing." She put her feet up on the coffee table. "I met this one guy for lunch the other day. He spent the whole time talking about his ex-wife and how he was still holding out hope that they would get back together. I went through a whole package of Kleenex mopping up his tears."

Shawna widened her eyes in disbelief. "He didn't!"

"Oh yes, he did," Katherine insisted. "And then there was the guy who admitted that he was moving back in with his mom. He moved out to try this dating thing and he realized he preferred living with her. He was sixty-seven!"

"Come on, you're making that up." Shawna giggled. "A severe case of failure to launch."

"You laugh, but you haven't had to sit through a coffee date when the guy talked on and on and on about his job and never once asked me about my work. I never drank my coffee so fast and didn't ask for a refill." She cringed at the memory.

"Are you at least having any good meals?" Shawna asked.

Katherine shook her head. "So there was this one guy who asked me to choose the restaurant. When he got there, he didn't like the table. It was too close to the window and there was a draft. Then he went through the menu. He couldn't have that because he was allergic to shellfish. He couldn't have that because he was gluten sensitive. He couldn't have that because it contained peas. He couldn't have any dairy because he was lactose intolerant. Poor guy couldn't find a thing he could eat on the menu. We had a drink and left. He didn't contact me again."

"I don't know how this works. Do you just connect with the guys that like you?" Shawna asked.

"No, I can 'like' guys, too. Vanessa made me promise that I would try to put myself out there so I 'liked' a few guys. It took courage to make the first move," she said. "Talk about a blow to my self-esteem. They didn't 'like' me back."

"Oh no, I'm so sorry." Shawna comforted her. "That must have hurt."

"All the guys that I've had coffee with, or dinner or lunch, have on paper looked like a great match, but when we meet, it's all wrong." Katherine mused, "And I keep thinking about Richard and how he matched up perfectly with who I 'should' be interested in and look at how that turned out."

"Maybe your 'shoulds' are not what you want or need."

Katherine thought about Jeff. Outwardly he was not a match, but he was everything she wanted. Kind, intelligent, funny, moral, loving.

Shawna watched Katherine's face. "Where did you go?"

"Hmm?"

"You drifted away just then."

Katherine felt herself blush. "If you must know, I was thinking about Jeff. And wondering why I'm bothering with this dating app."

Shawna sat back and studied Katherine. "Maybe you've already found what, or who, you want."

"I'm beginning to believe that, too."

# Chapter Sixty-Nine

Katherine stared at the letter from the University of Delaware. *This is it. This is either my next step or it's back to the drawing board.* She reflected on her last interview with the English Department. Her presentation with the faculty on her research had been well received. The meeting with the Dean had gone well. Conversation with the students and faculty over lunch had been lively. It would be a great place to spend the next year and, with any luck, the visiting position would convert to permanent the following year.

There was risk in this plan. There was no job security with a visiting position. It was only a one-year appointment. She was giving up a tenured position — some of her colleagues thought she was crazy since many faculty viewed tenure as lifetime employment. She had never seen it that way. The security was nice, but she was confident that she could find an equally or even more satisfying job if she left.

Her department chair had been shocked when she had resigned. He asked her if she was still overly emotional from her divorce and whether Stan thought this was the right decision. *Good grief! How dare he accuse me of being "overly emotional." Insinuating that I couldn't possibly be thinking clearly.* Stan was her ex-husband – he wasn't making any decisions for her. Period.

Pursuing this visiting faculty job was the right thing for her to do. She had played it safe for most of her married life, putting Stan's career ahead of hers, staying in her tenure track position when she really wanted to see what else she could do with her degree and experience. Now was the time to try out some other opportunities. The visiting position would be a good transition from her current tenured professorship. If it came through, she could continue teaching the courses she loved and working on her research book as well as building her creative writing portfolio. She set the letter down on the counter and circled around it, examining it from all sides. *I want to open it, but I'm afraid.*

And she would only be an hour away from Jeff. He was not the primary reason she was doing this, but he was certainly a consideration. She wanted to see where this thing with him could go. She wasn't ready to commit a hundred percent. She still didn't trust her own judgement about men given her experiences with Stan. And then Richard, the snake. She hoped the Securities and Exchange Commission could use the testimony that she and Michelle's colleague gave them about Richard's behavior.

If the visiting came through, she would pursue the business incubator in Newark, located next to the university. They had already agreed to have her give a workshop on the ten essential components of a successful business plan. She hoped that would lead to a consulting position to review business plans like she had been doing in Washington. That is, *if* the visiting came through. She held the letter up to the light to see if she could see what was inside. *It's not very thick. I don't know if that's good or bad.*

She shrugged. *And if it didn't come through...* Well, she could continue to work at the incubator in D.C. They told her she could work additional hours and they would pay her a small stipend. She was very grateful to Shawna — the divorce settlement gave her financial stability. She knew that not every divorced woman had that luxury. Working at the incubator would keep her occupied and still allow her time to work on her research and her creative writing. Then next year she could apply for other jobs.

*But look how this all came together so easily and quickly. It has to be a sign, right?* The opportunity at the University of Delaware had fallen into her lap when one of their English faculty was awarded a Fulbright fellowship for next year. A friend she met at the American Literature Conference a few years ago called to see if by chance she might be interested in a visiting. It had been a whirlwind of interviews over the past two weeks.

That's why she hadn't told anyone that she was applying. Not Jeff. Not even Shawna or Beth. She didn't want to get Jeff's hopes up. And she didn't want Shawna and Beth to be disappointed for her. If this didn't work, there would be other opportunities. *But I really, really want this to work!*

Katherine tore open the letter. "We are pleased to inform you that you have been selected for a one-year visiting position."

# Chapter Seventy

"Michelle, I can't believe you worked another miracle." Katherine signed the rental agreement with a flourish and handed it back to Michelle. "This house is right for me."

"For you, I would move mountains. I'm so glad you're coming back to Rehoboth. We've missed you so much at our Sunday night meetings. And our 'girls' dinners in' haven't been the same since you've been gone. No one makes lasagna like you do." Michelle stepped to the printer to scan the agreement and email a copy to Katherine.

Katherine laughed. "Thanks. Well, I owe you dinner when I get moved in."

Michelle said, "I'm going to hold you to it. What a whirlwind! I can't believe you came in, spent the day looking at rentals, and made a decision so quickly again."

"You did all the hard work finding the possible places. I trusted you to give me three good options that met all my criteria. Which you did. It was hard to make a choice because they were all good, but the house on Dodds Lane in North Rehoboth was the best of the lot."

"As soon as you called me, I called the owner who is a friend of mine to see if they had found a new renter yet. I told them about you, and they didn't even list it."

"Lucky for me, you have great friends."

Michelle handed Katherine a canvas welcome bag and an envelope. "Here are your keys. And the bag has a coupon book for several businesses around town, an application for a library card, a magnet for your refrigerator with all the emergency numbers you'll ever need, and some other swag."

"This is a nice touch. How come I didn't get one last time?" Katherine teased.

"Because you were renting from Jeff, who wasn't a client — I did it for him as a friend. Speaking of Jeff, have you told him yet?" Michelle asked.

Katherine hesitated. "No, I'm going to surprise him. I'll call him this weekend now that I have a place to live."

"Have you talked with him at all since you left?"

"No, we agreed that I would call him when I was ready to come back. It took me awhile to get there, but I'm ready now."

"What does that mean?"

"It means I want to build a relationship with him. I missed him terribly. I care a lot about him. I think I even love him. But I wasn't ready for anything permanent in January. I needed to get that divorce albatross off my back." Katherine walked to Keurig to make herself a cup of coffee. "And I had to figure out what I was going to do for the rest of my life — at least what I'm going to do for the next few years."

"I'm glad you came back. For what it's worth, you and Jeff seemed to have a good thing going." Michelle tidied up her desk as she watched Katherine settle back in the yellow and blue floral loveseat.

"We did. We do," Katherine agreed. "We've been writing real letters since January. Paper and pen, not even emails. I love the way he expresses himself. I treasure every one of his letters and cards. And I have a lot of them! He sent at least two or three a week!"

Michelle, envy in her voice, said, "I'd love to have someone write me a letter. It's such a lost art. And such an intimate way to get to know someone deeply."

Katherine put the keys on her key ring. "Okay, I've got to hit the road and get back to D.C. Graduation is this weekend. I have to clean out my office and say goodbye to a few people. Then I have to pack up my apartment, which won't take long. The biggest challenge will be deciding what to bring from my storage unit. If it gets too hard, I may bring everything."

She peered into her swag bag and pulled out a notebook with a pen attached. "This will be great for all the lists I have to make." She dug around a little more and came up with a list of furniture stores in the area. "I'm so glad the owners left most of their furniture while they build their new place. At least I won't have to worry about that right away." She laughed ruefully. "Even though I left most of the furniture and furnishings in the old house, you'd be amazed at how much stuff I have in storage. Three sets of china — mine, my mother's, and my grandmother's!"

Michelle nodded. "I know how that goes. I've lived in the same house for thirty years. I can't imagine what I would do with my mom's china and my grandmother's crystal if I ever decided to downsize. They have such meaning to me."

Lost in thought, Katherine looked out the window. "Mm hmm. . . I'll be able to hang my Great Aunt Blanche's cuckoo clock that's about a hundred years old. Stan didn't want it in our McLean house so it was boxed in the attic. I loved that clock because it reminded me of her. She was such a pioneer!

Born in 1896, she was the first woman in our family to get a master's degree. And she took an around-the-world cruise when she was in her forties and didn't get married until she was fifty. She was such an inspiration." She snapped out of her reverie. "Sorry for rambling. The stuff I have in storage means a lot to me so probably most of it will come."

"I can see where you get some of your values," Michelle said. "You'll be here June 15?"

Katherine gathered all her things and stood up. "That's the plan. The movers are coming early that morning. I hope to be here by late afternoon."

Michelle hugged her. "Welcome home, Katherine."

# Chapter Seventy-One

Katherine paced to the window and back in her tiny Foggy Bottom apartment. She didn't want to disappoint Stella, but Katherine knew this was the right decision for her. Marcie had a great business plan. And she had all the resources she needed to build a great business. Katherine knew Marcie would succeed. The Savvys would offer her friendship and moral support. Maybe even invite her to join the Savvys. *She would probably fit right in.*

After nights of soul-searching, she realized that she didn't want to leave academia. She loved teaching, researching, and writing. Working full-time as a consultant helping start-ups was tempting. The money was good. Marcie had offered a very generous retainer. But part of the joy of doing the work Katherine had been doing with the incubator and the pro bono work the Savvys had been doing in Rehoboth was helping women who had a big dream of starting their own business. These women didn't have the resources to hire consultants to help them get started. That's where the Savvys came in.

Katherine smiled. That look of wonder made everything worthwhile when the Savvys helped Tammy write a winning application for a $50,000 grant. Tammy went forward with her plan to start her own Pilates studio to work specifically with clients with neurological conditions and clients with sports injuries. She was highly educated and professionally certified. She had been teaching Pilates for fifteen years. She had all the qualifications and experience. *And she had a vision.* She just needed help with the business side.

Beth connected Tammy with the Chamber and SCORE, the Small Business Administration's network of volunteer expert business mentors. Brittany wrote a great advertising strategy. Michelle found her the right space on the ground floor of a small strip shopping center with plenty of parking. Isabella walked her through the permits she needed. Cassandra promoted her business in her bicycle shop. Tammy was soundly beating her modest revenue projections after three months in business. *I'm so glad we could help her. She's really our first success story.*

Katherine anxiously glanced at the clock. Stella would be here shortly. Katherine had asked her to come to dinner after her conference ended. The last time they had talked Stella said she was ready to leave the bank and do this start-up consulting full-time. Katherine wasn't sure how her own decision would affect Stella.

The front door buzzer startled Katherine out of her revelry. She spoke into the intercom. "Yes?"

"Hi, Katherine. It's Stella."

"Hey, Stella. Come on up." Katherine buzzed open the inner door.

Stella rapped on the apartment door moments later.

"Come in! I'm so glad you could make it. How was the

conference?" Katherine took Stella's jacket and stashed her briefcase in the closet. "Where is the rest of your stuff?"

"The conference was great. My brain is about to explode. You know how it is when there are terrific speakers talking about innovative programs other banks are doing." Stella paused. "I was going to drive back tonight and decided it would be too late so I'm staying an extra night at the hotel. And that way we don't have to rush dinner. Unless you have other plans this evening?"

"You are my plans. Now I don't have to worry about serving you wine. Let's go into the living room. I've got some cheese and crackers to have with our drinks. Dinner is in the oven and will be ready in about twenty minutes."

"I hope you didn't go to too much trouble?" Stella asked.

"No trouble at all. I miss cooking for other people. When it's just me, I often have a salad or takeout. I haven't made my eggplant lasagna in a long time. I was going to send some home with you when I thought you were going back tonight, but I'll freeze the leftovers instead and bring some to you later."

"Later? When are you coming to Rehoboth?"

"Have a seat and I'll tell you everything that's going on." Katherine handed Stella a plate and poured her a glass of wine. "First, tell me about the conference."

Stella bubbled about everything she had learned over the last three days. "The Gold Sponsor for the conference was Accenture. They presented data about innovations in banking. "What got me jazzed was what some banks are doing to help SMB — Small and Medium-sized Businesses."

"Like what?" Katherine passed Stella a plate of phyllo puffs filled with goat cheese.

"Mmmm, so good." Stella munched on the puffs.

Around bites and sips, Stella went on. "There's an Italian bank that offers the same level of personalized financial services and relationship managers to SMB that they do for their large corporate clients. Too often multiple small businesses are assigned to one relationship manager, and they only have so much time to spend with each of them. Their needs are not always met."

She talked about a Canadian bank, in partnership with another company, providing "Virtual Chief Operating Officers" to small businesses who couldn't afford, or need, a full-time COO. She raved about how some banks were making better use of their facilities to help small businesses — like using their conference rooms for co-working spaces or allowing small businesses to set up pop-up operations inside the bank for finance-related services like tax preparation.

Stella took a sip of wine. "I could go on and on about everything I learned. Like I said when I got here, my brain is about to explode!" She drew in a deep breath and collected herself. "If banks are going to survive, they're going to need to think about how we can serve our customers, especially SMB, better and differently. I've got a big job ahead of me."

Katherine looked up in surprise. "What do you mean?"

"I've got a new role at the bank," Stella said sheepishly. "That's one of the reasons I attended this conference. I'm the new Vice President of Innovation and Strategic Development."

"Congratulations! That's terrific!" Katherine said. "Cheers!"

"You're not upset that I'm not going to leave the bank and go full time into start-up consulting?" Stella fretted.

Katherine laughed. "No, not upset at all. In fact, I've been worried about how I was going to tell you that I wasn't going to do it full time either!"

Stella looked so relieved. "The bank execs must have heard I was getting restless. They made me a great offer. Basically, I get to identify new products and services. Be a change agent.

Champion strategic initiatives. It is going to be so much fun!" She rushed on, full of enthusiasm.

"I'm happy for you," Katherine said. "I've been wrestling with the decision since we first talked about Marcie's business plan. It would be very exciting to work with her because she's such a visionary and so well connected in her field. And it's a hot thing right now — talent management of remote workers in different countries with different tax policies, hiring practices. If she can make that whole process of hiring, paying, developing, providing benefits as easy as she promises, she's sitting on a gold mine."

Katherine pulled the lasagna from the oven. "But I realized I would miss teaching. And writing. And working with the small business women we've met from that presentation we made for the Chamber. I love helping them realize their dreams. And I especially want to help the ones who don't have resources. Who are bootstrapping their way into their own businesses."

"I know what you mean," Stella shook her head vigorously. "I think about the two young women we helped get a grant to expand their bakery. They had so many online orders, they couldn't fill them fast enough. And that's where I think I can help at the bank. There are other funding sources that I can partner with to help these fledgling businesses get off the ground."

Katherine plated the lasagna and pulled the green salad from the refrigerator. Waving to Stella, she invited her to sit down at her tiny table.

"But does this mean you're staying here?" Stella asked.

"No, that's the thing. I gave my notice to the university a couple of weeks ago. Don't tell anyone yet — but I was offered a visiting position for a year at the University of Delaware." Katherine glowed with excitement. "It's just for a year, but there's a strong possibility it could turn into a permanent position. But even if it doesn't, there are other universities in the area. I'm ready to take a chance and see where this goes."

"Are you moving to Newark? What about Jeff? When are you moving?" Stella bombarded Katherine with questions.

"Hold on. Hold on. I've already worked with Michelle and rented a place in North Rehoboth. As a visiting professor, I have fewer administrative responsibilities. I'm going to do Airbnbs Tuesday and Wednesday nights since I'm teaching Tuesdays and Thursdays. Then I'll work remotely on Mondays and Fridays in Rehoboth."

"Michelle knew, and she didn't tell the rest of us?" Stella frowned.

"I asked her not to. I want to be the one to tell Jeff. And this has happened pretty quickly," Katherine said. "You know Jeff and I agreed that we would take a break while I figured out what I intended to do?" Stella nodded.

Katherine reached for another piece of garlic bread. She lifted the wine bottle toward Stella, silently offering a refill. "I've got a date with Jeff next weekend. I'm going to tell him then what's going on and that I'm ready."

"Ready for what?" Stella nodded her thanks, clearly enjoying the Montepulciano d'Abruzzo.

"Ready to come back and see where this thing with him can go. I was pretty lost last year. I'm stronger now. I'm clearer about where I want to be. Leaving my old job and getting the visiting position is a big step. I did it for me, not for Jeff, not for anyone else, just me." Katherine folded her napkin and placed it next to her plate. She grabbed her wine glass and leaned in. "I know that sounds a little selfish, but I needed to prove to myself I could stand on my own two feet."

"I'm very impressed," Stella said. "I can see — we all can see — how much more confident you are now. I'm sorry you had to go through the divorce, but you've clearly come out the other side stronger." She beamed at Katherine. "When are you moving back to Rehoboth? We have to have a party!"

"I'll be there in a couple of weeks. I have so much to do between now and then!" Katherine's mind whirled as she thought of the tasks ahead of her. "The moving van is coming with most of my stuff on June 15!"

"Don't worry. You've got a whole slew of friends that are ready to help in any way we can."

Katherine hugged Stella. "You all are so important to me. Your support and friendship have given me a shoulder to cry on when I needed it, and I needed it a lot last year. Or an ear to listen to me rant about Stan. I always felt I could count on you all to help me get through whatever crap was going on." She reached for a tissue. "I'm still very emotional." She blotted her eyes. Stella patted her hand.

Katherine cleared the table and pulled the panna cotta covered with blackberries out of the refrigerator. "And you helped me laugh again. How cathartic was it to laugh ourselves silly over those *Mind the Gap* challenges. Do you remember Beth trying to demo The Carlton dance? Or when Isabella was trying to hum the theme song to Ghostbusters?"

Stella chuckled. "We need a rematch. Michelle's cheating. Her grandchildren are coaching her."

"Ah ha! That explains how she knew the Nae Nae and the Dougie, let alone The Floss." Katherine poured two cups of decaf coffee.

"Aren't we the pair?" Stella said. "We were both so worried about upsetting the other because we each decided not to do the start-up consulting full time. And here we are with two great alternative futures."

Katherine high-fived Stella. They chatted more about the conference until Stella said it was time for her to leave.

"Conference days like these are both exhilarating and exhausting." Katherine called her a Lyft and asked her to text when she got to the hotel. Turning out the lights after she heard from Stella, Katherine realized how happy she was. Her future was bright and she felt like she was finally going home.

# Chapter Seventy-Two

Katherine smoothed her hair and checked her lipstick one more time in the visor mirror. She sat on the street in front of Jeff's house, watching the minute hand move so slowly toward 6:00. Heart racing, she fretted. *Is this the best way to tell Jeff I've moved to Rehoboth?* She had hinted in her last letter that she had exciting news she hoped he would be happy about, but she hadn't received a response from him yet. His letter no doubt in the mail.

Thinking about his letters brought a smile to her face. She would miss them. Every week since January, usually on Tuesdays and Thursdays, she had mail from him. His notes were filled with local gossip and stories about the other Savvys. After the "small talk," he told her how he was feeling. The first few letters were a little awkward, but after a while, he started revealing how important his grandparents had been to him. His parents were great, but his grandparents, particularly his grandfather, had inspired Jeff's love of serving people by giving them great food. It wasn't just that they had "sold" their café to him, but they transferred their values to him. They truly reveled in knowing their customers and making the best comfort food they could. They measured their success by how many regulars they had. The ones that came back time and again were their greatest source of pride. *I can see why Jeff's customers love him — they know that he truly cares about them.*

He also shared how much he missed being a part of Chelsea's life on a daily basis. He was sorry that his marriage had ended in divorce, not that he still pined after Shannon, his ex-wife, but that the divorce hurt so many people — Chelsea, Shannon, himself. He never wanted to go through that again. If he ever married again, he would do things differently. He would make sure his marriage was his top priority. Katherine knew she wouldn't play second fiddle to his career if they stayed together.

Katherine thought about his vulnerability. He was so concerned that Chelsea might be scarred permanently by the divorce. Both he and Shannon had tried to keep things as normal as possible but shuttling back and forth from her house to his house had to be hard on Chelsea. He didn't want her to resent him or avoid commitment and marriage just because her parents didn't stay together. *I love how much he wants to make sure Chelsea is okay.* She grimaced. *I wish Stan cared as much about Vanessa and Anthony. Let it go. I can't make him do the right thing.*

She chuckled when she thought about the funny cards and "gifts" he sent her, too. One week she got a five-pound box of Dolle's saltwater taffy with her favorite flavors — key lime, peanut butter pie, banana cream, chocolate latte, peppermint patty, and caramel apple. She couldn't look at another piece of taffy after she ate the whole box in almost one sitting. *But they tasted so good.*

She thought about the sand bucket and shovel with a bag of sand and a note to "come build a castle with me." *Subtle but a clear message.* Then a bag of sea glass that he had collected to "remember the treasures that are waiting for you." She thought about that last kiss they shared before she left. That was a treasure she remembered and wanted more of. A mermaid-shaped flashlight to "help you find your way home." *I'm coming home now.* Whimsical and thoughtful, his gifts made Katherine laugh and feel loved.

*It's time.* She took a deep breath. As she stepped out of the car, Jeff threw open the front door and shouted, "I wondered how long you were going to sit there."

Katherine's gaze took in his crisp white shirt with the rolled-up sleeves and the faded blue jeans that hugged his strong, muscular legs. His warm brown eyes and the smile that filled his face. He strode down the sidewalk and wrapped his arms around her.

Burying his nose in her hair, he whispered, "God, how I've missed you."

Katherine pulled back so she could look in his eyes. His feelings were so clearly reflected there. She stretched up and put her lips on his, tenderly at first and then with more passion. Breathing heavily, she broke the kiss. "I've missed you so much."

"I can't tell you how happy you made me when you wrote you were going to be in town this weekend. What's your happy news? How long are you staying?" Jeff kissed her again. He looked over her shoulder. "Did you get a new car?"

"One question at a time. Are you ready to go?" She started backing down the sidewalk, tugging him with her.

"Hold on. Where are we going?" Jeff asked. "If you want to stay in, I'll order Grotto's pizza. And then we can talk or whatever," he said, waggling his eyebrows.

"That sounds very tempting, but I have a surprise for you," Katherine said mysteriously. "Yes, I did get a new car. That old

Volvo was on its last legs. I love my Hyundai Tucson. It's a hybrid so it gets great gas mileage, which is going to be very important to me later."

He admired the sporty SUV. "Very snazzy. Love the bright blue color."

"I know. It reminds me of the ocean." Katherine beamed. "Stan always bought black or dark gray cars — 'professional' colors. This is as far as I could get from those dull colors. And that's the last we'll be talking about him tonight."

Jeff squeezed Katherine's hand. "Is the car your surprise?" She shook her head no. "Well, don't keep me in suspense." He gazed at her expectantly.

"Come with me."

Jeff pulled the door closed and followed her to the car. He admired the leather seats and surround view monitor. She described the safety features like the blind spot sensors and the automatic stop. She showed off the heated steering wheel and the Bose audio system. After Jeff found his favorite Sirius classic rock station, he looked up. "Where are we going? I didn't know there were any restaurants in this neighborhood. Is it new? How did they get zoning? This is a residential area."

"You sure do ask a lot of questions. Have a little more patience."

Jeff looked around the neighborhood, searching for a restaurant sign. When Katherine pulled into the driveway of a lovely sand-colored cottage with bright blue shutters, Jeff said, "Are we having dinner here? Who lives here?"

"Can you grab that bag in the back seat?" Katherine hurried toward the side door, keyed in a code, and pushed the door open. "Come on in."

Very confused, Jeff entered the sunny yellow kitchen. Garlic and oregano smells wafted through the air. Two blue and white place settings graced the breakfast nook that looked out over the patio fire pit surrounded by lush landscaping and a stone fountain. Katherine opened a drawer and handed Jeff a wine opener.

"What is going on?" Jeff asked impatiently.

"Open the wine, please, and I'll tell you everything," Katherine said. "Let's go into the living room."

Jeff stopped in front of the pictures of Vanessa and Curt and Anthony and his family. "Why are your pictures in this living room?"

"Because I live here now," she said excitedly. "Maybe it was a bad idea to spring this on you. But I wanted to show you how ready I am. I'm renting this house. The owners and I have an agreement that my rent will go toward the purchase price if I decide to buy this place, kind of an informal land contract. They're building a new place in Florida so they left it mostly furnished. They'll actually move their things out later this summer which will give me time to buy my own."

Jeff paced the living room. "I don't understand. You didn't want to commute to Washington before. How is this going to work now?"

She grabbed him as he went by. "Sit down, please, and let me explain. You know the last year threw me for a loop. Stan's betrayal. His pregnant girlfriend. Quibbling over the house. The divorce. A big portion of my life was turned upside down." Jeff stroked her arm. *He's always been so understanding.*

She sighed. "And I felt my empty nest acutely. Vanessa and Curt are married and living halfway around the world. Anthony and Sonja in Atlanta. My children don't need me in the same way anymore." Jeff pulled her in for a hug.

Katherine pulled back, keeping her arms around his chest. *He feels so good. So solid. So warm.* "And then I met you. And Beth and the rest of the Savvys. My life revolved around you all and I was happier than I've been in a long time."

Jeff stroked her cheek and encouraged her to go on.

"When I went back to Washington in January, I was torn. There was my old life. Even though it was different, I was comfortable. I knew my colleagues. I understood the politics of the university. I knew my way around the area." She gazed at Jeff. "But I realized I didn't want 'comfortable' anymore. I want you. And the me I was when I was living here. I liked that Katherine."

"I like that Katherine, too. A lot," Jeff murmured. "But I still don't get how this is going to work. Are you going to drive back and forth to Washington every week?"

Katherine smiled. "No, I quit my job—"

"What!" Jeff interrupted.

"I have a new job. I have a visiting appointment at the University of Delaware starting in the fall."

Jeff was speechless, holding her away from him as if trying to make sense of what she was saying.

Katherine waited anxiously for his reaction. She rushed on. "It's only for one year, but there's a possibility it will be converted to a permanent position. It's risky, but thanks to you and the Savvys and Vanessa and Shawna and my own self-work, I'm confident that everything will work out. Even if the position doesn't get extended, I'll find something else." She searched his eyes trying to determine what he was thinking. She kept talking. "Because it's a visiting, I'll have fewer administrative responsibilities and they've given me a Tuesday-Wednesday-Thursday schedule. I may rent a room there in the winter to avoid the bad weather. Otherwise, I'll drive back and forth to teach."

*I wish he would say something.* Katherine plucked up her courage. "I know it's what you proposed in December, but I didn't want to drive back and forth to my old life. I wanted to start my new life — with you."

Jeff shook himself. Katherine watched expressions flit across his face — confusion, excitement, concern. Hope. "Wow. So many changes. Are you really okay with all this?"

Katherine nodded. "I am. What I've learned over the past few months is that I have the freedom to decide what *I want*. And have the confidence to go after it." She looked at Jeff. "What I want is to be here with you and see where we go. Changing jobs gives me the opportunity to do that and do what I love — teach, write, research."

Jeff looked down at his lap. He seemed to be struggling to say something. *Maybe his feelings have changed.* "Are you mad that I didn't tell you sooner? Are you okay with me living here? I didn't want to be presumptuous and ask to move back into your place."

Jeff wrapped his arms around her. "First, I am rapturously happy that you're living here. Pretty big word for a business guy, huh?" He grinned. "Second, I like what I see in this house. I'm hoping I get to see a lot more of it."

"Fishing for a tour?" Katherine relaxed a little.

"No, fishing for my own key," Jeff said suggestively.

"That's yours." She reached into her pocket and handed him a key. The oven timer dinged. "The lasagna's done. Let's have dinner and then I'll give you the tour."

Jeff stood and took Katherine in his arms. "I love your surprises. I would have been disappointed if we were having dinner with other people. I want you all to myself tonight."

She led him back to the kitchen. They bantered about whether lasagna should sit for five minutes after it came out of the oven. Jeff argued that it needed to sit so it would be nice and firm. Katherine said she liked it slightly runny. They compromised by taking her piece out first and getting Jeff's piece out later.

With eyes full of love, Katherine watched Jeff clear his

plate, using the fresh-baked bread to sop up the sauce. Her heart overflowed with happiness. "Thank you," she said.

"For what?"

"For being you. For waiting for me. For believing in us. I finally found home."

Thank you for reading Katherine's story, *Finding Home*, the first in the Rehoboth Beach series. Turn the page to read an excerpt from the next in the series, *Love Rekindled*, Beth's story.

Want to keep up with my new releases? Join my newsletter, Deborah's Musings, at https://deborahsmithcook.com/ and receive news about pre-release sales and other temptations.

# Love Rekindled

## Beth's Story

Beth's gray eyes widened in shock. *It can't be.* She ducked behind the science fiction shelf and chanced a quick look. *It sure looks like him. Same deep red hair color. Longer though and styled differently. Same profile — strong chin, defined cheek bones.* She glanced at his hands and groaned. *Same crooked pinky finger that he injured playing a pick-up game of basketball. How many times did I hold that hand and stroke that finger? Too many to count.* She turned and almost ran to the break room. "Katherine, can you take over the counter, please?"

"What's the matter? You look like you've seen a ghost." Her part-time employee at Browseabout Bookstore, and new best friend looked up from her lunch.

"I have...seen a ghost, sort of." Beth stuttered. "What is he doing here?" She paced the usually soothing room and peered through the crack in the blue ticking window curtains. The bookstore looked like it always did on a Saturday morning in June, full of flip-flop clad beach worshippers picking up their next book for a hot day in the sand, moms and dads enticing their little ones away from the stuffed animals that would not fare well in the salt water with promises of sand sculpture beach toys, locals coming in for the latest copy of the *Cape Gazette*. Muttering to herself, "I don't think he saw me."

"Who is here?" Katherine's normally poised and collected boss, the bookstore manager, was visibly flustered. Beth stole another quick peek through the curtain. Her soft gray curls quivered as she nervously wrung her hands. "I've never seen you this rattled. Is it a customer you've had trouble with in the past? Do I need to call our security guy?"

Beth sat down heavily next to her. "No. No. It's not that." She twisted her purple spiral elastic key bracelet around and around her wrist, growing more and more agitated, glancing anxiously at the door. "He's just...he's just...my fiancé."

"What?" Katherine, shocked, exclaimed. "Fiancé?" She rushed to the window to get a look. "I don't see anyone. Did you get engaged I wasn't looking?"

"Ex-fiancé. He's my former fiancé." Beth moaned. "I haven't seen him in forty years since I stood him up at the altar." She sunk down in the chair and put her hands over her head. Glancing at Katherine who looked like she didn't know whether to laugh or be worried, she pleaded. "Can you please just take care of the front for a little while? If a tall, red-headed, slightly gray, good-looking guy asks for me, tell him I'm not here. Please?"

Katherine drew in a deep breath. "Okay. I'm going. You can stay here and hide for now. But after work, you've got some 'splaining' to do."

The store was busy all afternoon. Katherine ducked into the breakroom after an hour or so and told Beth the coast was clear. No one that fit the description of her former flame was still in the store. Beth timidly crept out, looking left and right, checking around every shelf. Satisfied that he was gone, she threw herself back into her work. *That's what I've always done — put my work first.*

One after another, customers came in looking for the latest James Patterson or David Balducci. Others came in not knowing what they were looking for. Beth probed to see what was on their minds, what they needed, or what they wanted. Then she would steer them to the right section and right author or give them a couple of choices that she thought would work. The harried moms and dads were more difficult — they just wanted something, anything, to occupy their little ones so they could have a few minutes of peace. After flashing the lights to let everyone know the shop was about to close, the last straggler mom thanked her profusely when her daughter fell in love with the punch out dinosaur book.

Beth dragged out the closing procedures as long as she could, hoping Katherine would just forget about her earlier meltdown. Procrastinating, she finished counting the cash drawer a second time. Out of the corner of her eye, she watched Katherine drum her fingers on the counter. Under control now, she had been hoping that her friend would just let it go. But it didn't look like that was going to happen. *I'll just tell her the bare minimum. I don't have to go into all the gory details.* She didn't need to know her parents still haven't forgiven her. And she didn't have to tell her how much she had dreaded, and longed for, the moment she would see Andy again.

"Okay. That's enough. I counted it, too, and it's the same as it was the first time. Stop stalling." Her beautiful brown-haired, green-eyed friend called her on her behavior. "Let's get out of here so you can tell me what's going on. Do I need to call an emergency meeting of the Savvys or do they already know the story?"

Beth mentally clicked through the list — Michelle, Cassandra, Stella, Isabella, Brittany — all good friends who volunteered together to mentor women-owned small businesses. Cassandra and Brittany were out of town, but the others were around. They would come running if Katherine called them. *I can't get into it with everyone. I've kept this a secret for so long. If he hadn't come into the bookstore, I could still keep it a secret.*

Beth closed the drawer firmly and shut down the register. Looking at her friend, she sighed, "No emergency meeting. No, they don't know. It was a long time ago. Can't we just chalk it up to a little shock? I'm feeling much better now. It was probably a one-time fluke that he was here. He doesn't live here. He's in Wilmington."

Katherine gently pulled her out from behind the counter. "You were shaken up. And while you say you're all better now, I think it's interesting that you know where this guy lives even though you haven't seen him in forty years." She pushed Beth toward the office. "Go get your purse. For all the times you listened to my sad story when I was going through my divorce last year, and because you're going to be my maid of honor when I marry Jeff in a couple of weeks, it's my turn to listen to you."

Balking, Beth hesitated. "It's water under the bridge." Katherine gave her a stern look, one that probably terrified her students if they tried to turn a late paper. "Okay, fine." Beth reluctantly flipped the open sign over to closed, turned out the lights, and trudged out the door.

~

Follow Beth's story by joining my newsletter, Deborah's Musings, at https://deborahsmithcook.com/.

# Acknowledgments

Writing this acknowledgments page may be harder than writing the novel. What if I miss someone?! There are so many people to whom I am grateful for their love and support. I don't think my words can adequately express my appreciation. If I neglect to mention anyone, please know that it was unintentional and that someday in the middle of the night, I'll sit up and say, "Darn. I forgot about XX." Then I'll fret and stew that I've hurt your feelings. Please understand it's the sign of a slightly overwhelmed mind.

This book is dedicated to my husband, Joel, who encouraged and supported me throughout this process, not minding when I would hole up in the basement, who would cook dinner when I had "just a little more to finish," who brainstormed and shared research with me, and generally assured me that this was the right time to do this. His love, courage, and support allow me to reach for my dreams.

And to my immediate family — my son, Hunter, who read a very early version and gave me kind, constructive comments, and my daughter-in-law, Gabrielle, who reassured me that em dashes, en dashes, and hyphens were perfectly okay in fiction, and Xavier, the smartest, sweetest, cutest grandson in the world who fills me with joy and makes me laugh. My dad, Hayden, who at 92, is finishing his third novel and with whom I've had so many conversations about plot and character development.

My sister, Cheryl, read an early version and found a whole duplicated chapter!

Janet was my weekly Friday night accountability partner. She kept me honest when I reported my weekly word count and was such a great cheerleader and support.

The book would not be what it is without my beta readers — Sophie, Chris, Cheryl, Pam — who sent back great constructive comments and texted me quotes from pages that they particularly liked. It was so reinforcing.

Kitty Bucholtz, my book doula and editor, and a good friend, edited the book with a fine-tooth comb. She taught me everything I didn't know about point of view and dialogue tags and cleaned up the double spaces after periods — what can I say? I'm that old and that's what I was taught. The book is so much better thanks to her. Kitty's *Finish Your Book* Group Coaching (https://kittybucholtz.com/writers/) provided weekly motivation and inspiration.

Working with 100covers.com was a pleasure. They were so accommodating as I, like Goldilocks, found the cover that was "just right."

And my own Savvys — the Fabulous Five (Pam, Maya, Joan, and Rachel — I'm the fifth) the Minis (Sophie, Chris, Ellie, Mary), my Working Out Loud group (Pam, Leen, Tina), Peg, Janet, and Cheryl. You have inspired me, comforted me, made me laugh, shared your kindness and wisdom. My life is so much richer because you're in it.

Finally, this is for all the strong, wise, mature women I've met throughout my career who lead interesting, heart-full lives. You inspire me with your determination, courage, and kindness. We know love isn't just for the young.

# A Note From the Author

A novel is a work of fiction. It springs, or is sometimes dragged, from the author's imagination. None of the characters in this book are real. They are created from people I've known, people I've read about, or just people I've made up.

I love to read books about real places. It tickles me when I can say, "I've eaten there." Or "I've walked down that street." Rehoboth Beach, Delaware is a real place. I've researched it since 1994 when we took our two young sons to the beach for the first time over my husband's spring break in March. It was unbelievably cold. We stayed in the Boardwalk Plaza right on the boardwalk so it was a short walk to the beach. We decked the boys out in flannel shirts and sweatpants topped with yellow rain pants and jackets and made them wear yellow dish washing gloves tied on with rubber bands. They looked like miniature hazmat workers, but they had fun. That trip was the start of our life time love affair with Rehoboth.

Browseabout Books is my favorite place. I am much like Katherine — they could pay me in books just for the pleasure of working there. We've had many wonderful dinners in the restaurants the Savvy's frequented — Eden, Back Porch, Blue Moon, Salt Air — and many others. Grotto Pizza is our first night tradition, too. And we've consumed more than our fair share of Dolle's taffy.

We've walked the boardwalk many times. In fact, I did part of my training for my first marathon on the boardwalk, doing several two-mile loops at the crack of dawn before the boys woke up.

Besides the hands-on, in-person research, I visited the Chamber of Commerce and learned much about the economy and business environment. Since I started writing, I joined the Rehoboth Beach Writers Guild. My office is piled with stacks of local newspapers and marketing materials.

A confession — I'm a former professor of strategic management so I do research. I did a Master Class with David Balducci where he showed us the amount of research he does for his books — three-inch binders for one topic in the book. Six or seven binders per book! And then he showed us how all that research might only be one paragraph in a 90,000-word book.

Arghh! But there's so much I want to share about what I learned about romance over sixty. Or female entrepreneurs over sixty! The bicycle business especially for women. Brewpubs. Using Pilates for neurological conditions. Dating app scams. My editor had to tell me so many times — "That's interesting, but does it advance the story?" No. No. It doesn't. But I want everyone to know what I know! (You'll notice I rebelled a few times and left some of the good stuff in...) At any rate, suffice it to say, any errors are my own, but this book is as factual as possible.

# About the Author

When Deborah Smith Cook is not writing, she's reading. Or walking. Or having coffee with friends. Or going on "adventures" with her grandson. Spending time with family and friends. Or spending time at the Delaware beaches. And getting to Paris as often as she can. It's a pretty full life.

She lives in Northern Virginia near Washington, D.C. with her husband and a menagerie of backyard wildlife — the occasional fox, deer, pileated woodpeckers, and a myriad of other birds.

In her writing, she is passionate about "seasoned" or "mid-life" stories and romances — whatever we call these things about people over sixty. She believes love is for any age, not just the young.

She's all about pro-aging (not anti-aging), embracing our wisdom years. Her role models are all the women who don't believe they're "too old" for anything. In the non-writing part of her professional life, she's helping women figure out what their next step is after retirement.

Have you had in the back of your mind that you'd like to start a business? Keep reading to try out Katherine's Business Plan outline and make that dream a reality. And check out Cassandra's Bicycle Maintenance Tips, too!

Learn more about Deborah at her website https://deborah-smithcook.com/. She would love to hear from you at Deborah@Atheseus.com.

# Katherine's Business Plan Outline

You don't need a lengthy business plan to start your business, but there are good reasons why you should have a plan written down. Research published in the Harvard Business Review [1] found that entrepreneurs who write business plans are 16% more likely to succeed than those who don't plan. Given how many small businesses fail, every percentage point that helps you succeed is worth it. Why do you need a business plan?

- Articulate your vision clearly and succinctly.
- Give you a roadmap of next steps and priorities. To keep moving forward, we need to know the first step, then the next step, and the next, and so on. Breaking your plan into doable actions will help you avoid the dreaded "OVERWHELM."
- Ensure you won't be blindsided by key success factors in the functional areas that make up a small business. If you want to have a bakery, it's not enough to make great cupcakes. You also need to

know about supply management, marketing, cash flow — we'll touch on each of these areas below.
- Obtain outside investors or loans. They want to see that you know what you're doing. A good plan can show that.

There are many templates and formats for business plans from one-page plans to multi-chapter plans. One of my favorite books is *Bird by Bird* by Anne Lamont. The gist of it — she advocates breaking a big project in manageable bites. In the case of her child's project, it was working on each bird, and then moving to the next.

Don't look at how long this outline is. Just take it section by section, item by item within the section, and before long you'll be done. If you get stuck on an item, go on to the next. Sometimes you just have to let something "sit" until you're ready to write about it.

Another tip — give yourself a schedule and a deadline. For example, "I'm going to write at least an hour a day and plan to complete this draft in thirty days." Or fifteen minutes or a half hour or forty-five minutes. Or twenty-five days or sixty days or whatever works for you. Committing to a specific time period will help you prioritize this and work your other commitments around it. Setting a deadline will give you an endpoint. If you're like me, nothing motivates me more than a deadline. Just be sure you're being realistic — if you can only swing ten minutes a day, schedule ten minutes a day. If it's going to take you a year to finish your plan, that's your deadline. Make it work for you.

Here are the basic components of a business plan.

I. Executive Summary: I find that it's most useful to write the Executive Summary after you've completed the other sections. This is a brief overview, usually no more than a page, that describes the product or service solution you are offering, your ideal customers, why your solution is differentiated, or unique, and what outcomes you expect. You want this to capture the attention of your potential lenders or investors.

II. Organization Overview: In this section, you will provide more depth about your organization. (I will use "organization," "company," and "business" interchangeably. Here you will share your mission and vision statements as well as your goals and how you'll measure your progress on those goals. You should also talk about any key human resources such as partners or employees that are instrumental in the success of your business. Finally, identify the legal structure for your business — sole proprietorship, limited liability corporation, cooperative partnership, or S corporation.

III. Market Opportunity: This is where you discuss the market opportunity you've identified, the gap or problem that you are solving, the industry characteristics, the competition, your strengths and weaknesses, and how you have differentiated your product or service.

IV. Competitive Advantage: Discuss how your product/service is uniquely positioned to meet the needs of your target customers. How is your product/service differentiated from your competitors?

V. Marketing and Sales: This section addresses how you will market and sell your product, generate leads, promote your product/service, and your sales strategy.

VI. Operations: In this section, you will describe how your product or service will be made or performed, how you will support your customers, how you will collect payments, how you will staff your organization, what kind of facilities you need, how you will source materials for your product/service, what technology you will be using.

VII. Financial Plan: In this section you will describe your

revenue forecast and your projected expenses that will determine your projected profitability. Begin with your projected startup costs. Follow that with your projected profit and loss statement. Be sure to include a cash flow statement to reflect cash coming in and going out.

Now that you've finished all the sections go back and write your Executive Summary.

Good luck!

~

### *Resources for Women Entrepreneurs*

Just a few of the many resources available to women entrepreneurs. This is by no means exhaustive, but just a taste of what's out there. You don't have to do this alone. There are organizations and individuals who want to help you get your business started.

Tory Burch Foundation (https://www.toryburchfoundation.org/) provides educational resources — videos, articles, webinars — and access to capital as well as fellowship/mentoring programs. Their current initiative is #EmbraceAmbition.

SCORE (https://www.score.org/) SCORE's mission is "to foster vibrant small business communities through mentoring and education." They provide experienced business mentors.

Goldman Sachs 10,000 Women (http://tinyurl.com/292tupv7) provides "education, mentoring, networking, and access to capital."

SCORE (https://www.score.org/women-entrepreneurs) has dedicated resources to help female entrepreneurs.

Small Business Administration (SBA) (https://www.sba.gov/local-assistance/resource-partners/womens-business-centers) offers specific guidance to women entrepreneurs.

AARP has curated a list of resources for women entrepreneurs. (https://employerportal.aarp.org/small-business-resources/women-owned-resources)

Lisa Masiello has curated a global list of resources for women entrepreneurs. (https://www.lisamasiello.-com/business-resources-for-women-entrepreneurs)

Ш "Research: Writing a Business Plan Makes Your Startup More Likely to Succeed" by Francis Greene and Christian Hopp, July 14, 2017. https://hbr.org/2017/07/research-writing-a-business-plan-makes-your-startup-more-likely-to-succeed. Accessed January 6, 2024.

# Cassandra's Bicycle Maintenance Tips

Nothing beats having a great bike mechanic to make sure your bicycle is in tip-top condition, but there is a lot you can do yourself to keep your bike cruising smoothly.

First things first. Where should you start? With the right tools. Carry an on-the-bike repair kit that contains at a minimum a small multi-tool, spare tube, tire levers, hand pump, Allen, and crescent wrenches. You can handle just about any emergency with this basic tool kit.

Second, take a bike maintenance class at your favorite bike shop. Learn how to do things the right way. It's a much faster way to get up to speed on what you need to know. Know how to change a tire. There's always a chance you'll get a flat when you're riding so you have to know how to do this yourself.

Now, what's your basic checklist?

1. Tires: Check the tire pressure at least once a week and keep them at their optimal pressure. Also check for worn spots or embedded objects like little pebbles.

2. Wheels: Make sure your wheels are securely fastened

and the nuts and release mechanism is secure. If your wheel wobbles when you spin it, take it to the bike shop to get it trued.

3. Brakes: Check that your brakes only hit the rims and not the tires and that they provide the right pressure to stop the wheel. Make sure they are not worn down.

4. Cables: Check your cables to ensure they are not frayed or corroded. Lube the cables lightly before putting them back in the cable housing.

5. Gears: Run through your gears before you start your ride to make sure shifting is working properly and the chain doesn't slip.

6. Chain: Keep the chain lubricated. Your chain should be cleaned with degreaser once a week and then every link lubed. Wipe off the excess and make sure the lubricant doesn't get into the brakes.

7. Frame: Check the nuts and bolts holding your bike together. Make sure everything is tight.

8. Lights: Check that the lights are working. Make sure the reflective tape is in place.

9. Tape: Replace your handlebar tape regularly to make sure you have a solid, comfortable grip.

10. Saddle: Keep your saddle from squeaking by lightly oiling the saddle rails.

11. Clean: Clean your bike often especially if you've been riding on wet roads, dirt paths, or salt-treated winter roads. Make sure it is completely dry. Your bike will actually last longer if it's clean.

Even if you do all this basic maintenance regularly, at least once a year take your bike in and have the professionals make sure all the major parts are working properly. Now go enjoy yourself on a well-maintained bicycle.

www.ingramcontent.com/pod-product-compliance
Lightning Source LLC
Chambersburg PA
CBHW031839310726
48972CB00005B/1338